AF594133

Wolves of the Northern Rift

A Magic & Machinery Novel

Jon Messenger

THIS book is a work of fiction. Names, characters, places and incidents are the product of the authors' imagination or are used factiously. Any resemblance to actual persons, living or dead, business establishments, events or locales is entirely coincidental.

Wolves of the Northern Rift

Cover Design by:Whit & Ware Design
Typography by: Courtney Nuckels

"It is much easier to be a hero than a gentleman."

-Luigi Pirandello

CHAPTER One

THE WHIRLING BLADES OF THE ZEPPELIN PROPELLERS hummed within the passenger cabin, as the inflated transport drifted over the frozen landscape below. Frost clung to the windows, leaving tendrils of ice crystals reaching toward one another from their respective corners of the panes of glass. Despite the heat within the undercarriage cabin, the cold blanketed the hull of the craft.

Within one of the private rooms of the large cabin, Simon Whitlock drummed his fingers impatiently on his top hat, which rested on the table between him and his associate. Simon looked out the window, though the glass fogged almost immediately from his warm breath. He rubbed it with his suit sleeve, leaving a damp smear over the glass.

Frustrated, he sat back and pulled on the chain that dangled from his waistcoat. The pocket watch on the end of the chain slid from his vest pocket and spun lazily in the air. Simon grabbed the watch delicately and pushed the button on top. It swung open, revealing the timepiece on one side and a royal crest etched into the silver of the other. A photo of a dark-haired woman had been placed over the crest, concealing much of it. He only halfheartedly read the time before clicking the watch closed and replacing it in his pocket. The motion of brushing his suit aside revealed the butt of the silver revolver, tucked firmly in a shoulder holster. Simon hastily pulled his jacket back over the weapon and looked at his partner.

"How much longer is our trip?" Simon asked, interrupting his associate from his studies.

Luthor Strong looked up from his stack of papers on the table and arched an eyebrow inquisitively. Reaching up, he removed his wire-framed glasses, placing them gingerly on the table atop the strewn papers.

Without replying, Luthor looked out the window, admiring the snow-covered mountains over which they flew. A cold draft washed over him as he leaned closer to the window, and he shivered. He reached up absently and scratched the thick muttonchops that covered both cheeks.

"You have many virtues, sir," Luthor said as he settled back into his plush bench seat, "but patience has never been one. We still have a few hours remaining. You could easily pass the time by resting your eyes or, if you don't feel the inclination for sleep, you could pass me your blanket if you have no intention to use it."

Simon frowned. "You have a cold nature about you, and I'm not referring only to your body temperature."

He pulled the blanket from the bench beside him and passed it to Luthor, avoiding the oil lamp that burned merrily in the center of the table. Simon stared at the shorter man as he removed his jacket, folding it neatly beside him. Luthor buried himself in the thick, wool blanket, pulling it up to his chin.

"You can't possibly be that cold," Simon chided.

Luthor smiled at his friend. "Oh, I can assure you that it's entirely possible to be this cold, though I might not have believed you if you had told me it was the case before we left." He looked down at the papers spread before him. "Couldn't we have received an assignment along the southern coast? I hear they still have yet to pull out their winter jackets."

Simon smiled back at the apothecary. He reached up and stroked the pencil-thin moustache just above his lips. "If you were so fortunate to choose your own assignments, you would never leave the coastal resorts."

Luthor tapped his nose knowingly. "But not you, sir. The waters never did agree with you, did they?"

Simon shivered at the thought of the endless ocean. "Never. Luckily, we don't choose our assignments. We follow the will of a higher power."

Simon leaned toward the window and clutched a velvet cord that dangled from the top. With a gentle tug, the thick curtain descended over the pane of glass. Though the room darkened considerably, there was an immediately noticeable difference in temperature as well.

With a satisfied sigh, Luthor pulled his arms free of the blanket.

"Speaking of assignments," Simon said, leaving the sentence hanging.

Luthor cleared his throat and retrieved his glasses, placing them on the end of his nose. He lifted a few pages, their surfaces covered with tight, small, and meticulous writing. Setting them aside, he retrieved a folder concealed beneath them. Turning it so Simon could see, he pulled open its front cover, revealing more word-covered pages. Simon could see the corners of black-and-white photographs intermixed with the papers.

"We received reports of a supernatural occurrence within the city of Haversham, near the western coast, on the edge of White Lake," Luthor explained.

"And the occurrence?"

Luthor looked up from the pages. "Werewolves, sir."

Simon sighed and shook his head. "Werewolves. Of course it is."

He reached out and brushed aside the papers, revealing a few of the pictures underneath. They were headshots of regional dignitaries whom Simon assumed had filed the reports with the monarchy, but he found no actual evidence of the reported werewolves.

"Luthor, dear chap, how many of these so-called supernatural occurrences have we investigated thus far?"

Luthor shrugged. "Six? Seven? Let's see, there was the vampire of Dormuth Castle."

"Which turned out to be merely a political coup against the seated governor."

"The swamp creature."

"A large lizard, to be sure," Simon replied, "but hardly supernatural in origin."

Luthor counted on his fingers. "The rising dead, the mischievous pixies, the ravenous hound, and the Grand Wizard of Templeton."

"Lest you forget the mummy in the catacombs," Simon added. "All debunked as charlatans." He sighed and rested his elbows on the table. "When I took this position, I imagined myself as a stalwart defender of the crown, keeping our kingdom safe against the invading magics of the southern continent. Instead, I'm exposing fraudulent wizards who are no more adept at magic than a common circus juggler."

"The threat from the south is real, no matter the false reports we've received thus far." Luthor removed his glasses and wiped the lenses with a handkerchief. "The Rift exists; it tore its path right through the center of their continent, nearly splitting it in two. Because of it, mystical creatures of all sorts plague their land. You may be unimpressed with the assignments we've been given to date, but we're keeping our kingdom safe. It only takes one of the magic creatures to slip past our borders to cause panic throughout the lands."

Simon sighed and sat back. He knew the dangers of the Rift. It had been twelve years since the Rift first appeared, tearing through the Kingdom of Kohvus. They had felt the earthquakes hundreds of miles to the north, within their own kingdom. Simon had only been a young man then, barely into his teens, but he remembered the horror stories of creatures of legend crawling from the Rift. The magic it had introduced was a contagious toxin that infected first Kohvus, and then neighboring lands. They had closed their own borders, severing trade and tourism with the southern continent, but they lived in constant fear that the same mystical nightmares could reach past their borders.

"Tell me more about this report of werewolves," he said flatly.

Luthor turned the folder around and quickly read the report again. "The report was sent by Governor Godwin, on behalf of a Mister Gideon Dosett, a local business owner. Mr. Dosett operates a number of oil drilling companies, operating around White Lake. The reports of werewolf sightings are all a result of recent attacks on his drilling and refinery stations."

"They were probably just hungry wolves or local competition sabotaging his operations."

"A number of local politicians actually agree with you, sir. Mister Marrith Tambor, head of the Miner's Guild, and Mister Nathanial Orrick, president of the Artisan's Union, both think the report is rubbish and unfounded."

"Still," Simon bemused, "the crown thought there was enough evidence to support sending an Inquisitor to investigate."

"Apparently, Mr. Dosett holds some sway with the local governor. The governor placed his considerable political weight behind the allegations in this report."

Simon stared into the flickering flame. “Even so, I think it far more likely that we’ll discover another fraudulent claim. Disproving these werewolves should take little effort on our part.”

Simon pinched the bridge of his nose and furrowed his brow, like he was in pain. Luthor set aside the report.

“Are you feeling ill?”

Simon shook his head. “It’s just a headache. I think it’s the altitude. The thin air doesn’t agree with my body.”

Luthor pulled his doctor’s bag from the seat beside him and set it on the table in front of him. Despite his caution when setting it down, it still clinked as glass vials bumped together. Unclasping the top of the bag, he pulled it open.

“Please, Luthor, none of your pharmaceuticals today.”

“Your head hurts from an imbalance of air. Too much nitrogen from the height and not nearly enough oxygen. I can mix something that will remedy your ailment.”

Simon knew better than to argue with his friend. He sat back against the seat and let the apothecary work.

Luthor removed an empty vial and an eyedropper from the bag. He slid a rubber bulb onto the back of the glass pipette and drew some dark liquid from one of the concealed jars within his bag. With a measured squirt, he filled half the empty vial. The man whistled quietly to himself as he worked blissfully, drawing a few more odd chemical concoctions into the dropper. When he was done, a dark, viscous liquid sloshed in the vial.

He reached across the table, offering the mixture to Simon. “Please drink the whole vial.”

“I think ‘vile’ is a more accurate form of the word,” Simon replied halfheartedly. Despite his protests, he took the liquid and sniffed it. He immediately wrinkled his nose at the foul-smelling brew. “Are you sure this is absolutely necessary?”

“Trust in your doctor,” Luthor said. “I haven’t tried to poison you yet.”

Simon swirled the thick liquid. “But you reserve that possibility for the future?”

“Drink.”

Simon brought the vial to his lips and threw his head back. The liquid burned as it rolled past his throat. He coughed and sputtered as he fought for a breath. As his lungs finally relaxed and the mixture settled warmly in his belly, he found his headache quickly receding.

"I always doubt you, and you never cease to amaze me," Simon said appreciatively. "What did you put in this?"

"A little of this. A little of that. Mainly a liquid distilled from the flowers of the poppy plant."

Simon felt the stresses of their assignment lifting from his mind. "Well, whatever it was, you're a miracle worker. I owe you thanks."

Luthor shook his head and quickly changed the subject. "Don't discount the possibility that these werewolves are real. All our myths are based to some degree on fact."

Simon looked up at his assistant. He had hoped they were done with this discussion. "Are you saying that werewolves, vampires, and zombies are all real?"

"Potentially. Someone had to create the legends once upon a time. To know that these same creatures are now pouring from the Rift lends credence to the stories of old."

"Then these magical creatures have escaped from the Rift before."

"Again, potentially. Never to the degree that they are now escaping, mind you, but I find it hard to believe that a realm of magic has existed in parallel to ours for so many thousands of years, yet there has never been a bleeding between the two."

Simon considered his reply but didn't get a chance to answer, as there was a soft knock on their door.

"Enter," Simon said.

The door opened, and a steward bowed slightly. "Forgive my intrusion, gentlemen, but the pilot wanted me to inform you that we are approaching the dock at Haversham."

"Thank you," he replied, and the steward quickly shut the door behind him.

Simon reached over and pulled the velvet rope, lifting the heavy curtain. Both men immediately felt the biting chill of the wintery air seeping through the thick, glass window. Despite their discomfort, they leaned closer and peered through.

The city of Haversham was a squat town but spread over a couple of miles. A wall like a castle parapet ringed it, though it served little defensive purpose. It kept the strong arctic winds and drifting snow at bay. Within the confines of the city, the streets were fairly clear of the constantly falling snow.

On the horizon, Simon could see one of the oil refineries owned by Mr. Dosett. Even from a great distance, it looked like a twisted steel cage, with external piping emerging and running along the building's perimeter before vanishing once more into an access tunnel. Spouts of flame burst intermittently from tall smoke stacks, and black smoke belched high into the air.

"There's the tower," Luthor said, pointing awkwardly out the window at a structure directly ahead of the zeppelin.

Simon craned his neck and could barely see the four-story port tower jutting out of the deep snow. He could feel the hum beneath his feet lessen as the pilot turned off the rear rotors, and the zeppelin began to drift forward on its own stored momentum. Cries rang out as they reached near the edge of the tower. Ropes were thrown from the zeppelin and caught by thickly clothed workers, who expeditiously tied them to cleats on the flat upper platform. When the lines went taut, the zeppelin lurched.

Luthor gathered the paperwork and stuffed it into an over-the-shoulder bag. He closed his doctor's bag with the same faint clink of glass and slid out of the booth. Simon stood while Luthor retrieved his suit coat. Together, they reached into the overhead compartment and pulled down thick, fur-lined jackets. Simon had no other bags in their compartment. Once he was dressed, he opened the door and entered the busy hallway.

Well-dressed men and women filed into the hallway. He stepped out of the way, letting an older couple pass by. As he waited for Luthor to finish collecting his bags, Simon slipped his top hat onto his head and affixed it in place with a pat. It sat slightly canted on his head in a style all his own.

Luthor struggled through the doorway, shifting his weight back and forth, as his bags caught on the doorframe. Simon shook his head and reached out, slipping the over-the-shoulder bag from Luthor's side.

By the time they were in the hallway, it was nearly empty. Most of the other passengers had already disembarked through the far gangplank. The closer they got to the exit, the colder it seemed to grow. The wind cut through even their thick coats and rushed up their pant legs. Simon shivered and pulled his coat closer. As he felt the chill wash over his ears, he wished his top hat covered those as well.

As they turned at the end of the hallway, Simon had to raise a hand to cover his eyes. The brilliant sunshine reflected off the snow, temporarily blinding him. As he blinked away the spots in his vision, Luthor paused beside him. The apothecary slipped something over his glasses and smiled. Simon looked over to see dark lenses clipped onto his assistant's wire-frame glasses. The lenses blocked out the light. Luthor stepped past him and stepped lithely onto the sloped gangplank.

Simon shook his head and followed, walking carefully down the slippery, wooden ramp. Crossbeams added footholds but his smooth-bottomed shoes still slipped on the wood in between. His hands grasped the cold ropes until his knuckles grew white.

They stopped at the bottom of the ramp. A worker passed before them wearing heavy contraptions on his back. Rubber hoses jutted from the contraption, connecting different steel and brass containers to one another. A smoke stack protruded up over the man's shoulder, belching black smoke into the air. One of the hoses ran over the man's arm and connected to a nozzle in his hand. With a squeeze of the nozzle, a gentle flame poured onto the dock's frozen rooftop. The warm flames quickly melted the ice, leaving the surface wet rather than slippery.

With the ice cleared, they were ushered into a building at the end of the flat rooftop. Stepping inside was like entering a sauna. The heat practically struck Simon physically, making him stagger. After exposure to the harsh wind outside, entering the building was a welcome relief.

A sword-bearing guard stood at a table straight ahead and motioned for the two men to approach. As they reached his table, he gestured for them to place their bags on the table.

"Paperwork please, gentlemen," the guard said.

Simon reached into his coat and pulled out a folded piece of paper. As he unfurled the paper, the guard could see the ribbon and wax seal at the bottom. He didn't need to read the page. Pressed into the center of the deep red wax was the royal seal.

The guard immediately grew flustered, and he bowed his head respectfully. "Forgive me, Inquisitor."

"There's nothing to be forgiven," Simon said, clearly enjoying this aspect of his station as Royal Inquisitor. "You were merely doing your job. Now, I believe you were expecting us?"

"Of course, sir," the guard said. He spun on his heels and motioned excitedly toward another guard near the far door. "You have an escort awaiting you in the lower tunnels, Inquisitor. The governor is expecting you for dinner this evening."

The other guard approached, equally flustered. Simon gestured for Luthor to follow the arriving guard, and they approached the stairwell that would lead into the tunnels that ran beneath the city.

CHAPTER Two

THE GUARD LED THE TWO MEN INTO A WOODEN elevator. When they were both safely inside, he pulled an extendable metal cage across the door and latched it into place. Reaching out, he pulled a lever that stood beside the door. Near its base, large, metal gears turned against one another as the elevator's brake was released. It vibrated, and then shook roughly, as the gears above it began turning. They slowly descended toward the subterranean tunnels. Simon occupied himself by watching the hammered copper wall of the elevator shaft slowly glide past.

"What about our other bags?" Luthor asked after he grew sufficiently bored with their descent.

The guard looked to the shorter man. "A porter has already procured your bags. They will be waiting for you when you arrive at the governor's estate."

Simon knew the answer to Luthor's question before he had asked it but knew that the apothecary was likely just passing the time. Their trip on the zeppelin had been long from the capital, and the dreadfully slow elevator ride wasn't the enthusiastic adventure he hoped it would be.

He looked around, admiring the craftsmanship that went into the car itself. Small reliefs had been expertly carved into the wood, leaving intricate patterns throughout each of the three main sides of the elevator car. The electric light hanging above them was encased in frosted glass, diffusing the harsh light. In another setting, the ride would have been a remarkable display, as Simon was sure the governor had intended it to be. Unfortunately, the capital was full of technological wonders, the least of which seemed to be the pulley-operated elevator.

The guard looked at the Royal Inquisitor, and Simon offered a smile he hoped expressed that he was pleased. The truth was that he would have much preferred taking the stairs down the four or five flights. In the time they had ridden the elevator, he could have been in the tunnels and halfway to the governor's estate. Sadly, he realized, pomp and circumstance often took priority over practicality.

After seemingly an eternity, the moving wall in front of them gave way and exposed the worked stone of the underground passageway. The elevator came to rest on the hard ground with a jarring stop and the guard unlatched the metal door, sliding it aside. Simon nodded to the man before stepping out of the car.

The reception beyond the door was more than Simon would have preferred. A precession of gubernatorial guards stood at attention on either side of the tunnel, their livery emblazoned with the governor's crest. A bespectacled man stood in the middle of the passageway, calmly adjusting the cufflinks that protruded from the ends of his charcoal-colored suit. He wore a bowler cap, tilted low in the front so that the brim nearly touched the frame of his glasses. Seeing Simon and Luthor, the man approached and extended his hand.

As Simon shook the man's hand, the governor's liaison introduced himself. "It's an honor to have you visiting our humble town, gentlemen. My name is Patrick Mulvane, advisor to the governor. He apologizes for not being able to meet you in person but his responsibilities often keep him indisposed."

"Inquisitor Whitlock," Simon said, making introductions. "This is my assistant, Luthor Strong."

Patrick arched his eyebrows in surprise. "Just the two of you, then? I was told a team of Royal Inquisitors would be responding to our request."

Simon placed his hands on his hips, feeling slighted at the insinuation that he and Luthor alone would be inadequate. "Mr. Strong and I are a team. The Inquisitors, too, are often so busy as to be indisposed when help is requested. Be glad that you received a response at all."

Patrick noticed the acidic tone and realized he had overstepped his bounds. "My apologies, sir. Perhaps it would be best if I led you to the estate."

"Perhaps that would be for the best."

Patrick led the way. As Simon and Luthor fell into step behind the man, the guards turned and followed, flanking the small group. Simon glanced at the heavily dressed guards with passing interest. The men kept their gazed locked straight before them, not bothering with a glance toward the two visiting dignitaries. Sabers bounced against their hips as they walked. Each of the guards held a flintlock rifle, the barrels of which rested against the men's shoulders, allowing for a regular arm swing while they walked.

Despite the swaying weapons, Simon nodded approvingly as he read the thin, metal plates affixed to the barrels of the rifles.

"What do you see?" Luthor asked, knowing the Inquisitors propensity for noticing minute details.

"They're carrying Renault flintlock rifles," Simon replied. "They're an exquisite brand. The boring in the barrel is practically unmatched for ball-firing rifles."

"Correct me if I'm wrong, sir," Luthor remarked, "but they have a price that matches their craftsmanship. Unless I'm mistaken, of course."

Simon shook his head. "You're not mistaken. Clearly, the governor spares no expense when it comes to his employees. It already tells me much about the man we are to meet."

The tunnel from the elevator merged into a wider passage. Like the one they had just left, the tunnel was smooth, polished stone, with lacquered wood support struts set intermittently throughout the corridor. Naked bulbs dangled from wires overhead and exposed copper cables ran across the ceiling, providing power to the long string of lights. Between the bulbs were oil-burning fires that provided pools of warmth to the cold, stone passageway. Simon alternated shivering from the chill and feeling bothered by the intense heat as they passed underneath the heat lamps.

Unlike the street above, the tunnels were alive with people and foot traffic. Wagons bounced merrily along the cobbled corridor floor and more people flooded from merging side passages.

"These tunnels are remarkable," Luthor said as he examined the craftsmanship of the smooth, chiseled walls.

Patrick glanced over his shoulder and smiled. "These tunnels were once a cave system that existed before the city was built. They extend beneath the entire city and beyond. Once they were discovered, they were smoothed and reinforced. Now they serve as a refuge for the citizens during particularly severe winter storms, when even our walls can't hold back the winter winds and massive snowdrifts."

"Remarkable," Luthor muttered again.

Simon looked over to his friend, who seemed enthralled with the architecture. "I wish I knew how long it would take before we can delve fully into our work."

Luthor looked over, and his eyes came back into focus. He coughed faintly to clear his throat. "We'll be required to have dinner with the governor at a minimum, as decorum dictates. Beyond that, I believe we'll be at his mercy."

"Forgive my prying," Patrick interjected, "but the governor does indeed have a dinner planned for you both. He's invited a number of local dignitaries to help welcome you to our land and to show his appreciation."

Simon reached up and ran his hand along his thin moustache. "Will Gideon Dosett be one of those dignitaries?"

"I should assume so," the advisor replied. "Mr. Dosett is one of the wealthiest and most influential men in Haversham."

"Where would I call on Mr. Dosett if I wished to speak to him during my investigation? Does he live near the governor's estate?"

If Haversham were anything like the capital, then every noble would have their residence near the ranking royal as they jockeyed for political favor.

"You wouldn't have to go far at all," Patrick explained. "Mr. Dosett was actually recently granted quarters within the estate."

Simon frowned and exchanged glances with Luthor. Though Haversham's governor was only a far distant cousin of the king, he was still a royal. Opening his home to a businessman, even one clearly as influential as Dosett, was unusual.

Simon noticed many of the pedestrians in the tunnel moved hastily out of the way at the sight of the governor's advisor and guards. They eyed

Simon warily from their places as he passed, as though untrusting.

The din of conversation grew as it echoed along the stone walls. Their tunnel suddenly opened into a massive, rounded hub, where a half dozen other tunnels converged into an underground marketplace. Vendor stalls were erected around the walls of the room, and merchants hawked their wares to the people who passed by.

Looking up, he could see the ceiling arched overhead as though forming a natural dome. Sunlight spilled from the top, which was open to the air above. A soft, white snow fell through the gap, collecting in a pile that was illuminated by the shaft of light from the surface. The snow melted quickly near the mounted heaters, and its water collected in vats submerged into the floors nearby.

Patrick led them across the room to a staircase carved into the stone. It was a much narrower passage, requiring the guards to follow single file behind the group. The stairwell twisted as it rose, and Simon could feel the cool breeze blowing through the passage. Though he had felt uncomfortable under the intense heat of the overhead lamps in the tunnel, he immediately longed for their warmth as the wind blew over him. Patrick seemed unfazed by the biting chill as he led the way. Soon, natural sunlight filtered over the rocks, illuminating the passage ahead.

The stairs ended at an open doorway, its glass doors propped open, that led out onto a wide, cobblestone street in the city. Though it seemed that the majority were wandering through the tunnels below, Simon found the surface streets equally busy as people moved from store to store, purchasing provisions.

People walked with a stoop, huddled in their thick jackets and fur-lined boots. Their carried groceries were tucked under their arms as they hurried home before their fresh-baked bread froze in the arctic air. Simon could feel the breeze blowing across him. It cut through his jacket and straight to his bones. He knew that the wind beyond the city wall was much worse as it howled down from the mountains and across the plains. He was glad that the majority of the wind was kept at bay by the walls, but he and Luthor were from a much more temperate region of the continent. He was woefully unprepared for the cold this far north.

"The wind can be difficult to adjust to," Patrick said, noting Simon's discomfort. "You do eventually grow accustomed to it."

Simon looked over to Luthor and wasn't surprised to see the man shivering uncontrollably. "You have a keen mind, Luthor, but you lack the constitution for winter."

Luthor frowned as he looked at his friend. "With all due respect, sir, this is why I've repeatedly insisted that we investigate reports only from the southern coast."

Simon laughed as he followed Patrick onto the street. Their walk was blissfully short. At the end of the lane, the road ended at a wrought-iron gate. It was already open, offering a view of the palatial estate that sat in the middle of the city. Turrets rose from the corners of the three-story building. Balconies protruded from most of the open windows, culminating with a giant terrace that covered much of the third floor, where the building itself was recessed. Stone gargoyles sat perched at any exposed corners, adding to the opulence of the manor house.

Though Simon was loathed to admit it, he was impressed. He had assumed that the governor had been assigned to this distant outpost because he was of low standing, despite the royal blood in his veins. He would have expected to see a more subdued home, one fitting the governor's station. The home before him rivaled many of the mansions owned by royals in line for the throne.

Valets opened the doors to the mansion as they approached, and the glittering chandelier that hung in the vaulted foyer entranced Simon. Light filtered through the thousands of crystals, casting dancing droplets of light that sparkled on the floor.

A footman approached and took Patrick's jacket before extending his arm for Simon and Luthor's as well. The men removed their thick jackets and draped them over the man's arm before he retreated into a nearby parlor.

A line of maids and footmen stood at rapt attention before the stairwell that curved gently to the second floor. Patrick paused before the butler, a stout man who looked to be in his mid-forties.

"Mr. Archibald," the advisor said. "Is everything in order?"

"Yes, sir," the butler responded with a polite nod of his head.

"Excellent. Let me introduce you to the Royal Inquisitor and his assistant. They will be our guests until such a time as their investigation into this dreadful werewolf business is completed."

That was the first time Simon had heard anyone else mention the beasts. He gauged the reaction of the staff and was surprised to see many of them involuntarily cringe in fear. He frowned at the obvious superstitious lot and felt more justified that his investigation would debunk yet another legend of yore.

"Very good, sir," the butler replied.

Patrick returned to the two men who stood just inside the doorway with their shoes dripping melting snow onto the hardwood floor.

"The governor will see you for dinner promptly at seven," he told them. "If you have any needs or wants, please let Mr. Archibald know. He and his staff are among the best you will find."

"Thank you for your generosity," Simon said.

With a bow, Patrick turned and disappeared into an adjoining room.

The butler introduced Simon and Luthor to the wait staff that would take them to their rooms. The footmen offered to carry their few remaining bags but Luthor adamantly refused, clinging tightly to his doctor's case.

They were led up the stairwell and onto the second floor. The walls were flourished with flowered wallpaper. Simon could smell potpourri seeping from underneath the closed doors that they passed, adding to the illusion of springtime in the land of perpetual winter.

When they reached the end of the hall, Simon's guide led him to the left while Luthor went to the right.

"See you at dinner then?" Simon asked as the footman unlocked and opened the door to his room.

"I'll knock on your door shortly before seven, if that's all right," Luthor replied.

Simon nodded and the two men parted, entering their respective suites. As part of his station as an Inquisitor, Simon had grown accustomed to being housed in large rooms. The size of the suite in which he found himself took his breath away. The door opened onto a living room, beyond which double glass doors led to one of the many balconies around the building. His bedroom and washroom were separated, with doorways leading to each on his right.

"I hope everything is in acceptable order for you, sir," the footman said.

"Everything is… remarkable."

"Very good, sir. Is there anything else you require?"

Simon shook his head. He fetched a silver coin from his coat pocket and handed it to the man. The footman backed out of the room, pulling the door closed behind him.

Walking into the room, Simon glanced into the bedroom and was pleased to see his leather bag already resting on a chest at the foot of his bed. He walked past the leather couch and pulled open the double doors. Stepping out onto the balcony, he admired the view. The squat buildings of the city were sprawled before him, their rooftops glistening as the sunlight reflected off the snow. It was a magical view, ruined only by another strong breeze that washed over him. Without his thick jacket, he felt his muscles seize in revolt. Simon hurried back inside, shutting the doors before he rushed over to the burning fireplace.

As his body warmed again, he pulled out his pocket watch and checked the time. Knowing he only had an hour before Luthor would call on him, he walked into the bedroom and began preparing for dinner.

CHAPTER Three

SIMON LOOKED IN THE MIRROR. HE TILTED HIS HEAD from side to side, examining his coifed hair, held in place by an obscene amount of hair grease. He pulled a comb from his pocket and ran it along the side of his head, smoothing out a stray strand of hair.

He had changed into a more formal suit for the dinner, leaving behind his pistol but retaining his pocket watch. He pulled the silver piece from his vest pocket and checked the time, frowning when he saw that it was nearly seven already. He tucked it away and walked to his suite's front door. As he pulled it open, he startled Luthor as the diminutive man exited his own room.

Luthor had tried his best to tame his wild mane of curly hair, but to no avail. Large curls stood out defiantly from where he had tried to smooth them against his head, and they draped over the upper half of his trimmed muttonchops.

"I thought you were going to knock on my door well in advance of our dinner reservation?" Simon chided.

Luthor brushed his hands together, cleaning off a white powder that clung to his fingertips. "I was, sir, but I lost track of time. I barely got myself dressed before meeting you here in the hall."

Simon stepped into the hallway and pulled his door closed. He reached across the divide and straightened Luthor's tie, which hung askew from the center of his neck. As he straightened the tie, he caught a scent of something foul in the air. He wrinkled his nose and glanced over his friend's shoulder.

"Do you smell that? It's atrocious. It's a mixture of spoiled milk and gangrene. Please tell me that isn't coming from your room."

Luthor blushed slightly and looked over his shoulder. "I accidentally broke one of my vials when I was unpacking. It's an unpleasant scent, to be sure."

Simon frowned. "Please don't tell me that was one of the liquids in that foul brew you gave me on the zeppelin."

Luthor pushed his glasses back up his nose but remained silent.

"Luthor?" Simon asked, arching his brow inquisitively. "It wasn't, was it?"

When the apothecary didn't reply, Simon threw up his hands in disgust and stormed down the hall.

"In my defense," Luthor said as he hurried to catch up, "you told me not to tell you."

"I swear that you're trying to poison me. You slip these terrible concoctions into my drinks just to kill me slowly."

"There are actually indigenous tribes along the far eastern shores that intentionally ingest poisons in an attempt to build a resistance to the natural venoms that exist in their flora and fauna. Despite a wide spread acceptance of the practice, only a very small percentage of them actually die."

"You find the most remarkable ways to try to defend your inane actions," Simon said. "I'm not an indigenous tribesman from the eastern shore. Please stop trying to poison me."

"I'd never poison you without your knowledge," Luthor said before reconsidering his word choice.

"I guess I should be pleased that my friends will stab me in the face, rather than stabbing me in the back."

They descended the curved marble staircase and were met at the bottom by the butler. He led them through an empty parlor, though Simon could smell the lingering scent of whiskey and cigars. He regretted being so late to the dinner and having missed the social hour leading up to the meal. It would have been a good opportunity to discuss his investigation with those involved or, at the very least, a chance to enjoy fine alcohol and a smoke.

The butler slid a set of double doors aside and stepped into the formal dining room.

"Ladies and gentlemen, Royal Inquisitor Whitlock and Mr. Luthor Strong."

The guests all slid their chairs across the floor and stood politely as the two men entered. A long table dominated the room, capable of holding far more than the dozen people that were currently seated. Most of the guests looked like couples—aristocratic husbands and wives who were enjoying the company of the local royalty. Simon gave them all only a halfhearted inspection, wondering if any of them matched the pictures buried in the report they received. The governor sat at the end of the table in the place of honor. The man was portly and leaned back heavily against the velvet-lined chair.

Though he was a cousin to the king, the two men shared very little similarities. They both had the same hazel-colored eyes and dark hair that ended in a widow's peak on their forehead. There were little comparisons beyond that. The king was a man who maintained peak physical conditioning through swordplay and boxing. It was possible that beneath the governor's borderline obese physique hid a man of similar musculature to the king, but Simon had his doubts.

The governor's cheeks grew rosy as he came face to face with the Inquisitor. Simon knew he had that effect on people. The position was one of great honor in the royal court but was viewed as little more than a witch hunter occupation by the common populace. Though Simon considered his approach to his investigations to have a more gentle touch than his peers, he knew the reputation of most Inquisitors. If there was a rumor of supernatural or paranormal activity, the Inquisitors became Death, riding into towns with the intent to destroy not just the mystical creature, but also anyone who stood in their way. The result had been fewer legitimized reports, despite Simon knowing that these monsters existed and appeared on occasion within their borders. Villagers would rather face their own fears and slay the monster alone, than call on an Inquisitor and risk their own lives even further.

"Inquisitor Whitlock," the governor said, "please come and sit by me."

The chair immediately to the governor's left was unoccupied. Simon looked at Luthor apologetically as his associate took his seat at the far end of the row of chairs. As Simon reached his seat, the governor waved for everyone else to be seated as well.

"Sit, sit," the rotund man at the head of the table said, patting Simon's chair. "It's so rare that we get visitors from the capital, and an Inquisitor no less. I must know everything. Tell me all there is to know about the city and my family."

Simon smiled politely at the man, but he felt dreadfully uncomfortable sitting beside the governor. He cared little for small talk and had never mastered the subtle nuances of political repartee. If left to his own devices, he would have arrived incognito and conducted his investigation from the privacy of a hotel room somewhere within the city. It was Luthor who served as Simon's protocol guide, letting him know what was demanded of him by his royal position.

"Yes," said a voice across from Simon. "Do tell us all about the capital and the royal family."

Simon turned toward the suited man sitting across from him. His dark hair was pulled back into a ponytail, which was tied in place with a broad ribbon. A frilly cravat protruded from the top of his high vest. His facial features were hard to discern, as he drummed his fingers together in front of his face. The intensity of his black eyes, however, seemed to bore into Simon.

"Mr. Dosett, I presume," Simon said with a nod.

Gideon Dosett nodded and raised his hand in a mock salute. "It appears my reputation precedes me."

"Your name is spoken in many of the circles around this city," Simon replied tactfully.

Gideon dropped his hands, exposing the abnormally red lips that had been concealed. Simon couldn't tell if it was the result of makeup or just a natural blush.

"You've heard only good things, I hope."

Simon nodded. "Only the most pleasant of descriptions, though my associate and I hardly came here to confirm rumored reputations."

He looked to the governor, expecting the man to respond. Since he was the dinner's host, it was his right to bring up the subject of the pending investigation. Such unpleasant topics weren't normally discussed during dinner, but Simon was already growing impatient. He had already overstepped his bounds by alluding to his mission.

The governor nodded. "The werewolves are a dreadful business and threaten the safety of our city. They've become a painful thorn in our collective sides. We're honored that the crown saw fit to grace us with an Inquisitor. Though, truth be told, I'm hardly the man with whom you should speak. Mr. Dosett's businesses suffer the worst from these assaults. The werewolves have destroyed, what is it now, three of your drilling stations?"

"Four," Gideon replied flatly. His lips pressed together until the blood drained from them. "Four drilling stations destroyed and over a dozen men killed. We are, indeed, lucky to have an Inquisitor looking into this unfortunate business."

Simon was flattered but still uncomfortable with the attention. Before he could respond, servants appeared with the meal's first course. Conversation forgotten, the entire table sipped their soup quietly, the still air broken only by the occasional slurp of the thin liquid.

As soon as they finished their soup, the servants appeared again and cleared away the plates.

"We visited the capital once, you know?" an elderly man remarked from further down the table.

Simon was glad to have someone else to talk to and turned with a broad smile toward the older gentleman. "I hope you found the capital to your liking."

His wife chuckled and placed a hand affectionately on his arm. They exchanged glances before the older man spoke again. "Heavens no. It was far too busy and full of people. We hardly ever had a chance to be alone with our thoughts, much less alone with one another." When he noticed the surprised looks from another couple, the man politely cleared his throat. "Forgive me, I get carried away sometimes. Things like that are hardly dinner conversations."

"There is no need to apologize," Luthor said. "I find the city to be oppressive sometimes. I grew up near the marshes of Narampoor, where your nearest neighbor was an hour's ride by train and even longer by horse and buggy."

"You'd fit in perfectly with us in Haversham," the man replied. "If you ever get tired of being around the busy city, you can always take the tunnels out of town and wander the ice flows for a while."

"I believe I would like that," Luthor replied.

"I want to ask about the Inquisitor's line of work," said the woman sitting beside Luthor, "but I fear it would be imposing. Would you mind?"

Simon could barely see her around her husband, but her powdered wig extended high above the man's head. "I don't mind at all, madam, but it's our host's right to allow such talk at the table."

He turned toward the governor, who glanced over to Gideon before waving his hand, permitting the topic to be broached.

Simon turned back to the woman. "What would you like to know, madam?"

The woman leaned forward, and Simon could see her painted face. Her skin was white, though her lips were a brilliant scarlet. Unlike Gideon, hers were clearly caused by an application of lipstick.

"Have you seen any monsters?" she asked.

"Gertrude!" her husband interjected.

"No, madam," Simon said quickly, before she felt embarrassed by the topic of conversation. "We have yet to see any real monsters."

"But surely this isn't your first assignment as an Inquisitor?" her husband asked.

Simon laughed. "No, sir, though every Inquisitor has to begin somewhere. Luthor and I have been on a number of missions thus far, but we have yet to encounter an actual monster. All our experiences have been debunking general tomfoolery."

"It's a fascinating life you must lead, Inquisitor Whitlock."

"Please, just call me Simon. I believe we're among friends here and can be slightly less formal with one another."

"We've heard so many stories of monsters since the Rift appeared but never saw one for ourselves," she continued. "I started to wonder if they truly existed until the werewolves, of course."

"The Rift and the monsters it produces are quite real, I assure you," Simon replied. "The issue is not whether they exist… but if people would recognize them when they saw them. The reason Inquisitors disprove so many reports of monsters in our kingdom is because people assume the monsters to be things of subtlety; that if they were to encounter them on the street, they'd look mostly like a man but with slight monstrous variations to the brow or the shoulders or the legs. The truth is, the monsters are far more, well, monstrous than people are wont to believe. They see a disfigured man and assume him a byproduct of the Rift when, in fact, he's just an unfortunate soul."

"The Rift has made people paranoid, jumping at shadows," Luthor expounded. "The majority of reports filed to the Inquisitors are proven false by the team deployed. Most of the reports are filed because the people involved either suffers from the vapors or hysteria."

"Which brings us to why you are with the Inquisitor," Gideon said with a smile. "I had wondered the purpose of an apothecary as a cohort."

"Indeed," Luthor said with a nod. "Vapors and hysteria are both treatable conditions through a regimen of chemicals or other pharmaceutical interventions. An apothecary is actually the perfect associate for an Inquisitor."

"You make a very solid argument," Gideon said. "I guess I must raise my glass to you both. We're truly lucky to have you here in Haversham."

He raised his glass and nodded to Simon. "To the Inquisitor," he turned toward Luthor, "and to the apothecary."

"Here, here," the other guests said, raising their glasses.

Simon raised his glass begrudgingly and looked toward the governor. The man took a long drink from his wineglass. He smiled broadly, as he pulled his glass from his lips.

"Here, here," he said.

The servants brought the main course, setting down a plate of beef. The smell was amazing, and Simon's stomach growled. He waited for the governor to take a bite before picking up his fork and knife and carving off a piece of meat. As he was lifting the food to his mouth, Gideon spoke again.

"So will you begin your investigation tomorrow?"

Wistfully, Simon sat his fork back down and glanced across the table. "That is our intent."

"What do you expect to find?" he asked.

Simon shrugged. "I won't know until I have a chance to inquire, though I presume I'll find that there is a much more rational explanation for these werewolves than something supernatural."

"You speak of the monsters beyond our borders but you're still very much a skeptic, aren't you?" Gideon asked. "You don't actually believe you'll find werewolves when you investigate?

"The basis of my work requires me to be skeptical. I still keep an open mind, however, and reserve judgment until after my investigation is complete."

Gideon turned toward Luthor. "You, however, seem like a true believer. If I didn't know better, I'd think you were actually excited at the prospect of finding a real monster during your visit."

Luthor scratched absently at his arm and furrowed his brow as he thought. "I am loath to admit, while in the company of an Inquisitor, that I secretly do hope to find creatures of legend when we are sent out on missions."

The guests at the table chuckled.

"Though it's our station to contain any magic that might threaten our lands, it's almost heartbreaking to prove that the mummy of the lower catacombs is nothing more than a pauper in ragged clothing scaring away grave robbers."

Simon picked up his fork and placed the meat in his mouth. Gideon took a long draw from his wine. As he sat the glass down, he licked the purple tint from his lips.

"You both seem to take your work very seriously," he said.

Simon swallowed and nodded. "Magic, in all its forms, represents a threat to the sovereignty of the kingdom. It must be discovered and, if it can't be contained, destroyed. It's the motto by which every Inquisitor lives."

"So you think our werewolves are a hoax?" Gideon asked again.

"Until I see one with my own eyes, I will believe them to be trickery of the mind."

Gideon smiled. "So you won't believe them real until you see one for yourself?"

Simon set down his fork again. "What game are you playing at?"

"We killed one during their last raid on one of my refineries. It's available for you to inspect, if you feel so inclined."

"My good man," Simon replied, "I must teach you which information to lead with when starting a conversation."

He slid his chair back, the wood screeching on the hardwood floor as he pushed away from the table.

CHAPTER Four

SIMON HELD HIS HANDS ALOFT AS LUTHOR TIED THE strings of the smock behind his back. With the apron firmly in place, the apothecary retrieved rubber gloves and slid them over Simon's hands. He flexed his fingers as he maneuvered the gloves into a more comfortable position. His hands immediately began to sweat within the thick rubber. The gloves kept him sanitary during autopsies but were uncomfortable and often ungainly.

A tall man opened the door to the tiled room and stepped inside. He wore a roughly hewn wool vest and slacks, with a stained, white dress shirt with the sleeves rolled up to the elbow. He had a hat in his hand that he twisted nervously in the presence of the Royal Inquisitor.

"Pardon the intrusion, sir, but it's arrived if you're ready."

"I've never been more ready," Simon replied. "Have them bring it in carefully."

"Very good, sir."

The man stepped aside and held the door open for a group of muscular laborers behind him. The men entered the wide doorway, each at the corner of a large burlap bag. Despite the strength of the men, they clearly strained under the weight of their cargo. They huffed loudly as they tried to walk, though the center of the bag drooped low to the ground and impeded their steps.

"Set it up here," Simon said, patting the metal table beside which he stood. "Be gentle with it."

The men moved to one side of the table and, in unison, hefted the bag onto the table. They let out an audible sigh of relief when the job was done and, with a polite bow to Simon and Luthor, exited the room.

The other man remained at the door, holding it open.

"Is this everything?" Simon asked.

"No, sir," the man replied and quickly looked over his shoulder. "There is a pair of boxes that go along with the… the…"

"Werewolf. It's fine if you say it. Unless there's something about werewolves I don't know, saying their name isn't going to bring it back to life."

"No, I would suppose it wouldn't," the man said, though he didn't sound confident in his reply.

He looked visibly relieved when two of the muscular men returned carrying wooden crates. The insides of the crates were lined with hay. Simon could see row after row of glass jars jutting from the hay, filled with a blue liquid. Floating within the jars were bloated organs of different natures.

The men set down the jars and hastily exited. The man at the door watched them leave before turning back to Simon.

"If there's nothing else, sir, I'll be taking my leave."

Simon was looking at the shape beneath the burlap bag and waved his hand dismissively. "On your way out, send in the doctor, if you please."

The door swung shut as Simon retrieved a knife from a table beside him. He cut carefully at the corded string holding the edges of the burlap bag closed. With each cut of the string, he was able to pull away more and more of the bag. Slowly, the white fur beneath the bag was revealed.

His work was interrupted as the door swung open again, and a man in a white coat entered the room. The doctor had tuffs of gray hair protruding from the sides of his head, though he was perfectly bald on top. Aside from his hair, the man looked surprisingly young.

"You're the doctor?" Simon asked.

"Mr. Parrish, at your service," the man replied. "I conducted the original examination of the creature."

"Very good. Please stand beside Luthor and be available to answer any questions that might arise."

Simon went back to his work, carefully cutting away the string holding the satchel closed. The work was boring, but Simon had incredible patience when it came to his work. With a final slice, he cut away the last of the cord. With little pomp or circumstance, he threw back the top half of the burlap bag, exposing the body within.

He looked down in awe at the sheer size of the creature. The wolf measured nearly six feet long, even with the slight curvature of its body caused by rigor mortis. The specimen's body was covered by coarse, white fur, the same color as the snow falling over the city. The only break in its otherwise pure white body was a dark brown stain just behind its front leg. Pushing the fur aside, Simon could see a smooth bullet hole from where it had been shot.

"The creature has the appearance of a common winter wolf," Simon said as Luthor quickly transcribed onto a notebook, "albeit unnaturally large. I measure it at approximately six feet in length, not including the tail. My estimation is that it stood nearly four feet in height while walking on all four paws."

He moved around to the head of the wolf and pulled open its mouth. Both sets of canines were missing. Bloodied stumps marked the places where the teeth once sat imbedded in the jawbone.

"Canines have been removed by—" He looked toward the doctor for an answer.

"The canines were already gone by the time he arrived for my examination. They're prized by local hunters, so I wouldn't be surprised if they were torn out right after the kill."

Simon nodded, assuming as much. The tongue was missing as well, though he could see the clean surgical incision where it had been cut from the mouth. He ran his hands over the wolf's cheek until he reached the eyes. As he presumed, the eyelids were stitched shut.

He stepped away from the table and turned toward the pair of wooden crates filled with jars. He lifted a couple from their resting places in the hay and examined their content. The creature's organs floated in a blue concoction. Simon noted the liver and stomach before putting the jars back down. He sorted through a few more jars before he found the eyeballs. Despite the blue of the liquid, the pupils still shone a bright sky blue.

"Previous autopsy of the creature has resulted in the removal of the internal organs. Luthor, please note that the creature had blue eyes, consistent with the anatomy of a winter wolf. The internal organs all appear to be in good condition, preserved as they've been in a solution of formaldehyde, but removal from the body makes it impossible to discern their original placement or the true internal anatomy of the creature."

The doctor raised his hand to speak, and Simon nodded to him. "I have extensive notes and diagrams of the autopsy. I can provide those for your review, which should provide you all the information you need about from where the organs were removed."

"That would be most beneficial. Luthor will coordinate with you following my examination."

Simon sorted through the rest of the jars, seeing nothing out of the ordinary. "Luthor, please continue transcribing. The organs are consistent, again, with those of a winter wolf, though slightly enlarged to match the increased girth of the creature itself."

"As you'll see from my diagrams," Parrish said, "the organ placement within the werewolf when standing on its hind legs is actually more consistent with a human than a wolf."

Simon frowned at the interruption. "I've found nothing so far to allude to this being anything more than a wolf, but my autopsy is not yet completed."

"If I may," the doctor said, "I think you're being a little dismissive. I think this is far more than a simple winter wolf."

"You may not," Simon replied harshly.

"Please at least check the opposable thumbs on the forelegs," Doctor Parrish added.

Simon shot the man a stern look, and the doctor shrunk from his gaze. Dejected, the doctor leaned back against the far counter.

The Inquisitor approached the table again and pulled the front leg toward him. It ended in a padded foot, though he immediately noted the longer than normal fingers on the end of the paw. He stretched the fingers from side to side, noting their flexibility. Despite the fur and the claws protruding from the tips of the fingers, even he had to admit that they were remarkable human-like.

Simon turned the paw upward and immediately saw the thumb

protruding from underneath. He reached up and grasped the thumb, tugging firmly to see if it was actually attached. When he received resistance, he ran his fingers along the digit, feeling the joint bone where the thumb connected to the creature's wrist. He expected to find stitching where it had been sewn in place, but the connection seemed complete. For argument's sake, he ran his hand further up the creature's front arm, checking for any stitching where a taxidermist might have worked to create the monster of legend. Finding none, he frowned slightly.

He knew he should have been ecstatic at the idea that he had found a true werewolf, but his training wouldn't allow him to grow too overwhelmed. A clinical mind, not an emotional one, was needed during his investigation.

"What do you think, Simon?" Luthor asked as his pencil hovered over the page. The Inquisitor had been surprisingly quiet for the past few minutes, leaving the apothecary little to write in the journal.

"Is it a werewolf?" Parrish asked.

Simon turned and approached the jars once more. He pulled one of them at random from the crate, removed its lid, and sniffed. He immediately recoiled and replaced the lid.

He turned toward the doctor. "Your work was sloppy. Removing the organs and keeping them in this concentration of formaldehyde ruins any possibility of me conducting a further examination. Furthermore, the specimen should have been preserved so a proper autopsy could have been conducted by an Inquisitor, rather than by a local physician. Now leave us. We have Inquisitor business to discuss in private."

The doctor looked crestfallen as he exited the room. Simon looked up to catch Luthor's disapproving stare.

"What?"

Luthor shook his head. "You were far too hard on that man. He was only looking for your approval of his work."

Simon huffed. "He bungled his examination and left little for us to work with. Anyway, he's a doctor. He shouldn't require my approval of his work to feel validated."

"You're a Royal Inquisitor, Simon. Your words carry weight."

Simon pointed toward the werewolf in an attempt to assuage his guilt. Luthor was right; the man was only looking for Simon's validation of his work. Despite his harsh reply, he had been impressed with the doctor's abilities during the autopsy. The lines were clean and despite the overuse of the preserving agent, the organs all seemed to be in good condition.

"Do you think it's real?" Luthor asked, knowing he wouldn't get much more of a worthwhile discussion out of his partner. "Or do you think that this is merely a large winter wolf?"

Simon lifted the front leg and held up the paw so Luthor could see the opposable thumb jutting from its wrist. "I've checked underneath the fur. I've felt under the skin for any internal stitches. I've found nothing. If this was the work of a taxidermist in an attempt to fool us, then I owe the taxidermist a drink. This work is exquisite and the best I've ever seen."

"The alternative is that this isn't a hoax. I think it's time we admit that as a possibility."

Simon cringed at the thought. Despite wanting to find monsters on his missions, the report had stated that dozens of these creatures had been attacking Gideon's businesses. If that were true, it wasn't merely a single monster that slipped across their border from the south. This was an infestation.

"I'm not ready to say that this is a werewolf. I reserve that decision until after we talk to Mr. Dosett's naysayers. There were plenty of people who believed this whole thing to be an elaborate farce. I have to assume Gideon was willing to present this corpse as evidence, and they still said he was wrong. Let's talk to them in the morning, and then I'll decide whether or not we notify the crown."

As they exited the examination room, Luthor bid Simon a good night before turning toward one of the back stairwells. He glanced up the stairs to make sure none of the servants were nearby, and then peered around the corner to ensure the hallway beyond was empty as well.

He absently scratched at his arm beneath his sleeve, much like he had done at dinner. Undoing his cufflinks, he pulled back his sleeve to expose the redness beneath.

In the center of his forearm, a puckered rune was carved into his skin. The flesh around it was enflamed and angry. He scratched at it again and frowned.

Looking around once more to ensure he was alone, he pulled down his sleeve and hooked his cufflinks. With a slightly nervous huff, he hurried up the stairs toward his bedroom.

CHAPTER Five

SIMON COLLECTED HIS THINGS AND PUT ON HIS COAT. He found Luthor waiting in the hall. The diminutive man had already retrieved his cane from among his belongings and now used it as they walked along. Though the cane didn't serve any medical purpose, Luthor used it in the past with some success as a defensive weapon.

"Do you think Misters Tambor and Orrick will provide some contrary evidence to the werewolf you just examined?" Luthor asked as they reached the top of the staircase.

Simon brushed off a piece of lint from his top hat. "On the contrary, I expect they'll provide me little I could not discern with my own two eyes."

"Then why visit them at all? If you're convinced that the creature we examined is not an elaborate jest, then wouldn't our time be better spent figuring out ways to destroy their... pack? It's the right word for a group of wolves, but does the same terminology extend to werewolves?"

Simon smiled. "I believe we're in new territory, Luthor. You have the distinct privilege of defining the vernacular."

Luthor grinned broadly. "Pack will suffice, unless I decide to invent a term more fitting. You still didn't answer my question, though. If you believe that what we saw could be a werewolf and you don't think the Union and Guild representatives will convince you otherwise, why are we paying them a visit?"

Simon glanced around as they reached the bottom of the stairs and entered the foyer. He couldn't see anyone around, but he still remained silent until they walked outside.

"Something about this isn't sitting well with me," he said when he was sure they were out of earshot. "I should have already notified the crown and sent in a preliminary report. If I thought there was a chance that an entire pack—to borrow your term—of werewolves existed in the region, I should be sending for a company of royal guardsmen. Yet, I find myself hesitating. I keep asking myself how so many creatures could have arrived on our shore without anyone noticing. If they did somehow circumvent our defenses, then what purpose are they serving? The oil production from Mr. Dosett's refineries can't be of such great impact outside our borders to warrant its destruction. I can't put my finger on it, but something about this situation seems slightly off kilter. Sorry my response is so vague, but I have little to go on other than my intuition."

"Your intuition hasn't yet served you wrong," Luthor replied as he used his free hand to pull his collar closed against the midday chill. "Let's hope that these gentlemen will be able to shine further light on the mystery."

They walked through the wrought-iron gates of the gubernatorial estate and into the city proper. Simon took a deep breath and enjoyed the cool air on his face. His concerns about the werewolves—potential werewolves, he corrected himself—weighed heavily on his mind. It was an exhausting business without being coupled with the politics of the mansion. He was glad to be away from the aristocracy and walking along the rough cobblestone streets.

Despite the temperature remaining well below freezing, it was relatively warm for the area. People were out on the regular streets as opposed to traveling through the shored tunnels underground. Simon wore no badges that marked him as a Royal Inquisitor, but people bowed respectfully as they passed. It seemed that rumors spread rapidly, especially in a small city like Haversham.

Luthor's cane clicked on the stone with every other step, sounding a cadence for their silent walk. Though Simon enjoyed the apothecary's company, he was only able to review the facts of the investigation when left to his own devices.

He wanted to believe the facts lay out before him but struggled to accept that werewolves were roaming the countryside. For the past twelve years, the king had done a remarkable job of keeping the spreading magic at bay, going so far as hiring the enigmatic Order of Kinder Pel to found the original Inquisitors.

Though the Order existed before the forming of the Rift, they had focused all their energies toward destroying the denizens of the world of magic, wherever they appeared. They seemed a perfect fit for what the king was proposing, though their fanaticism alienated many of the early supporters of the Inquisitors. Ten years later, few of the current Royal Inquisitors were still a part of the Order. Simon had been offered an apprentice position following his training, but he didn't care for the fact that everything they did was so cloaked in secrecy. Even the initiation ritual was an intensely guarded secret. In the end, Simon had passed on their offer, choosing instead to go directly into his partnership with Luthor.

With the Order operating throughout the kingdom, albeit behind the scenes in many cases, Simon had trouble believing that Rift creatures could have established such a foothold on the northern continent.

Simon and Luthor walked through an open square. A dry fountain sat in the middle of the area. A carved marble horse decorated the top of the fountain with its mouth open to spew water high into the air. He wondered if it ever got warm enough to enjoy a running fountain or if it had merely been installed for the sense of opulence.

The square was equally deserted of anything of note, other than a few couples walking through as a shortcut to their final destinations. Simon assumed this was normally a marketplace, though, again, he wondered if it was ever warm enough to justify standing at a booth for hours at a time.

"There's the tavern," Luthor said, pointing with his cane toward a painted, wooden sign dangling from an awning.

As they opened the door, a bell jingled into the mostly empty tavern. A few patrons looked up from their pints. Their glasses hung halfway to their mouth when they recognized the strangers.

"Our reputation precedes us," Luthor said.

"Apparently, they don't get many visitors in Haversham," Simon replied, "not that I necessary blame people. This wouldn't be my first choice of a place in which to build a summer home."

Luthor laughed softly but stopped when he saw two gentlemen stand from one of the back tables. The pair of strangers smiled broadly at the Inquisitor as they approached, and Simon quickly surmised they were the two men they had come to meet.

"Inquisitor Whitlock, I presume," said the stockier of the two men from beneath his bushy moustache. "I feel honored that you've taken time out of your busy investigation to speak with us."

Simon shook the man's hand, admiring the calluses and his firm grip. "Think nothing of it. You would be Mr. Tambor, I presume."

Tambor's eyes widened in surprise. "How did you know?"

"The placement of the calluses on your hand, being more toward the palm at the base of the fingers, lends itself more to a man familiar with the swing of a pick axe and, therefore, the head of the Miner's Guild. Had your calluses been more along the fingertips, I would have placed your profession as one of artistry, including a skill set that involved a more refined work. Had that been the case, I would have immediately known that I was speaking instead to Mr. Orrick."

He turned toward the other man, who rubbed his handlebar moustache with delight. "Mr. Orrick, to whom I now have the pleasure of addressing."

Tambor laughed heartily, his belly shaking with delight. "Remarkable. Simply remarkable. The reputation of the Royal Inquisitors is well earned, I'll grant you that. Please, come join us for a meal or, at the very least, a drink."

"We'd be delighted to join you."

Orrick tugged at his lapel as he fell in step beside Luthor. "Am I to understand that you are not an Inquisitor?"

Luthor looked up at the tall, thin man and shook his head. "I'm a pharmacist by trade. It is by pure happenstance that I have come to accompany Simon."

They took seats around the table. The waitress brought over a round of pints, the tops of which held a thick layer of foam. Simon watched a few bubbles rise slowly through the thick, dark stout before picking up his glass and taking a drink. The beer was bitter but quickly warmed his insides as it settled on his stomach.

Simon licked the flecks of foam that clung to his lip and smiled appreciatively to the two suited gentlemen. "This certainly hits the spot on a cold day like this."

Tambor chuckled. "They're all cold days around here. A good stout or a hot toddy is always on the menu."

Simon sat his hat down on the table in front of him and ran his fingers through his hair, pushing it back away from his forehead. "If I may, I'd like to discuss what brings my associate and me here today."

Orrick frowned and grasped his glass a little tighter between his long boney fingers. "The werewolves, you mean?"

"Yes," Simon replied. "In the report the crown received, you were both listed as the biggest opponents to the idea that there were werewolves beyond the city walls."

Orrick and Tambor exchanged knowing glances, but it was the heavyset man who spoke. "I fear the intent of our objection wasn't made clear in the report. We believe there are werewolves."

"Yes," Orrick agreed. "Of that, there's little doubt."

Simon sat back surprised. He drummed his fingers on the table as he collected his thoughts. "Perhaps I do not understand. The report said that you two opposed the idea that the city was under siege by these supernatural creatures."

"Exactly," Tambor said, nodding enthusiastically.

"Precisely," Orrick added.

Simon looked over at Luthor perplexed. "I'm not sure I fully understand."

Tambor leaned forward, resting his elbows on the table. "I assume the governor let you see the body of the werewolf, did he? There are more where that one came from, of that I'm sure. The difference is that I don't think they pose a threat to the city. We're not 'under siege' as you put it, which was why we objected to the exaggerated report submitted by the governor."

"By Mr. Dosett, you mean," Orrick corrected, nearly spitting the name like venom.

"But there have been numerous attacks," Luthor said.

"On oil refineries and drilling stations out near the lake," Tambor said.

"Owned by Mr. Dosett," Orrick added.

Simon raised a finger, silencing the group. He turned the index finger to his mouth and tapped his lips thoughtfully. "So your issue isn't with the werewolves, who you believe exist? Your issue rests solely with—"

"Mr. Dosett," they said in unison.

"Interesting," Simon said, as he motioned toward Luthor.

His assistant reached into his waistcoat and pulled out a notebook and pencil. Luthor began furiously taking notes as the conversation continued.

"Please explain," Simon said.

Tambor cleared his throat. "Every attack so far has been confined to property owned by Mr. Dosett. If the werewolves exist, and we have no reason to assume they don't, they have never bothered any of my mining operations."

"Nor have they bothered any of my artisans," Orrick said. "Leatherworking, cobbling, tailoring, and architecture all continue unabated and unhindered. Whatever the complaints of the werewolves, they reserve their bile solely for Gideon Dosett."

Simon felt mildly exacerbated. The two men at the table seemed oblivious to the issue at hand and the sole reason for Simon and Luthor's presence in town, which was the investigation of magical outbreaks. He was faced with one of the largest infestations identified to date, yet these two gentlemen treated it like it was nothing more than a general inconvenience, and one reserved for someone else.

"These are magical creatures beyond the walls of your city," Simon began, trying to keep his frustration in check. "As Luthor is keen to point out, these monsters seem to be based on the legends we all heard as school children. If they are to be believed, then these creatures are carriers of lycanthropy, which is highly contagious and transmittable through their saliva. You may not see them as an issue, but your entire town is teetering on the brink of destruction, especially if this infection spreads."

"Then we're correct in placing our trust in you, Inquisitor," Tambor said with a smile mostly concealed by his bushy moustache.

Simon sighed. "What is your issue with Gideon Dosett?"

"Where to begin?" Orrick said with a huff. "He came to town only six months ago and started buying property both within and outside of the city. It wasn't his purchases so much as the way the transactions occurred.

He bought businesses that had been in families for generations and paid a few coppers for every gold piece the land was actually worth. I don't know how he did it, but he swindled good men out of their livelihood."

"Did he strong arm them?" Luthor asked, looking up from the notebook. "Did he threaten them with physical harm or extort them? How come no one reported his behavior to the governor?"

"Because the governor is in his pocket?" Tambor said. When he noticed everyone's surprised expressions, he lowered his eyes. "It's the truth. Everyone's thinking it; they just don't have the fortitude to admit it to strangers, much less an Inquisitor."

"Making allegations of corruption against one of the king's cousins is serious business," Simon warned. "I'm assuming you have proof?"

Tambor refused to look up and meet Simon's stern gaze. "No, other than the man lives in the governor's own home. It's indecent, especially considering Dosett is clearly more than capable of purchasing his own home here in town."

Simon stood and retrieved his top hat from the table. "Gentlemen, I thank you for your time. Sadly, my associate and I must attend to other matters pertaining to our investigation. Please excuse us."

Luthor tucked his notebook and pencil into his coat and stood, nodding politely to both men before hurrying to catch up to Simon.

When the door jingled shut behind them, they stepped onto the street and started walking back toward the estate. Simon was visibly upset with the two businessmen, though he remained silent as they walked.

"They were merely speaking their mind," Luthor offered, breaking the silence. "We should be encouraging behavior like that."

"They weren't speaking their mind," Simon said. "They were expressing their petty jealousy and wasting our time. We have supernatural occurrences to investigate. We hardly have the time to listen to complaints about shrewd or even unethical business practices conducted by Mr. Dosett. If they think something immoral or illegal is happening, call a constable, not an Inquisitor."

Luthor nodded and let the issue drop as they walked. They passed back through the open marketplace and passed the dry fountain. As they intersected another major street, Luthor noticed a building on the corner that he had overlooked on their way to the tavern. He tapped Simon on the arm and pointed.

"It's a telegraph office. Do you need to send a report to the crown yet?"

Simon considered it. He was required to send regular updates to the Inquisitor head office as his investigation progressed, but he found it difficult to formulate a decent message just yet. Aside from the corpse, which he still wasn't entirely convinced was authentic, there was nothing worthwhile to tell.

"No, not yet," he said. "Though it's good to know where the telegraph station is located. I believe we'll be putting it to good use before all this is said and done."

"Then where shall we go from here?" Luthor asked.

"We try our best to get our investigation back on track. We came to investigate werewolves and by God, that's what we're going to do."

"What other evidence is there? We've seen all there is to see in the city."

"Exactly," Simon said. "If the city has failed to definitively prove the existence of werewolves, we'll go find evidence elsewhere."

Luthor frowned. "Would this 'elsewhere' be beyond the wall, in the territory of the werewolves?"

Simon smiled at his friend's discomfort. "Indeed it would be."

"I'm going to need a thicker jacket," Luthor sighed.

CHAPTER

THE TWO MEN ENTERED THE MANSION AND SHOOK the snow from their coats. The footmen appeared at their return and took their jackets before disappearing through the parlor door.

Mr. Archibald, the butler, approached and nodded to the men. "Would either of you care for a warm drink or perhaps something to eat?"

Simon shook his head and answered for the both of them. "Thank you, but no. I actually have a need to speak to Mr. Dosett. Is he in his office?"

"No, sir. Mr. Dosett is downstairs at the moment."

"Downstairs?"

"Yes, sir. I believe he is currently practicing his fencing. There is a stairwell down the hall just past the foyer. I can take you there, if you wish."

"No need," Simon replied. "We can find our way."

Mr. Archibald nodded and spun on his heel before disappearing down the hall.

The two men found the stairwell easily enough. The natural sunlight that filtered through the large windows on the house's main level slowly faded, replaced by the sterility of overhead electric lights. The stairs leveled, turned, and descended further as the pair walked toward the estate's lower level. When they finally arrived at the bottom of the stairwell, they were into the bedrock on which the mansion had been built.

A long hallway stretched before them, ending in ornately carved double doors. From behind them, Simon could hear the clash of blades and grunts of pain. Quietly, so as not to disturb the combatants, he pulled open the double doors and stood in their arch.

Two men, garbed in protective padding and wearing full meshed facemasks, slashed and parried one another in the center of a broad room. A blue sash hung from the belt of one of the swordsmen, while a red hung from the other. They wielded thin, metal epees, which clashed together as they parried.

"They're remarkable," Luthor stated quietly.

Simon stroked his chin as the two men engaged one another again. They quickly broke apart after a dizzying display of parries and ripostes.

"They're good," Simon whispered, "but the man with the blue sash is the far superior swordsman."

Luthor furrowed his brow and watched a second longer. The man in red thrust with his epee, which was turned aside at the last moment by the man in blue. A circle parry pushed the red man's epee wide, but he recovered quickly enough to block a thrust by the man in blue. To Luthor, they seemed evenly matched.

"I don't see an advantage one way or the other."

Simon pointed to the man with the red sash. "Watch him after their next engagement. The man in the red sash will immediately retreat, keeping their duel at a longer distance."

"He has the reach," Luthor noted. "Distance seems like the correct course."

"It would be, if the man wasn't scared. The man in blue is toying with him, closing the distance with every attack and working inside the red swordsman's defenses. The technique of keeping his distance is a sound epee technique if you can control the duel, which the man in red cannot. Instead of watching his sword, watch his feet during the next engagement."

Luthor watched as the man in red lunged forward, driving his epee toward the man in blue's heart. The blade was turned aside again, passing harmlessly over the blue man's shoulder. As Luthor watched, the man in red shifted his weight and hastily retreated as the man in blue pressed the offensive. The red swordsman's feet came dangerously close to the back line of the dueling ground.

"He's not trying to win by strikes," Luthor remarked of the blue swordsman's technique. "He's forcing the man in red backward until he crosses the back line."

"Exactly," Simon said with a smile. "Points are points in a competitive duel where your life isn't on the line. Whether it's through a strike on the body or forcing them past the line, a smart swordsman garners his victory through any means necessary. The man in the blue sash is a calculated fencer. This match will be over soon."

Seconds later, the swordsman with the red sash tumbled past the back line and raised his hands in defeat. The blue man turned his blade down, placing it against the padded floor. He reached up and pulled his helmet from his head, shaking his head as he did so. Gideon walked back to his own line and removed his blue sash, using it as a towel to wipe the sweat from his face.

"Well played, Jack," Gideon said as the other man removed his helmet as well. Jack's breath was labored as he walked toward the businessman. "You nearly had me a couple of times."

"Almost doesn't constitute a victory, sadly," Jack said.

The two men shook hands and stepped off the dueling mat. As they turned toward the door, they noticed their unexpected guests and paused. Gideon smiled broadly, as he patted his dueling partner on the shoulder dismissively. The man bowed and hurried toward the door. Simon and Luthor stepped aside, letting the man pass.

"Gentlemen," Gideon said as he approached. "To what do I owe this honor?"

"We came to ask your permission—" Simon began.

Gideon raised his hand, stopping him in mid-sentence. "Do you duel, Inquisitor?"

Simon frowned, irritated at being interrupted. He wasn't used to people stopping him during an investigation, even those who come from the kingdom's aristocracy.

"I've practiced," Simon replied.

Gideon pointed to the wall to Simon's right. As the Inquisitor looked, he saw gear neatly folded on a bench. A series of blunted swords were hanging above the bench on pegs. Gideon walked to the wall and ran his fingers across the blades.

"What is your preference? Epee? Foil? No, you appear to me to be a man who prefers the elegance of the saber."

Simon looked at Luthor helplessly, knowing it would be impolite to refuse the man's request for a duel. It was further complicated by the fact that he needed Gideon's blessing to go investigate the refineries that had been attacked. Though the businessman was charismatic and had been nothing but polite thus far, Simon hated being at someone else's mercy.

With a sigh, he removed his outer coat, handing it to Luthor. He undid the cufflinks, handing them to his friend as well before rolling up his sleeves.

"I have protective equipment that you could wear," Gideon said, realizing that the Inquisitor intended to duel without it.

Simon shook his head. "I watched you duel in your last match. I trust that you have the control not to stab me in the eye."

Gideon stiffened for a second, but he quickly relaxed and his smile returned. "Of course. Please, choose a weapon."

Simon walked to the wall and pulled down a pair of sabers. He swung them with practiced swings, feeling their weight and balance. The one in his right hand was too heavy, so he quickly replaced it on the wall. The other blade was lighter and sturdy with its weight centered just above the hilt. It was comfortable in his hand, and he slashed a few more times through the air before nodding appreciatively.

"I'm assuming I can trust you to do the same?" Gideon said, as he set his meshed helmet on the floor beneath the practice blades. "I am the face of my business. I would be most offended if you left a scar on that face."

"I wouldn't dream of it," Simon replied.

The two men walked to opposite ends of the dueling mat and took their places behind their respective lines. Simon raised the flat of his blade to his face in a salute, which was returned by Gideon. The businessman dropped into a wide-legged stance, turning his body sideways to provide the least amount of exposed torso for Simon to strike. He raised his rearmost hand into the air.

Simon tucked his left hand behind his back, placing it in the small of his back. He, too, turned sideways, though not to as severe a degree as the businessman.

"En garde," Gideon said.

Gideon lunged, driving his blunted blade toward Simon's chest. The Inquisitor shifted his weight and parried the strike, letting it pass inches wide of his shoulder. Though Gideon braced for a riposte, Simon let the strike go unanswered.

Stepping back, Gideon nodded appreciatively. The first strike was a test of one another's skills and he was pleased with what he saw, even if there was no counter. Simon watched the businessman settle back into his stance, awaiting the Inquisitor's response to his attack.

Simon feinted left before hooking his blade back toward Gideon's armpit. The businessman leapt backward, sweeping his epee in a circle and knocking Simon's saber to the side. He immediately shifted his weight to his back leg and lunged forward, thrusting back toward Simon's stomach. The Inquisitor was forced to take a couple steps backward as he parried back-to-back thrusts from the businessman.

Despite not connecting solidly, Gideon stepped back with a confident smile and settled back into his stance.

"You're talented with the blade," Gideon complimented.

"It appears as though I'm facing someone better than myself," Simon lied.

Gideon shook his head. He relaxed momentarily and pushed his hair out of his face with his free hand. "I don't believe that for a second. You're holding back. Don't, at least not for my benefit. I choose my competition carefully and consider myself a very good judge of character."

He raised his blade and saluted again. Simon returned the salute, and they both settled back into their stances.

"So is your investigation going well?" Gideon asked. "I'm assuming you at least now believe that the werewolves are real."

Simon shrugged and flexed his fingers on the grip of his saber. "To an extent."

The tip of Gideon's blade dipped slightly before righting itself. "I've provided you a corpse. What more do you require?"

Simon could hear the faint irritation in the man's voice. "Forgive me if I gave you the impression that I don't believe you. As an Inquisitor, I don't believe anything until I have seen it living and breathing with my own eyes. The advances in taxidermy make anything less than skepticism foolish for someone in my line of business."

As soon as there was a lull in the conversation, Gideon attacked. He shifted his weight to the right in a feint, but Simon read his attempt. As the blade came from the left instead, Simon was already waiting to knock the blade aside. Instead of the normal single strike before they separated, Gideon shifted his grip and slashed toward Simon's shoulder. Despite the epee's thin blade being designed for piercing, Simon knew even the blunted tip could tear his skin. He spun his saber and blocked the second attack.

Gideon pressed the advantage, thrusting the blade forward. Simon was forced to take a step back. From the corner of his eyes, he saw the back line of the dueling mat and dug in his heels before he was forced to concede defeat. Turning Gideon's blade aside, Simon slashed forward in a wild swing. The businessman easily dodged it but in his haste to avoid the blade, he staggered backward. Simon took a couple steps forward, giving him space from the edge of the mat.

Simon chose not to continue his attack, instead settling back into his stance. Haughtily, Gideon flipped the strands of hair that had come loose from his ponytail out of his face.

"So what is next for your investigation?" Gideon asked.

Simon stood from his wide-legged stance and stretched his shoulder with a broad rotation. "I'm glad you asked, Mr. Dosett. With your permission, I would like to visit the site of the last purported werewolf attack. I think seeing the site of the attack would solidify in my mind if these creatures are real or fake."

Gideon seemed put off, and he stood from his own fencing position. He frowned deeply and crinkled his brow. "A visit to the refinery? Royal Inquisitor, I have employees who fear going to work because they can't stand the thought that monsters may wait in ambush. Every day that we hesitate, it costs me money. How much evidence do you require before you request reinforcements from the crown?"

Simon arched a brow at the man. His experiences thus far had led him to believe the businessmen's happy façade was unflappable. To see him so passionate about his business gave Simon pause.

"Allow me to visit your operations," Simon countered. "If I find evidence that supports the insinuations in the governor's report, then I will request a company of soldiers be deployed to Haversham."

Gideon's smile returned. "Then it seems our conversation has reached an impasse until you've seen my refinery. Would tomorrow be good for you to depart?"

Simon saluted with his blade. "That would be perfect."

"Then shall we continue?" Gideon asked, settling back into his fencing stance.

Simon lowered his sword to his side and took a couple steps backward, crossing the edge of the dueling mat and disqualifying himself. He raised his blade in surrender.

Gideon stood with a huff and lowered his epee. "This is not a satisfactory conclusion to our match."

Simon bowed with a flourish. "Forgive me, but Luthor and I have much to do today if we leave in the morning. This is hardly a time to duel, wouldn't you agree?"

Gideon turned and walked off the mat. He hung his epee on the wall and collected the rest of his equipment before walking out of the room. Luthor nodded as the man pushed past him and stormed down the hallway. As Gideon passed, Luthor scratched absently at his arm.

Simon approached the near wall shortly afterward, hanging his saber on its hook. He reached up and wiped the sweat from his brow.

"So?" Luthor asked as he approached his friend.

"We leave in the morning," Simon replied. He took his coat from the apothecary and slid it over his shoulders. Fitting his top hat on top of his head, he canted it to the side.

As he started toward the door, Luthor placed a hand on his arm. "I don't understand. All Inquisitors spend years training with the blade. You could have easily beaten him."

"My dear Luthor, sometimes you learn far more from an opponent in the course of a battle, rather than in the man's defeat. A man like Mr. Dosett has little in his life besides his business and his pride. These werewolves have brought his business to a halt. Had I handily beaten him in our duel, I would have taken his pride as well. Take everything away from a man and you make him unpredictable. If there's one thing that makes my job difficult, it's unpredictable men."

Luthor smiled appreciatively. "So what did you learn about Mr. Dosett?"

"He places the well-being of his business above the well-being of his employees. His concern was with the money he was losing, and not the workers he's already lost."

Luthor turned and led them both into the hallway, back toward the stairwell. "Nothing personal, sir, but I could have told you that after our dinner with the man. He's not keen on interpersonal relationships."

"Fair enough. I also learned that he's offended whenever someone questions his integrity. The thought that his word wasn't good enough to make me believe in the authenticity of the werewolves made him irate, though he kept up a stoic visage."

"Again, sir, I believe that's fairly standard for every businessman in the capital. I wouldn't expect it to be different here, just because we're far detached from the bustle of the city."

Simon patted the man on the back. "Then I guess it's a good thing that I also learned that there's a secret door in the room we just left that leads into the tunnels beneath the city."

Luthor looked over his shoulder. "Really? Where?"

"There was dirt on the floor near the far wall, the type you would expect from the worked stone tunnels we passed through after we left the zeppelin."

Luthor smiled as they reached the bottom of the stairs. "Then I guess it wasn't a totally wasted trip."

"Go get some rest. I have the feeling that tomorrow is going to be a hard day for us beyond the wall."

CHAPTER Seven

IT WAS LATE AT NIGHT WHEN SOMEONE KNOCKED loudly on Luthor's door. The apothecary buttoned the sleeves of his nightshirt and pulled the bedroom door closed behind him as he hurried toward the front entrance to his suite. The curved glass of the peephole rested right at his eye level, and he peered through it. The hallway beyond was distorted but the well-dressed man on the other side was unmistakable. Luthor frowned as the Inquisitor leaned down toward the peephole, peering back through at Luthor. The warped lens made Simon's eye appear disproportionate to the rest of his face and elongated his narrow moustache.

With a sigh, Luthor pulled open the door.

"Sir, it's very late. Why are you knocking on my door at such an obscene hour?"

Simon rocked back on his heels so he wasn't stooped at a peephole that was no longer in front of his face. He smiled disarmingly at his friend. "I couldn't sleep."

"Neither can I, apparently," Luthor replied dryly.

"Good." Simon walked past his friend as though he had been invited inside.

"Please come in," the apothecary said after the fact. "What brings you to my room in the middle of the night?"

"Do you mind if I sit?"

Luthor motioned toward the couch. "Make yourself at home. Since we're both up, would you care for a drink?"

"Scotch, please. Better make it two fingers worth."

Luthor arched his eyebrow as he walked to the wet bar against the far wall. "Two fingers? It must be something serious on your mind."

"I honestly don't know if it's important or not, but I trust your advice on the matter. That is, if you have time of course."

"Clearly I have nothing but time," Luthor said as he poured drinks for them both. He carried the glasses over and handed one to Simon before taking a seat in one of the armchairs across from the sofa. "What's bothering you?"

Simon wrinkled his nose as a foul smell drifted past him. It was a similar sulfur smell to the one he had noticed coming from Luthor's room before. "That scent still lingers. It's horrific. Could the maids not get the smell of the broken vial out of your room?"

Luthor shrugged and looked toward his closed bedroom door. "They tried, but the smell is persistent."

"And horrific. Did I mention horrific?"

Luthor smiled and tried to get the conversation back on track. "You were about to tell me about what bothered you."

"We've been partners for nearly a year now, and everything we've seen can be easily explained as the shenanigans of a few men," Simon replied as he swirled the ice cubes in his drink. "This case, however, feels different."

"You're bothered by the idea that this case could be real?"

Simon stopped swirling his glass and looked up at his friend. "Aren't you? Doesn't it frighten you in the least that werewolves could have infiltrated our borders? It scares me something awful to think that this may be a precursor of something far worse."

Luthor leaned forward in his armchair, resting his elbows on his knees. "What if it is real? We wouldn't be the first Inquisitors to locate a real magical threat. The simple fact that the threats exist at all is why the Order of the Kinder Pel remains so powerful. They may be uncouth in their methods but there isn't a magical threat or malady that remains once they arrive."

Simon frowned and leaned back into the cushioned couch. "Little remains after the Kinder Pel finish, mystical or mortal either one."

"Is that what's bothering you as well?"

"If I send a telegram confirming the existence of werewolves in Haversham without being able to confirm that the threat is well contained, the Grand Inquisitor will dispatch the Order. I can't risk lives until I'm certain without a shadow of a doubt that the werewolves are real."

Luthor nodded. "Then let's make sure we are sufficiently convinced before we send that telegram. What do we know of the case thus far? We've seen a body."

Simon smiled, feeling once again in his element. "We've seen something that can still be explained as merely an exquisite taxidermy."

Luthor ran a hand through his muttonchops. "True. We know that these attacks, werewolf or not, have been localized to Mr. Gideon Dosett's businesses."

"Gideon Dosett," Simon replied flatly. "Something doesn't settle well with me at the mention of the man's name."

Luthor raised his glass. "Well, you'll get little argument from me."

"So you agree that something is amiss with Gideon?"

Luthor took a long drink of his scotch. He lowered the glass from his lips as the liquor burned down his esophagus. "I agree that something is amiss, though I'd be hard pressed to give you a specific reason."

Simon scratched his chin. "That, quite sadly, is where I find myself as well. I can't help but feel that he knows more about this investigation than he is letting on. He's withholding something; I sense it every time I speak with him."

"Then there's the business with the Union and Guild leaders," Luthor said dryly.

Simon huffed and took another drink. "While I don't think them completely wrong in their distrust of Mr. Dosett, I cannot abide them speaking ill of the governor. He's still family, albeit detached, of the king himself."

Luthor canted his head to the side. "We're speaking between friends, sir. You can speak your mind."

Simon smiled. "You know me far too well. Yes, something is wrong about the relationship between the governor and Mr. Dosett. They seem far too friendly with one another, speaking to one another as old friends rather than you would expect a businessman to speak to royalty."

"Then there might be something to the Union's and Guild's complaints," Luthor offered.

"Perhaps," Simon said with a coy smile, "but I'd never give them the satisfaction of knowing they were right. They needed to be reminded of their station as much as Mr. Dosett does."

Simon waved his hand dismissively. "At the end of the day, Mr. Dosett is inconsequential. His overtly friendly relationship with the governor doesn't matter. All that truly matters are the werewolves and whether or not they exist. Hopefully our trip tomorrow will shed some light on that issue."

"Agreed," Luthor replied. "Hopefully, we'll find something worthwhile. This whole mission is leaving a foul taste in my mouth. The sooner we can leave, the better."

Simon set his half-emptied tumbler onto the table between them and rose. Caught unaware, Luthor hurriedly stood as well.

"I've taken far too much of your time at far too indecent an hour," Simon said. "I shall leave you to your rest. As always, Luthor, thank you for your friendly ear and keen mind."

"Of course, sir," Luthor said, as he followed Simon to the door. "I would say 'any time', but I would prefer the next time you visit while the sun is still up."

They both laughed as Simon stepped into the hallway separating their two rooms.

"Goodnight, Luthor."

Luthor nodded. "Goodnight, sir."

He closed the door on the Inquisitor as the smile faded from his face. He pulled the deadbolt lock across the door, ensuring he wouldn't be disturbed again. Walking across the room, he reached the closed bedroom door and pulled the double doors apart.

Stepping into the bedroom, Luthor bent down and lifted the blanket that had been hastily tossed onto the floor. Beneath, the smeared remnants of a pentagram were still visible on the floor. The removal of the blanket released the scent of sulfur, mixed with the white powdered chalk on the ground. Luthor retrieved a piece of chalk and etched the circle again, strengthening the broken lines. When the pentagram was complete once more, he stood and walked into the center of the chalk design.

He raised his arms to the side and gently turned his head as though listening to a distant voice. For a long moment, he stood frozen in his position. Finally, he nodded slightly.

"No," Luthor said to the empty room. "He doesn't suspect."

He fell quiet again as he listened to the reply.

"Something is amiss," he responded. "That much is certain. There's a chance one of them is here, though if they are, no one suspects."

He nodded enthusiastically. "I have my suspicions as well and will let you know as the situation develops. Keep the Order at bay until I can complete my task at hand. I'll report back when I know more."

With his conversation completed, Luthor broke the circle of the pentagram with his toe, severing the connection. He returned to his bed and pulled out a pile of ancient, leather-bound books. Pulling open their covers, he began reading old stories and myths about werewolves.

Returning to his own room, Simon closed the door behind him. He knew he should go to bed, but sleep seemed to elude him. Instead, he went into his bedroom but bypassed the comfortable four-post bed. Kneeling beside it, he reached underneath and pulled out a darkly stained wooden case. He set it on the bed before retrieving a small key from his vest pocket. He slid the key into the lock and heard the click of the tumblers.

With the case unlocked, he lifted the lid and admired the contents. Sharpened wooden stakes sat against the top of the velvet-lined Inquisitor kit. A glass vial with a thick cork stopper rested beside that. A gold cross was embellished on the front of the vial. The rest of the case was filled with an odd assortment of acids and other weapons to use against the supernatural.

Simon found what he was looking for near the middle of the case. He pulled his silver revolver from its shoulder harness and released the drum. With a twist of his wrist, the ammunition drum flicked to the side of the pistol. He admired the copper casings of the bullets already loaded in the weapon.

Ensuring he was over the comforter, he tilted the pistol and let the six rounds drop to the bed. Reaching toward the middle of the case, he withdrew six new bullets. The casings were still copper, but the dull lead of the other normal bullets was replaced by a brilliant silver. He loaded the silver bullets into his revolver, noting the dozen other rounds that still remained in the case, just below a tooled metal plate that read, "Loup Garou."

Chapter Eight

THEY ATE BREAKFAST WITH THE GOVERNOR THE NEXT morning. Simon sat at the governor's left once again, with Gideon across from him. The rest of the guests from the previous dinner were gone, allowing Luthor a better seat of honor beside the Royal Inquisitor.

Simon stuffed a slice of eggs Benedict into his mouth and dabbed runny yolk from the corner of his mouth. He looked up as the governor spoke, though the man's attention was turned toward the businessman across the table.

"You look practically exhausted, Gideon," the governor said. "Another long night entertaining?"

Gideon smiled, but the mirth didn't extend to his eyes. "You know me, My Lord. The social life of the aristocracy never ends. There is always someone new to court."

The governor laughed heartily. "Say no more. Perhaps you'll take leave of your busy schedule today and spend time playing chess with me? It's not threatening and with you being tired, I stand a far better chance of beating you."

Gideon flashed a thin-lipped smile. "I've never been so tired that I couldn't beat you in a game of chess. Perhaps if you didn't open with the same risky gambit every game."

The governor laughed again and turned toward Simon and Luthor. "Tell me, Inquisitor Whitlock, what do you and your associate have planned for today?"

Simon glanced briefly toward Gideon before turning his attention back to their host. "We'll be going beyond the city walls today."

The governor choked and coughed roughly, as he tried to swallow a bite of food. "Beyond the wall, you say? The werewolves live beyond the wall. Good men have already lost their lives to those beasts."

Simon wiped his fingers on his napkin before setting it back in his lap. "All the more reason for us to go. I was sent to find out if these werewolves were real or not, and I simply can't make a decision one way or the other by remaining here."

The governor shook his head. "The bravery of the Inquisitors knows no bounds. Were it me, I would gladly remain safely behind these thick walls and let the savage werewolves have their frozen wasteland beyond."

Gideon flashed him an irritated glance, and the governor quickly fell silent.

"Were it not for my refineries and drilling rigs beyond the wall, he meant to say," Gideon corrected. "Of course, the governor has enough compassion to be concerned about the well-being of those men and women who work beyond the wall."

The governor stuffed a bite of bread into his mouth, squelching any possible retort.

"Of course," Simon said, saving him any further embarrassment.

"Though I am forced to agree with the governor," Gideon continued. "I do so wish you'd take my word on the validity of these monsters. It would save you an arduous trip into the arctic plain beyond the walls."

"Were it only the proof of their existence that I needed, then I would gladly take you at your word and enjoy another snifter or two of brandy in my suite," Simon joked. "Unfortunately, the matter is far more serious than that. If these werewolves are real, then I must know how they got into our lands. If they slipped through our sea defenses, then there's a weakness that must be closed before it's exploited further. If the werewolves are real, then are they the vanguard for a larger invasion? For what purpose have they come here, of all places? No insult intended, of course."

"Of course," the governor replied.

"These are the questions that must be answered before I can satisfactorily conclude my investigation. It's not merely a confirmation that magic has infiltrated our lands. It's answering the question of *why* magic has infiltrated our kingdom."

"Then let me ensure you are safe and expedited on your journey," Gideon interjected. "I have a sled master in the stables near the northern gate. There's no one quicker in Haversham. I'll send word for him to be at the ready. He is at your disposal and will take you wherever you need to go."

Simon nodded. "You are most kind." He took his napkin from his lap and neatly folded it before setting it on the table. "I guess we really must be off. I'm sure Luthor and I will have an exhausting day ahead of us."

The governor and Gideon rose from their seats politely as the Inquisitor and apothecary excused themselves from the breakfast table. Walking out of the room, they let the door close softly behind them. They walked into the foyer, and the butler appeared with their coats and hats. After collecting their garments, Luthor walked to the front door and retrieved his cane from a rack. The apothecary patted his inner pockets, ensuring the vials he had retrieved from his doctor's bag that morning were properly secured.

With Luthor out of earshot, Simon turned to Archibald. "Forgive me for bringing up a difficult subject, but it appears your maid staff is doing an inadequate job with their cleaning."

The butler arched his eyebrows in surprise. "Indeed, sir? Please let me know what shortcomings you've noticed, and I'll ensure they are rectified immediately."

Simon leaned in closer and glanced to Luthor as the apothecary affixed his bowler cap on his head. "My associate spilled some caustic-smelling chemicals in his room, and the scent lingers despite numerous attempts at cleaning it."

The butler cleared his throat hoarsely. "That's impossible, sir. Mr. Strong has strictly forbidden any of my maids from entering his room without his expressed permission, which he has yet to give."

Simon furrowed his brow and stared at his friend. "My apologies,

Mr. Archibald. It appears there has been a misunderstanding."

"Think nothing of it, sir."

"Are you coming?" Luthor asked from his place by the door.

"On my way," Simon replied.

He joined Luthor at the door before they walked into the wintery outdoors. As they walked down the building's front steps, Luthor stifled a yawn. Simon arched his eyebrow toward his partner.

"I hope you're not tired as a result of my intrusion last night," he said.

Luthor shook his head as he finished his long yawn. "If only I could place the blame solely on you. Sadly, I had trouble sleeping even after you left. It seems I had quite a bit on my mind."

Simon stuffed his hands into his jacket pockets and lowered his head against the biting breeze. Despite the tall walls around the city, the wind was still strong enough to threaten to pull his top hat from his head. Luthor, who wore a bowler cap with a far shorter profile, merely pulled down the brim to keep his eyes from watering in the cold.

"What's on your mind, pray tell?" Simon asked as they walked toward the front gate of the estate. Not for the first time, he wished Haversham had some of the autobuses that had become the technological rave in the capital city.

"I wonder about the truthfulness of the werewolf mythology," Luthor replied. "Everyone knows the story of silver being the bane of werewolves. There's also the more alchemical myth of Wolf's Bane being harmful to the monsters, though I have yet to discover the best way to administer the proper dosage, or if there is a proper dosage at all. It seems so simple to call a plant Wolf's Bane and assume everyone knows its uses."

Simon laughed. "Always the scientist, aren't you?"

Luthor frowned. "So says the trained medical doctor and forensic scientist. In this regards, I prefer to think of myself as a historian. While most of the texts pertaining to werewolves have been nothing more than horror stories used to scare children, they were clearly based in some sort of truth. More importantly, most stories refer to werewolves as people who were infected with lycanthropy. If true, that would mean that it's an infection rather than a state of being. Perhaps there's a cure somewhere in the natural world for their disease."

Simon ran his hand across his thin moustache thoughtfully. "Perhaps the cure resides in the Wolf's Bane?"

"Perhaps," Luthor replied thoughtfully, "but I have only a small amount of *Aconitum* root with me. If there are as many werewolves as Mr. Dosett claims, the quantities I have would hardly be enough to treat the entire population, even if a cure could be devised from the plant."

"Then perhaps we could use a small amount merely as a test, if we captured a live creature."

Luthor nodded. "Perhaps, though I would need time to purify the root."

They passed through the estate's main gates. "Would it not be effective as it is now?"

Luthor shrugged. "It would be effective, but not for what we want. Pure *Aconitum* root is lethal even in smaller doses."

"I guess 'Wolf's Bane' is an accurate moniker, then."

The wind kicked up again as they passed beyond the estate, and Simon found himself clinging both to his top hat and to his coat as it threatened to fly away. He looked to his associate, who was similarly huddled against the biting wind and using his cane as support on the cobblestones.

"The weather seemed to have turned against us," Simon remarked. "Perhaps we'd be better suited in the tunnels."

Luthor nodded his agreement, and the pair made for one of the cavern entrances. The street-level entrance barely resembled a cave opening. It looked far more like an autobus stop, with glass doors framing the front of a squat gray-stone building. It was fairly nondescript, and Simon would have potentially passed right by it unaware had it not been for the handful of people that entered and exited the small structure.

Simon held the door for the apothecary before following the diminutive man inside.

The entrance to the tunnels was the same they had exited from earlier. They soon found themselves in the expansive underground hub and were once again surprised by the mercantile world that existed just below the barren surface streets.

The hub was a chaotic whirlwind of noise and activity, with people hurriedly arriving and departing down the myriad of interconnecting tunnels. Simon felt temporarily overwhelmed until he caught sight of a carved stone sign protruding from one of the side tunnels. It read—Western Gate. Simon followed the curve of the cavern until he found the next major tunnel to the right and led Luthor in that direction. He nodded happily when he read, "Northern Gate" on the carved sign.

Once beyond the hub, the din of conversation died away. They passed a few other pedestrians and even a wagon clattering along the hard stone and packed dirt floor. They nodded politely to the people they passed but continued strolling toward the distant gate in relative silence.

Simon felt genuinely apprehensive about their trip beyond the wall. Though the trip itself would be arduous, it wasn't the strain of the journey that had him concerned. He knew that one way or the other, he should be able to confirm the presence of werewolves by the time they returned to Haversham. Though he had trained for years as an Inquisitor for the sole purpose of identifying and eliminating magical threats, the idea of coming face to face with one was almost horrifying. More than that, he knew that confirming the identity of the werewolves was only the beginning of his mission. If they truly were the spearhead of a much larger invasion, then he knew just how dangerous today could be for both Luthor and him.

Lost in his reverie, he didn't notice they had arrived at the spiral staircase leading to the northern gate until Luthor tapped him politely on the arm. Simon looked up at the natural sunlight filtering down from the man-made shaft to the surface and smiled. Whatever was to come, he knew he had no choice but to face it with a smile on his face. It wouldn't do at all for a Royal Inquisitor to appear scared in the face of a paranormal threat.

Their booted feet clanged on the metal spiral staircase as they climbed toward the surface. Simon made the mistake of placing his hand on the railing and immediately regretted that decision. It was colder than ice and seemed to sap the strength from his hand. Even the short grasp of the frigid metal left his fingers stiff. He flexed them cautiously as he continued to climb.

By comparison to the streets in front of the gubernatorial estate, the streets where they exited near the northern gate were considerably warmer. The arctic wind that seeped over the top of the tall wall surrounding the city drifted down and over the streets this close to the wall. They were happily protected from the cold breeze. Even so, Simon still noticed the puffs of warm air escaping his lips with every breath.

"It's impressive," Luthor said, craning his neck to see the top of the city wall.

Simon followed his gaze and admired the height of the stone barricade. Though most of the houses within Haversham were at most two-stories tall, the protective barrier towered over them at nearly forty-feet high. He performed some mental calculations as he examined the size of the supporting base stones and realized that the manual labor required to move the thousands of tons of stone to such a remote location must have been an incredible feat. He mentally catalogued it as something of interest he'd have to research after he returned to the capital.

As they were admiring the wall, a fur-cloaked man approached the pair.

"Excuse me, gentlemen," the gruff man said. "Would you be the Royal Inquisitor and guest?"

Luthor smirked. "I'm a guest."

"Meaning no disrespect," the man quickly added.

Simon smiled politely at the man, immediately understanding that proper etiquette was clearly not the man's forte. His exposed face was lined and weathered from exposure to the howling winds beyond the wall. It was deeply tanned except for rings around each of his eyes that matched the circumference of the dark-tinted goggles dangling from around his neck. The coarse growth of a beard was unkempt but, Simon surmised, probably incredibly warming while moving along the frozen tundra.

"He took no disrespect," Simon replied. "Would you be the sled master that Mr. Dosett sent us to find?"

"Aye, that would be me." The man pulled off a thick mitten that covered his hand and extended it. "Theodore Parrish. I'm the sled dog master for Mr. Dosett's businesses beyond the wall."

Simon shook the man's hand. "A pleasure, Mr. Parrish. I'm—"

"I know who you both are, begging your pardon for the interruption. Everyone in town knows about the Inquisitor and the apothecary that have come to take care of the werewolf menace."

Simon and Luthor exchanged pleased glances. The more word spread of their presence in Haversham, the easier it would become to interview people and conduct their investigation.

"Well then, Mr. Parrish, it seems that we are at a disadvantage. This seems to be your area of expertise, so we defer to you. What do we need to do first for our trip outside?"

The sled master looked over the two impeccably dressed men. "The first thing you'll need is warmer clothes. You'll freeze to death wearing those fancy threads." He jutted his thumb over his shoulder. "I have some winter jackets, extra gloves, and goggles you can use during the trip. Just follow me, if you will."

Parrish led the two men down the street until the massive northern gate came into view. The two metal doors stood impractically tall, towering nearly a dozen feet over Simon's head. Thick metal studs protruded from the door's frame at regular intervals, fastening the immense metal crossbeams in place. Fingers of ice crept through the seam between the doors, reaching half a dozen feet into the near side of the doorframe.

A pair of workers stood at the base of the door with heavy packs slung across their backs. Simon had seen similar contraptions earlier when they disembarked from the zeppelin. As he watched, black smoke belched from the tall smokestacks that rose above the men's shoulders. The nozzles in their hands hissed for a brief moment before flames erupted to life. The warm flames poured onto the protruding ice between the doors, instantly turning the icy tendrils to water.

"I told them we were coming," Parrish explained without prompting. "They're getting the doors ready to open so we can leave."

"Metal doors seem like an odd choice," Simon remarked, "especially since they seem so prone to freezing."

Parrish looked over his shoulder as they passed the gate. "Have you ever seen a wooden door on a cold, cold night? They seal shut tighter than a virgin's…" He glanced back and forth between the two curious gentlemen. "Well, let's just say they seal real tight. There isn't a flamethrower in existence that will get them pried apart."

The sled master led the two men to a sturdy, wooden barn not far from the northern gate. It was a stout building with narrow, horizontal windows near its insulated tin roof. A door was closed along the front of the building; it was large, though the massive gate doors dwarfed it.

Parrish pulled open the barn's front door, and the three men were greeted by the barks and yelps of the sled dogs within. Simon stopped at the threshold, letting his eyes adjust to the dim lighting within. He could see an oil lantern hanging from a post to his right, but it was unlit. The only light filtered through the narrow windows up high.

The barn was partitioned, with a dozen pens lining either side of the building. The wooden doors that separated the pens from the main thoroughfare were short, stopping just above Simon's waist. Hounds' heads peered from above the doorways as they rested their paws on the top of the wooden planks, alternating between panting enthusiastically and barking incessantly.

The sled master led the two men past the kennels to where heavy, knee-length winter parkas hung from hooks. He pulled the coats from them, revealing a pair of thick mittens and tinted goggles beneath.

"You'll need these for the trip," Parrish said. "I recommend leaving behind your fancy hats. They won't do you any good once we're past the gate. You're far more likely to lose them in a snow drift."

Simon reluctantly removed his top hat, placing it on the wooden table before him. Luthor followed suit, placing his bowler cap beside it.

"You might want to leave behind the cane as well," Parrish offered to Luthor. "It won't do you any good in the snow or on the ice."

The apothecary looked down at his cane and shook his head. "I think I'll keep it, but thank you kindly for the offer."

Parrish shrugged. "Suit yourself. You gentlemen get dressed while I get the dogs hitched to the sled. I'll come get you when we're ready."

As Simon and Luthor slipped on the thick parkas, Parrish manhandled a long, wooden sled from a storage closet at the end of the kennels. It had a pair of thatched seats on its frame and shiny metal skis attached to its underbelly. Though the sled appeared handmade, it also seemed extraordinarily sturdy and well maintained.

"Are you sure you're ready for this, sir?" Luthor asked as he fitted mittens over his hands. He struggled to grasp his cane after his hands were bundled against the cold, eventually settling for holding the haft under his arm.

"Are you asking if I'm prepared for the cold or the werewolves?" Simon asked as he slid the goggles over his head, letting them rest at his neck in an imitation of Parrish.

"Either or both."

"I believe it was you who said you'd much prefer an assignment to the beach resorts than one to the arctic western shore," Simon said. "After spending some time in Haversham, I'm far more prone to agree with you."

Luthor laughed and pulled up his own hood. The fur lining seemed to disappear against his thick muttonchops. “If we encounter the werewolves?”

Simon shrugged. “It’s a bridge we’ll cross when we come to it.”

“I don’t think the werewolves, if they are real, will appreciate the bridge we’re offering.”

Simon grew intensely serious. “Then we’ll burn the bridge to the ground… with them on it.”

The yipping and barking grew in intensity as the sled master began hooking up the dogs to the harnesses. The distraction broke Simon’s intense mood and brought a smile to his face. He noted the irony of the situation. The dogs they were using to pull the sled were all descended from wolves. It seemed a slight conflict of interest that they should pull a Royal Inquisitor as he investigated proof of their kin.

“We’re just about ready,” Parrish called from the front of the barn. “If you gentlemen would like to join me, we’ll be on our way.”

Simon pulled up his fur-lined hood. He looked back longingly at his top hat.

“My hat will be fine if I leave it here?” he asked.

Parrish shrugged noncommittally. “No one in their right mind would steal from Mr. Dosett. It’ll be fine here.”

The two men walked to the front of the barn, as Parrish led the dogs through the front door. The sled was already attached and bounced along the cobblestone street. Simon kindly closed the barn door behind them before catching up to the others as they headed toward the northern gate.

By the time they arrived, the gate was unfrozen. Water pooled on the ground at its entrance like a lake, though the liquid was already refreezing into a sea of ice. Steam rose in waves from the heated metal as it cooled quickly in the frigid air. The workers with their now-quieted flamethrowers stepped aside and absently wiped black soot from their cheeks and foreheads. Simon nodded appreciatively to the men but paused when he reached for the brim of his hat. He frowned disappointedly at the lack as the sled stopped at the door.

“We’re ready,” Parrish called to the two workers. “Open the doors.”

The workers gripped a long, metal bar that protruded from one of the doors. Their hands were covered with heat-resistant gloves that still sizzled as they came in contact with the metal. They pulled firmly against the door. Slowly, they began to separate and a sliver of light could be seen from the far side of the gate.

Parrish pulled his goggles into place on his face and both Simon and Luthor hurried to follow suit. As the crack widened on the door, the light pouring from the other side was blinding. The sun reflected off the smooth sheet of virgin snow, reflecting its brilliant white light onto the trio.

"Climb aboard," Parrish said to the gentlemen. He motioned to the two seats on the sled, as he climbed onto the protruding ends of the metal skis behind the seats.

Simon and Luthor took their seats just as the door was pulled fully open. As they sat in the wicker chairs, the full force of the arctic wind struck them. Their exposed faces went immediately numb from the chill and despite their thick parkas, they both shivered from the cold.

With a loud yelp, Parrish drove the dogs forward. The animals gleefully bounded through the gate, throwing Simon and Luthor into the backs of their respective seats. The dogs raced out onto the snow and turned slightly to the left, tracing the edge of the frozen lake against which the city had been built.

In the distance, Simon could see the tall, blackened spires of the oil refinery. Spouts of flames leapt from the stacks, rising high into the air before falling apart into black soot.

With the cold burning his cheeks and lips, he buried his face in the thick fur of his collar. The flames belched again from the pillars, and Simon regretted his presumptuous conversation with the governor. Perhaps waiting out his assignment within the warmth of the estate wouldn't have been a bad plan after all.

CHAPTER Nine

THE SLED DOGS BARKED HAPPILY, AS THEY BOUND through the thick, powdery snow. The metal skis on the bottom of the sled carved through the dunes of snow like a skiff through ocean waves, riding up the crest of the snowy hill before careening wildly down its leeside. Simon held his breath as he felt the sled slide unabated across an icy patch. As quickly as it slid, the dogs pulled the ropes tight and the sled lurched forward once more.

Simon didn't care for this mode of transportation. Looking at Luthor's pale expression in the seat next to him, he assumed the apothecary would agree with his assessment.

"How far is it to the refinery?" Simon called back over his shoulder.

The sled master bent his knees and lowered himself until his face was mere inches above the backs of the wicker seats.

"Say again, sir?" he asked.

Simon cleared his throat and felt the burn of the cold air against his dry esophagus. "I asked how much longer the trip would be."

The Inquisitor looked at the refinery in the distance. It had grown closer during their trip but still seemed an eternity away. With the brilliant glare of the morning sun reflecting off the ocean of snow before them, he had no way to tell the passage of time. He assumed their trip had already been a few hours at least but was relying on an unreliable internal clock.

"About an hour," Parrish replied. "Maybe a little longer if the ice along the edge of the lake has weakened. Our path is the most direct but relies on the flightiness of the shifting ice floes."

"An hour," Simon muttered. He turned back toward Parrish and spoke loud enough for the man to hear him. "How long have we been traveling thus far?"

Luthor turned his head at the question, clearly eager to hear the answer as well.

Parrish shrugged. "Thirty minutes? Maybe a little less."

Luthor practically melted into his seat. Simon turned back with a huff and felt his stomach churn in response to the answer. Though he felt nauseated before he spoke to the sled master, the man's response seemed to cause a revolt in Simon's gastric tract.

He felt a large lump form in his throat and tried unsuccessfully to swallow the queasiness. As he felt the urge to vomit growing, he turned back to Mr. Parrish.

"Would you mind terribly if we stopped for a while?" he asked.

He couldn't read Parrish's facial expression behind the thick hood and tinted goggles, but the man's frown was unmistakable. Simon expected to hear the man's disapproval but was surprised when the sled master stood to his full height and barked unintelligible orders to the sled dogs. The animals rushed over a few more snowy mounds before their quick sprint became a slow cant. Eventually they came to a stop, panting and glancing around curiously.

"Mr. Dosett said that I was to follow your every request during your investigation," Parrish said, no longer having to yell to be heard. "If you gentlemen would like to stop, we'll most certainly stop."

Simon tried to stand, but his legs felt weak and unsteady. He pushed off from the armrests of the wicker chair, managing to rest on his knees in the snow. Simon finally managed to roll out of his seat and sat for a moment on his hands and knees in the snow. Though it never happened, Luthor watched him intently from the far side of the sled, expecting his associate to vomit into the pure white snow.

"I thank you," Simon said as he climbed to his feet. "It seems my intestinal fortitude isn't what it should be. I'm surprised, to be honest.

I've ridden in autobuses, zeppelins, trains, and many other forms of conveyance. It surprises me that the sled ride would be so detrimental to my constitution."

Parrish shrugged. "Some people just have trouble when their conveyance, as you said, is being pulled by living creatures. They're unpredictable and have a tendency to pull you from side to side a bit more than you're used to. I would be lying if I said you were the first to grow ill on one of my trips."

"Well, I appreciate your honesty," Simon replied.

He turned toward the frozen lake, the edge of which began just down a gentle incline from where he stood. The snowy bank led seamlessly onto the crystal blue, icy surface of the lake. As he watched, Simon could see dark shapes moving beneath the ice, though it was hard to tell if it was something living or just blocks of ice trapped beneath the frozen surface.

He lifted his gaze and looked out over the frozen tundra. The lake stretched across his vision with the far shore barely visible in the distance. Beyond the shoreline, the ground rose toward mountain peaks to the north. The arctic wind rolled down from the mountains and poured unhindered across the flat ground. The realization that the wind was still blowing strongly across him made Simon shiver.

He was about to turn away when his eyes fell to the foothills across the lake. Small tendrils of smoke rose from the valleys between the rolling hills, rising up like black pillars into the frigid air. Simon raised his hand over his eyes, blocking out a little more of the glaring sunlight and stared toward the rising smoke.

"Mr. Parrish?" Simon called.

The sled master climbed down from his perch and walked around the sled. Luthor followed the sled master; he was suddenly interested in Simon's observation.

"Sir?"

Simon pointed toward the smoke. "I see smoke rising from across the lake, as though rising from campfires or the like. Are there people living out here?"

Parrish nodded. "There are indigenous tribes that still live in this inhospitable land. They're uncivilized brutes, living in portable leather homes and surviving off the land by hunting the few wild animals that survive in the tundra. I wouldn't give them too much of a thought, sir."

Simon shook his head. "The werewolves live out here as well, don't they? How is it that the tribes haven't been slaughtered by the werewolves?"

"Nothing is saying they haven't been, sir."

Simon pointed to the smoke. "They're clearly still alive. If you were being hunted by werewolves, would you light campfires and draw the attention of every predator in the area?"

Parrish shrugged unconvincingly. "Mayhap they've found a way to live in peace with the monsters."

"Magical creatures don't know how to live in peace," Simon replied flatly. "That's why they're considered monsters."

Parrish sighed. "I don't know what to tell you, sir. I haven't had much interaction with the natives. All I know is that the werewolves prefer to attack Mr. Dosett's businesses. What they do on their free time in between ruining Mr. Dosett's factories, I couldn't tell you."

Simon stared at the smoke and struggled to see any movement. He wanted to see signs of life, proof that the indigenous tribesmen were still alive.

"Come, sir, we should be off," Parrish said as the man turned back toward the sled. "We still have a journey ahead of us, and I'd like to have us back in the city before nightfall. If you think it's cold now, you won't want to get caught in the tundra overnight."

Simon nodded and reluctantly turned away from the view of the foothills. Walking back to the sled, he stopped beside his wicker seat. He stared across at Luthor, who blanched at the thought of being flung around by the sled dogs once more.

"I hope our pause gave you a chance to steel your resolve," Simon said with a laugh.

Luthor frowned and climbed into his seat without a reply. Simon took his seat beside his friend, but his gaze fell back to the wisps of smoke rising from the foothills in the distance.

"Did you find something worth your time?" Luthor asked.

"Like I've replied many times during this short investigation," Simon said, "I don't know. I have, however, discovered yet another mystery. This whole area seems like an onion. Every layer peeled back reveals another layer and another obstacle."

"Like an onion," Luthor said, "every layer peeled away is giving me another reason to cry."

With another sharp shout, Parrish drove the dogs forward. The sled lurched and began its endless bouncing as they raced toward the refinery.

The refinery was far more intimidating the closer they got. The snaking pipes and hoses looked like a myriad of limbs from a demonic abyssal creature, forcing its way from the depths of the frozen earth. The belching flames from the tall smokestacks sounded like horrific roars of anguish.

Simon pulled his collar tighter over his nose and mouth as he began smelling the smoky scent in the air. He frowned as he noticed the dark discoloration on the snow, growing more marred and stained the closer they got to the refinery.

The sled dogs weren't keen on approaching the factory either. They threw their heads from side to side and began sneezing. The sled jerked with each sneeze as the dogs pulled awkwardly on their harnesses. The Inquisitor felt for the animals. They longed to run freely across the frozen tundra rather than be confined near the industrialized structure. As much as Simon loathed riding any longer on the sled, he agreed with the dogs. Between the two options, the choice to ride along the tundra was much preferred to standing in the ashy shadow of the serpentine building.

Parrish pulled the dogs to a stop as a parka-covered man emerged from the main entrance of the factory. He had a handkerchief pulled up over his nose and mouth and a pair of goggles over his eyes. Simon couldn't see any of his features. Not even a wisp of hair was hanging free of his deep hood.

"This is as far as I go," Parrish said as they came to a stop. "My dogs don't like being too close."

"Understandably so," Simon replied. "How will we contact you when we're done here?"

"I'll be watching. Once you come outside, I'll come and get you both."

Simon and Luthor climbed free of the wicker seats and stepped aside as Parrish turned the sled around. The dogs grew visibly more excited as they turned away from the refinery and faced the open snow beyond.

"Best of luck to you both," Parrish said. "I hope you find what you're looking for."

With a yell, the dogs began running, pulling the sled far away from the falling soot. Simon and Luthor watched the sled hurry away before turning back toward their liaison.

The man reached up with gloved hands and pulled down the handkerchief, revealing the thick beard beneath.

"Good afternoon, gentlemen," he said, wringing his hands uncomfortably. "I'm led to believe that you are the Royal Inquisitor?"

"Even in a thick parka, it appears my reputation precedes me," Simon joked.

"I'm Mr. Tanner, the refinery foreman. Why don't we head inside where we can talk in some warmth?"

Simon couldn't remember the last time he heard a better idea. He nodded enthusiastically and followed the foreman as he led them through the doors and into the dark interior.

As soon as he crossed the threshold into the building, Simon felt blanketed by the warmth. Potbellied stoves burned brightly on either side of the doorway, cutting through the chill of the invading winter breeze. The smoke pipes leading from the stoves glowed cherry red from the heat, radiating across the three men as they paused in the doorway.

Simon sighed blissfully as he pulled down his goggles and pushed the hood from his head. Snow dropped from his hood and piled on the floor at his feet. He shook his shoulders, dropping free the remaining powdery accumulation from his parka.

"If only all of Haversham were this warm," Simon remarked. "You have made this whole trip worthwhile with this single moment."

The foreman laughed nervously. "Then let's call this inquiry concluded and be on our way."

Simon looked over to the man in surprise. "Is that what you think this is? Do you worry that this is an inquiry?"

"Begging your pardon, sir, but you are a Royal Inquisitor."

"True, but this is an investigation, not an inquiry," Simon corrected. "You are hardly on trial. I merely want to inquire…" He paused and frowned at his own choice of words. "I merely want to ask about the most recent werewolf attack on your facility. You have nothing to fear from me."

Mr. Tanner cleared his throat and forced a smile. "Forgive me, sir. We don't always receive the timeliest reports so far removed from real civilization. There is—"

"A reputation amongst the Inquisitors," Simon interrupted. "We're horrible men; reapers encased in petticoats, carrying notepads instead of sickles but no less deadly. Is that about right, Mr. Tanner?"

The foreman blushed. "That about sums it up, sir."

Simon and Luthor both laughed. "Again, you have nothing to fear. While I would be lying if I said that there weren't Inquisitors that lived up to that retched reputation, my associate and I are hardly those types of men. Show us what we want and we will be on our way with the least of interruptions to your work."

Tanner seemed visibly relieved. He motioned toward a steel staircase leading up to an upper office. Simon and Luthor followed him, letting their boots clank loudly on the metal stairs. In stark contrast to the freezing cold outside, the factory was overtly warm. He even felt sweat beading on his brow with the parka becoming burdensome as they walked. Despite the pungent aroma in the air, he was glad to be indoors.

They entered the foreman's cramped office. Tanner closed the door behind them, though large pane glass windows offered a broad view of the factory floor below.

"Can I take your jackets, gentlemen?" Tanner offered. "You will both die of heat stroke if you stay in those massive parkas much longer."

He stripped off his own jacket, hanging it on a peg beside his narrow desk. He took both their parkas as well as they pulled them free and hung them beside his own. Simon took a seat on the hard chair across from Tanner, feeling like himself for the first time since leaving the governor's mansion.

"I'm sorry," Tanner said to Luthor, who still stood by the closed door. "We don't have much of a budget, or need to be honest, for furniture in the refinery. Please take my chair. I don't mind standing while we talk."

Luthor dismissed his offer with a wave of his hand. "Don't be silly. I've just spent far too much time seated during the world's most uncomfortable transport from Haversham. If I don't sit for the next century, it'll still be too soon."

Simon retrieved a notebook from his jacket pocket while Luthor did the same. The apothecary also pulled out his glasses and placed them on his face, frowning as the lenses fogged over in the warmth of the office. Retrieving a pencil from the book's bindings, Simon tapped its graphite tip against his tongue in anticipation of answers to his questions.

"Mr. Tanner, I know you're a busy man. I'll try to keep my questions brief so that you may return to your work."

"I thank you, sir," the foreman replied.

"Your factory has been attacked recently by these purported werewolves, is that correct?" Simon asked.

"Twice."

Simon looked up from his notepad. "Twice? They seem to have a keen dislike for your specific refinery."

Tanner laughed derisively. "It's not just my refinery, sir. Every refinery and drilling operation has been attacked numerous times by these creatures. We're actually lucky, being the closest operation to the city. The guards respond the quickest to my needs, meaning that the beasts seem hesitant to do more than passing skirmishes."

"Have you seen these beasts?"

"With my own two eyes," the foreman said. "Terrible beasts, they are."

"In your own words, please describe them to me."

Tanner sat back in his chair and crossed his arms over his chest. "They're werewolves."

Simon frowned and set his pencil on the top of his notebook. "Mr. Tanner, please refrain from such generalities. Assume you're speaking to a man who knows nothing of mythology or creatures of legend. Assume that speaking a simple word like 'werewolf' would mean nothing to me. Describe them as you would to a child."

Tanner shrugged. "They're huge beasts, standing as tall as a man when they're on their hind legs. Their bodies are covered with white fur like the snow, making them virtually impossible to see as they approach the refinery. Each of their hands end in long, sharp claws, which is capable of piercing the steel of the factory's walls as easily as they do a man's flesh."

Simon nodded, confirming what he had already seen with the first corpse he examined. "Their attacks hardly seem to have caused any lasting damage to this facility."

Tanner's demeanor immediately changed. He frowned deeply and furrowed his brow. "These attacks have killed half a dozen of my men. That may not seem like much to an aristocrat like you, but in a facility like this, that's nearly a fifth of my operating staff. We got a few replacements for those we lost, but we're still working understaffed. The longer these attacks go on, the less likely anyone is to take the jobs on the refineries. The only other option is if people like Mr. Dosett and the governor authorized armed guards around every facility beyond the city wall, but no one will approve those sorts of expenses. So while our refinery may seem in fine working order to an outside observer like yourself, that's solely a testament to the hard work of the reduced staff that I have on hand, that they are able to keep the facility operating at their best efficiency while covering double shifts."

Simon swallowed hard. "Forgive me, Mr. Tanner. I clearly spoke without thinking and meant no disrespect."

Tanner seemed to relax as he realized to whom he was talking. "No, sir, I spoke out of turn and with bile. My outburst was uncalled for."

Simon smiled disarmingly. "On the contrary, your outburst has been the first moment of pure honesty I've encountered since beginning my investigation. I appreciate the insight you've offered."

The Inquisitor stood and put away his notebook. "If you would, Mr. Tanner, I would very much like to see any damage your facility incurred during the most recent attack."

The foreman stood and retrieved their parkas. He led them out of the office and back down the steel stairwell. A few workers moving palettes of supplies looked up with soot-covered faces at the odd pair following the foreman from the building. The trio paused at the entrance and stood for a brief moment between the potbelly stoves, soaking in the warmth they offered. With an audible sigh, Tanner pushed open the door.

While the cold had been harsh before, having been inside in the warmth made the arctic blast far worse this time around. Simon immediately shivered involuntarily as he felt his sharp mind temporarily freeze. The haze over his brain quickly receded, but he was left feeling miserable. He pulled his hood further over his face and tried to disappear into its warmth.

The foreman led them around the building. On the far side, the recent damage was immediately visible. The concrete that formed the core of the building was marred by long gashes. The pipes and hoses that Simon had admired from afar were twisted and torn upon closer inspection. He knew immediately that he had misspoken when they were in Tanner's office. The building had suffered severe damage, much of which had yet to be repaired. The hoses sat silent and still, where they should have been channeling refined oil into storage vats below ground.

Simon unclipped his parka as far down as he dared and reached into the pocket of his suit jacket beneath. He pulled out the notebook, holding it in one of his mitten-covered hands. He struggled to pull the pencil free, finally jerking on it with so much effort that it flew from his fingertips and disappeared into the nearby snow bank. Simon frowned as he stared at the small hole it had left in its wake. There was a brief moment where he actually considered digging in the snow after it, since he didn't have another instrument with which to take notes.

"Please, sir," Luthor said, pulling an extra pencil from his small bag, "take one of mine before you do something you'll regret immediately afterward."

Simon smiled and took the nub of the pencil Luthor offered. "You know me far too well. Do you happen to have the compass and protractor handy as well?"

Luthor opened his over-the-shoulder bag once more and sorted through, pulling out both the metal instruments. Simon took the tools before turning back toward the claw marks on the wall.

"What is he doing?" Tanner asked as he stepped beside Luthor.

Luthor raised a finger to his lips.

Simon took the metal compass and held the two free-floating ends of the measuring instrument to the scars on the wall. Pulling the tool away from the wall, he lowered it to his notebook, annotating the width of the marks. He confirmed his findings with similar claw marks along the wall before collapsing and putting away the compass. He returned to the first set of claw marks and retrieved the protractor. He took angle measurements of the claw marks, noting his findings in the notebook beside the claw measurements.

"What exactly is he expecting that to tell him?" Tanner asked.

Luthor hushed him more audibly.

Simon put away the second tool and stepped away from the wall. He raised a hand and scratched his chin thoughtfully as he looked at the marks. To everyone's surprise, he howled loudly. Luthor and Tanner jerked in shock. Simon immediately raised his hand and slashed it downward, mimicking the claw gouges in the concrete. With his arm returned to his side, he spun quickly on his heels and marched over to the inquisitive pair of men.

"From the angle of the slash, taking into consideration an arm length similar to that of a man and no abnormalities in the general paw structure of the werewolf, I have deduced we're dealing with at least four different creatures, standing at a height of between five foot and six inches and six feet and two inches tall, all with claw width of approximately an inch and a half."

Luthor annotated the findings in his notebook underneath their other research discoveries to date.

"Mr. Tanner," Simon said as he put away his notebook, "thank you ever so much for sacrificing your time and answering our questions. Luthor, if you would be so kind, please signal for Mr. Parrish. I believe I would like to examine one of the refineries further away from the city to see if my findings are similarly confirmed."

CHAPTER Ten

THE RIDE TO THE DRILLING STATION BEYOND MR. Tanner's refinery was blissfully quicker than the trip from the city. Simon tried to review his notes during the brief trip but gave up after realizing the futility of the effort. His head kept bouncing one direction while the notebook in his hand bounced the other. Looking down and attempting to read was only aggravating his nausea. He unbuckled the top of his parka and slid his notebook away before turning his attention back to his snowy surroundings.

He expected to arrive at another serpentine refinery like the one they had just left, but he was very surprised when they instead approached an open-air operation underway. A tall, narrow, wire-framed pyramid rose from the frozen ground, towering over the group as they approached. A single thick, metal tube ran through the heart of the pyramid, extending into the earth. A myriad of workers encircled the drilling operation, barking orders or manhandling the rig into place.

The closer they got to the rig, the louder the din of yells and conversation. The men around it wore thick parkas similar in design to the ones he and Luthor wore, but they were filthy with grease and crude oil.

Simon and Luthor climbed from the sled as soon as it stopped. Unlike the refinery, no one left their post and approached the visitors. As Simon watched, the men worked as smoothly as the machine that they tended. Men lathered grease onto the exterior of the drill. With a wave of their hands, other men pulled levers and the interior pipe began spinning. Gray smoke mixed with rocky debris erupted from the drill tube. The men nearby turned their heads away and covered their mouths until the dirty air settled.

Simon walked toward the men, though he doubted any of them had even noticed the Inquisitor's arrival. He paused behind the man that seemed to be observing and calling out the occasional order. The sound of the drill carving through the bedrock beneath the permafrost was deafening this close to the operation. Simon flinched at the noise and suddenly realized why no one heard them arrive.

He considered tapping the man on the shoulder, but he wasn't sure he wanted to distract him from what appeared to be a crucial stage of their drilling. Instead, he and Luthor stood just past his shoulder so that they wouldn't even be seen in passing by his peripheral vision.

"Pull it back," the foreman yelled, his voice barely rising above the grinding of the drill bit. "Slowly. Just ease it back a couple feet."

The men pulled up on the switches they'd been holding down. The drill reversed the direction of its spin, and the terrible metal on stone sound Simon had been hearing eased immediately.

"It's close now," one of the men greasing the drill called back. "You can feel it breaking through the last of the bedrock."

"How much further?" the foreman asked.

One of the men standing further to the side looked up from a table, where cylindrical coring samples were strewn in front of him. He held a finger in a notebook, marking his latest calculation. "It should be no more than three feet, sir, though I expect we'll be passing close to the iron deposit."

The foreman nodded. "That's what I expected. We're close, gentlemen, but that doesn't mean we need to get overzealous. We'll drive the drill slowly until I'm sure we're clear of the iron deposit before we make our final push. If anyone pushes too quickly and breaks the drill bit, I'll send you personally to Mr. Dosett to ask for more money."

The men all laughed before returning to their respective jobs. With a wave of his hand, the switches were thrown and large gears spun, twisting a massive screw and descending the drill once more. The sound of metal on stone returned immediately, and even Simon's thoughts were consumed by the noise.

Unbeknownst to the foreman, Simon and Luthor continued to stand behind the man as they admired his smooth-running operations. The drill continued to descend slowly, inching forward as it carved through the thick limestone.

The foreman's gaze traced upward, reaching to the full height of the rig. Simon followed it, wondering exactly what the man was waiting for. As he watched, a single spurt of black liquid shot from the top of the hollow tube attached to the drill. Simon canted his head to the side as another small geyser of oil erupted from the rig.

The foreman turned to Simon and Luthor, catching them both by surprise since they had no idea the man knew they were even there. "You both may want to back up. This is about to get messy."

The three men walked back to where Parrish waited with the sled dogs. No sooner did they turn back toward the rig than oil sprayed wildly from the top of the structure. The black liquid sloshed over the sides of the metal frame and dripped down on the men below. The workers bellowed with glee at the sight of the oil.

"Stop the drill," the foreman yelled. "Clamp it down. I don't want to lose any of our payload."

The men worked feverishly, spinning large wheels affixed to the side of the drilling tube. The erupting volcano of oil slowly petered back to a small geyser before turning into nothing more than an intermittent drip of the fluid.

With the rig clamped down, the foreman turned back toward the Inquisitor and apothecary with a broad smile. "I'm sorry I wasn't able to properly welcome you earlier, though I can't think of a more proper introduction to the work we're doing here. Do you work for Mr. Dosett?" The foreman's expression suddenly fell. "About what I said earlier about Mr. Dosett, I meant no disrespect. I was merely joking with my men."

Simon held up a hand. "I don't work for Mr. Dosett. My name is Royal Inquisitor Whitlock."

The man's expression didn't improve at the revelation of Simon's official title.

Simon cleared his throat awkwardly, having forgotten that not everyone showed him the deference to which he'd grown accustomed when announcing himself.

"My associate and I are merely conducting an investigation into the tales of werewolves in the area. Since you and your crew are more mobile, I had hoped you might be able to share some insight into your own experiences."

The foreman nodded. "We've seen them, but never up close. They've slinked around the edges of our camps as we were checking out some other drilling sites, but as soon as they were found to be dry, we moved on and never saw them again."

Simon stroked his chin as he listened intently, mentally annotating a few more interesting facts. Luthor seemed far less interested in the man's words as he stood beside the Inquisitor. He lazily spun his cane between his fingers as he stared out across the tundra.

Luthor took a step forward, letting the icy cover to the powdered snow nearby crunch under his thick-soled shoe. He was about to take another step when he saw something dark in front of him. His gaze drifted toward the snow at his feet, where a large droplet of spilled oil had stained the pristine white snow. Luthor stopped spinning his cane and used the tip of it to press into the inky spot. He withdrew the cane, and its tip ran black with crude.

"You've never actually seen one of these werewolves up close, then?" Simon asked. "You couldn't actually confirm what they looked like?"

The foreman shrugged. "They were as big as a man and covered in white fur. I presume they could have been a person in an elaborate wintery garb, but in this instance, it actually seems more likely that they were werewolves."

Simon frowned at the man. "You realize that statement is preposterous. It is never more likely that what you saw was a mythological creature rather than just a man in a suit. That mentality is exactly why Inquisitors are in such great demand, often for the most nonsensical and mundane of reasons."

Luthor looked up again, his gaze tracing the distant foothills. He furrowed his brow as he realized something was amiss. It took him a moment to realize that the thin trails of smoke coming from the campfires were no longer visible, as though all the fires had been simultaneously extinguished.

"Simon, sir?" Luthor said.

"If the idea of werewolves were so preposterous," the foreman countered, "you certainly wouldn't be investing so much time and energy determining their authenticity. You would have sent a simple telegraph back to the capital announcing a lack of evidence to support the allegations of monsters and then flown back home at your earliest convenience. The fact that you remain is a clear proof that at least an iota of you believes they're real."

Luthor saw movement in the distance as something as white as the snow rushed from one snowdrift to the next. He clutched the pommel of his cane tighter as he tilted his head to be heard without taking his eyes from the scene before him.

"Sir, begging your pardon, but I believe we're about to be under attack."

"If I truly thought the werewolves were real," Simon retorted, "I would have sent a telegraph demanding a team from the Order of Kinder Pel. You and half the town are alive only because I had the common decency not to send that message."

From the leeside of a snow bank, a wolf emerged. Even from a distance, the creature was enormous. Thick muscles rippled underneath its smooth coat of snowy white fur. It padded along the top of the hill on all fours. Its lips twitched as it stared at Luthor, who stood transfixed in place. As the winter wolf turned away from the apothecary, he noticed a bandolier wrapped around the creature's waist. He furrowed his brow only for a moment before the wolf turned back, this time standing on only three legs. Its other front leg was held aloft, holding the stock of a flintlock rifle. Pushing off with its other front leg, the werewolf rose to its full height on its back two legs and pulled the stock of the rifle into the crook of its shoulder. It lowered its head and sighted along the top of the rifle toward where Simon and the foreman argued with one another.

Luthor turned and ran toward the pair. He leapt, striking Simon from behind and driving him into the snow as a gunshot rang out. The foreman lurched backward and clutched at his shoulder. Blood seeped from between his fingers as he collapsed into the snow.

"Luthor," Simon said while facedown in the frigid snow, "please get off me."

Luthor hastily moved from atop the Inquisitor and Simon turned his head to the side, spitting out a mouthful of partially melted powdery snow.

"A thousand apologies, sir, but I believe we're under attack," Luthor explained.

A second gunshot rang out, and they both heard the whizz as it flew dangerously close over their heads.

"I notice as much," Simon said. He rolled over and climbed quickly to his feet. "Arm yourself and go defend the drill workers. I don't think they have much more in the way of weaponry than the wrenches and hammers at their disposal in the toolkits around the workstation."

"Very good, sir," Luthor said as he rushed toward the rig.

Simon climbed to his feet as another gunshot rang out. The lead bullet struck the metal framework around the drill site, resounding loudly across the empty frozen plain.

The Inquisitor could see the werewolf atop the hill with the butt of its rifle driven into the snow. It tilted a powder horn, knocking some of the black granules into the end of the barrel. The wolf looked up and met Simon's gaze as it tore off a small swatch of fabric, shoving it into the barrel ahead of another lead bullet.

Simon's attention was pulled away from the reloading werewolf as another of the creatures bounded over a nearby snow bank and sped toward him. Shocked from his stupor, Simon reached up and attempted to unclasp the top of his parka. As before, he found the task nearly impossible while wearing the mittens. His fingers fumbled with the metal clasp unsuccessfully.

He looked up to see the werewolf sliding gracefully down the backside of the snow mound, landing only on its hind legs. It grasped the hilt of a long knife tucked into its sheath at the wolf's waist. In a fluid motion, it pulled the shining steel blade, holding it nimbly between its fur-covered paw and its dewclaw, which Simon noted was long and limber enough to act as a thumb.

In frustration, Simon stripped off the mittens, tossing them to the ground at his feet. The werewolf stepped forward, slowly at first, but gaining speed as it ran. Though the metal clasp was extremely cold to his unprotected hands, Simon unclasped the top latch of his parka and slid his hand into its warm interior.

The werewolf lowered its head and charged, baring its teeth and exposing the elongated canines. Simon fumbled inside his parka but didn't break eye contact with the monster as it rushed toward him.

The creature leapt easily over the abandoned table of coring samples and sprinted the last two-dozen feet toward Simon. As it neared the Inquisitor, it raised the long knife over its head.

Simon's fingers finally closed around the handle of his revolver, and he drew the weapon fluidly from his parka. In practiced motion, he pulled back the hammer nearly simultaneously with squeezing the trigger. The first round struck the werewolf in the gut, causing it to stumble during its long stride. No sooner had the first rapport rang out than Simon pulled the trigger again. The second and third rounds both struck the werewolf in the chest.

Momentum carried the monster forward, though Simon doubted it still had the strength to strike him. It swayed unsteadily as it took one last step before finally pitching forward at his feet.

Simon looked down at the creature and sighed with relief.

Another gunshot rang out, and the snow at his feet exploded upward. Simon raised his head and saw the werewolf on the hill hastily reloading his long rifle. The creature used its teeth to tear off the top of the powder horn, and it tilted it toward the lip of the rifle.

Simon adjusted his stance and straightened his firing arm. He closed one eye as he took aim and squeezed the trigger. The bullet struck the powder horn as the werewolf turned it upward. The black powder within ignited from the impact, exploding in a giant fireball that consumed the wolf. When the smoke cleared from the top of the hill, Simon could see no sign of the insolent monster.

He turned his gaze elsewhere and sought a new target.

Luthor rushed into the drilling operations, ducking as a lead ball struck the framework directly above his head. He slid to a stop beside the central drill, digging the tip of his cane into the ice to stop his momentum. He looked around for the site workers, but he appeared to be alone. Most had fled away from the werewolves, thinking that putting distance between themselves and the monsters would save their lives. Sadly, the creatures merely adjusted their charge to intercept the fleeing workers.

Luthor was alone under the framework pyramid around the drill. He could see a few of the werewolves rushing across the tundra, though most gave the actual drilling site a wide berth. A few gunshots cut through the air, though Luthor struggled to identify exactly where the sounds were originating.

He glanced around quickly to make sure no one was watching him. With a wave of his hand, a translucent shield encompassed his left hand. Luthor muttered under his breath as he continued the incantation, covering himself with a protective spell. Though it wouldn't stop the razor-sharp claws of the beasts, it would hopefully let him survive the creature's first salvo.

As he turned away from the drill, a tall shadow fell over him. A werewolf stepped into one of the entryways between the metal legs of the rig. It towered over the much shorter man, though it wasn't the creature's height that had Luthor worried. The werewolf carried a flintlock rifle that was already trained on him.

"Damn it all to hell," Luthor muttered as the werewolf pulled the trigger.

Flames leapt from the end of the rifle as the lead ball flew from the barrel. Luthor's eyes couldn't trace the trajectory of the bullet, but he felt it as it connected with his spell. The translucent light around him sparked madly, like steel striking flint. Sparks erupted from its impact, but the spell miraculously held. The lead ball was turned aside, passing within an inch of his left hip. It struck the drill behind him with a hollow thud before dropping to the snow.

Luthor let out a sigh of relief but frowned as the werewolf howled into the air and charged at him.

He raised his cane in defense, but the werewolf ignored the paltry weapon. He swung the rifle like a club, connecting solidly with Luthor's chest. The protective spell flared again but, weakened as it was, it sputtered and failed. While it absorbed some of the kinetic energy from the impact, Luthor was tossed from his feet. He felt ribs crack and break beneath his thick parka as he slid unceremoniously on his back through the snow and ice.

The werewolf growled as it rushed at him again, in an attempt to finish off the prone man. Luthor waited until it was close before rolling quickly to his side. The werewolf drove the butt of the rifle into the snow where he had lain moments before.

Despite the pain in his ribs, Luthor rolled to his feet, brandishing the cane. The werewolf seemed unimpressed as it bared its teeth again.

Luthor swung the cane like a club, striking the werewolf across the face. The creature reared back more in surprise than in pain. Pressing his advantage, Luthor raised the cane above his head and swung sharply downward.

A white, furry claw shot up and caught the cane in the middle of its arc. Luthor tugged on the cane, trying to free it from the werewolf's powerful grip, but to no avail.

With his cane gripped firmly in one clawed hand, the werewolf snapped its jaws forward, closing the razor-sharp canines over Luthor's exposed forearm. The residual magic of his spell kept the powerful jaws from snapping bone and severing his arm, but the teeth still sank deeply into his flesh. Luthor bit back a scream of pain, as he felt blood seep into the underside of his parka's sleeve.

The werewolf growled gutturally as it tried to bite down further into his arm. Luthor hoped he never had to hear the crunching sound again. The bite was accompanied by a flare of pain as the monster shifted its jaws back and forth.

Luthor winced as he stared into the creature's dark eyes. It looked back at him with malevolence, though he saw a spark of intelligence behind its animalistic façade.

"I'm truly sorry for this, old chap," Luthor said through clenched teeth. "Nothing personal."

The werewolf cocked its head to the side as though it understood the apology. Luthor winced once more at the creature's movement, his arm still latched between powerful jaws.

Luthor released the cane with his trapped arm but grabbed it with his free hand quickly before the werewolf could pull it away. He pressed a button on the side, releasing the cane's pommel and the rapier that had been concealed within the haft of the walking instrument. With a practiced flourish, Luthor slashed across the werewolf's forearm. It dropped the rest of the cane and howled in pain, clutching its damaged arm with its free hand. Its howl freed Luthor's injured arm, which dropped weakly to his side.

A turn of the blade dragged the rapier across the creature's stomach. Though it lacked the strength to cut through the thick fur and hide more than a few inches, the slash drew an angry red line of blood across the monster's gut.

Whimpering with surprise and pain, the werewolf dropped the rifle in its uninjured hand and covered the seeping blood on its belly with its claw. With a surprised and angry glance at the apothecary, the werewolf turned away to flee. Luthor took the opportunity to drive his point home with another slash across the shoulder blades of the retreating creature.

The magical creature dropped to all fours and bounded through the powdery snow. Luthor waited until the werewolf had disappeared over the nearest snow bank before he lowered the tip of his rapier. He glanced around and was glad to see that he was alone once more.

He saw the rest of his cane resting half submerged in the snow. He reached down to retrieve it, groaning softly as he felt pressure in his broken ribs and the anguish rolling through his bitten arm. He knew that when he was finally alone, he'd have to use a spell to repair the damage. It wouldn't do for him to be incapacitated during their investigation.

A werewolf in the distance howled, and the noise was picked up and echoed by the rest of the pack. Simon watched as the werewolves rushed hurriedly through the snow, disappearing back the way they had originally come. Much of the white fur of the wolves was stained red with fresh blood. Simon didn't envy their task ahead, as they sought out survivors of the drilling crew.

The foreman was alive, Simon was happy to note. The lead bullet had pierced the man's shoulder cleanly, exiting through a hole in his back not much larger than the entry wound. Simon found some fabric used for packaging the coring samples and used the cloth to pack the man's wound. He groaned but didn't resist the treatment.

Simon dropped his gaze to the foreman and tried to smile reassuringly. "Good news, you won't bleed to death before the city guards arrive. In fact, there is even a good chance that you won't die even after they arrive, though I wouldn't place much faith in the ill-trained country doctors at your disposal back in Haversham."

Before the foreman could manage a stinging retort to what had to have been the worst bedside manner he had ever experienced, Simon noticed Luthor approaching and stood.

Luthor staggered through the snow, favoring his broken ribs and clutching his bitten arm close to his chest. His face bore a smile, though it only thinly veiled the pain.

"Are you all right, Luthor?" Simon asked.

"I've certainly been better."

Simon reached over and stuck his finger through a hole in Luthor's parka. Pushing deeper into the parka, his finger emerged from a similar hole on the backside of the coat.

"Good Lord, man. You were nearly shot," he remarked.

Luthor looked down, noting that the passage of the bullet passed less than an inch from piercing his side. He had been so intently focused on his other injuries, he had nearly forgotten about the gunshot.

"Had I been a fatter man—"

"—the sled dogs would have never been able to drag you through the snow in the first place, saving you the discomfort of the motion sickness you experienced. You also would have never been attacked by, dare I say it, a werewolf," Simon concluded. "Be thankful you're in such good shape."

"It appears to be both a blessing and a curse," Luthor joked, though he wasn't sure how much Simon had spoken in jest. "Has anyone ever told you that you speak quite a bit when you're nervous?"

"My mother," Simon said wistfully. "Quite often, actually. More than you realize, or I realize, or anyone realizes, really."

Luthor placed a hand on the Inquisitor's shoulder, though lifting his arm caused him pain as well. He let go and slipped his hand into the inside of his parka. His fingers came in contact with a viscous fluid and, for the briefest moment, Luthor was sure he had suffered far more injuries than he originally believed. As soon as his fingers brushed against the broken glass of the vial, he felt simultaneous relief at not being injured and anger at the loss of more reagents. Feeling deeper into the pocket, his fingers found the other vials concealed within. He fetched a vial of amber liquid and sloshed it around before handing it to his friend.

"Drink this," Luthor ordered. "It will calm your nerves."

Simon took the vial but looked at it dubiously. "What did you put in this elixir?"

Luthor smiled. "It's scotch. I find the vast majority of ailments can be fixed with the right application of alcohol."

Simon hastily uncorked the vial and drank its contents in a single swallow. He shook his head as the alcohol burned the back of his throat, but it also warmed his belly and helped clear his mind. He handed the empty vial back to the apothecary.

As Luthor retrieved the vial with his healthy arm, Simon's gaze fell to the one cradled protectively.

"What has happened to your arm?" Simon asked.

Luthor swallowed hard, as though he was reticent to tell Simon the truth. Begrudgingly, he pulled up his sleeve. The bleeding had already stopped, though tacky blood was smeared across his forearm, matting the fine hairs. The bite marks were puckered and rimmed in an angry red as though an infection were already burning through the apothecary's skin.

"Forgive me, sir," Luthor said quietly. "I was bitten."

Every child's tale about the infectious bite of a werewolf poured through Simon's mind. He had heard enough werewolf stories to know that the lycanthropy was passed through the saliva. A bite could turn a normal man into another of the magical creatures like a disease. A cold lump formed in Simon's chest as he looked at his apologetic companion. He shook his head softly, hoping beyond hope that the stories were just that—stories. He wasn't sure what he believed of werewolf mythology, and he told himself that the legends surrounding the bite of the creature could be nothing more than folklore. He sighed, however, knowing that he was forcing himself to believe that his accomplice wasn't going to turn into another of those monsters. He had no way yet to know, one way or the other.

"Luthor?" he asked, knowing that the hanging question was enough for his friend.

"It hurts, to be certain," Luthor replied, "but I don't think it's anything worse than a bad injury. I certainly don't feel like howling at the moon, if that's what you're insinuating, though for good measure, it might not be a bad idea to lock me away somewhere safe once we return."

Simon sat down heavily in the snow but kept his eyes trained on his friend. "This is a fine mess."

The Inquisitor looked around the destruction caused by the werewolves. Luthor followed his gaze initially but grew distracted at the sight of the one Simon had shot, now lying dead, facedown in the snow.

The apothecary pointed at the remains. "It seems we can put the argument of authenticity to rest now."

"Yes," Simon sighed, "there's no doubt in my mind that magical creatures have invaded our kingdom." His gaze fell again to Luthor's injured arm, which was, once again, covered by the thick parka. "We must make haste back to Haversham. I'll find Mr. Parrish at once. I'm not sure how he'll manage, but we'll have to make due with a third passenger for the ride home."

CHAPTER *Eleven*

LUTHOR GRIMACED AT EVERY BOUNCE OF THE SLED AS it raced back toward Haversham. Though it was hidden from Simon's view, the magic coursing through Luthor's blood had already begun healing the broken bones and damaged skin on his forearm. By the time they reached the city, the bite marks would be scabbed over and the infection better controlled. For now, however, each bounce sent new waves of pain racing through his body.

Their riding position was far from ideal, only adding to the apothecary's discomfort. Their legs were draped over the husky body of the werewolf, leaving their knees pressed nearly to their chins as they sat in the wicker seats. Mr. Parrish's sled wasn't made to hold more than the two passengers, so the addition of the werewolf corpse had required some creative positioning.

Simon stole a glance at his friend, leaning forward to see around the sled's only other addition: the flintlock rifle dropped by the werewolf Luthor fought. The apothecary sensed eyes upon him and glanced over at the Inquisitor.

"You're staring at me again."

Simon didn't bother denying it. "I know it makes me sound heartless and uncaring, but I'm intrigued about the process of transformation, if it really is to happen. Do you feel anything unusual? Anything at all that might be the early signs of an incubation period?"

Luthor frowned. "Ever the scientist, aren't you, sir? You know, sir, I do feel unusual."

Simon arched an eyebrow inquisitively.

"I feel an indescribably level of anguish, though I can guarantee every bit of that is related to the dozen or so new holes that are adorning my arm and not, as you so callously hoped, associated with early stages of lycanthropy. If it's all the same to you, sir, I would greatly appreciate being able to focus on this investigation. If I am going to become a werewolf, I might as well serve some purpose other than future dissection."

Reaching over, he patted the flintlock rifle resting between them.

"Do you recognize it?" Luthor asked.

Simon's gaze fell to the rifle as though he were scrutinizing its features, though it was unnecessary. He had recognized the model of firearm the moment it had been placed between them.

"It's a Renault," Simon said.

Luthor nodded. "A fine quality weapon to be in the hands of savage monsters."

Simon frowned, though his eyes were unreadable underneath the tinted lenses of his goggles. "Especially considering I've only seen this caliber weapon in the hands of the governor's personal retinue."

Luthor ran a hand across his thick muttonchops. "Could the werewolf have possibly taken the weapon from a slain guard?"

Simon furrowed his brow as he looked at his friend. "There is always a possibility, though I remain skeptical. During the brevity of our stay, I have yet to see the gubernatorial guards further away from the estate than the elevator during our welcome. Though if one of Governor Godwin's guards was assaulted within the confines of the city and everyone simply failed to mention such crucial information, I will be very put out."

"Then how did a werewolf come to possess one of their rifles?"

Simon bit his bottom lip thoughtfully. "How indeed, my good fellow."

Luthor saw the pensive look spreading across Simon's face and knew the Inquisitor was formulating a theory. Simon had worn a similar expression shortly before revealing the elaborate series of marionette wires used during their case involving pixies. The apothecary waited patiently for Simon to elaborate, but the Inquisitor instead glanced back toward the distant city walls.

Luthor let his gaze follow Simon's as he pulled his arm close against his chest.

"We've now confirmed the presence of mystical creatures in Haversham," Luthor said loudly over the whipping wind. "What will you do now?"

Simon stroked his chin and shook his head. "The proper procedure of an Inquisitor would be to notify the Order immediately and await further instructions."

Luthor swallowed hard, nervous for his own safety. "I sense that there's a 'however' in your response."

"However, I don't know what to report."

Luthor looked over at his friend. "You don't know what to report, or are you hesitant to tell the Order that your companion might be infected with the very disease you came to investigate?"

Simon kept his gaze stoically ahead. "They seem like two sides of the same argument."

"Forgive me for playing the Devil's advocate, but we've seen the werewolves. We've met them face-to-face. For God's sake, our feet are resting on the remains of one as we speak. What more do you require to be satisfied?"

"A reason," Simon replied, driving his fist into his palm. "I require a justification as to why these monsters are attacking isolated drilling and refinery sites and not the city itself. Do you remember when the governor's assistant told us the tunnels led beyond the wall? Why wouldn't the werewolves simply use the tunnels to enter the city, where they could do the most harm?"

"A personal hatred for Gideon Dosett, perhaps?" Luthor surmised.

"That would be my assumption, but it's all conjecture. Before I send a telegraph back to the Order, I want to ensure I have all the facts."

Luthor shook his head. "Procedure dictates you contact them the moment you have any indication of magic. They won't like this delay, nor will they accept your excuses without bitter disapproval."

Luthor blanched slightly as he continued. "And what if they contact you instead, demanding an update of your investigation? What will you tell them, about the werewolves and about me?"

Simon turned his gaze back to the jostling landscape. "That will just have to be a bridge we cross when we come to it."

Luthor let his gaze follow Simon's to the desolate frozen tundra over which they raced. "For what it's worth, thank you," Luthor said. When Simon didn't reply, the apothecary cleared his throat and continued. "It's more than just a quest for information, isn't it?" he asked.

"If I send a telegraph with no more information than that werewolves exist, you and I both know what the Order will do."

"They'll send Kinder Pel," Luthor answered.

Simon nodded. "The Order of Kinder Pel is a little, shall we say, heavy handed. If Inquisitors are surgeons, tactfully exercising the magic from our kingdom, they're performing said surgery with a mallet."

"Do you fear for the lives of the denizens of Haversham, should Pellites arrive?"

"Nothing so altruistic, I'm afraid. While I do worry about their well-being, I'm far more concerned with the werewolves themselves. A pack of werewolves of this size, assuming what we've seen today is but a fraction of their full strength, is clearly an advance force, but of what, I cannot say. Before I can release the tactless Pellites on Haversham, I have to know why the werewolves are here. Sadly, the Order of Kinder Pel doesn't share my concerns. They'd destroy any further evidence and our investigation—the reason 'why', mind you—would disappear forever."

Luthor turned toward the Inquisitor sternly. Though Simon refused to return Luthor's hard stare, he read his companion's confused expression well enough. He understood the apothecary's concern. Simon was ignoring the written doctrine of his order by continuing his investigation, especially without notifying the crown. Luthor was right that the Order wouldn't be happy about this breach. Despite the fact that Simon didn't envy the conversation he'd have with the Grand Inquisitor upon their return to the capital, he knew his path was righteous.

"If we are to uncover this mysterious reason why to which you keep alluding, what do we do once we get back to Haversham?" Luthor asked.

Simon patted the corpse under their feet. "We start by conducting a right and proper autopsy. Then I think it'll be time to have a more candid conversation with Mr. Dosett."

"And then, sir?"

"And then we discover whether or not you and the next full moon are to become intimately acquainted."

Luthor nodded in satisfaction and leaned back in his wicker chair as the sled raced over the frozen ground.

CHAPTER Twelve

SIMON HUNG HIS PARKA ON THE HOOK AS THE SLED dogs yipped from their respective kennels. He shook gently as though mentally dusting off the snow that had accumulated during their trip. Like returning to an old friend, the Inquisitor affectionately retrieved his top hat and placed it, canted, on top of his head.

He joined Luthor outside as the apothecary supervised the loading of the werewolf corpse onto the back of a wagon. Luthor quickly climbed up onto the back of the wagon and unfolded a coarse, woven blanket. He winced as he draped it over the wolf, ensuring all of the white fur was concealed. Once the deed was done, he drew his bitten arm closer to his chest protectively.

"We should take you to the doctor," Simon remarked, gesturing toward Luthor's wounded limb.

Luthor shook his head. "It's nothing, sir. A doctor will give me nothing that I can't produce more effectively on my own. I merely need to return to the estate and my doctor's bag."

Simon stepped forward and stared up at his companion. "The role of the solemn hero is unbecoming on you, Luthor. You will do me no good if the wound gets infected."

Luthor looked down, appreciative of his friend's genuine concern. "I appreciate the sentiment, but it'll heal far better on its own. I can dress the wound properly once we're safely returned to the gubernatorial mansion. I promise, sir."

Sensing the end of Simon's protests, Luthor grasped the wooden side of the wagon and began lowering himself to the frosted cobblestones below. As Luthor climbed down from the horse-drawn wagon, the driver approached the Inquisitor. The portly man's gaze struggled to remain on Simon, as he repeatedly looked toward the covered monster as though expecting it to rise from the dead at any moment.

"It's thoroughly deceased," Simon reprimanded the man. "It poses no threat to you. However, failing to follow my instructions could be detrimental to your future employment."

The man brought his gaze immediately back to the Royal Inquisitor. "Of course, sir."

"You are to take the body back to the governor's estate with all haste. Mr. Strong and I will be accompanying you the whole way and will answer any questions that may arise. You are to stop for no one and no matter the inquiry that may arise, under no circumstances are you to remove or allow to be removed that blanket before we arrive. Do you understand my directions thus far?"

The man nodded.

"Good. Then let's be off."

Simon scrambled into the front seat beside the driver as Luthor climbed himself onto the open back of the wagon. His feet dangled over the back as he pressed his weight down onto the loose end of the blanket, ensuring it wouldn't rise up as they rode off.

The driver swung himself onto the wagon. It started with a lurch, and its wooden wheels clacked along the cobblestone street. The ride through the town was blissfully quick and uneventful, though Simon's stomach churned at every wary eye that watched the Inquisitor pass. He could sense the growing suspicion as to the contents of the wagon, though he kept his expression stoic toward their scrutiny. He politely tipped his hat to anyone who stared for longer than a brief moment.

The gubernatorial guards let the wagon pass into the estate without question, and the battered cart pulled in front of the house as though it were a nobleman's carriage. Simon climbed hastily from the seat and approached the front door.

"Find Mr. Dosett at once," he demanded of the guards. "Tell him we have need of his autopsy room once more."

Before the guard could turn to leave, Simon grabbed his arm and forced him to turn. "And find some burly chaps who can carry a great weight. We'll have need of their services as well."

Simon returned to the wagon but walked around to the back, where Luthor sat nervously. His legs swung back and forth and his gaze was distant.

"You look deep in thought," Simon remarked.

"It's supposed to be a full moon tonight, you realize," Luthor stated. "I took note of the lunar patterns as soon as I was told our mission, in case the effects of the full moon did have an impact on the transformation of these creatures."

Simon lowered his voice so the wagon driver couldn't overhear. "And you fear tonight you will become a beast?"

Luthor shrugged. "I'm not sure what I think, though I believe a werewolf loosed in the mansion would create an unfortunate panic indeed. All attempts to keep the Order of Kinder Pel at bay would be for naught if the governor himself reports a direct attack."

"If it's a transformation you fear, then tonight I will lash you to your bed with the best seaman's knots I can recall. I can't say you'll sleep at all comfortably, or at all, for that matter, but you will be better… contained, shall we say?"

Before they could continue their conversation, the front door to the estate opened and Gideon appeared. He rushed down the steps and approached the back of the wagon. Without a word to the two gentlemen, he lifted the back corner of the blanket. At the sight of the dead werewolf, he smiled broadly, dropped the blanket, and patted Simon appreciatively on the back.

"Well done, gentlemen," he said excitedly. "Well done."

"I wouldn't grow too excitable at this one creature's death," Simon responded. "This one death hardly outweighs the cost to your business or men who were run off or worse during the attack."

Gideon waved his hand dismissively. "We can always rebuild a drill, but until these creatures know that we'll hunt them and stop them at every turn, then all our actions are for naught. You've delivered them a great blow today, and I can't thank you enough."

"You most certainly can thank us," Simon corrected, "by having this corpse delivered to the surgical suite in the basement. I would like to conduct my autopsy, a proper one, this time."

"Of course," Gideon said. He turned toward the door and motioned for a pair of large men to join them. The two brutish workers wrapped the corpse fully in the blanket before lifting it from the wagon with strained grunts.

Gideon led the way through the foyer, much to the chagrin of the butler who stood impassively to the side. The frown etched on his face was evidence enough of his feelings of a monster being towed through his clean antechamber.

The doorway to the basement was open, and both Simon and Luthor followed the parade of workers down the winding steps. At the bottom, Gideon led the group into a familiar sterilized room. The werewolf's corpse was placed onto the metal table and unwrapped. The two large men struggled to shift its weight and pull the blanket from underneath it, only successfully doing so after Simon offered his assistance.

With the blanket removed and the body on display, Gideon dismissed the two workers and turned toward Simon.

"What shall we do first?"

"We won't be doing anything," Simon quickly corrected. "Mr. Strong and I will be conducting this autopsy in private."

Gideon frowned, clearly not used to being so readily dismissed. "I would like to stay, if it's all the same."

His words carried weight, as though spoken by someone who did not intend to be denied. Luthor turned away from the growing battle of wills and absently scratched at his arm.

Simon stared blankly at Gideon for some time before finally shaking his head. "I'm sorry, Mr. Dosett. My stance is very firm in this situation."

If possible, Gideon's frown deepened for a moment before he nodded submissively. "Very well. Though I would appreciate a full report of your findings. If this autopsy can assist in eliminating the werewolf threat once and for all, I would like to be kept informed."

"That would be acceptable," Simon conceded.

Gideon stared a moment longer before turning and walking out of the room.

Both men sighed in relief, glad that the battle between the iron will of Simon and the oozing charisma of Gideon didn't last longer than it did. By the time Simon turned back toward Luthor, the apothecary had already laid out a series of surgical instruments on a rolling table beside the corpse. He reached up above his head with the arm on the opposite side from his fractured ribs and pulled down a shower nozzle. Even so, the movement sent a brief spark of pain through Luthor's side, despite the magical healing coursing through his body. A squeeze of the handle produced a quick spray of water. He released the nozzle and let it retract back toward the ceiling.

"Where shall we begin, sir?"

Simon looked around the room until he spotted a microscope set against the wall. "Before we conduct the autopsy, I would like to examine the creature's blood. Can you draw a vial for me?"

"Of course, sir," Luthor replied, retrieving a syringe from the table.

"While you are at it," Simon continued, "draw a vial from yourself."

Luthor's hand froze above the syringe and he looked back at his mentor. "Sir?"

"If these creatures are carrying pathogens that, as you presume, are transmitted through its bite, than there should be traces of this disease in your own blood as well. I would like to confirm if you are or are not infected."

"Of… of course," Luthor stammered.

Simon walked past the table and picked up a long stick wrapped at the end in a cotton swab. He moved to the creature's mouth and crouched in front of it. The werewolf's mouth was agape as it had died, and its tongue hung flaccid from between its sharp teeth. Simon inserted the cotton swab and soaked up samples of the monster's saliva in the absorbent cotton. Satisfied, he stood and walked back to the microscope. He smeared the saliva onto a glass slide and slid it under the lens of the machine. A turn of the handle adjusted the mirror beneath until it caught the light, reflecting it through the slide and into the microscope's lens.

"Here are your samples," Luthor said from behind Simon.

Without looking up from the microscope, the Inquisitor motioned to an empty rack beside him. "Place them there, please. They're properly labeled so I know which is whose, correct?"

"Of course," Luthor replied. Simon heard the clink of the glass vials settling into the wooden slots. "Is there anything else I can prepare in advance of the autopsy?"

Simon lifted his head from the microscope's eyepiece and glanced at his clearly nervous companion. He knew Luthor's concerns, though he found the man's worrying unnecessary and a bit presumptuous.

"I fired three silver bullets into the creature. Could you please retrieve the bullets for me? I'd like to see the condition of the shells and any affect they might have had on the surrounding tissue."

"Gladly," Luthor replied, clearly glad to have something to keep him occupied.

Simon removed the saliva slide from the microscope and picked up the nearest blood sample, which was labeled with Luthor's name. A dropper beside him offered the means to collect a droplet of the apothecary's blood. Like the saliva before it, he smeared it onto a slide and placed another on top of the sample, spreading and trapping the red fluid. He slid it quickly under the microscope.

"Elevated white blood cells," Simon said after a moment's examination. "Though that's easily explained by the trauma you recently suffered. Good concentrations of red blood cells and platelets. No clear sign of any abnormalities or pathogens. Luthor, your blood says that you're in overall good health, albeit fighting off an infection that I can only assume stems from the bite on your arm."

"I do so hope that's the case, sir," Luthor said as he pulled the second silver bullet from the corpse.

Simon repeated the procedure with the next vial of blood, that which had come from the werewolf. He slid the slide under the microscope and looked through the eyepiece. As the blood sample came into focus, Simon frowned.

"This bullet has splintered," Luthor said from behind him. "It'll take some time to collect all the pieces."

When Simon didn't reply, the apothecary turned curiously toward the Inquisitor.

"Sir?" he asked. "What do you see?"

"Normal red blood cell count," Simon said quietly, just audibly enough for Luthor to hear. "Elevated white blood cell count and concentrated platelets. I was hardly trained in zoology during my Inquisitor training, but this blood looks decidedly, well, human to be honest. Luthor, are you sure this blood came from the werewolf?"

"Of course, sir. What's the matter?"

Simon shook his head. "There's no sign of any pathogens in this creature's blood. I would have expected to have found something buried in the werewolf's blood that would indicate the potential for a spreading infection."

Luthor blanched at the news. "Perhaps their disease really is magical in nature and not scientific. Perhaps there isn't anything to observe under a microscope."

"And perhaps you will still turn into one of them," Simon concluded. "That's your real concern, is it not?"

Luthor didn't reply, but he didn't have to.

"Did you find anything abnormal in the tissue surrounding the bullet wounds?" Simon asked.

Luthor shook his head. "They appear to be normal by all indications."

"No abnormal inflammation or weeping of pus?"

"None, sir."

"Most odd," Simon replied. "I don't think the silver had any effect on the monster. I can find no antigens in his blood against the invasion of silver in his system. He appears to have died of a normal series of gunshot wounds."

Simon spun in his chair so he could face his companion. "If the myth of silver being positively deadly to a werewolf can be debunked, then perhaps spreading their disease through their bite might also be nothing more than over exaggerated hearsay. You may be nothing more than a man who was unfortunately bitten by a wolf."

Luthor looked up and offered a weak smile. "I certainly do hope so, sir."

"Excellent. Now that that's settled, let's conduct an autopsy."

The organs were stacked neatly on trays beside the hollowed-out remains of the werewolf. Simon brushed his gloved hands on his bloodstained smock, smearing viscera across his covered torso.

"What can I bring you, sir?" Luthor asked.

"The scalpel, if you please."

Luthor ran the instrument underneath the spray of water, washing away the gore that clung to its exterior. With a quick pat dry, he handed it to Simon.

The Inquisitor ran his gaze across the collection of organs, settling finally on the engorged stomach. He deftly sliced into the soft organ. A wave of partially digested food and bile poured from the pierced stomach, filling the bottom of the raised pan in which it sat. Simon handed the scalpel back to Luthor before sticking both hands within the stomach. With a jerk, he pulled the remaining contents onto the tray.

He used the back of his hand to brush aside the clinging digestive juices, exposing the creature's final meal. Simon arched his eyebrow curiously, as he picked up a partially chewed but evidently sliced piece of vegetable.

"Could you get me the glasses?" Simon asked, his eyes never leaving the tuber.

Luthor picked up a pair of jeweler's glasses. A series of lenses clung to the wire frame, each with increasing magnification. Simon lowered his head as Luthor approached, allowing the shorter man to set them comfortably on his face.

"Which lens would you like?"

Simon tried his best to look at the options dangling just beyond his periphery. "Let's start with three times magnification."

Luthor flipped down the appropriate lens over his left eye and stepped away.

Simon raised the plant root in front of his face and stared at the scoring across its surface. He rotated the plant slowly, examining it from different angles.

"Most curious," he muttered.

"What is, sir?"

Simon looked up as though surprised Luthor was still in the room. He raised the root over his head as though celebrating his find.

"The incisions on this root weren't made by the creature's teeth or claws, as I originally assumed they would have been," Simon explained. "The lines of the cuts are far too precise. These were cut with a tool, most likely a knife of some craftsmanship."

Luthor shrugged noncommittally, stealing some of Simon's thunder. "These creatures were using rifles with relative ease. It hardly seems unlikely that they'd have the ability to manage a flintlock rifle but suddenly lack the manual dexterity to cut a vegetable with an ordinary knife."

Simon frowned and dropped the vegetable into the tray. He brushed aside more of the stomach's contents. His hand paused, however, when he found a partially chewed piece of meat. The blackening around the edges of the meat caught his attention. He lifted it from the tray and brought it to his nose. Despite the foul stench of the creature's stomach acid, he could still discern the faint underpinnings of char.

"That's truly disgusting," Luthor remarked, wrinkling his nose at the filth that Simon held to his face. "I really wish you wouldn't do that, or at the very least warn me before you do so that I might leave."

"Oh you of little faith," Simon mused to his companion. He set the meat back in the tray and removed his glasses, oblivious to the blood he smeared on the delicate lenses. "We've been assuming that these werewolves are, to some degree, savages, correct? That despite their use of tools and their opposable thumbs, they're magical monstrosities?"

Luthor nodded. "Findings that are supported by the accounts from Mr. Dosett and the governor."

"Exactly," Simon replied excitedly. "We've been told that they eat the flesh of their victims raw like their wolf cousins. But this meat isn't raw, Luthor. It's been cooked, as though over an open flame."

Luthor arched an eyebrow and ran his hand across his muttonchops. "So you're insinuating that they're civilized? That they've set up a settlement somewhere in the frozen tundra?"

Simon smiled his damningly knowing smile as he pulled off his entrails-stained gloves. With the gloves removed, he untied the smock and dropped it on the countertop beside him. He turned sharply on his heels and walked toward the door.

"What do you know?" Luthor asked, hurrying to keep up.

"I know nothing. I only presume to know."

Luthor stopped at the doorway in frustration and watched his mentor walk calmly down the hallway. "Are you really going to do this to me again? Just simply walk away with a wealth of conjecture and theories bouncing around your head while leaving me completely in the dark?"

"A hunch is only a hunch until supported by scientific evidence," Simon called back over his shoulder. "Scientific evidence is what separates us from the mystical monsters that have escaped the Rift."

"Then where are you going?"

"To see Mr. Dosett. We owe him our findings."

"And from there?" Luthor asked, exasperated.

Simon paused and stroked his chin. "Perhaps after that we'll get lunch."

"Lunch? I ask for answers and all you offer me is lunch?"

Simon began walking again, climbing the stairs that led to the main floor of the mansion. Luthor hurried to catch up.

"I truly do hate when you do this," he yelled, ensuring his mentor heard his displeasure.

CHAPTER Thirteen

"CAN YOU AT LEAST GIVE ME A HINT AS TO WHAT YOU discovered?" Luthor begged as they climbed the last of the winding stairs from the mansion's basement. "An inkling with which to satisfy my indelible curiosity?"

"Patience, Luthor," Simon chided. "I am still missing a few pieces of the puzzle."

Luthor frowned. "That's far better than me. I'm still not sure what picture the completed puzzle is supposed to reveal."

The doors at the top of the stairs were closed but unlocked. Simon pulled them inward and stepped into the hallway that ran between the kitchen and the foyer.

"Mr. Dosett will be able to provide a few more of the answers we seek," Simon continued. "That's why we are going to visit him now."

As they entered the foyer, the butler emerged from the sitting room with a severe expression on his face. He stopped curtly in front of the pair and nodded to them both.

"Gentlemen," Mr. Archibald said, "forgive my interruption. A telegraph came for you while you were out, sir."

He handed an envelope to Simon, who took it hesitantly. The

envelope wasn't sealed, and the yellow telegraph could be seen jutting from its folds.

"Thank you," Simon said quietly before stealing a glance at the apothecary.

"Do you require anything else?" the butler asked. When Simon shook his head, the man turned in place and disappeared back into the sitting room, pulling the sliding doors closed behind him.

"What will you do?" Luthor asked, his eyes never leaving the envelope in Simon's hand.

Simon glanced down at the telegraph. "You mean if it's actually from the Order? What will my response be?"

Luthor nodded.

"Well, I don't know," Simon replied. "I haven't read it yet to know what they want."

"You know damn well what they want. They want to know why you've failed to update them on your investigation."

Simon looked pensively at the envelope, as though weighing his options.

"Sir, I'm begging you not to do something foolish," Luthor chided. "I'm ready to accept my fate, but I won't let you fall on your sword to protect me. Read the telegraph and give them the appropriate response, including informing them of my affliction."

"Which we haven't even confirmed yet that you have," Simon corrected.

"Sir, you're arguing semantics. Do the right thing."

"Right is so arbitrary," Simon muttered, as he pulled the yellow telegraph from the envelope.

His eyes darted quickly across the minimal lines of typed font. He furrowed his brow for a brief moment before his entire expression relaxed considerably. A faint smile pulled at the corners of his mouth as he lowered the telegraph.

"What does it say?" Luthor asked.

Simon brought it back up to his gaze. "Dearest Simon. Stop. I hope this finds you well. Stop. I worry that I haven't yet heard from you. Stop. Please write me at your earliest convenience. Stop. With all my love, Veronica."

Luthor visibly shook as he lowered himself down onto the bench against the wall. His face brightened with a smile before he let out a shaking, nervous laugh.

"A love letter? I've been worrying myself into an ulcer all because you got a love letter from your lady caller?"

His laughter grew louder as he tilted his head backward. Simon's expression didn't change; he arched an eyebrow in Luthor's direction as the man suffered his hysterics.

"I thought it was rather sweet of her to check on my well-being," Simon remarked.

Luthor wiped a tear from his eye and stood. "It was the most generous thing I think that woman has ever done for you. And her timing was utterly impeccable." He grasped Simon by the shoulders and shook him firmly. "Do give Veronica all my love when you respond."

"I didn't think you cared for her."

Luthor shrugged. "I don't, but for this moment, I am truly in love with her."

"She doesn't share your distaste, you know. She genuinely likes you."

"Good for her."

Simon frowned. "What is it you don't like about her?"

"You're an Inquisitor, sir. You deserve to be courting a lady of class, rather than one of such dubious reputation."

Before Simon could reply, Luthor turned toward the stairwell that led to Mr. Dosett's office. "Come, sir, we have work to be done."

Simon shook his head as he followed the apothecary up the stairs. "You're a very odd man, Luthor."

"You have no idea, sir."

Gideon's office was a pristine comment on modern opulence. He waved them into the expansive suite as soon as he noticed the Inquisitor standing in his doorway. Simon and Luthor entered and took seats on the near side of the broad oak desk that dominated the center of the room.

"I'm waiting with bated breath to hear your findings," Gideon said.

"Do you have any scotch?" Simon replied.

Gideon paused, taken aback by the sudden change of conversation. "I believe so."

Simon rubbed his throat dramatically. "Science always seems to leave me parched."

Gideon seemed put out as he stood and walked toward the liquor cabinet behind him. He stood before the assorted bottles of alcohol for a moment, staring at Simon through the mirror mounted on the wall. Eventually, he pulled a bottle and glass from the shelf, pouring a healthy amount into the tumbler. He walked back and set it in front of the Inquisitor.

"Now can we please get down to business? My time is very valuable."

Simon motioned to the room around them. "So I surmised. Yes, let's get down to business. We concluded our autopsy of the creature, but have left with little useful knowledge about their weaknesses. I killed the creature in question with silver bullets, which seemed to have no effect on the werewolf's physiology. They seem like a sturdy lot, but susceptible to death by normal means."

Gideon stared as Simon blankly. "That's all? You turned this autopsy in a practical circus of enthusiasm and fanaticism; I would have expected something far more remarkable in your findings."

"I approached the autopsy with theories, but science doesn't exist to be shaped to fit a theory. Theories are proven or disproven by the scientific process. In this instance, our assumption was disproven. However, even in failure, we advance our knowledge."

"Enough of your Inquisitor rhetoric!" Gideon barked angrily. "I'm not interested in hearing about the hundreds of things that you didn't discover. I need to know a way to end the threat of these werewolves once and for all. Have you found anything that can help me or not?"

"Not, I'm afraid," Simon said.

"And yet I see no movement on your part toward requesting more Inquisitors."

"I don't think we've reached that point yet in our investigation."

Gideon slammed his hand down on the table angrily, though it spurred no response from Simon, who remained impassive. "I don't understand you, Inquisitor! You have all the proof you need. I offered you a corpse, and it wasn't good enough. You faced the monsters yourself and killed one. You performed the autopsy yourself and concluded that the beasts are real, that it isn't some elaborate hoax on our part. Yet, you still persist in delaying your report. What more could you possibly need?"

"A rushed investigation begets poor results," Simon said flatly.

Luthor looked over toward his mentor cautiously, sensing the open hostility from Gideon.

Taking a deep breath, Gideon pushed loose hairs from his face, affixing them in the ponytail tied at the back of his head. "You infuriate me, Mr. Whitlock. Perhaps you aren't the capable Royal Inquisitor that I thought you to be. Perhaps it's time the governor sent a second request for assistance, citing your incompetence and bumbling of this investigation."

Simon merely shrugged noncommittally. "Perhaps, if that's what you feel would best serve."

Gideon sat back in his plush chair and frowned. He drummed his fingers together in front of his face, as though contemplating Simon's bluff. "You surprise me, Inquisitor, in more ways than one. But be forewarned: you're not the only one here full of surprises. If the Inquisitors are impotent in this situation, I will find my own creative means to deal with these monstrosities. I'll leave you to continue your so-called investigation, but you'll remain out of my way as I eliminate the werewolf threat once and for all."

Simon nodded and stood abruptly. "I apologize that I wasn't able to offer you more insight."

Gideon waved his hand dismissively. "I'm not sure why I expected anything more from you."

"Very good, Mr. Dosett. We'll be taking our leave now."

Simon turned without offering his hand and walked out of the room. Luthor hurried to keep up, his gaze lingering on Gideon a moment longer, though the businessman never looked up from his desk. As they exited the room, Simon pulled the doors closed behind them.

"I'm not exactly sure what just happened," Luthor said matter-of-factly.

"We briefed Mr. Dosett on our findings."

Luthor shook his head. "It was more than that. I don't understand why you insist on instigating him so."

Simon turned toward his friend as they reached the top of the stairs. "Mr. Dosett assumed that we came here to give him information. He was sadly mistaken. I wasn't here to give him information, but rather to extract information from him."

"In your inevitably infuriating manner, no less," Luthor remarked. "So what have we—or should I clarify by saying 'you'—learned?"

"The werewolves have an insatiable hatred for Mr. Dosett, but we have yet to discern why. Mr. Dosett knows that he's the target of their rage but, far more importantly, he has the means to eliminate these monsters. He practically said so just now. If he has the means, then why weren't these werewolves destroyed long ago? Why even bother contacting the crown and the Inquisitors in the first place?"

Simon began descending the stairs with Luthor at his side.

"You have another assumption about this as well, I presume?"

Simon nodded. "Mr. Dosett sits in a place of power within this estate—nay, this whole town—and yearns to know everything that happens. He holds far more sway than a man of his stature and position should dictate. What we've done today is set smoke to the rabbit hole. He will eventually come up for air, once the smoke grows too thick."

Luthor frowned and placed his hand on his friend's arm as a warning. "Normally when you smoke a creature from its hovel, you do so with the intent of bashing in its skull when it finally reveals itself."

Simon didn't return Luthor's gaze but shook off the apothecary's hand. Luthor sighed heavily and followed him down the stairs.

Before they reached the foyer, the governor's advisor burst through the front door. He looked excitedly toward the two gentlemen descending the steps and waited patiently for them.

"Mr. Mulvane," Simon said with a broad smile. "We haven't seen you since our arrival in Haversham. I assume you were looking for the two of us in particular?"

Patrick nodded. "I've been looking for the two of you throughout the city. You can imagine my surprise when I heard you had gone beyond the wall and my even greater concern when I heard that you had been attacked. As soon as I was notified you returned, I've been searching the city thoroughly, though I've had the devil of a time finding you both."

"Do take a breath, sir," Luthor offered, "before you pass out here at the base of the steps. Inquisitor Whitlock is a fine forensic scientist, but he's far more comfortable autopsying the dead than reviving the living."

Patrick blanched, clearly not acknowledging Luthor's dry humor.

"Forgive my companion," Simon interjected. "He jests. For what reason were you looking for us?"

The advisor cleared his throat and retrieved a white envelope from his jacket's inner pocket. He offered it to Simon, who admired his and Luthor's names written in elaborate calligraphy on its surface.

"The governor is hosting his annual Winter Ball this evening. He would like to extend an invitation to attend to you both. He would be delighted to have you as his guests of honor."

"Thank you for the kind offer, Mr. Mulvane," Luthor began with a polite smile, "but—"

"Will Mr. Dosett be in attendance as well?" Simon interrupted.

"Of course," Patrick replied. "He's present for all the governor's gala events."

"Then please let him know that we are honored by his invitation and will most certainly be present."

Simon walked past Patrick and entered the sitting room, leaving Luthor to glare after his friend from his place on the stairs.

CHAPTER Fourteen

LUTHOR TUGGED ON THE CRAVAT THAT BILLOWED against his throat. His mop of hair was slicked against his head, leaving only his muttonchops untamed. He reached up to run a hand through his hair, but Simon knocked it aside.

"Stop fidgeting," he chided. "You're acting like a child who abhors dressing up for Sunday services."

Luthor frowned but lowered his hand to his side. The pair stopped at the landing between the second and third floors in the mansion. Above them, they could hear soft string music drifting down from the grand ballroom.

"I feel preposterous," Luthor complained.

"You look preposterous, but that doesn't mean you have an excuse to mess with your well-manicured features."

"You should have let me wear my bowler cap, at the very least."

Simon smirked at Luthor's request. "It's impolite to wear a hat indoors. Try not to think of this as an obligation, but rather as an extension of our investigation. I have a strong feeling that many of our queries will be revealed before we retire for the night."

The servant at the top of the stairs motioned for Simon and Luthor to advance. They climbed the stairs side by side, Simon in his well-fitted, black, three-piece suit, and Luthor tugging endlessly on his coarser, tan, wool jacket. As they reached the third floor, the servant pulled aside a heavy cloth curtain that separated the ballroom from the rest of the house. A cacophony of sound rolled from the room, overwhelming the pair.

Ladies in long dresses milled about beside their dates, their bouffant hair rising to ever increasing heights as though the rise of their hairstyle signified their societal standings. The gentlemen were all similarly dressed to Simon and spoke to one another in boisterous tones, while servants drifted through the busy ballroom serving glasses of champagne. A string quartet sat on a raised dais, playing soft music to which a few couples danced.

"Ladies and gentlemen," a man announced from just inside the ballroom, "I present Royal Inquisitor Whitlock and his companion, Mr. Strong."

The faces in the room turned toward the entryway, as Simon and Luthor begrudgingly stepped past the curtain. The doorway opened onto a small ledge, from which a few stairs descended to the ballroom's official floor. The two men walked calmly down the steps as previously interrupted conversations resumed throughout the room. A few nobles positioned close to the stairwell paused to shake the Inquisitor's hand as he passed. Simon nodded politely as they introduced themselves, surely intent on befriending someone so closely associated with the crown and the capital city, but Simon forgot their names as quickly as they said them.

Simon's gaze drifted over the room until he spotted Governor Godwin. The heavyset man sat at a head table near the far side of the room, laughing heartily to whatever witticism Mr. Dosett offered. The thin businessman sat on the governor's right, as he had done at the dinners.

A servant passed them, and Simon deftly snatched two glasses of champagne from the tray. He handed one Luthor.

"What is our plan for the evening?" Luthor asked. "Do we in fact have a plan, or are we merely mingling until you've deduced the answers to the mysteries of the universe after witnessing nothing more than the shade of mud smeared on the bottom of a man's shoe?"

Simon turned curtly toward the apothecary. "Luthor, I'm noticing a very blatant amount of hostility. You're being rather rude at the governor's party."

Luthor tilted back his glass and drank most of it in a single long draw. "I joined you as your traveling companion because I have a deep rooted fascination with the occult and mythology. I find true happiness in a book or in a wicked brew that I can create from local flora. I understand books. I understand plants. What I don't understand is people. Therefore, when you force me into a room full of not just people but arrogant nobles and men of affluence, I find myself quite out of my element. So forgive me if you perceived a hint of insolence because I clearly meant it to be much more pronounced."

Rather than seeming upset, Simon tilted his head back and laughed. "That's why I like you so much. Please, don't let me keep you confined in the middle of the room. I believe there's a balcony that you could explore that would be better suited to your tastes, though I'm sure it's a bit frigid for standing outside."

Luthor smiled, though the humor wasn't reflected in the rest of his expression. "I'll take my chances with the frostbite. Better to risk the cold in the air than be exposed to the ice in some of these men's veins."

Luthor touched his forehead in a salute before making his way across the room. The tall doors that separated the main ballroom from the outer balcony swung open briefly as the apothecary stepped outside. In that short moment, Simon could feel the arctic chill wash through the room. He understood his companions dislike for such formal occasions, but he struggled to understand why anyone would rather risk their death in the cold rather than enjoy good food and spirits.

Simon wandered through the room, shaking hands politely but never letting his gaze drift for too long from the governor and Gideon. Despite his chiding of Luthor, the apothecary was correct. Simon didn't truly have a plan, though he knew that observing Gideon would offer the best chance at discovering what the businessman knew about the werewolf attacks. Contrary to Luthor's opinion of him, Simon showed surprising understanding of the importance of attending formal events like the governor's Winter Ball. Though he generally lacked decorum at such events, Simon could be political if it suited his purposes.

As he reached the far side of the room, Simon turned and caught sight of two very familiar faces. The tall Mr. Orrick of the Artisan's Guild and stocky Mr. Tambor of the Miner's Union stood merrily by one of the hors d'oeuvres tables, laughing at one another's jokes. Of all the people he expected to see at the Winter Ball, he was most surprised by these two, who were such outspoken opponents of both the governor and Mr. Dosett.

A guest of cold wind washed over Simon once again, and he shivered involuntarily.

"Have you conceded that it's more comfortable indoors?" Simon asked without turning toward the apothecary.

Luthor's teeth chattered, and he rubbed his arms to promote the return of circulation to his extremities. "I concede nothing."

Simon motioned with his now-empty champagne glass toward the two men. "Do you see who else has graced this soirée?"

Luthor saw the two men and frowned. "They seem like the least likely people to be in attendance."

"My thoughts exactly. You asked me previously if I knew what I was searching for tonight? I believe I'm now ready to answer that question."

The duo walked back through the crowd, approaching the two guild leaders. Upon seeing the Inquisitor, their faces brightened considerably.

"Inquisitor Whitlock," Tambor said with a firm pat on Simon's shoulder, "it's very good to see you again."

Orrick pulled a glass from the table beside him and offered it to him. "We weren't sure we'd see you here tonight. You seemed so thoroughly committed to your investigation, we were sure you'd be locked away in some dark laboratory running experiments."

"Quite on the contrary," Simon said as he took the filled glass from Orrick. "I'm quite in my element at parties like this. I must confess, however, that I'm more than a little surprised to see you both here. When last we spoke, you weren't exactly fans of either of our hosts."

Tambor waved his thick fingers as though brushing aside such nonsensical thoughts. "We spoke out of turn. You were right to chastise us at the time."

Simon arched an eyebrow. "So you've made amends with the governor and Mr. Dosett?"

"We had a meeting with Mr. Dosett shortly after we spoke at the tavern," Orrick explained. "He was courteous enough to let us voice our concerns. In return, he offered concessions and, in the end, made an offer that neither of us could refuse."

"You yourself said during our last meeting that he swindled families out of their property and businesses by offering coppers against the real value of the land."

Orrick shrugged, his handlebar moustache bouncing with the movement. "I was mistaken."

Simon clenched his fists. "You both practically spit venom at even the mention of his name."

"We erred," Tambor replied with an irritatingly jovial smile. "We judged him too harshly."

"You filed reports with the crown contrary to Mr. Dosett's accounts. Your reports were practically the reason the Order of Inquisitors were so intrigued with this specific investigation. I'm here as much on your contrary accounts as I am from the governor's initial report."

"No one feels worse about wasting your time than we do," Orrick said. "If we had the ability to turn back the hands of time, we would have certainly voiced our support for Mr. Dosett's accusations."

The red on Simon's face began at the neckline of his suit and crept slowly to his ears before finally crashing onto his cheeks in splotchy patches of crimson.

"Good day, gentlemen," he said through clenched teeth.

Orrick and Tambor nodded to the Inquisitor, as Simon spun angrily on his heels and stormed away. Luthor didn't bother returning their polite nods, feeling no need to smooth the waves Simon was creating.

"Can you believe those bastards?" Simon stammered as the elegance of the language eluded him.

"If you were searching for something out of sorts at the party," Luthor offered, "I believe you found it."

"Not two days ago, they were the vocal minority. Now, they're even more sheep, catering to Gideon Dosett's every whim. They stand there with the same glassy expression as the governor, on bended knee and bent ear toward every—"

Simon stopped in mid-sentence. The pause took Luthor aback, and he had to look at his mentor to ensure the man was still feeling healthy.

"Sir?"

Simon shook his head. "I've been a fool, Luthor. I've allowed myself to become flustered for all the wrong reasons. Let's forget about Misters

Orrick and Tambor. Let them cater to Mr. Dosett if they so desire. You and I should be enjoying the night's festivities."

Luthor frowned and ran his hand nervously through his greased hair. "Did you take an imaginary blow to the head that I somehow failed to observe?"

Simon laughed. "Not at all, dear friend. Our encounter with Orrick and Tambor was far more revealing than you could possibly imagine. It may not be your proverbial smear of mud on the bottom of a man's shoe, but it was as close to a smoking gun in this case as I've seen thus far."

Simon looked over only to realize that Luthor hadn't heard much of what he had just said. The apothecary's gaze was set across the room. Simon followed his gaze and saw a splash of red against the otherwise powdered white skin and wigs of the women in attendance.

The woman's tresses of unkempt red hair framed her narrow face. She had tried to pull it back into some semblance of order, but it fought free of its confines as though from its own volition. The tendrils of free hair fell to the dark leather corset pulled tightly around her waist. It ended in a long, flowing red dress that match the fiery copper color of her hair.

Though she was attractive in her own right, she stood in such an unpolished stance—with her hands placed on her hips as she stared with an expression that bordered between anger and fear—that Simon was immediately intrigued.

"Do you know her?" the Inquisitor asked.

Luthor shook his head. "I've never seen her before, though she's stunning."

Simon shrugged. "She's plain. For an unrequited bachelor who constantly ridicules my relationship choices, I would expect you to select a better mate."

Luthor shot Simon a glance devoid of amusement. Simon merely shrugged and looked back at the redhead. Her gaze hadn't wavered since they first noticed her. Her eyes remained locked on something across the room. Simon tilted his head to the side in an attempt to estimate the recipient of her hatred and was stunned when his gaze drifted to the head table. Truly, if looks were daggers, she would have been flaying the governor and Mr. Dosett alive.

"You know, Luthor, I believe I owe you an apology. This stranger with whom you seem infatuated has suddenly piqued my interest as well. Why don't you get us all drinks while I introduce myself?"

CHAPTER Fifteen

SIMON WALKED TOWARD THE REDHEADED WOMAN while Luthor begrudgingly went for more drinks. The Inquisitor skirted the edge of the dance floor as couples waltzed around the polished wooden floor, though his eyes never left the strange woman. Throughout it all, her eyes never left the head table.

As he approached her, a servant with a tray of champagne happened by. Simon grabbed a pair of flutes, holding one in each hand. He stepped innocuously to the woman's side and turned toward the head table as well. From her periphery, she noticed the tall man and frowned.

"I'm not interested," she said gruffly. Her accent was thick and her words seemed muddled as she barely opened her mouth to speak.

"You don't even know why I'm here," Simon replied calmly.

"Nor do I care," she said curtly. "Whatever you're selling, I'm not interested. Just go away."

Simon offered her the champagne glass, but she refused to even look at the drink. "You're not being at all polite."

The woman turned sharply toward the Inquisitor. "Nor am I trying to be. I've made myself quite clear that I'm not interested in your company. Do the gentlemanly thing and oblige a woman's request. Kindly go away."

Simon set her champagne flute down on the table beside him and took a slow drink from his own. With a satisfied sigh, he set his half-empty glass down and turned toward the woman, flashing a broad smile.

"Sorry," he said, "but you're far too interesting to leave be."

The woman sighed dramatically and turned her attention back to the head table. She took a step away from him but he merely followed suit, stopping beside her once again.

She threw up her hands in disgust and turned back to Simon. "Why are you even talking to me?" she asked. "There are plenty more attractive women here with whom you could discuss the finer points of aristocracy."

He looked to the other women, who fawned over their dates as they paraded around the dance floor. "The other women here are draped over their dates like pieces of jewelry, like they're struggling to be the most fashionable new bracelet or fanciest pocket watch. They lack a sense of self-worth, as though their mere existence is defined by the political station of their date for the evening. You're something different, independent and abrasive. Frankly, you intrigue me."

The woman frowned. "I'm not intriguing. I'm boring and should be duly left alone."

"Quite on the contrary," Simon replied. "Everything I know about you is intriguing."

"You know nothing about me."

"Again, on the contrary. I know you're one of the locals, are you not? I don't mean one of the people who have settled in Haversham. I mean those who lived here long before the city was more than a trading outpost in an inhospitable land."

She looked at him suddenly, startled.

Simon raised his hands, begging her to remain calm. "I'm not a threat to you. I'm merely remarking on the texture of your skin, which shows signs of extended exposure to strong winds, rather than the polished alabaster of the other women in the room. The lines at the corners of your eyes are indicative of someone who squints against the glare of sunlight reflected off snow. I know that you have an unhealthy interest in the governor and the businessman who even now laugh irritatingly at the head table."

She turned toward him slowly, her eyes widening in surprise. Simon acted as though he hadn't noticed her obvious concern as he continued.

"I know that you're an imposter and feel that you don't belong at this event. Your eyes constantly dart around the room, as though searching for that certain someone who will march over and reveal you for the charlatan you are before summarily and unceremoniously removing you from this Winter Ball."

The woman's pale skin blanched even further, and her lower lip quivered in fear.

Simon turned toward her, his soft expression hardening. "And I know that you've been exceedingly rude to a Royal Inquisitor."

The woman tried to turn away, but Simon grabbed her painfully by the wrist.

"Let me go," she hissed, as she struggled against his iron grip.

Simon was surprised by the lithe woman's obvious strength. Though his hand remained firmly affixed around her wrist, he struggled to maintain his balance as she pulled away.

"I don't want to have to hurt you," she threatened.

Simon shook his head and pulled her closer to him. "You couldn't if you tried. Why don't you calm yourself and tell me exactly why you're here."

The woman shook in his arms. Simon glanced around the room and saw a few faces turned toward their direction as she struggled against his grip. He slipped a hand around her waist and forced her to step to the side and onto the dance floor.

"Quit struggling, unless you want to draw the attention of every person in this room," Simon warned. "If you wish to remain inconspicuous, you'll do exactly as I say."

Simon stepped back, pressing on the small of her back as he did so. She obliged, taking a step forward, beginning a slow waltz with him on the far corner of the dance floor.

"Are you going to kill me?" the redhead asked nervously.

"You've hardly given me good cause to kill you. Is there a reason I should be considering that course of action?"

The woman shook her head slowly.

Simon took her right hand and placed in on his shoulder. Taking her left hand, he held it properly out to the side so they looked more like a formally dancing couple.

"Then let's begin at the beginning, shall we?" Simon asked. "What shall I call you?"

The woman sighed in surrender. "Matilda Hawke. Mattie."

"Excellent, Mattie. Now why are you at the Winter Ball? Do you intend harm to the governor or Mr. Dosett?"

Mattie blushed furiously, the color quickly replacing the paleness that had previously overcome her. "You wouldn't believe me if I told you. I'd be wasting my time trying to explain it to you."

Simon shook his head. "Don't presume to know my mind. Explain."

Mattie set her jaw, the muscles beneath her cheeks flexing and relaxing in frustration. "Gideon Dosett is not what you think he is. He's a monster."

Simon spun Mattie in beat with the string quartet. As she came back around, he slipped his hand around her waist and pulled her close once again.

"I believe you," Simon said matter-of-factly.

Mattie stared into his eyes, her own narrowing as she weighed her options. "I believe that you believe me."

"Good. Mildly convoluted, but good. So you came here to, what, harm him?"

"I… I don't know," she admitted as she was forced to look away. "I guess I just had to see him for myself."

"What has Mr. Dosett done to you that has filled you with such loathing? You look practically ready to skin him alive."

"It's not just what he's done to me, it's what he's done to my entire tribe," she said quickly, the words spilling from her. "In just a few months, he's managed to destroy what we've built for generations. He marched into our villages, one after another, using his silver tongue…"

Her words trailed off as she glanced over Simon's shoulder. Despite his attempts to keep her dancing, her feet seemed rooted to the floor. Simon turned slowly and looked over his shoulder. At the top of the entryway stairs, a small contingent of armed guards stood, scanning the crowd. The servant at the door spoke to the captain of the guards in a hushed tone before turning and scanning the room. As the servant's eyes fell upon Mattie and Simon, he pointed excitedly. The captain followed his gaze before stepping quickly down the stairs.

"Please," Mattie begged, "you have to let me go. Don't let them catch me."

“There appears to be trouble coming your way, sir,” Luthor said from Simon’s side.

The apothecary held three glasses, delicately balanced in his grip. Mattie turned sharply toward Luthor, who merely smiled awkwardly.

“Luthor, Mattie,” Simon said. “Mattie, Luthor.”

“Please,” Mattie said again.

Simon looked at the redhead and saw the petrified look painted on her face. He stepped back and bowed slowly.

“Miss Hawke,” he said. “It has truly been divine dancing with you this evening.”

Mattie shook with relief. Leaning in, she kissed his softly on the cheek. She held her place and spoke softly in his ear.

“Find out what Mr. Dosett has done to my tribe and you’ll understand our hatred. More importantly, you may start to understand just what type of monster he truly is.”

She stepped back and curtsied to Simon. “Thank you for the dance, Inquisitor, but I must depart. Please don’t follow me.”

Mattie nodded quickly to Luthor before walking hurriedly toward the doors to the balcony. The captain of the guard pointed toward her and yelled for her to stop. The redhead kicked off her high-heeled shoes and ran barefoot across the floor, as the guards struggled to push their way through the crowd.

The quartet stopped playing, and the dancers ceased their movement. The entire room turned their attention toward the indigenous woman fleeing from the pursuing guards.

Luthor set the forgotten drinks on the table and turned toward the Inquisitor. “You’ve done a fine job scaring off yet another woman.”

“Surprisingly, it’s not my fault this time.”

The apothecary paused as he saw Simon’s gaze flicker between Mattie and the guards. “Sir, I know that look all too well. She quite distinctly asked you not to follow her.”

“Never have I met a request more eager to be blatantly disregarded. Come, Luthor, I believe our services are about to be needed.”

The duo set off in chase. Mattie threw open the doors to the balcony, and a blast of arctic air rushed through the ballroom. She hurried barefoot onto the balcony, stepping in the soft coating of powdered snow that covered the long veranda.

The guards exited the ballroom just as quickly with Simon and Luthor on their heels. Mattie ran to the far end of the balcony and leaned out over the railing, glancing at the plummeting three-story drop to the frozen ground below. She spun back toward the ballroom, only to face a row of guards blocking her escape.

Simon struggled to see past the captain, who stood at the center of the line. Beyond, he could see a frightened Mattie, who shivered as much from fear as from the biting cold.

"Halt," the captain yelled out. "Stay where you are."

Mattie took a step back and glanced over her shoulder once more, as though debating the merits of leaping from the tall balcony. Her gaze fell on a smaller balcony extending from a room a floor below her, though the leap was nearly twenty feet.

"I told you not to move," the captain said. "One more step and I'll fire."

The captain drew his pistol, as the other guards drew their swords. He trained his weapon on the scared redhead as she glanced around once more for an escape.

"He's going to kill her," Luthor whispered. "You have to do something."

Simon glanced toward the captain and saw the man slowing his breath as he took aim. His finger shifted as he prepared to pull on the trigger of his flintlock pistol.

The Inquisitor lashed out, striking the captain's wrist just as the man fired. The shot went wide, ricocheting off the stonework just to the right of Mattie's head. She ducked involuntarily as stone debris showered over her.

The captain wrenched his hand away from Simon and spun angrily toward the Inquisitor. A brief flicker of recognition gave the guard pause, but his anger quickly flooded back into his face.

"What are you doing?" the captain yelled. "You're going to let her get away!"

"Who?" Simon asked. "The harmless unarmed redhead you nearly shot dead in cold blood?"

A low growl caught Simon's attention. Both he and the captain turned slowly toward Mattie, who was doubled over as though in pain. Simon was certain the bullet had ricocheted high, falling harmlessly near the wall rather than striking her. Still, she exhibited all the signs of having been shot.

Mattie suddenly stood upright as though she were a puppet on the end of strings controlled by a tactless marionette. Her arms jerked, and her head flopped to the side. One of her hands flashed to her chest and she drug her fingernails across her skin, leaving bloody tracts in their wake.

Simon felt nauseated at the sight, and he could see Luthor raising his hand to his mouth in disgust.

Mattie's hand rose to her chest again, scraping her nails again over the same spot on her chest. Long strips of flesh tore free, dangling over her tight corset as she scratched herself once again. Instead of blood in the wounds, stark white fur jutted from the holes left on her body.

"Stop her before she transforms!" the captain yelled. The guards remained frozen at the sight of the self-flagellation for a moment longer before responding to his request.

The redhead grasped the edges of her wounds with both hands as she threw her head back in pain. She let out a piercing howl as she pulled the skin apart. It ripped, falling away in sheets like a present being unwrapped during the holidays. The corset tumbled to the ground, falling beside the discarded skirt.

The werewolf stood at the end of the balcony, snarling at the guards who suddenly rushed toward her. The creature that had once been Mattie turned toward Simon, locking eyes with him briefly. She suddenly turned and leapt over the railing.

Simon and Luthor rushed forward in pursuit, reaching the balcony just in time to see the werewolf leap from the lower room's narrow balcony and land gracefully on the ground far below. Dropping onto all fours, like they had seen at the drilling site, the werewolf sprinted across the lawn of the estate and disappeared into the city proper.

"What have you done?" Gideon screamed from behind the jumbled collection of guards and Inquisitor.

Simon turned as the businessman stormed toward him. "You let that monster get away!" Gideon yelled, his face a brilliant crimson.

Simon shrugged noncommittally. "With all due respect, Mr. Dosett, I had no idea the woman with whom I was dancing was in fact a werewolf. I guess the better question would be for how long have you known that the monsters we were hunting had the capability to transform? That seems like a far more interesting line of questioning, since you obviously felt it necessary to exclude that knowledge from any of our discussions."

Gideon clenched his teeth, grinding them back and forth behind his narrow, bloodless lips. "If she causes any death or wonton destruction within the city, I'll hold the Order of the Inquisitors personally responsible."

The businessman spun on his heels and stormed back inside the ballroom. A few patrons lingered at the doorway a moment longer before stepping back inside as well.

The captain glared at Simon and Luthor briefly before ordering his guards back inside, leaving the Inquisitor and apothecary alone on the frigid balcony. Simon watched them depart before turning back toward the estate's grounds across which Mattie fled.

"It seems this investigation is growing progressively more complex," Luthor remarked.

"Indeed, though you know what I find most interesting?"

Luthor shrugged and shook his head.

Simon smiled as he patted his friend on the shoulder. "I find it absolutely uncanny, Luthor, that of all the women you could have selected at the ball, you happen to find the only werewolf in the crowd. You either have the most remarkably good or incredibly bad taste in women I've ever seen."

Simon gestured toward the exit to the ballroom as his jovial demeanor melted away. "Come, Luthor. We have work to do. If Gideon Dosett won't tell us more about what he knows of these monsters, I believe it's time to demand such answers from the governor himself."

CHAPTER Sixteen

SIMON STORMED UP THE STAIRS WITH LUTHOR IN TOW, still dressed in their finery from the Winter Ball. Though the Inquisitor didn't speak a word, the red flush across the back of his neck prominently displayed his seething rage.

At the top of the stairs, he pushed through the closed double doors, startling Patrick Mulvane as the governor's advisor stacked papers on his desk in preparation for retiring for the evening. A stack of folders tumbled from the desk and spilled across the floor, much to Patrick's dismay.

"The hour is late, gentlemen," he said. "Is there something I can assist you with?"

"Yes," Simon said through clenched teeth, "you can get out of my way so that I may pay a visit to Governor Godwin."

Patrick eyes flickered to the doorway behind him, across which drapes had been pulled. The movement was incredibly subtle but didn't escape Simon's gaze. Without awaiting the advisor's reply, Simon stomped toward the doors.

"You can't go in there," Patrick said quickly, moving to block the Inquisitor's way. "The governor's not in. He was tired after the ball and departed straight to his quarters."

Simon didn't stop. Patrick moved himself against the doors, spreading his arms as though to block the entirety of the entrance.

"I said he wasn't available. Please show proper decorum and leave at once."

Simon grabbed the advisor by the collar and pulled him close. "What you said was that he wasn't in his office. Now you're saying he's not available. I'll give you a chance to revise your story once more before I use you as a knocker while I open the door anyway."

Patrick swallowed hard, his Adam's apple bobbing as he stared in the angry face of the Inquisitor. Luthor stepped forward, placed his hands on the advisor's shoulders, and gently moved the man aside before he got himself into further trouble.

The way now cleared, Simon grasped the door handles and pulled both doors toward him. The light curtains billowed as the doors flew open. Across the office, sitting behind his chair and clearly not surprised by the late visit, sat Governor Godwin.

Simon stared intently at the portly man. Even from the distance, he could see a thin sheen of sweat on the man's brow. Though the governor tried his best to appear calm, he drummed his fingers impatiently on the table with one hand while absently straightening his fountain pen with the other.

"What can I do for you, Inquisitor Whitlock?" the governor asked.

"I suspected the truth, you know?" Simon began as he stepped into the room. His angry façade had faded, replaced by his normal stoic demeanor. "There were signs—pieces of the puzzle that I had to build on my own."

"I'm not sure to what you're referring," Godwin replied.

"The werewolves, my good man. Do keep up. More importantly, there were signs that the werewolves were more than just mindless, savage brutes terrorizing your region. I would have brought all my findings to you earlier, but I didn't see the point. You see, had you been aware that the werewolves were able to walk among you in human form, you most certainly would have told me. It would have been your sworn duty as a member of the Royal family."

Simon's voice began to rise, the anger creeping back into his words. "Certainly, a cousin of the king himself wouldn't withhold such crucial information to an Inquisitor's investigation, would he? Honestly, what would be the point? What could he possibly have to gain from lying and impeding an active investigation?"

Simon turned his attention fully toward the governor, who remained silent in his plush, high-backed chair. The Inquisitor locked his hands behind his back and strolled into the room.

"I found it odd when we first arrived, that you had so many foreign guards under your employment. With such a rich, indigenous population, it would only make sense to find cheap labor from the region in which you hoped to rule. What good would a governor be if he alienated the locals during his tenure? That alone was odd, but not suspicious."

Simon strolled to the large window overlooking the courtyard below. The wind had picked up, carrying powdered snow across the road leading to and from the manor. It was practically indiscernible from what he had to assume was grass beneath the larger snowdrifts on either side of the path.

"On our way to the drilling sites, I noticed the campfires in the distance. I even remarked to Luthor that it was odd that the indigenous population and the werewolves could live in a form of stasis, if not peace with one another. Yet, when performing the autopsy on the wolf I slew, I found cooked meat in its gut, the likes of which would have been cooked and charred over a campfire."

He turned away from the window and stared at the governor. The heavyset man glanced back and forth between Simon and Luthor nervously, drumming his fingers with an ever-increasing cadence.

"You can, of course, see where all this is leading. The werewolf that Luthor fought dropped a special brand of rifle, its kind I've only seen carried by your personal retinue. That's when it struck me. Perhaps you had indeed hired the indigenous population to serve on your gubernatorial guard. Perhaps their desertion coincided remarkably with the first reports of werewolf attacks around Haversham."

Simon walked over and rested his hands on the governor's desk, leaning forward until he could smell the rotund man's sour breath, as though he had imbibed far too much alcohol during the evening's festivities.

"All my suspicions were founded this evening, of course. You, yourself, saw the woman transform before our very eyes, flesh tearing away to give room for the strong, fur-covered body. Her narrow face ripping as the beast's elongated maw burst forth. While I stared at the creature in horror, knowing it had been a diminutive, red-haired woman not moments before, you and Mr. Dosett seemed far more upset that she had escaped."

The Inquisitor lowered his voice, as to ensure his words carried the extra weight. "Which begs the question, for how long have you known the truth?"

The governor looked over, making eye contact with Simon. His pupils were dilated and beads of sweat dripped visibly from his brow. "I don't have to answer your inquiry. You forget yourself. You forget to whom you're talking." With every word, he grew more emboldened. "I'm the governor, cousin to the king himself. How dare you interrogate me as though I were a common criminal?"

Simon slammed his open hand down on the table, and the fire that had grown in the governor's belly extinguished itself immediately. "I have not forgotten who you are! Perhaps it is you who have forgotten your place. The king, your cousin, charged me to conduct this inquiry. It is the king, your cousin, who fears the infiltration of magic into our kingdom. What do you think our king will do if he found a member of his own family impeded my investigation? Do you believe he would turn a blind eye to your transgression because of your relationship? I've been to the capital city, Governor Godwin. I've seen nobles dragged into the square, and I have seen their heads taken from their shoulders for less!"

The governor blanched as Simon's final words echoed in the broad room. The portly man raised his hand to his neck subconsciously and rubbed the soft flesh.

"This will be the last time you and I have such a conversation, sir," Simon said, his voice deadly calm once more. "You will tell me what you know about the werewolves, all of it."

Simon took a seat in one of the two chairs across from him and motioned for Luthor to sit in the other. The apothecary took his seat, but his eyes shifted toward the Inquisitor.

The governor coughed and fidgeted with his formal attire. "It began a few months ago. We noticed some of our local guards missing from their posts. We inquired as to their absences, of course, but none of the tribespeople seemed any the wiser as to their whereabouts. It wasn't long before nearly all the locals were missing from their positions, both within this estate and without. We, that is, Mr. Dosett and I, cornered one of the last remaining locals here in the home. The woman, a maid, sought to evade us, but Mr. Dosett was far quicker. When cornered, the queerest thing happened, an event that you yourself witnessed this very eve. The maid tore away her dress until she wore only her unmentionables. Then, as though her own skin had become a prison, she clawed at her flesh until the werewolf concealed underneath burst free."

The governor retrieved a handkerchief from his desk and blotted the sweat from his balding head. "You can imagine my shock and horror. Luckily, I had at my side Mr. Dosett, who responded far quicker than me, or even the guards I had at my disposal. Mr. Dosett drew his blade and struck the creature down where it stood."

Realization dawned on Simon, and he nodded understandingly. "That was the first creature I viewed, the one that had already been autopsied before my arrival."

"Indeed, it was. The attacks began shortly thereafter, I assume in retaliation for the death of one of their own kind."

Simon stroked his thin moustache for a moment, as he absorbed the governor's explanation before shaking his head. "I don't believe that is a legitimate justification. Their attacks are far too precise and localized to be something as simplistic as revenge based. There's something you're not telling me, something that will assist in finding an answer to the question that has plagued me since my arrival—why."

For the briefest of moments, the governor seemed prepared to elaborate, but then his eyes grew mysteriously distant and his jaw went slack. Simon leaned forward in time to see the man's pupils dilate further.

"Governor Godwin?" Simon asked cautiously.

The governor sat in his chair unmoving, staring at a point between Simon and Luthor, but clearly unseeing through glossy eyes.

"He seems afflicted," Luthor remarked as he moved his hand into the governor's line of sight, to no avail. "He practically appears under the influence of a powerful sedative."

Simon shook his head. "I've seen something similar while I apprenticed during my training. A local snake oil salesman had an uncanny ability to work a crowd into a virtual frenzy at the mere mention of purchasing his placebo chemical mixture. It was a remarkable gift, one that we believed to be supernatural until we observed his powers of hypnosis. The results of those under the hypnotist's sway appeared similarly to how the governor now appears to us."

"He's hypnotized?" Luthor asked. "But how and when?"

"I could only begin to speculate. The hypnosis itself is merely a theory, though his reaction could have been triggered by my line of inquiry."

Simon slammed his hand down on the desk once again. "Governor Godwin," he said loudly.

The governor was startled, jumping slightly and blinking away the slack-jawed expression. "Forgive me, gentlemen. I appear to have dozed momentarily. It was a long night full of excitement, what with the ball and the werewolf. What was your question again?"

Simon stared at the man for a moment before offering a polite smile. The Inquisitor stood, Luthor following suit immediately afterward.

"You do seem quite drained, Governor," Simon offered. "Why don't you retire for the evening and get some rest? My questions were not so important that they couldn't wait until another time."

"Yes, of course," the governor mumbled, still seeming to struggle to gain his bearings. "Rest would do this weary body some good. Again, forgive me for my absentmindedness. I believe it merely comes with age, though I would leave that prognosis to a more qualified man."

Simon laughed politely. "We will speak again, Governor. Have a good evening."

The Inquisitor and Luthor walked out of the room. Despite his reason to excuse himself from the conversation, the governor didn't get up from his chair but remained in place, staring at the two men as they left.

In the antechamber, Patrick frowned as the two men passed. Once they were nearly to the office's outer doors, he slipped into the governor's office, pulling the doors closed behind him.

As Simon opened the outer doors and they both stepped into the hallway beyond, Luthor turned sharply toward his friend. "Exactly what just happened?"

"As I said while we were still in the stupefied presence of the governor, I believe the man has been hypnotized."

"By whom?"

Simon arched an eyebrow and glanced disapprovingly at the apothecary. "Do you truly need to ask that question? Has it not made itself readily apparent already?"

"Gideon Dosett."

"Gideon Dosett," Simon confirmed. "A strong relationship with the governor has clearly served him well during his rapid expansion into Haversham. If he is a hypnotist, it would also explain why Misters Orrick and Tambor seemed so quickly drawn under his spell. Yes, it all does seem to make a remarkable amount of sense."

The two men descended the stairwell, their booted feet clicking on the marble steps.

"Except that it doesn't explain why the werewolves despise him so," Luthor said as the reached the second floor landing, on which both their rooms were located. "Certainly some innocuous hypnosis isn't justification for the amount of damage they've caused to Mr. Dosett's various businesses."

Simon frowned as he considered Luthor's comment. "No, I wouldn't assume so. Nor would I assume that the werewolves would justify killing so many of Mr. Dosett's employees simply because some of their number fell under his thrall."

They walked down the hall, approaching their respective rooms. An image of a brash, redheaded woman flashed through Simon's mind.

"Mattie said that if we understood why the werewolves hated him so, then we could finally conclude our investigation. If the members of this estate have mental reservations from answering our questions, then tomorrow we'll have to seek the answers elsewhere."

Simon pulled a key from his pocket and slid it into his door. With a turn, the door clicked open. Luthor did likewise, though he paused in his open doorway. His eyes locked on the window across the living room and the stars that reflected through the glass.

"Sir," Luthor said in a panic. He glanced hastily around his room, searching for rope or similar cord. "The moon is rising. If the change is to occur, it'll happen soon. Quickly, you must restrain me."

Simon slipped his key back into his vest pocket and smiled at his companion. "My dear Luthor, the moon rose while we were still at the party. Clearly it holds no sway over you, nor are you evidently infected with lycanthropy."

Luthor released a breath and his shoulders slumped with relief. As quickly as his relaxation appeared, his shoulders tensed once more. "You knew that evening would come while we attended the party. You risked uncountable lives by taking me there on tonight of all nights."

"I had a hunch that we would be able to debunk your concerns of a transformation."

"A hunch, sir?" Luthor asked, visibly shaken. "It's terribly irresponsible to risk lives on nothing more than an educated guess."

"A correct educated guess," Simon corrected.

Luthor shook his head. "Hindsight is hardly a justification for irresponsible behavior. There's no way you could have known."

"Just as there was no way I could have foreseen the indigenous population being the werewolves, and yet I did. Someday, you'll learn to trust me. Perhaps after we expose Mr. Dosett for the criminal he is."

"You're unconscionable. Good night, sir," Luthor said. "Sleep well but do be cautious, especially in regards to Mr. Dosett. If he has this remarkable ability, it behooves us to approach him with caution when we are forced to confront him. It won't do us any good to solve the mystery, only to fall under his spell."

Simon cringed at Luthor's blasé use of "spell". Though the werewolves were clearly mystical in nature, Simon was perfectly content thinking that the reason for their incited anger was something far more mundane.

"Until tomorrow, Luthor. Sleep well."

Simon stepped into his room, closing the door behind him.

CHAPTER Seventeen

LUTHOR SAT AT THE DINING ROOM TABLE THE NEXT morning, looking far more refreshed than he had in days. Having found himself not infected by the werewolf's bite, he had fallen quickly to sleep and awoke energized.

He took his knife and spread marmalade onto the toast in front of him. Taking a bite, he savored the crisp orange flavor. Setting the toast back down onto his plate, he glanced over his shoulder but saw no one coming. Despite the late morning hour, Simon still hadn't made it downstairs.

Luthor picked up the Capital Gazette and read the headlines. For a moment, he arched his eyebrow in confusion. He had read these headlines before, shortly before he and Simon departed the capital on their trip to Haversham. His gaze fell to the date. The headlines were familiar because it was the very newspaper he had read before their departure. Very possibly, the stack of newspapers had been carried on their zeppelin.

With a disappointed sigh, Luthor folded the paper and set it back down on the table.

The sound of heavy footsteps on the stairwell startled him as he reached for his tea. He glanced over his shoulder just as Simon reached the foyer. The Inquisitor noticed Luthor and waved excitedly for him to hurry along.

"Come along, Luthor," Simon said as he placed his top hat on his head. "We're off."

"No breakfast for you this morning then, sir?" Luthor asked as he took a rather large sip of his still hot tea.

"There's no time. Far too much demands our attention today."

Luthor sighed and set his teacup gently down in its ornate saucer. He stood, gathering up his napkin from his lap and dabbing the corners of his mouth. As he set the napkin over the toast, he nodded appreciatively to the servant, who hurried to clear his plate.

He turned toward the door to see Simon tapping his foot impatiently. Luthor gathered his coat, hat, and cane before joining him.

"I presume you have a plan for today?" the apothecary asked.

"I spent quite some time thinking about our predicament last night, staying up far too late into the night. That is hence why I slept so late this very morning."

"And to what determination have you come?"

Stepping out the door, they tried to acclimate to the biting cold. They nodded to the guards on either side of the door before stepping into the lane that led to the estate's main gate. "Miss Hawke told me to find out why the werewolves disliked Mr. Dosett."

Luthor smirked. "I believe she used some less tactful language."

Simon continued as though he hadn't heard the interruption. "I was reminded of our conversation with Misters Orrick and Tambor as well, where they decried Mr. Dosett for purchasing land and businesses at such a low cost; land and businesses, I might add, that had been in families for generations. If he is a hypnotist and is using his abilities for nefarious purposes, that would explain people's willingness to sell their properties for mere copper pieces."

Luthor shoved his hands in his pockets and lowered his head against the wind. "It's a perfectly viable theory, but what does it have to do with the werewolves?"

It was Simon's turn to smirk. "Who do you think owns the land on which Mr. Dosett's businesses are drilling?"

Luthor smiled. "A keen observation. How do we prove it?"

"In a town controlled by the crown, it's the law that a meticulous record be kept of all land transactions. Haversham will have a Hall of Records, in which will be the sales transactions. If Mr. Dosett truly did cheat either his fellow citizens or the indigenous people out of their land, then there will be evidence in the records."

They walked through the city, opting again to stay above ground rather than moving through the tunnels beneath the city. Though it was bitterly cold, the surface streets were nearly deserted and lent itself to private introspection as they walked.

Simon led the way, taking them through turns seemingly at random. Before long, they walked past the telegraph office. Simon's eyes lingered on the building for a brief second before they moved past it.

Before too long, they stopped in front of a one-story brick building. A pair of columns flanked the front doorway, supporting a jutting stone awning. A bronze plaque, the corners of which were coated in a faintly blue frost, hung from the brick edifice just left of the doorway. The simplistic words read—Hall of Records.

Luthor grabbed the protruding door handle and pulled the door open, stepping out of the way and gesturing for Simon to enter. He stepped inside, taking off his top hat and brushing off the accumulated snow. As the door swung shut behind him, he was temporarily blinded by the general dimness of the building's interior. Blinking away the lingering spots that danced in his vision, Simon took a deep breath and was welcomed by the familiar scent of oiled leather and ancient parchment.

As his vision cleared, he noticed a bespectacled, gray-haired woman watching them both inquisitively. Her finger was poised over a ledger, marking her place.

Simon smiled and approached the desk behind which she sat. "Good morning, madam. My name is Inquisitor Whitlock. This is my associate, Mr. Strong. We're here to examine some of your records."

The woman glanced slowly over her shoulder toward the row after row of leather-bound ledgers neatly stacked on wooden shelves. She turned back toward Simon and Luthor equally slowly.

"Perhaps you could be more specific, sir."

Simon rubbed his red-rimmed eyes and leaned back in his wooden chair. Lifting his left hand, he rubbed his index finger against his thumb in an attempt to remove the dark ink that had stained his skin. When he realized the stubborn ink wouldn't be removed so easily, he surrendered and retrieved the leaking pen from atop the parchment beside him.

The Inquisitor jumped as Luthor slammed two more thick tomes onto the wooden table between them.

"This is impossible," the apothecary complained. "Just reviewing the ledgers from the past year would require a staff of dozens. These are perhaps the most thorough ledgers I've ever had the displeasure of coming across."

Simon tapped the end of the pen on the parchment, noting the dozens of sales to Gideon Dosett that they had already located within the books.

"Haversham, for all her faults, is a town of thorough record keeping," Simon agreed. "The information we have retrieved thus far has been most telling, though. It leaves little doubt in my mind that Mr. Dosett has been purchasing land through some means of coercion."

When Luthor didn't respond, Simon continued vocalizing his concerns. "This is further begging the question, however, of how did Mr. Dosett manage to hypnotize practically the entire town. You don't think it's possible that he has employed some sort of device, do you? Perhaps he is utilizing something to amplify his ability, in order to affect so great and diverse a group of people." He tapped next to a number of names. "It seems highly unlikely that he personally visited so many people throughout the city, hypnotizing them one at a time, though I guess anything is possible for a sufficiently dedicated villain."

The Inquisitor looked up and realized that Luthor's face was buried in one of the tomes. "Luthor, are you even listening to me?"

"Admittedly no," Luthor responded as he excitedly tapped the list before him. He looked up with a smile. "I haven't heard a word you said, though I promise it was for a good reason."

He spun the ledger so that Simon could read its contents. Before Luthor could point at the section in question, Simon located the interesting sales transactions.

"These sales were all made within days of one another," he remarked, dumfounded. "Three copper pieces for seventy acres. Eight copper for over one hundred. These prices are preposterous! This is more than just underhanded business dealings—this is outright criminal behavior."

Luthor nodded. “My sentiments exactly. Mr. Dosett paid the tribes not even a handful of copper pieces for huge tracts of land. At least for those within the walls of Haversham, there was the illusion of equitable costs. Not with the tribes, however.”

Simon continued to look over purchase after purchase. “This list goes on and on. How much land do you suspect he purchased from the tribes?”

Luthor shrugged. “A quick estimation—all of it. I would be surprised if the indigenous people even owned their campsites in the foothills of the distant mountains.”

Simon whistled in amazement. “It’s no wonder the werewolves despise him so. Though they may be abominations, I at least can respect their desire to destroy everything Mr. Dosett has built on their stolen lands.”

“Did you notice the names of those who sold the lands?” Luthor asked. “I found that fairly telling as well.”

Simon looked at the list once more, following a further column that identified from whom Gideon purchased the land. Though the names were unfamiliar, the title of “Chief” preceded each. There were at least seven unique names listed for different land sales.

“Tribal leaders?” Simon asked.

“That would be my assumption, sir. Not only did he hypnotize one or two of the leaders, he evidently hypnotized them all.”

“They would have been hypnotized as a group, which would be the only acceptable explanation as to how they all sold their lands within forty-eight hours from one another. I would wager that if we delved deeper into these records, we could find evidence of a meeting of tribal elders shortly before these sales took place.”

Simon ran his hand through his thin moustache as he slowly nodded, deep in thought. Luthor watched for a moment before daring to interrupt his mentor’s train of thought.

“I’ve seen that look before, sir, usually moments before closing a case.”

“Indeed, Luthor,” Simon said. “I have the evidence I require. I believe it’s time to confront Mr. Dosett.”

Simon’s expression darkened slightly. “I believe that we have also answered the ‘why’ to this case, the question to which I’d been seeking an answer for far too long. It’s now time to send that telegraph to the Order of Inquisitors."

Luthor blanched, though Simon failed to notice. "Very good, sir."

Simon stood and closed the dusty books, leaving them stacked haphazardly atop the table. He retrieved the handwritten list of sales from beside his elbow and folded the parchment, slipping it into his inside jacket pocket. Luthor stood as well and walked around the table, joining his friend. They walked toward the entrance to the building, passing the elderly woman as they did.

"I hope you found what you were looking for," she said politely.

"That we did and far more, madam," Simon replied. "We greatly appreciate your hospitality and your forgiveness for the mess we left in our wake."

"You would hardly be the first."

Simon placed his hat on his head and tipped its brim to her before walking back into the glaring sun and frigid winter winds.

CHAPTER Eighteen

THE TELEGRAPH OFFICE SEEMED WELL USED AND BUSY, especially early in the morning. Simon and Luthor waited patiently behind a row of people sending telegraphs to their loved ones in distant cities and towns, encouraging them, one and all, to visit their quiet hamlet of Haversham. They moved forward at a slow pace, shifting a few steps every time someone completed their telegram and left the building.

Simon's mind swirled with the case before him. It all painted a clear picture of deceit on the part of Gideon Dosett, though Simon still struggled with a different question of why. He no longer wondered why the werewolves hated Mr. Dosett; that reason was evident from the sales in the ledger. Instead, he began wondering why Mr. Dosett would risk the ire of the werewolf tribes. At the time of the land sales, he had to have known their true nature. Yet he still risked his fiscal and physical health by robbing the monsters blind.

Eventually, there was only a single man standing in line ahead of the men. The hunched gentlemen walked to the counter, rubbing his balding head nervously.

"What's your destination, sir?" the telegraph operator asked politely.

"Wollen Hall," the man said in a shaky voice. "The telegraph is addressed to a Mr. Peter Bronwell, my brother."

The man behind the counter wrote down the name onto a yellowing piece of paper. "And what would you like the message to say, sir?"

The balding man cleared his throat. "Dear Peter. Stop. Great job opportunity in Haversham. Stop. Working for Mr. Gideon Dosett's oil refinery. Stop. Bring the entire family. Stop. Your loving brother, Quincy."

The man's message struck a chord with Simon. He furrowed his brow as he tried to compile the pieces of an ill-fitting puzzle, but one whose picture was steadily becoming clearer by the minute.

As the balding man paid and stepped out of line, the man behind the counter gestured for Simon and Luthor to advance. Instead, Simon spun brusquely on his heel and impolitely pushed his way past the other customers waiting in line. Luthor, dumbfounded, hurried to catch his mentor.

"Sir?" Luthor asked as they exited the telegraph office. "I thought you were inclined to send a telegraph."

"I've been a fool, Luthor," Simon said, striking his fist into his open hand.

"You've been called many things in your time as an Inquisitor, sir, but a fool was never one of them."

Simon turned toward the apothecary and fiddled anxiously with his thin moustache. "Gideon Dosett is a villain; I think we can both agree to that fact."

"Indeed," Luthor agreed.

"Yet, though a villain, has he ever tried to impede our investigation? Has he placed any roadblocks in our way that would keep us from learning the truth? Quite on the contrary, he's been more than forthcoming with evidence. He provided the first werewolf corpse for us to examine. He provided a sled and driver to take us wherever our heart's desired beyond the city walls. He had to know that we would find the ledgers eventually. Yet he hid nothing from us. Does that sound like logically devious behavior?"

Luthor arched an eyebrow. "Admittedly not, though I don't follow your reasoning or your sudden departure from the telegraph office."

Simon scowled at his own blindness and ignorance. "What is the only thing Gideon Dosett has requested, time and time again? What was the only demand he made following the first autopsy, and the second, and following our trip into the tundra? What would be the only thing he would request were I to present the evidence we uncovered at the Hall of Records?"

Luthor smiled knowingly as the realization dawned upon him. "He only requested that we send our telegraph requesting support from the Order."

"And what would have happened had I sent that telegraph, confirming the existence of werewolves in Haversham?" Simon asked, guiding Luthor toward the answer.

"The Order of Inquisitors would have gladly obliged. They would have sent numerous teams. Had the Pellites received word of this discovery, teams from Kinder Pel would have arrived as well."

"And an exceptional hypnotist like Mr. Dosett would have brought them all under his sway, as he'd already done the governor and many of the business leaders within Haversham. He would have created a personal army, one that would have granted him a fairly direct line of access to the crown itself."

"That's why he hypnotized the governor," Luthor said. "He knew he was a cousin to the king, though obviously he overstated their relationship. With the governor giving him no further leads—"

"He requested an Inquisitor," Simon concluded. "We were pawns in his malicious game. We were literally a few feet from handing over the crown to a devil of a man like Gideon. I abhor the thought of what would have happened had I sent that telegraph as intended."

The two men paused and let the realization of their situation settle. Simon took a deep breath and looked away, staring down the road without seeing anything beyond the brim of his top hat. He prided himself on his intellect and both cognitive and deductive skills. To have been so readily played for a fool sat very poorly with him.

"If we are, in essence, cut off from the Order," Luthor queried, "then what shall we do?"

When Simon turned back toward his friend, his face reflected his steely resolve. "We will confront Mr. Dosett. If we can't garner the support of the rest of the Order without endangering the kingdom, then we'll simply have to handle the situation ourselves.

Luthor coughed politely, breaking the spell of brash confidence that Simon was exuding.

"I sense that you have something to say," the Inquisitor remarked flatly.

Luthor removed his bowler cap and scratched at his mop of hair. "Meaning no disrespect, of course, sir, but I fear there's a very important fallacy in your otherwise masterful plan."

Simon frowned. "And that would be?"

"The entire reason we can't send our telegraph is because Gideon would simply hypnotize those that responded to your request for reinforcements. Every Inquisitor that arrived would become enthralled by Mr. Dosett."

"Which is exactly why we can't send the telegraph."

"Begging your pardon, sir, but you're an Inquisitor. If you and I go and face Mr. Dosett alone, what's to stop him from simply hypnotizing you and making you send the telegraph?"

Simon laughed. "Hypnotism works on the weak-minded and weaker-willed, of which I'm neither. Strong minds like mine are immune to such parlor tricks and other frivolities. Now come, Luthor, we have an investigation to complete."

The Inquisitor turned on his heel and started walking toward the governor's estate. Luthor frowned and glanced quickly over his shoulder, ensuring no one was watching. He pulled up his sleeve slightly, revealing the lower edge of the rune of warding carved into his arm. The inflammation he had seen before had receded and the thin, puckered lines of the rune looked as fresh as the day it had been burned into his skin. He quickly pulled down his sleeve and hurried after his mentor.

Simon knocked politely on the closed door leading to Gideon's office suite. He could hear the man shuffling within but opted against barging into his office like he had done to the governor the day before. After a few moments of waiting, Gideon opened the doors. He immediately frowned at the sight of the Inquisitor and apothecary.

"To what do I owe this visit?" Gideon asked matter-of-factly. "Are you here to berate me as you did the governor last night? Shall you interrogate me? Perhaps you should go ahead and tie me to the chair and torture me until I talk."

Simon waved his hand dismissively, not even acknowledging Gideon's obvious irritation. "Nothing so severe, I'm afraid. We've come only to talk."

Gideon stood in the doorway a moment longer before stepping aside and inviting the two men into his office. Simon and Luthor took their seats in front of the oak desk again, while Gideon walked around and sat behind it. The businessman leaned back in his chair and brought a finger thoughtfully to his lips.

"So if not an interrogation, then why are you here?" Gideon asked. "You've shown a clear disdain for my concerns thus far, I can't imagine you have much more to offer me."

"We know about your purchase of the lands beyond the wall," Simon said bluntly. "We know you conned the tribes—the werewolves—out of their lands for far less than it was worth."

Gideon shook his head. "If you know that, then you also know that their land was sold to me willingly by their chieftains. Every business venture I've entered into since my arrival in Haversham has been well documented and above reproach."

Simon laughed derisively. "If that were the case, I certainly wouldn't be here today."

Gideon lowered his hand and leaned forward, placing his forearms on the table in front of him. "What, exactly, do you think you know, Inquisitor?"

"I know that you cheated a lot of hard-working men and women out of their livelihood, all in an attempt to expand your rapidly growing fortune."

"I didn't cheat men and women," Gideon hissed through clenched teeth. "If I cheated anyone, it was werewolves—monsters of the worst kind, straight from the Rift itself. You, of all people, should know that. How many of these monsters have you now faced personally? Yet you become fixated on my business dealings, while ignoring the more painfully obvious threat to the sanctity of our kingdom. Any Inquisitor worth his salt would have already requested support from the Order. Any Inquisitor worth a damn would have already ensured that Haversham was crawling with Inquisitors, slaughtering these werewolves one and all."

Simon dragged his fingers on the table, oblivious to Gideon's rising infuriation. "Except that you and I both know that I won't do that. You and I both know that I won't risk bringing more Inquisitors into this town before I ensure it's safe for their arrival."

"Safe from whom?" Gideon screamed.

"From you, Mr. Dosett," Simon replied calmly, a stark counterpoint to Gideon's anger. "I've learned many things about Haversham and her operations since arriving a few days ago. I know far more than I did from the dossier that I read on the zeppelin ride from the capital. Most importantly, I know what you are."

Gideon froze, the flush of anger draining from his face. His eyes narrowed dangerously and he stood, not aggressively, but cautiously. Gideon turned away from the two men and walked to his liquor cabinet against the back wall. He stared at both men as he retrieved the scotch and a single tumbler from the cabinet.

"So you think you know what I am?" Gideon asked defiantly. His eyes gleamed maliciously as he watched the two men through the mirror.

Luthor seized his arm as a lance of pain pierced him to the bone. He bit his lip to suppress the groan of surprise and anguish.

"You're a hypnotist," Simon said. "You've brought the leaders of this city under your thrall in a play for power. The governor, the leaders of both the Artisan's Union and Miner's Guild, and I'm sure countless others, have been brought under your hypnotic sway. We're here to put an end—"

He was interrupted as Luthor flinched again, squeezing his forearm so tightly that the hand beneath the rune was ash white. Throughout his anguish, his eyes, wide with surprise, never left Gideon's reflection.

"Is everything all right, Luthor?" Simon asked quietly, irritated at the interruption.

"Forgive me, sir," the apothecary replied through gritted teeth. "I seem to have taken suddenly ill." He stood abruptly and tried to step around the chair, stumbling as his heel caught the chair's leg. "I believe I must retire to my room until this abysmal feeling passes."

"If you feel that's for the best," Simon said, his previous irritation giving way to genuine concern. He couldn't remember the last time he'd seen Luthor taken ill, or if he ever had, for that matter. For the first time since the apothecary was bitten, Simon wondered if the lycanthropy was infectious after all.

"Perhaps you could do me the honor of escorting me back to my room, sir, in case I'm suddenly taken faint during the walk."

Simon shook his head. "The walk is brief, and there are plenty of servants that can assist if you require aid."

Luthor's cheeks turned rosy. "I believe I'd be better tended with your assistance, sir, rather than a stranger that I might pass along the way."

Simon stood and turned toward his friend. "There is an investigation to conclude," Simon said quietly, his irritation returning. "If you're ill, get rest and drink plenty of fluids. I'll check on you once this business is completed."

Luthor clutched the Inquisitor's lapel, pulling him in close enough that Simon could hear his harsh whisper. "Don't trust him. There is far more to Mr. Dosett than meets the eye."

Simon gently removed Luthor's hand from his jacket and smiled reassuringly. He spoke loudly enough that Gideon could hear his response. "This won't take much longer, I promise. I'll check on you once this nasty business is concluded. There are just a few more things I'd like to discuss with Mr. Dosett."

Luthor looked over his friend's shoulder as he backed slowly out of the room. Gideon's eyes never left the apothecary; they bored into him with an unholy intensity.

"I couldn't agree more," Gideon replied impishly. "I believe there are a few more things left to discuss, Inquisitor. Don't worry, Mr. Strong, I'll send him along to you shortly."

CHAPTER Nineteen

LUTHOR HURRIED THROUGH THE HALLS WITH HIS arm clutched to his chest as though it were broken. Another wave of pain rolled up through his shoulder and pierced his heart. His breath froze in his throat as he leaned heavily against the hallway wall until the pain subsided.

"Are you well, sir?" a servant asked from behind him.

Luthor angrily waved the man away before pushing off from the wall and continuing toward his room. The apothecary glanced over his shoulder to ensure the servant had disappeared from view before he risked pulling up the sleeve of his jacket.

Beneath the thick fabric, the warding rune on his arm burned a furious red. The puckered scaring looked new, as though it had recently been burned into his flesh, as opposed to the faded scar it normally appeared to be. Most disconcerting were the black tendrils that spread from the edges of the rune. They ran like dark veins, stretching away from the scar and spreading far enough up his arm that they disappeared beneath his jacket's sleeve.

Luthor unbuttoned the top pair of buttons on his dress shirt and slipped his hand beneath the open collar. He could feel the heat radiating off his skin and knew the black threads stretched deep into the muscles of his neck and chest.

He coughed, and it sounded raspy and wet in his lungs. For a second, his vision swam as he tried to focus on the doorway to his room. Blinking furiously until his vision cleared, he staggered to his door. His fingers felt thick and numb as he attempted to retrieve his keys from his vest pocket. As his fingers finally closed around the wide metal, he pulled the key free and with fumbling and shaking hands managed to slip the key into its lock.

The interior of his room was blissfully cool compared to the stifling warmth in the hallway. He shoved his door closed carelessly, ignoring the thunderous sound it made as it slammed shut behind him.

Stripping away his suit jacket and vest, he tossed them onto the couch. He fumbled with the cufflinks on his shirt for some time before they finally slipped free. The dress shirt and undershirt came off equally as quickly as the suit and both were discarded with as much care.

Feeling slightly more himself in the magical coolness of his suite, Luthor walked to the washbasin set in front of the vanity across the room. Crystal clear water swirled in the stone basin, and Luthor gladly dipped his hands into the water before splashing it across his face. He allowed a handful of water to pour over the back of his neck and run down his back. He barely gave a second thought to the water as it soaked into the back of his pants.

Standing upright, he observed his reflection. As he surmised, the black tendrils stretched up his forearm, weaving an intricate pattern across his bicep and shoulder before settling in a latticework of webbing across his chest. Numerous black threads culminated above his heart, leaving a wide, dark stain on the skin of his chest.

The tendrils accentuated the dozens of other small runes and scars that laced his chest and torso. He knew an equal number marred his back, each with their own purpose, though many existed merely to keep him from ever growing ill. He frowned at his reflection, the boyish face standing in stark contrast to the battered body. Though he hated lying to Simon—and he had worked incredibly hard to always remain shirted when in the Inquisitor's presence—he doubted Simon would fully understand his predicament.

Wordlessly, he walked into his bedroom and retrieved his doctor's bag. The vials within clinked as he brought the bag into the sitting room and dropped it onto the vanity beside the basin. Opening it, Luthor drew forth a number of glass tubes with varying colors of liquid within. Some had labels written in clear handwriting. Some had words written in a language known by few others, chemicals and plant extracts from rare fauna found only on distant continents. Still others weren't labeled at all, their opaque liquids clinging to the side of the glass as though straining toward the cork that kept them in place.

The apothecary selected a few of the vials and pulled free their stoppers. Pouring with little thought to exact measurements, he added a rainbow of chemicals to the basin's water. The clear blue quickly grew cloudy and dark, first turning a muddy brown before swirling to an inky black. Bubbles rose to the surface of the water. As they popped, white smoke hissed out of the bowl, pouring over the surface of the vanity before drifting to the floor.

When the surface of the water finally settled and no more bubbles rose through the dark depths, Luthor pulled a long needle from his bag and pricked his index finger on the same arm as the rune. A large, abnormally dark droplet of blood formed on his finger, and he squeezed the skin until it dropped into the bowl with a foul hiss. The water immediately cleared, returning to its crystal blue. Not a trace of the dark liquid remained.

Luthor reached into the bowl and scooped a handful of the clear water. As he poured it onto his forearm, the black tendrils washed away as though they were nothing more than soot. He claimed a washcloth from the cabinet beside the vanity and dipped it into the water. Using the cloth, he scrubbed the rest of his arm and chest. With each wipe, huge swaths of black threads disappeared. The cloth grew dirty and each dip into the basin left the water slightly darker than it had been the time before.

Before long, his skin was renewed and looked as fresh as it had been before their encounter with Gideon Dosett.

Satisfied, Luthor toweled dry before collecting his dress shirt. He left the other articles of clothes on the couch as he buttoned his shirt closed and laid down the stiff collar.

He stormed into his bedroom and unceremoniously threw aside the rug that rested on the floor at the foot of his bed. The chalk outline of the pentagram was broken and streaked, but the general shape still remained intact.

A piece of chalk sat beneath the ottoman. He wrapped his fingers around it and pulled it from the shadowy recess. With quick strokes, Luthor redrew the pentagram on the wooden floor, fixing the smeared lines. With the symbol redrawn, he walked to the side of the bed and dropped to his knees. He reached under the bed until his fingers closed on a small suitcase. Pulling the leather case out, he unlatched its straps. The interior was full of candles and incenses. The wafting smell of herbs struck him immediately, and he quickly collected a handful of candles and a small box of matches before hastily closing it once more.

The five candles were placed at the corners of the pentagram and lit one by one. Their flickering light danced over him as he took his place in the open center of the star.

Luthor closed his eyes and stretched his arms out beside him. The air grew electrified as a hum echoed through the bedroom. The lines of chalk glowed with an inner light, illuminating the room in a faint blue glow. Pulses of energy raced along the ley lines of the chalk outline.

The hum in the room grew to a roaring crescendo before crashing into silence. Luthor stood unmoving a moment longer before he spoke.

"He's here," he said to the empty room. "I've seen him with my own eyes. What would you have me do?"

He tilted his head to the side as he listened to the response. Luthor slowly shook his head.

"Forgive me, but it is not nearly that simple," he replied. "The demon has his claws in everything in Haversham. To separate the demon from the town would be virtually impossible at this time. He would march on me with an army of unwilling thralls."

Luthor frowned as he listened again. His arms drifted to his side, and he placed then frustratingly on his hips.

"Absolutely not!" Luthor hissed. "You sound like the Order of Kinder Pel when you say things like that. You sent me to find the five. I have located the first. If you trusted me thus far, then trust me to complete the task at hand without further interference."

He didn't wait for the full reply before he spoke again. "The Cabal can do whatever it deems necessary, but it will do so without my blessing or support. I trust in the Inquisitors to help, even if they are ultimately unaware of their true mission and how it inadvertently coincides with our own. Inquisitor Whitlock has yet to disappoint me; he won't do so now."

Before he could say more, someone knocked softly at the door to his suite. Luthor raised his head sharply, though he couldn't see the door from his place in the pentagram.

"Someone's here," he said to the empty room. "I must go. I will contact you again when I have had a chance to further study the demon. Until then, await my next communication."

The apothecary kicked the edge of the pentagram, breaking the circle. The blue light immediately faded from the room. The dim light of the candles seemed unimpressive when compared to the magical ley lines that had been glowing moments before.

The person knocked again as Luthor bent down and began extinguishing the candles, one after another. He slid the candles beside the chalk beneath the dust ruffle on the bottom of the ottoman. The rug was tossed back over the emblem as the person impatiently knocked for the third time. Luthor looked down at the wrinkled throw rug and considered fixing it, but another knock drew him away.

He pulled the door shut behind him as he walked to the suite's front door. Peering cautiously through the peephole, he saw Simon waiting stoically on the other side of the doorway.

With a smile of relief, Luthor unlocked the door. He hated leaving Simon alone with Gideon, but the pain in his arm had been exquisite. He had been unable to remain in the man's presence any longer without passing out from the strain put on his body by the protective wards. Seeing Simon alive and well gave him hope.

Luthor opened the door and smiled broadly.

"Simon, I'm glad to see you," he said curtly. "There is much that you and I need to discuss. Please come in."

Simon stood unblinking. With a fluid motion, he pulled the silver-plated revolver from his hip and pointed it at the apothecary.

"Simon?" Luthor said in disbelief.

The Inquisitor tilted his head to the side as he squeezed the trigger.

CHAPTER Twenty

LUTHOR STRUCK SIMON'S HAND AS THE PISTOL FIRED. The bullet screamed past his ear before striking the mirror above the vanity. Mirrored glass crashed onto the table and shattered as it struck the hardwood floor beneath. The apothecary quickly grasped Simon's hand before he could bring the revolver to bear once more.

The Inquisitor's face was a blank slate, staring unblinking at Luthor with eyes that were dilated until his normal blue was consumed by the black of his pupil.

"Stop this," Luthor hissed as he tried to hold back Simon's hand. Simon tried his best to turn the barrel of the pistol toward the apothecary, despite Luthor's pressure on his wrist. "This isn't you, this is Gideon Dosett."

Simon tilted his head to the side once more before raising his leg and kicking Luthor in the chest. Despite the close range, his heeled foot carried impressive weight, lifting Luthor from his feet. He slammed down onto the coffee table in the recessed sitting room, smashing through the sturdy wooden table.

He clutched his chest and coughed painfully as his back felt as though it were ablaze. He could feel ugly bruises spreading across his shoulder blades and ribs.

With his hand free of Luthor's clutches, Simon raised the pistol again, pointing it at the prone apothecary. The Inquisitor pulled back the hammer on the back of the revolver as he took aim.

Despite the throb behind his eyes, Luthor quickly waved his hand and the air before him shimmered as though a pane of warped glass had divided the room. Simon, who stood impassively on the far side of the shimmering wall, looked distorted with features out of proportion to the rest of his body.

The report of the pistol firing was muffled through the mystical divider. Sparks flew as bullets struck the protective wall in rapid succession. The ricocheting rounds struck the walls to either side of the doorway, splintering the plaster in puffs of white, chalky smoke.

Simon pulled the trigger until the hammer fell to a dry click on an empty cylinder. He turned the weapon to the side and stared at it inquisitively, as though struggling to comprehend why the weapon would fail to fire. Without any emotion on his face, he tossed his beloved revolver aside, letting it clatter and slide to the bedroom door.

He marched forward, as Luthor struggled to stand. The Inquisitor's body struck the shimmering barrier, barely slowing as he passed through its glassy exterior. Luthor frowned at the sight. He hadn't the time to create a proper barrier, one that would have kept Simon at bay for longer. Instead, he had hastily erected one that would stop projectiles. Simon's physical form, however, passed through with minimal resistance.

Luthor stepped backward, stumbling through the wreckage of the former coffee table.

"Fight it, Simon," Luthor begged. "Gideon has you ensorcelled. You're an Inquisitor, for God's sake! Show them that your will is stronger than a man's hypnotic magic."

Simon didn't appear to hear Luthor's plea. Once through the near side of the barrier, he strode toward the apothecary. Luthor struck his hands as Simon reached out to him, but to no avail. Possessed as he was, Simon was far stronger than the much shorter man was.

The Inquisitor's hands closed over Luthor's neck, squeezing tightly and closing most of Luthor's windpipe. The pressure was exquisite, and he could feel Simon's fingers biting into the sides of his neck. A trickle of air seeped between the Inquisitor's fingers and Luthor's lungs began to scream for more, unsatisfied with the minimalistic oxygen they received.

Simon squeezed harder, and speckles of light danced in Luthor's vision. The diminutive man stared at his friend and felt wildly unnerved by the expression on his face, one completely devoid of his previous humanity. His intricate mind had been reduced to a machine, following a single command, much to Luthor's chagrin. He doubted appealing to the man's humanity would have any chance of success.

Despite his growing lack of oxygen and the drumming of his pulse that seemed to be growing exponentially in his ears, Luthor closed his eyes and focused his breadth of magic within him. The palm of his hand began to radiate its own unnatural light. He raised his hand until the palm was even with Simon's chest.

"Forgive me, sir," he croaked through his practically closed throat.

He placed his palm against Simon's chest, and the air between them was filled with blue sparks. The Inquisitor's hands immediately left Luthor's throat as the man was rocketed backward. He was propelled only a few feet before striking the invisible barrier. Simon's body, now flying like a projectile, was denied access through the wall. Instead, yellow sparks were added to the previous blue and the air was filled with an acrid smell of burnt hair and clothing.

Simon ricocheted from the barrier and crashed unapologetically into the couch, tumbling with the furniture as it turned over. He rolled along the floor, his momentum carrying him forward, before coming to a rest near Luthor's bedroom door.

Luthor rubbed his throat and coughed hoarsely. Though the hands were gone, he could feel the heat and feel the minor indentations where Simon's fingers had pressed against his soft skin.

The apothecary cringed as he saw smoke rise from the back of his mentor. He hurried around the fallen furniture and crouched at his side, pressing a finger to Simon's carotid artery, checking for a pulse. He sighed with relief as he felt the steady rhythm of a heartbeat. Licking his fingers, Luthor pinched a strand of smoldering hair, extinguishing the nubile flame.

For a moment, Luthor merely crouched above his friend and watched his body rise and fall with each labored breath. He doubted very much that lying on the floor was in any way comfortable, even for a man who had so recently tried to murder him. The apothecary glanced around and realized the entire main room of the suite was in shambles. The vanity mirror was shattered. Bullet holes marred the plaster walls near the doorway. The couch and Luthor's articles of clothing that had been draped across it were upended. The doorway to the room itself was still wide open. Luthor quickly rushed to the door and glanced out into the hallway.

At the end of their hall, the butler stood hesitantly, shifting his weight from foot to foot, as he stared nervously. At the sight of Luthor, the man relaxed considerably and smiled. He approached Luthor's open doorway, but the apothecary raised his hand to keep him at bay.

"Is everything all right, sir?" the butler asked as he stopped in the middle of the long hallway.

"Of course," Luthor lied. "There's nothing going on that should alarm you."

"Sir, begging your pardon, but we heard gunshots."

Luthor bit his lip as he stared at the butler and the menagerie of other servants gathered at the mouth of the hallway. "You are absolutely correct, of course, though it's all a great misunderstanding. Inquisitor Whitlock merely dropped his firearm, and it discharged. It's an older weapon, sadly, and it carries a sensitive trigger."

The butler looked thoroughly unconvinced, but he nodded all the same. "I shall send someone at once to clean up your room and repair any damages."

"That won't be necessary," Luthor said hastily. As the butler frowned and furrowed his brow, Luthor quickly added, "Not today, at least. I believe the Royal Inquisitor could use some rest after the start he suffered during the accidental discharge. Tomorrow would be optimal to send someone by, say at ten in the morning?"

The butler bowed slightly at the waist. "Very good, sir. I shall have someone come by promptly at that time."

"Very good," Luthor echoed.

As the butler turned away with one final cautious look over his shoulder, Luthor quickly closed the door and turned back to the devastation. He sighed heavily as his eyes fell on Simon's still unconscious form, knowing he would have to deal with his mentor sooner rather than later.

Luthor sat on the edge of the couch, which he had painstakingly righted, and placed a damp rag on Simon's forehead. The Inquisitor stirred slightly and his eyes flickered beneath closed eyelids, but he remained unconscious. Luthor left the damp cloth where it was and walked to the vanity, where his doctor's bag rested. He stepped gingerly through the shards of broken glass, pushing many of them out of the way with the toes of his dress shoes.

The bag was still open from where he had treated his own infection earlier. A few shards of mirror jutted from the depths of the bag, and he removed these carefully. A quick inspection ensured none of the vials had been broken during the fight, nor had any become uncorked during the room's upheaval.

An empty glass sat on the side of the washbasin. Luthor blew out a few small slivers of mirror and wiped out the interior of the tumbler with one of the few remaining clean washcloths. With the glass sufficiently cleaned, Luthor set it on the counter and began withdrawing tubes of liquids from his bag.

The stopper was removed on the familiar extract of poppy, and a thin layer of the yellowed liquid was poured into the bottom of the glass. He pulled a small paper envelope from the side of his bag and unfolded a corner. With a tap of his finger, a small amount of white granules dropped into the glass and began to immediately dissolve. A larger beaker filled nearly to the brim with distilled water was removed from the corner of the deceptively small bag. Luthor poured a couple finger's worth of water into the glass. The white powder vanished in the water, and the coloring took on only the faintest of yellows from the poppy extract.

Luthor glanced over his shoulder and was relieved to see Simon still asleep. He doubted Gideon's control over the Inquisitor would be so easily broken as by physical violence. In fact, he was rather certain that physical violence was exactly the trigger that drove Simon forward in his attempt to murder Luthor.

Turning his attention back to the doctor's bag, he slipped his hand into a hidden compartment along the side of the bag. He pulled out a cloth drawstring bag. As he untied the cord holding it closed, the aroma of earthy rot assaulted his senses, mixed with the faint underpinning of an overbearing sweetness. He withdrew a few twigs of an unidentifiable plant and dropped them into the glass.

The water hissed as the blade-like leaves struck the surface of the fluid. The plants ignited, glowing a vibrant blue as the flora charred and quickly dissolved. The water turned a deep blood red before the dark color swirled away, leaving behind a brown liquid.

Luthor leaned over the glass and breathed in its scent. The smell of pungent scotch filled his nostrils, and he smiled appreciatively. Luthor retrieved the glass from the table and walked back to Simon.

He sat on the edge of the couch near Simon's hip. Leaning forward, he slipped his free hand beneath his head and raised the man to a seated position. The Inquisitor's lips were faintly parted in his slumber, and Luthor wasted no time pouring a modicum of the false scotch into Simon's mouth.

The Inquisitor sputtered as the alcohol struck the back of his throat. His eyes opened in surprise and his hands flew to his mouth as he coughed painfully. Spittle flew from his lips, and he indignantly wiped the strands of mucus from his mouth with the back of his sleeve.

Simon's eyes were full of confusion and anguish, a far cry from the automaton that had assaulted Luthor minutes earlier.

"Did you just pour scotch down my throat as I slept?" Simon managed between rough coughs.

"Forgive me, sir, but it was a necessary evil," Luthor replied calmly. He observed his friend but didn't see the murderous intent reflected in his actions.

"A necessary evil?" Simon echoed. His eyes scanned the room, adding to his burgeoning disorientation. "Where am I, Luthor? Is this your room?"

Luthor stood from his spot on the edge of the couch, allowing Simon to remove his feet from the couch and sit properly on the cushioned furniture. Simon grasped the sides of his head as soon as he sat upright in an attempt to suppress the piercing ache behind both eyes.

"It is," Luthor said. He furrowed his brow in concern. "Can you look up for me, sir?"

Still attempting to brush away the cobwebs that so thoroughly coated his every thought, Simon blindly obeyed. Luthor noted the series of bright red blood vessels enveloping the sclera of both eyes.

"Dear Lord," Simon muttered as he lowered his gaze once more. "What happened to your room?"

Luthor knelt in front of his mentor so that he might look into Simon's eyes. "Sir, do you genuinely have no recollection of this very night's events?"

Simon shook his head, perplexed. "I remember visiting Mr. Dosett and you taking suddenly ill. After that I remember… nothing."

Luthor placed his hand on Simon's shoulder and raised the glass. "Drink some more of this. It will help immensely with your headache."

Simon took the glass but examined it hesitantly. "Is it worth inquiring what's in this brew?" He sniffed the glass and arched his eyebrow in surprise. "Aside from scotch, which is readily apparent."

"Poppy extract to control the pain," Luthor replied.

"Naturally," Simon said with a smile.

"Powdered willow bark to help with the inflammation."

Simon took a draw from the glass before Luthor had to explain any of the other more mysterious ingredients. The Inquisitor sighed as the alcohol ran over his raw throat.

"Is it helping, sir?" Luthor asked.

Simon nodded. "Impressively so." His gaze fell to the brilliant red finger marks on Luthor's neck. "My good chap, I believe it's time you told me what in the bloody hell has happened."

Luthor looked Simon sternly in the eyes. "You attacked me, here in my room. Don't worry, sir, it wasn't of your own volition."

Simon blanched before turning scarlet red. "That in no way sets my mind at ease. Are you insinuating that I fell under the sway of a mere hypnotist? Have I truly become so simpleminded that a parlor trick such as having me stare at a swaying watch would so readily put me under—?"

"Sir," Luthor interrupted, "I don't believe you were hypnotized."

"I don't understand. You said I did this not of my own volition. If not hypnotized, then what would overcome me that I would assault my dear friend and yet have no recollection of the event?"

Luthor motioned toward the half-finished glass resting forgotten in his hand. "Drink more, if you please. I believe it will help restore some of those lost memories."

Simon looked down at the liquid once more before finishing the drink in a single large gulp.

"Tell me again, sir. What do you remember of this evening?"

Simon furrowed his brow as he struggled to remember. "I told you once already. I remember confronting Mr. Dosett, and then I remember you growing ill and asking me to accompany you back to your room. Is that when this happened?"

"Concentrate," Luthor reprimanded. "Speak less and focus more on retrieving those lost memories. Again, tell me what you remember."

"I remember nothing else," Simon chided. "We went to Mr. Dosett's office to confront him about being a hypnotist. He poured himself a drink, and you fell ill."

"What happened following my departure?" Luthor prodded.

Simon shook his head. "Mr. Dosett returned to his desk and then… I just can't seem to remember."

The Inquisitor rested the cool glass against his forehead. The pounding of his headache had receded to a barely noticeable hum and his eyes no longer ached when he looked toward the lamps in the room, but he still felt out of sorts.

Luthor sighed and stood, pushing splinters of the broken table away from him with his heel. He absently raised his hand to his neck, rubbing the red marks on his skin.

"Wait," Simon said excitedly. "I feel like the veil holding back my memory is receding ever so slightly, as though I'm on the cusp of remembering something very important."

"Do go on," Luthor said. He knew that Simon had to arrive at the answer on his own, rather than being told the truth.

"He sat down and began to explain how we had misconstrued the facts of the case. I scoffed at the notion that I could misconstrue facts, as though it were in any way in my nature."

Luthor crouched again. "Then what happened, sir?" he asked quietly, his voice barely louder than a whisper.

"Then he… he said something," Simon said, though the difficulty remembering was evident as he pursed his lips in thought.

His eyes suddenly flew open in shock, and his breath froze in his throat. "Oh dear God!" the Inquisitor said breathlessly. "It wasn't what he said. It was him or, more precisely, it was what he became."

"What did he become?" Luthor goaded.

"His skin turned black like the night and from his forehead, curved horns like a ram's grew, curling into a spiral around his ears."

Simon reached forward and grasped Luthor by the collar. "My good man, I've been the greatest of fools. Gideon Dosett isn't a hypnotist at all. He's—"

"A demon," Luthor replied sternly.

CHAPTER Twenty-one

"YOU KNEW," SIMON SAID ACCUSINGLY.

"I… well, sir, I—"

"You knew he was a demon, and yet you left me to my own devices in the presence of such a monster." Simon tried to set his empty glass down but quickly realized that the coffee table was in shambles. "It all makes perfect sense now. You taking suddenly ill in Gideon's office wasn't because of a bout of gastrointestinal distress. It was a façade by which you could escape his presence. Why, Luthor? Why would you abandon me to his clutches?"

"I was mortified!" Luthor hastily responded. "Yes, sir, I saw what he truly was. As he looked into the mirror, the illusion melted away and I saw the abysmal beast beneath."

Luthor crouched before Simon, ensuring the Inquisitor could see his sincere concern. "In my defense, I tried my damnedest to get you to leave with me."

"Clearly, I should have heeded your advice."

Simon stood and walked toward the vanity, intent on finally setting down his drained tumbler. Halfway across the room, he paused. His gaze fell to the silt residue floating amidst the few droplets that remained in the bottom of the glass.

"He had me under his sway," Simon said. "While I was still aware of my actions, I could feel his words in my mind like the fingers of a puppeteer, pulling my strings. All the facts remain a bit obfuscated, but I remember clearly that it wasn't so much that he controlled my body. I genuinely felt obligated to kill you. No, that's not quite accurate either. I genuinely wanted to kill you, on behalf of Gideon Dosett."

Luthor swallowed hard and nodded. He slowly rose from his crouch and took Simon's place on the couch. "It must have been horrible, especially looking back on your actions in retrospect."

Simon nodded without turning toward his friend. "Oh, it was, which is why it's all the more confusing as to how you are still alive."

"Divine intervention?" Luthor offered.

Simon scoffed at the idea. "Rubbish. I don't mean how did you survive, though that question vexes me as well, since I am clearly the better swordsman and excel at martial combat. I simply mean, why aren't I still trying to kill you?"

"Ah, that I can answer. The drink in your hand, sir, contains an odd concoction of extracts, powdered bark, and a few other insignificant ingredients. Taken apart, they're good for pain, inflammation, and little else. Combined, however, they become a potent blend capable of shattering the demon's hold over your mind."

"Alchemy trumps mysticism?" Simon asked, his skepticism evident. "Your brew was capable of shattering the monster's hold?"

Luthor shrugged. "You're a man of science who prefers to let facts and evidence speak for themselves, rather than to be open to loose interpretation. What does the evidence tell you?"

Simon frowned and finally set his glass on the vanity beside the washbasin. "I cannot refute your claims, Luthor. I came to this room to kill you and though the memory of what transpired once I passed through the doorway remains unclear, I am clearly no longer a thrall of the demon."

Luthor stood, using the toe of his shoe to push more of the debris away from the couch. "Moreover, sir, the brew will keep Gideon Dosett from regaining control over your mind. While no one is happier that you have returned to your former self than I, sir, and I realize you have had little time to absorb the evening's events, but there is an elephant in the room that needs to be addressed. What do we do now?"

Simon shook his head. "I honestly don't know. I've prided myself on my keen mind, a mind trained by the Inquisitors to withstand torture and even mystical probing without faltering. Yet Gideon Dosett brushed aside my defenses as though he were brushing newly fallen snow from his lapel. I can't in good conscience—"

Simon attempted to step further away from the vanity, but his knees buckled. He braced himself against the marble countertop as he clutched his chest.

"Luthor?" he asked as the apothecary rushed to his side. Luthor slipped his hand under Simon's armpit to support the Inquisitor's weight. "Luthor, did you strike me in the chest? It hurts like the dickens!"

"Forgive me, sir, but it was unavoidable. You were trying to kill me at the time."

Simon rubbed his chest again. "You are deceptively strong. I believe I have a cracked rib."

Luthor led him back toward the couch. "Perhaps you should sit again."

"Don't be preposterous," Simon said, brushing aside Luthor's supporting hand. "We don't have time for that. What I was trying to tell you before I was overcome with a bout of discomfort was that the demon would know quickly that I've failed. He will surround himself with other servants. We cannot in good conscience harm the citizens of Haversham for no other reason than they are unwilling pawns of this demonic creature."

"Then what would you have us do?"

Simon ran his fingers through his unkempt moustache. "Though I'm loathed to admit it, we need space in which to think. That space is clearly not in this estate and, dare I say it, I can't think of a place in all of Haversham that is safe enough. There is no telling how far Gideon's reach has extended."

"If not Haversham… sir, you can't be serious."

"Yes, my good chap, I'm very serious. There's only one group in this land that I can say with all sincerity are not enthralled with Gideon Dosett."

They packed quickly, taking only belongings that could be carried hastily in over-the-shoulder bags. Luthor carried little in the way of supplies, opting instead to keep his doctor's bag close at hand. When they were done, they gathered just inside the door of Luthor's suite.

"I assume you have a plan," Luthor remarked.

"I always have a plan," Simon said, before adding, "It just may not be as well formulated as I would have hoped."

Luthor stood impassively for a second before sighing in exasperation. "Would you do me the honor of enlightening me? We have truly moved beyond the time where you do your cryptic deductions while leaving me in the dark."

Simon smiled sympathetically toward his friend. "We will leave the city by means of the tunnels. At this late hour, they'll be practically abandoned."

"Excellent," Luthor replied. "Then we'll need to leave with the utmost haste. We have the cover of darkness, which should work in our favor."

Simon shook his head. "If we move toward the front door, we'll be spotted almost immediately. If we attempt to hurry across the open courtyard of the estate, we'll most certainly be spotted. In either scenario, we'll be captured long before we make it to the tunnels."

Luthor frowned deeply. "You're an infuriating man. You realize this, of course? Why propose using the tunnels if you're only going to immediately point out the numerous faults in your own plan?"

"I bring up those inevitabilities to frame the simple fact that we'll have to find another way into the tunnels."

"What other way? How else can we get into the tunnels if not…?"

Luthor's voice trailed away as a brilliant smile spread across his face. "You cheeky bastard. You're referring to the entrance in the fencing room. You mean to use Gideon's own secret passage."

Simon's smile matched the apothecary's. "I told you that sometimes an opponent gives away more than he intends. Still, the way will be treacherous. As we make our way into the basement, trust no one, least of all anyone to whom Gideon himself has introduced us."

"Are we ready, then?"

"We are." Simon grasped the door handle but let his hand fall away. "Do try to relax, Luthor. I've never met a man who looked less incriminating."

Luthor laughed nervously. "Is it that noticeable?"

"You actually look like you're about to steal something."

Luthor took a deep breath as Simon opened the door. The hallway beyond their rooms was empty as far as Simon could see. The hallway ended at the landing for the stairwell, which spiraled gently to the foyer. Though he had moved back and forth to his room when packing his meager belongings, he anticipated resistance every step of their journey.

They exited the room in silence. From the corner of his eye, Simon could see Luthor practically bending at the waist as he fought an internal struggle against actively sneaking down the hallway. Simon walked upright with a soft smile on his lips, as though their late night stroll was nothing out of the ordinary.

The landing was empty, and a quick glance over the railing confirmed that the stairwell was as well. The duo padded quietly to the top of the stairs, walking gingerly on the woven rugs that lined the floor. The stairs were unadorned, exposing the white marble. Simon's first step onto a stair clicked loudly as his cobbled sole struck the floor. It echoed through the vaulted room, and both men cringed. They paused for a moment, straining to listen for any approaching footsteps. When they were satisfied that there was none, they continued down the steps with more caution.

The foyer, as with the stairwell, was empty. Simon didn't fully appreciate how late it was until he realized that the entire estate was asleep. They turned sharply from the base of the stairs, heading toward the hallways that housed the stairs down to the basement. Luthor stopped suddenly and hurried toward the front door. His cane jutted from the open top of a tall, bronzed cylinder. As he withdrew it, the metal tip of the cane grazed the edge of the barrel, and the noise rung faintly across the room.

"Did you hear something?" a voice asked from outside the front door.

"What did it sound like?" another voice replied.

Simon and Luthor froze in place, Simon scowling at the apothecary. They were exposed in the open foyer. A shadow fell across the pane of glass beside the front door. The glass itself was frosted and nearly impossible to see through, though the guard evidently tried his best to look into the mansion's interior.

"I didn't hear anything," the second guard said. "You're being paranoid."

"Paranoid, my arse," the first said. "You heard Mr. Dosett's orders. If we spot the Inquisitor or his companion, we're to shoot them on sight."

Simon swallowed hard, his Adam's apple bobbing. The shadow remained in the window for a few seconds longer, seconds that felt like an eternity to the two men frozen in place like statues carved out of the very marble that surrounded them.

"You're probably right," the guard finally said. "I'm just hearing things."

The shadow disappeared, and both men let out breaths they'd been holding. Simon motioned quickly for Luthor to follow and the two men hurried quickly, albeit quietly, toward the next stairwell.

They rushed down the last set of stairs, unconcerned about any sounds they might make. The hallway was illuminated, but the rooms to either side were unlit. Luthor shivered as they hurried past the autopsy room. The mixture of stale blood and viscera in the air mixed with the eeriness that came from the pitch black of the room. He practically anticipated a monster to come charging out and attack them. Gladly, his fears never came to fruition.

Simon reached the fencing room at the end of the hall and fumbled around the interior wall until his hand closed on a light switch. He flipped the brass knob upward, and the harsh overhead lights flickered to life.

Though the secret door he had noticed earlier was to his left, he skirted the right wall until he reached the rack of fencing swords. He withdrew the same saber he had used earlier, swinging it gracefully in his grip as he admired the weight once more. Retrieving its scabbard from the rack as well, he strapped it comfortably around his waist.

"Take one," Simon offered in a whisper. "You might very well need it before this night's through."

Luthor detached the pommel of his cane, exposing the blade concealed within. "I'm already sufficiently prepared, but thank you all the same."

The two men hurried across the floor to the left wall. Simon stooped low, brushing his hand across small granules of dirt ground into the floor.

"It's here," he said. "Look for a lever or switch of some kind that will release the door."

The wall was barren aside from a single sconce mounted just above Luthor's head. A naked light bulb glowed in the stand, and the copper wiring disappeared into the wall. He looked over to Simon, who ran his hand over the unseen edges of the invisible doorway, searching for a pressure plate or recessed section of wall, which could be depressed. Luthor turned his gaze back to the sconce.

"Certainly it can't be this simple," he remarked out loud. Simon paused to look at the apothecary.

Luthor reached up and pulled on the sconce. It slid easily forward, tilting at an angle as he pulled down. A metal arm protruded from the back of the sconce and disappeared within the wall. As it reached a forty-five degree angle, a click sounded and the secret door glided inward.

"The wall sconce?" Simon asked. "It seems a bit clichéd."

Luthor suppressed a laugh at the absurdity. "Indeed, but I give credit where credit is due. If you are to live in such utter opulence and you don't have a wall sconce secret door or a passage that can only be exposed behind a fireplace or bookshelf, then certainly you're spending your money incorrectly."

"Come," Simon chided as he stepped into the tunnel.

They hurried down the tunnel, which was illuminated by evenly spaced electric lanterns mounted on the walls. A multitude of exposed pipes ran overhead and copper tubing coated the walls, disappearing occasionally into the rock face only to reemerge a few feet further down the passage.

The tunnel ended abruptly into one of the side passages that ran beneath the city. From the collection of loose dirt on the floor, very unlike the packed dirt floors of the main tunnels, Simon surmised the tunnel was rarely used.

"Which way is the exit?" Luthor asked.

Simon glanced down both lengths of tunnel. Both directions were equally well illuminated but revealed nothing worthwhile.

"Supposedly many of these tunnels terminate beyond the city wall. At this point, we pick a direction and hurry."

They turned left and rushed away from the estate's secret entrance. Their side tunnel merged with one of the main passages, which allowed easier movement as they progressed beneath the city proper. As Simon had deduced, most of the tunnels were empty. The citizens of Haversham were asleep in their homes, blissfully unaware of the fleeing fugitives.

A few people traversed the same tunnels down which they walked.

The people offered strange glares as the two men walked hurriedly past. Though Simon knew that he was being unnecessarily paranoid, he swore their gazes lingered longer than they should have and carried with them a bit of malice. He smiled and tipped his hat to the men and women but received no niceties in response.

He could feel perspiration forming in his hair underneath his hat, though it had nothing to do with the ambient temperature. Simon realized he was operating in the dark, so to speak. He and Luthor had approached Haversham well informed, having researched werewolves in mythology and in a more logical context. Demons, however, were outside his realm of knowledge. For all he knew, Gideon's influence over his thralls had nothing to do with distance. The glares he was receiving, he realized, could just as easily be a result of new orders being received from the demon, who still resided safely and comfortably in the governor's estate. He was far more concerned about how wide Gideon's influence reached. Though he and Luthor were more than capable of handling even possessed townsfolk, he doubted his skills against the entire population of Haversham.

"This way, sir," Luthor said, nodding toward a side passage.

As soon as they turned, Simon understood why Luthor chose this particular passage. The arctic winds howled down the tunnel, passing through his jacket as though it didn't exist. They both wore the same thick jackets with which they'd flown to Haversham on the zeppelin. The jackets had been warm enough for passage through the city, but he was doubtful once they moved beyond the inordinately tall protective walls.

"Are you sure about this, sir?" Luthor asked, echoing his own concerns. "There has to be another option."

"There is only one group in this region who hates Gideon Dosett more than you or I. Their hatred alone is enough to warrant my trust, even if that trust is temporary and wholeheartedly situational dependent. However, are you asking if I would like to find another solution other than to place my trust in the werewolf clans? You're damned right I would."

He looked down the tunnel and pulled his jacket tighter around his body. "Sadly, I can't think of another option."

Simon stepped ahead of Luthor in the narrow tunnel and walked, head down, into the frigid wind. He pulled his watch from his pocket, noting that the night was almost gone and with it their concealment from prying eyes. Simon glanced apologetically over his shoulder. "Come on, Luthor. It certainly isn't going to get any warmer standing around waiting."

CHAPTER Twenty-two

SIMON SHIVERED UNCONTROLLABLY AS THEY BROKE through the thick, powdered snow. Their feet sank until their knees were covered, and the moisture soaked through their pants legs. He pulled his jacket closer around his body, but it did hardly any good. The voracious wind cut through the woven fabric, chilling them to the bone.

He raised a hand to cover his eyes, but it did nothing to negate the brilliant glare from the snow itself. Simon glanced enviously toward Luthor, who had affixed his tinted lenses to his glasses. Though the apothecary could see better than Simon, his skin was still a vibrant red and his lips already looked chaffed and cracked, with a tinge of blue along the rim of his mouth.

"This was a fool's errand," Simon said loudly to be heard over the wind. "I'm the greater fool for thinking it a worthwhile plan."

"I won't deny we very likely marched toward martyrdom, sir," Luthor replied, "but I would rather take our chances finding the tribesmen than fall victim to Gideon Dosett and his vile magic."

Simon frowned and looked away. His body ached in a way that he was sure Luthor didn't understand. Though he was stoic, he felt drained to his core, as though Gideon's demonic magic had pulled from his very soul. His thighs burned with every step and his breathing became more and more labored.

"How far do you suppose we've traveled?" Luthor asked.

Simon glanced over his shoulder at the city, now far in the distance. His eyes trailed from the high city walls to the sun, glaring overhead. "Ten miles, maybe fewer."

Luthor flexed his fingers as he tried to ball them into a fist, but the swelling in his knuckles limited his movement. "Dare I ask how far we still have to march?"

"To the foothills?"

Simon turned his gaze to the distant mountains. He mentally calculated the distance, comparing it to Haversham behind them. He internally groaned at the realization of how far they still had to go.

"Not far," he lied to his companion. "It should be about the same distance, perhaps a little less."

Luthor nodded, though Simon could see the skepticism on the man's face.

Simon lifted his leg weakly from the deep snow and took another step. They were cresting another snow bank, and Simon always advanced with more caution near the top. In most instances, the height of the dunes was caused merely by an accumulation of snow. A wrong step could send him sinking to his chest in the thick powder or, worse, over his head in snow. He knew the numbness that had spread through his feet and shins from the damp cold there. He was loathed to imagine how cold his body would be if he were completely submerged in snow.

To his satisfaction, the top of the snow bank held as he stepped forward. The powder beneath his shoe compacted, lending him a platform from which he could support his weight. Simon raised his other foot from the snow and placed it beside the first so that he was standing at the top of the dune.

"Do keep up," he said, glancing over his shoulder at the struggling, shorter man. Where the snow reached to Simon's knee, it was nearly to Luthor's groin. The man shivered involuntarily with each downward step. "The quicker we reach the foothills, the quicker we can warm ourselves by a fire."

"Or the quicker we can be skinned alive by a pack of werewolves,"

Luthor corrected. "You seem to have quickly forgotten that these creatures aren't prone to kindness toward an Inquisitor. They did try to kill us."

"True, but your lady friend also tried to help us expose the demon for what he truly is. The enemy of my enemy is my—"

A rumble ended Simon's sentence. The snow beneath his feet shifted, and the crest of the snow bank collapsed. Simon tumbled forward as the snow underneath him cascaded down the steep backside. His feet flew out behind him, and the Inquisitor fell into the snow. For a second, Simon teetered on the tip of the collapsing bank, his face half concealed by the powdery snow and his hands clawing for purchase. As quickly as he landed, however, he disappeared from view as the small avalanche continued to claim his dune.

Luthor scrambled to the top of the evaporating mound in time to watch Simon tumble through the drift. The drop was far longer than Luthor would have surmised as they climbed up the leeward side of the hill. With the snow beneath giving way, the drop was nearly vertical, ending on the frozen surface of the lake below.

Simon saw the world spin wildly as he tumbled head over feet. Snow filled his mouth and coated his skin. It stung his eyes as he tried to gain his bearings, and he was forced to close them tightly. He spread his arms and legs to make a wider surface area and he was quickly able to halt his tumbling, though he still slid amidst the snow toward the frozen ground below.

The falling snow struck the surface of the frozen lake and piled into a mound through which Simon ploughed. His momentum carried him out of the snow bank and he slid in a circle, his arms and legs still spread, before coming to a stop on the icy surface.

Slowly, he opened his eyes. He stared at the deep blue and aquamarine of the sheet of ice. Light filtered through it, reflecting in the large bubbles that floated just beneath its frozen surface. Through the heart of the ice, a web of cracks and fissures ran in all directions.

Simon's breath froze as solidly as the ice beneath him. He saw the still-flowing water far beneath him through the ice, drifting lazily away from where he lay. Despite the frigid cold that was permeating his body, he remained paralyzed at the sight of the water.

"I'm coming, sir," Luthor yelled from above. "Stay where you are."

Simon coughed, forcing air back into his lungs. "Don't worry. I have no intention of moving a muscle," he replied, though his answer was far too quiet to be heard.

Luthor trudged a few dozen feet to his right until the slope of the snow leading to the edge of the lake was more gradual. He tentatively stepped onto the edge of the lake. Though the ice beneath his feet groaned from the weight, he didn't hear the telltale snaps of breaking ice. Moving slowly, keeping his feet in constant contact with the icy surface, Luthor skated toward his prone mentor.

Simon shivered until his muscles felt like they were on fire. He wasn't sure his body would respond even if he tried to stand, though he still had no intention of trying. The idea of standing above unknown depths of murky lake water with God only knows what swimming hungrily in its depths was horrifying enough. Knowing that the only thing keeping him from discovering first hand was a sheet of ice, the depth of which varied from region to region, was paralyzing.

"I'm almost to you, sir," Luthor said as he skated slowly closer. The man's arms were held parallel to the ice as he tried to maintain his balance as he moved along the slippery surface.

Simon watched the man through squinted eyes. The glare of the sun off the ice was even more severe than off the snow itself. He had heard stories about snow blindness in his travels, though he thought the idea of succumbing to such an ailment was so miniscule that it hardly warranted concern. Now, the thought that he might lose his sight was as equally frightening as standing on ice.

As Luthor grew closer, the ice beneath them both groaned. Water sloshed through existing fissures in the lake's surface, as their weight forced the icy surface lower into the water.

"Stop," Simon demanded. "For God's sake, stop!"

Luthor paused and regained his balance. "Sir, you're going to have to stand at some point. You can't remain prostrate forever."

"I think you underestimate my strength of will."

Luthor frowned. "You're wet and cold already. The longer you lay there, the more likely your joints and muscles will freeze. Once that occurs, there isn't a power in the kingdom that will get you moving once more. You need to stand."

Simon sighed. "Of course. Let me… well, let me just collect my thoughts."

His thoughts consisted of little more than envisioning himself breaking through thin ice and sinking into the depths of the lake, the freezing water constricting his chest as his lungs screamed for air. His hands would struggle feebly to pull him back to the surface, but the underwater currents would have taken him far from his hole. His fingers would claw at the ice above him, falsely finding hope in small cracks that offered no relief until, inevitably, he died beneath the frozen surface.

"Sir?" Luthor asked, shattering his waking nightmare.

"Give me a moment, won't you? Has anyone ever told you that you're far too demanding?"

Luthor sighed but remained where he was.

Despite Simon's better judgment, he placed his palms against the ice. His muscles screamed in protest as he began lifting himself. His hands slid slightly from side to side, making standing even more difficult than it already would have been for Simon. The ice groaned and small cracks formed near the pressure points on his hands and knees. He finally placed his feet beneath him and managed to stand on the slippery surface. Bending low and retrieving his top hat, he placed it on his head. Though he currently cared little for the hat itself, he knew that it would trap heat escaping his head, which would grant him a modicum of warmth.

"Get me back to the snow," he demanded.

Luthor shook his head and looked apologetic. "That's not our best course of action, sir."

"Frankly, I don't give a damn about our best course of action. I want off this accursed ice."

Luthor placed his hands on his hips. "Sir, you're already wet and cold. If you think that I also haven't noticed that you're still weak from your encounter with Gideon, then you're a fool. If we go back to the closest shore, we'll have to trek for some time to skirt the lake. Your body will never survive. Hypothermia, frostbite, or both will claim you long before we come within miles of the mountains."

Simon scowled at his companion, but Luthor was unfazed.

"If you wish to survive," the apothecary continued, "we'll have to cut across the lake. It'll save us hours of travel, hours that you can't spare, I might add."

Simon looked across the frozen lake, much of which was concealed by a layer of powdered snowfall. He groaned louder than the ice beneath his feet.

"I once worried that you'd poison me in my sleep," Simon said. "Now I realize that was a foolish fear. You're far more diabolical. You're clearly planning to torture me to death."

"With all due respect, you complain like a woman. Now come on, sir."

Simon stood for a moment longer before gingerly following Luthor across the ice. "I can't help but feel that you don't think I'm actually due much respect at all. If we survive this—"

"When we survive this," Luthor corrected.

"If we survive this, you and I will have need to redefine our relationship."

"I truly can't wait for that conversation, sir."

They moved painfully slowly across the ice. The trip seemed far longer to Simon than it had been to reach the lake from Haversham. He tried to flex his toes within his shoes but couldn't tell if he was successful or not. Everything beneath his knees felt numb with an accompanying dull ache in the bones. His fingers were beginning to feel equally as pained, as though he had a sudden acute onset of arthritis in his knuckles.

By the time they reached the far shore, the toll on both men was severe. Their lips were blue and quivered with each breath. Eyelids hung low as the bodies of both yearned for sleep. Their arms hung limply at their side, and their feet shuffled along the ice less because of their desire to skate over the frozen surface and more because their legs lacked the energy to lift them higher.

As Luthor's foot crunched through the partially frozen covering of the deep snow, he sighed with discontent. Though the climb off the frozen lake was gradual, it was still a steady incline, one that neither man was eager to tackle.

"It won't be much further now, sir," Luthor said, though his words were slurred through numb lips.

Simon merely grunted his response. He was certain the trip had taken its toll on Luthor, but he doubted the apothecary understood the level of his soul-aching weariness. The iron will of which Simon had often prided himself had been replaced by a morose acceptance of his fate. Despite his efforts, he was certain he was going to die facedown in the snow.

He stepped into the snow and even the loose powder seemed to pull at his feet. His pants legs were stiff where the moisture had frozen them solid. Each movement cracked and calved some of the clinging ice from his clothing, though he knew it would quickly be replaced once more.

Reaching the tip of the incline beyond exhausted his body. Simon lifted his leg to step and his numb foot caught on the snow bank. Stumbling forward, he dropped to his knees. He placed his hands out to catch himself, only to have them disappear in the deep snow.

Luthor appeared by his side, slipping his arms beneath Simon's armpits and pulling him upright with surprising strength.

"Leave me, Luthor," Simon muttered. "You clearly have far more strength than I do remaining. Go and find the werewolf tribes. See if they'll send someone to retrieve my remains."

"That's absolute rubbish, sir," Luthor said, crouching at his side. "I have no intention of leaving you. Now come on and get to your feet."

"I can't," Simon replied. "I'm defeated. I should have never brought you out here. We should have taken our chances in Haversham, confronting the whole of the city if necessary. Had we died then, it would have been a far bit better a fate than to die alone and forgotten. We're going to perish here and no one, probably not even the werewolves themselves, is going to find our bodies."

Luthor grasped Simon by the shoulders and shook him violently. The Inquisitor raised his eyes to his friend. "We're not defeated yet. We just need to go a little further, but in order for that to happen, I need you to get to your feet. Now get up."

Simon shook his head and it earned him another violent shake from Luthor in response.

"Stop shaking me, damn you."

"I'll stop shaking you when you quit wallowing in your own self-pity and stand up."

"Just let me—"

He was interrupted with another violent shake.

"Stop that!" Simon barked angrily.

Luthor smiled. "There's the fire in your belly that I've come to know. Now get on your feet."

Simon shifted his weight so that he could free a foot. He placed it in the snow for support. "I'm growing to greatly dislike you. The word 'hate' has been bantered around in my mind lately."

"Excellent, sir. Your hate will keep you warm."

"So will beating you senseless, I presume."

Luthor laughed though it quickly turned into a ragged cough. "If that's what it takes, then I'll accept my punishment."

Simon forced his other leg beneath him and stood awkwardly. None of his limbs felt as though they were cooperating fully, as though he were standing on artificial limbs that had never been properly fitted.

He took a step and nearly fell again. Only Luthor's quick grasp kept him from collapsing fully into the snow.

"I've got you, sir."

Simon shook his head. "How is it that you still have any strength at all, Luthor? I have a weariness in my chest the likes of which I've never felt before, yet you still have the strength to support my weight."

"I never had the displeasure of being entranced by a demon. It's taken more out of you than you are willing to admit."

"Maybe so," Simon said wearily. "Maybe so."

He planted his feet beneath him once more and looked toward the horizon. The mountains still seemed impossibly far away. The slowly setting sun cast deep shadows over their peaks, only adding to the illusion of their distance.

As he tried to step again, his legs simply gave out and he dropped heavily to the snow. Not even Luthor's support could keep him upright, and they both fell to their knees.

"I'm done, Luthor," Simon sighed.

"No, you're not. You just need to get up and moving once more. Once the blood flow returns to your limbs, you'll feel perfectly revived once more."

Simon shook his head. "Your pathetic motivational speeches aren't going to work this time. I don't even have the strength to stand."

The Inquisitor started to lean backward, and Luthor caught his head before he could fall completely into the snow. Simon's eyelids fluttered as he struggled to remain conscious.

"Sir, you can't fall asleep. I can't carry you, and I certainly won't leave you here. I need you to wake up."

"Forgive me," Simon said quietly. "Forgive me for being so foolish. We should have never come."

"Sir," Luthor said. He struck Simon's cheek with some force, leaving bright red fingerprints across the man's face. Even with the strike, Simon refused to fully open his eyelids.

Despite what Simon believed, Luthor was equally as exhausted. The protective runes on his body kept him warmer and prolonged his energy beyond normal human means, but their power was nearly expired. The same ache that Simon felt was creeping into every iota of Luthor's body.

The cold was a living beast, enveloping them both. Its seedy fingers were creeping into Luthor's mind, clouding his ability to concentrate. He looked down at his friend and noticed Simon's eyes fully closed. His chest barely rose and fell with each respective breath, and his skin felt icy to the touch. If he wasn't warmed soon, he knew Simon would die of exposure.

Luthor looked to the snow beside Simon and tried to summon a mystical flame, one that could burn without wood for fuel and even on top of the moist snow. Sparks flickered at the ends of his fingers before a small wisp of flame appeared. As he extended his fingers toward the surface of the snow, however, the flame danced briefly before evaporating into a small puff of white smoke. He tried again, but the sparks refused to light. Under normal circumstances, summoning a flame would have been child's play, but his clouded mind refused to focus enough for his magic to coalesce.

Had he still been able to cry, Luthor would have shed a tear. He curled his arms around Simon and pulled the Inquisitor close to his body, hoping their shared warmth would help the man survive even a few moments longer.

Darkness enveloped Luthor and for a moment, he feared he fell asleep and the sun had set. He looked up to see the silhouette of a man blocking the setting sun. Fur lined his body and a flintlock rifle rested comfortably in his hand, the stock of which was pressed to his hip.

Luthor turned his head and noticed more of the natives surrounding him, pointing spears and knives threateningly toward the exhausted pair.

"Please," Luthor managed through a dry throat and cracked lips. "Please, we've come to seek your help."

The tribesman in front of him lifted his rifle from his hip, spun it gracefully in his hand, and drove the stock of the rifle into Luthor's face. The apothecary was unconscious long before he fell backward into the snow.

CHAPTER Twenty-three

LUTHOR OPENED HIS EYES TO AN INKY BLACKNESS. Panicked, he looked to the side only to realize something was pressing against his face. He reached up tentatively and his hand closed on fur. Grasping the fur, he pulled the blanket away.

Sunlight streamed through a small hole above him, though wooden poles jutting from the narrow hole above bisected the light. The air around him was warm and smelled of a combination of wood smoke and lye.

Disoriented, he sat up in the pile of furs that made his bed. A fire crackled merrily in the center of the animal hide-covered tent. Though the beam of light from above and the small campfire provided illumination, the dome-like tent was mostly shadowed.

A soft moan beside him alerted Luthor that he wasn't alone. He glanced over quickly and found Simon buried similarly in furs, though the Inquisitor was sleeping soundly. Luthor leaned over until his ear hovered an inch above Simon's face. Slowly, gently, he felt the man exhale. The rush of air against the side of his face made Luthor far happier than he believed possible.

"Sir?" Luthor asked, gently shaking the Inquisitor's shoulder.

Though Simon responded with a faint groan of displeasure, he didn't awaken. He pulled away the blanket and found Simon dressed in an odd assortment of furs and hides that covered most of his exposed skin. Looking down, he noticed that he was similarly dressed.

Simon groaned again, and his brow furrowed in discomfort. Luthor returned Simon's blanket, tucking it in affectionately around the man's chin. Simon immediately relaxed and fell back into his deep slumber.

Luthor stood and looked around the room. His eyes had adjusted quite a bit since awakening, and he could now clearly see the thin outline of a hide doorway on the opposite side of the fire. Standing stoically by the door was a tribesman, dressed in similar furs but carrying a short, wickedly pointed spear.

"Excuse me," Luthor said as he walked around the campfire. The smell of smoke and lye grew stronger the closer he got to the edge of the tent. "Do you understand me?"

As he grew closer, the guard raised his spear, pointing it at Luthor's chest. He said nothing, but his eyes narrowed dangerously.

"I see that you clearly do understand me, even if you don't speak the language. Where are we?"

The guard said nothing.

"I refuse to be one of those incessant fools who speaks slower or louder merely in an attempt to get you to understand me better. Was it you that treated my friend? He was suffering from hypothermia and what I have to assume was acute onset of frostbite. Is he better now?"

The guard remained silent, the tip of his spear unwavering.

Luthor looked down at his own hands and noticed that they were red and slightly inflamed, but otherwise healed. He didn't know whether to attribute it to whatever healing was done by the tribesmen or to his own supernatural ability to heal, but he was grateful to be healthier.

Luthor placed his hands on his hips in frustration as he faced the guard again. "Is there someone with whom I could discuss this matter? Are we your prisoners or are you our benefactors?"

He took a step forward, and the guard extended his arm until the tip of the spear pressed against Luthor's chest. Despite the thick fur shirt, he could feel the sharpened metal tip biting into the flesh beneath.

"Fair enough," he said. "You've made your point. You're clearly more the former rather than the latter. So what shall I do in the meantime?

Shall I just stand here and wait until you feel more talkative?"

The spear was pulled away from his chest. Using its tip as a pointer, the guard motioned toward the pile of furs on the floor.

Luthor looked at the furs before looking back to the guard. "So you do understand me after all? Very well, I'll play the part of your patient captive until your boss arrives."

Luthor returned to the furs and sat down beside Simon. He placed his hand on the man's forehead and was pleasantly surprised to note a lack of fever. Though Simon wouldn't yet wake up, it was because of his body's need to regenerate rather than fighting against a burgeoning infection.

The wait was blissfully short before the tent flap was thrown aside and the room flooded with natural sunlight. Luthor turned and noted a much smaller silhouette at the door. The person who ducked under the opening was much shorter than the muscular guard watching the prisoners. As the newcomer entered the room, the light from the campfire danced across her features.

The red from the fire matched her red hair. Her features were weatherworn but still remarkably attractive. Though she looked starkly different in native furs as compared to the stately dress she had worn to the governor's Winter Ball, there was no mistaking it was the same woman. This was the same woman, Luthor had to remind himself, who had subsequently transformed into a werewolf before throwing herself off the third-story balcony.

She smiled as she realized that the apothecary was awake and made her way around the fire. Luthor climbed to his feet as she approached, though he was suddenly feeling less attracted to her than he had at the ball.

"We were never properly introduced," Mattie said, extending her hand. "My name is Mattie."

"The werewolf," Luthor replied, staring at her hand.

She slowly curled her finger and withdrew her hand. "If such titles make you happy then yes, I'm Mattie the werewolf."

Luthor's hard expression softened as he glanced over his shoulder to where the Inquisitor slept soundly. "You rescued us, I presume?"

"We watch Haversham intently, recording anyone who enters or exits the city. We saw you both escape through one of the tunnel entrances. When you collapsed in the snow, yes, we rescued you and brought you both here."

Luthor raised his hand to his face and touched the skin beneath his eye. Though it had mostly healed already, it was still tender to the touch.

"I recall it being a fairly violent rescue from my perspective. Still, we both owe you a debt of gratitude." He motioned toward the guard, who remained stoically at his post. "Though I'm under the distinct impression we are not your honored guests."

Mattie looked over her shoulder toward the guard. "He's unfortunately a necessary precaution, until we can decide what sort of threat you both pose."

Luthor pointed toward Simon. "The Inquisitor is sound asleep, still recovering from his wounds. We're clearly not a threat."

Mattie frowned and glared at Luthor. "Perhaps I misspoke. We're deciding what sort of a threat *you* are."

Luthor was taken aback. He placed his hand on his chest in mock indignation. "Me? I'm hardly a threat."

Mattie looked over his shoulder and saw Simon stir. "Perhaps this is a better discussion for outside."

She turned and walked toward the tent flap. The guard pulled it aside for her, allowing her to pass through. Though he glared at Luthor, he didn't impede his exit.

Luthor was forced to raise a hand to block the glare as he stepped outside. The sun was once again burning brightly overhead. His eyes had adjusted to the dim light of the tent's interior, and the brilliant sunlight was practically blinding. He still had his glasses on his face, but the tinted lenses were missing.

"How long was I asleep?" he asked, realizing that it was at least the following day.

"Two days now," Mattie replied.

She walked away from the stunned apothecary and approached a central bonfire. Thick logs, brushed free of collecting snow, were placed around the fire like benches. The fire itself roared taller than Luthor, its flames licking the sky and sending a cloud of black smoke toward the mountains nearby. Around him, natives wandered between similarly formed dome tents. Though some appeared to be family, most of the people he saw were warriors, carrying rifles or spears.

"Two days?" Luthor asked in disbelief.

"You were tired and clearly needed the rest," Mattie said as she stopped near the bonfire. Her red hair billowed as waves of heat rolled over her. "We saw no reason to disturb you."

"Where are we?" he asked.

"No," Mattie replied. "It's about time we change the dynamic of this relationship. You are our guests and I have far too many questions that you will answer in turn."

Luthor suddenly felt very aware of all the warriors surrounding him, carrying their assorted weapons. "Very well."

"Why are you here?"

Luthor gestured toward the people around him. "I think you know why we're here. There were clearly founded reports of werewolves in this region. Simon is an Inquisitor, and we were assigned to discover the truth."

"That's only partially true," Mattie said. "If you were only searching for werewolves, you would have finished your investigation by now. Clearly, I transformed before your eyes. Furthermore, you wouldn't have snuck out of the city in the dead of night, like thieves. What were you running from?"

Luthor bit his lip as he stared at the redhead. "The same thing you have been, unless I'm mistaken."

Mattie turned toward him and smiled. "Then you now realize the threat Gideon Dosett poses?"

"Far more than I believe even you do."

Mattie stared at him intently, as though attempting to decode his cryptic last statement.

Luthor quickly changed the subject. "You said inside that you thought I was a threat."

"I said we were deciding how much of a threat you were," she corrected.

"But I am right in assuming that you believe me to be a threat?"

Mattie's gaze narrowed as she continued staring at him. "We had to undress you to warm you and treat your frostbite. I saw the marks on your body."

Luthor paled. "You'd do well to forget what you saw. Whatever you think it was, you're sadly mistaken."

"I know what you are," she continued.

Luthor clenched his teeth and walked toward her. He grabbed her by her arm and pulled her in close. One of the tribesmen nearby clenched his spear and stepped forward threateningly. Mattie raised her hand and shook her head, letting him know she wasn't in trouble.

"You know nothing about me," Luthor said.

"You're a wizard," Mattie said, not intimidated by the short man. "Those are runes, aren't they?"

The color returned to Luthor's face in a bright crimson, and he let her go.

Mattie jutted a thumb toward the tent in which Simon slept. "Does he know?"

"No!" Luthor said brusquely. "No, he doesn't, nor will he."

"Who are you? And I don't mean what's your name and I certainly don't mean the farce about how you're an apothecary. Who are you really?"

Luthor took off his glasses and wiped their lenses with the lapel of his fur-lined parka. He chewed on his bottom lip as he worked, as much to delay the inevitable as to actually clean his glasses. He wondered how much to actually reveal to her before quickly realizing that he had little option. He was her prisoner, and they needed her help.

"I work for a shadow organization known as the Cabal of Mages," he said finally, albeit hesitantly.

Mattie shook her head. "I've never heard of them."

Luthor laughed nervously. "They wouldn't be a very good shadow organization if you had. Do you know of the Rift and the threat it poses to our kingdom?"

Mattie shrugged but continued watching Luthor cautiously. "I've heard the stories. It's a passage to a world of magic. Vile monsters have escaped from its depths."

"You're right, but only partially so."

Luthor sat down on a log near the central campfire. He patted the spot beside him, inviting Mattie to sit. She looked at him for a moment before deciding he wasn't a threat. Sitting down, she stared at the obviously strained man. Luthor looked around them and noticed the wary eyes of a number of guards standing nearby, ready to strike at the apothecary.

Luthor replaced his glasses on his face. He then held up his hands, balling them into fists while keeping them a foot apart. "The Rift is a vestibule between our world and a world of magic, but it's not the world of magic you presume. This realm of magic isn't a fantasy world full of mischievous gnomes, prancing elves, merry dwarves, and benevolent human kingdoms. The realm of magic is a place of nightmares, full of vile monsters."

"Like werewolves?" Mattie asked sarcastically.

Luthor frowned. "Yes, but not like you and your ilk. The werewolves on the other side of the Rift are savage beasts who rip men limb from limb and devour their flesh. No offense to your kind, but they're exactly what we thought you were when the Inquisitors received the governor's report."

"I'm happy to disappoint."

He took a deep breath before continuing, smashing his fists together until his fingers overlapped. "When our worlds smashed together and the Rift tore the Kingdom of Khovus asunder, it opened wide a gateway to the realm of magic. This realm is full of deadly creatures, like the werewolves we assumed you and your kin to be. Yet none of the creatures are nearly as dangerous as the demons that rule that land."

He stared at Mattie with an intensity that startled her.

"The five demon lords ruled that land for a millennium with ruthlessness. If you imagine the creatures that have escaped the Rift, think then about the type of beasts that would have to exist to rule over them as unchallenged kings."

Mattie swallowed hard. "Is it these demons that you seek?"

Luthor dropped his hands to his side and nodded. "It's the demons that the Cabal was created to hunt. Despite what you might think about those of us who wield magic, not all of us seek the destruction of our world. Many of us are simply victims of a spreading infection of magic, much like you and your tribesmen. The Cabal, however, knows the threat these demons pose. The Rift has granted them a chance to expand their kingdom into our world."

"That's why you became an assistant to an Inquisitor, isn't it?" she asked knowingly.

Luthor smiled. "Can you think of a better way to investigate reports of magical activity, to hunt the very demon's presence that the Cabal was created to uncover? Even if Simon is not the Inquisitor assigned to such a report, I am in a position to overhear the constant reports spread between the Inquisitors within their keep."

"You say that the Cabal—that you—hunt these demons. Then they're already here?" she asked.

"Closer that you would believe."

"You mean here?" she said as she pointed to the ground at her feet, though to her credit, she didn't sound nearly as surprised as Luthor would have believed. "There's one of the demons in Haversham, isn't there?"

Luthor nodded. "I didn't arrive with any suspicions that there would be, but I was quickly surprised by his presence." He ran a hand along his chest. "These runes on my body are protective wards, meant to alert me to the presence of dark magic. There has been one man's presence in which the runes constantly reacted."

"Gideon Dosett," she surmised.

"Very good. He is, by definition, a silver-tongued devil, with the ability to sway men's minds with his spoken word. Yes, I was alerted to Mr. Dosett's use of dark magic almost immediately."

Mattie furrowed her brow. "Then why not destroy him at once?"

"For a multitude of reasons. First and foremost, I can't reveal myself without putting myself in harm's way and exposing the Cabal. I care greatly for Simon, and he's perhaps the most liberal of all the Inquisitor's of whom I've encountered. Even so, Simon is beholden to them. I wouldn't want to put him in that position unless absolutely unavoidable. Secondly, I had no way of knowing if Gideon was merely a wizard or a demon. While I would have stopped him had he been a mere dark wizard, the means to handle a wizard are far different than the techniques for handling a demon."

"But you're convinced now?" she asked.

Luthor shivered. "I've seen his true form, as has Simon. There is no doubt in my mind that Gideon Dosett is a disguise, covering one of the demon lords straight from the Rift."

They sat in silence as Luthor's gaze fell on the blazing bonfire in front of them. His eyes reflected the dancing flames as he stared off into the distance.

"Does the Cabal know?" she asked finally. "Will they send someone to stop him?"

Luthor's gaze didn't leave the flames. "They know. Though I was interrupted in my last conversation with them, they were alerted to the demon's presence. And they won't send anyone else. They've already sent one of their best."

He looked over, and Mattie was stunned to realize he was talking about himself. “You really are full of surprises, Luthor. So the Inquisitors know nothing of the Cabal?”

Luthor laughed sadly. “Our goals may be more aligned than the Inquisitors realize, but they wouldn’t hesitate to destroy my order if they knew we existed.”

Before Mattie could respond, one of the tribesmen ran up to the pair. “Your friend is awake.”

CHAPTER Twenty-four

SIMON WAS STILL UNDER HIS BLANKET WHEN LUTHOR and Mattie arrived, though his eyes were open and he was clearly alert. His gaze of bewilderment turned to joy as his companion entered the domed structure.

"Luthor," Simon croaked through a dry throat.

"Can we get him some water?" Luthor asked Mattie.

"Of course," she replied before slipping back outside.

Luthor walked over to his friend and sat heavily on the pile of furs beside him. Simon slipped his hand free of the blanket and grasped Luthor's, squeezing it tightly. He immediately winced and withdrew his hand, glaring at the offending limb as though it had caused him great personal harm. Which, in truth, it had.

"How are you feeling?" the apothecary asked.

Simon coughed to clear the phlegm from his throat. "I feel as though all my extremities have been passed through a meat grinder and only loosely reformed into their previous shape."

Luthor glanced at the Inquisitor's exposed hand. Though the skin didn't appear darkened with frostbite, small blisters covered most of his fingers near the fingernails. In contrast to Luthor's hands, which while red had healed quickly, Simon's still appeared painful.

"They'll heal in time, sir. I'm just glad you're alive."

"You as well," Simon replied as he slipped his hand beneath the blanket.

Mattie pulled the tent flap aside and stepped into the room. Simon glanced past Luthor and caught sight of the redhead as she brought him a leather water skin.

"You," Simon remarked.

"Are you surprised to see me, Inquisitor?" Mattie asked as she knelt beside him.

"Pleasantly so," he replied, taking the water skin from her and drinking deeply. He rolled to his side, spewing water and coughing violently.

"What was in the skin?" Luthor asked as he reached for the water skin.

Simon quickly pulled it away, clutching it to his chest. As his coughs subsided, he glanced at his companion.

"The water is fine," Simon explained. "It's my own fault for attempting to drink too quickly. I was overzealous."

Luthor sighed with relief and sat back on the furs.

Simon shifted his gaze to Mattie. "You must think me a walking contradiction. What Inquisitor actively seeks a werewolf for help?"

Mattie smiled. "The same type of Inquisitor that takes a chance on a werewolf at a formal ball. The type of Inquisitor who finds the decency within himself to believe a werewolf he barely knows, rather than assuming her silver tongued."

"I was right to trust in you," Simon said flatly. "Gideon Dosett is indeed a dangerous man."

"More than a man, if Luthor is to be believed," Mattie replied.

Simon exchanged a glance with the apothecary before continuing. "I assume Mr. Strong has told you what we discovered?"

"That Mr. Dosett is a demon, yes, which explains many of our problems with the man."

"Yes, I intended to ask you about that," the Inquisitor said. He forced himself up on an elbow so that he was nearly eye level with Mattie. "We discovered that your chieftains sold nearly all your lands to Mr. Dosett a few months ago."

Mattie nodded and joined Luthor on his fur-lined bed. "Shortly after Gideon arrived at Haversham, he requested a meeting with the tribal leaders. He offered them work with wages that were hard to refuse."

"If a deal seems too good to be true," Luthor said, leaving the end of the quote unfinished.

"And it was," Mattie replied. "Hindsight being what it is, I can now say that Gideon used his demonic abilities to sway their minds. They willingly sold our lands for a mere pittance."

Luthor furrowed his brow. "If your chieftains were under his spell, what happened to them?"

Mattie raised her chin defiantly. "We killed them. We tried to free them from his hold but to no avail. In the end, we knew they would have preferred death over a life of servitude, especially knowing that Gideon Dosett was dangerous enough without a personal werewolf army."

Simon nodded. "As I surmised. As a result, you've declared a personal war on the man and his businesses?"

"Our new chieftains have devoted their lives to destroying that which Gideon builds with his blood money, constructing drilling operations on our stolen lands."

"Then you're not a chieftain?" Simon asked.

Mattie laughed heartily. "Me? No. I was born to immigrants who came to Haversham looking to establish themselves in a nubile town. They both died during an outing beyond the city walls when an ice shelf gave way. I survived and was taken in by the tribe. As such, I'm best suited for reconnaissance inside the city, since I lack their naturally tanned skin and dark hair. No, our chieftain is a stern woman who you will meet in due time."

"A woman?" Simon remarked, surprised.

"Is there a problem with that?" Mattie quickly asked defensively.

Simon raised his hands painfully. "No, none at all. It just caught me off guard."

Luthor cleared his throat, slicing through the intensity that had suddenly appeared. "Forgive me for prying, but how is it that you became werewolves in the first place? Clearly you weren't born to it, were you?"

"You mean since I was born of immigrant parents but still became a werewolf?"

"It's not… well, that is to say, it's not contagious, is it?" Luthor asked, acutely aware of the healed scars on his forearm.

"Nothing so vile," she replied.

Luthor exhaled with relief.

"It happened quite unexpectedly, shortly after I came to live with the tribe. Two men argued over a kill and one suddenly grabbed his chest as though struck. As he straightened again, his hand tore away large strips of flesh, revealing the stark white fur beneath. One transformation led to more. In all, nearly half the tribes on the tundra became the werewolves we know today."

"It must have been horrifying," Simon said morosely.

Mattie lowered her gaze. "It was. We're not complicated people, Inquisitor Whitlock. For all of you with your fancy technology, magic is an abomination. It's why you and your order even exist. For those of us who live on the fringe, however, magic is a disease, a plague that leaves us unclean. Magic isn't the abomination here. To those that didn't transform, we were the abomination, to be shunned. The day that I realized I was one of the werewolves, I lost some very close loved ones."

Simon looked at Luthor. "Then we were right. This isn't an invasion from the Rift. Magic has become an airborne contagion."

"Then aren't we all at risk, sir?" Luthor asked.

"I believe the more poignant question is whether or not we're already infected."

Silence fell between the two men. Mattie glanced back and forth inquisitively, unsure of how their conversation would continue.

Simon drank again from the water skin before setting it aside. "We have to notify the crown of our findings. I have to find a way back to the telegraph office with all haste."

"Wait," Mattie interrupted. "You can't send them a telegram. You know now that we're not monsters; at least we're not the type that they fear from the Rift. You may seem understanding, but somehow I doubt that the rest of the Inquisitors will be quite as forgiving. If you contact them, you're condemning us all to death."

"Ms. Hawke, my hands are tied," Simon replied, recalling her surname from their introduction at the ball. "I promise you, however, that I intend to contact them not to warn about you and your ilk, but to warn them about the demon prowling Haversham and to warn them that magic has infiltrated our lands."

Mattie looked alternately crestfallen and defiant. “I want to believe you, but I find it difficult. Even the best of intentions can go awry when you’re dealing with fanatics like the Order of Kinder Pel. I know you believe you’re doing the right thing, but whether or not you leave this camp isn’t up to you or even me. Our chieftain will have to make that decision.”

“Then let me speak to her,” Simon said.

A commotion arose outside the tent, a sound like barking and howling emerging from the otherwise quiet exterior.

Mattie glanced over her shoulder. “It seems like you’ll have your chance sooner than expected. Chieftain Kidnip has returned.”

CHAPTER Twenty-five

MATTIE LED THEM OUT OF THE TENT. WHAT HAD previously been a sparsely populated village was now teeming with life. Warriors roamed between the tents, restocking supplies and sharpening spears. As they noticed Simon and Luthor, they glared at them both with unconcealed hatred.

Despite the obvious anger, Mattie seemed unperturbed by the looks they received. She walked them past the smaller domes toward a larger tent set against the mountainside. The larger dome dwarfed those around it and extra pelts draped its exterior. Guards stood on either side of the grand entrance, their rifles at the ready.

"We're here to see the chieftain," Mattie told the guards.

The two men exchanged looks before they stared at the Inquisitor and his companion. One of the men spit on the ground, as though the mere sight of Simon left a sour taste in his mouth.

"She's expecting you," the other guard replied.

Simon practically anticipated one of them striking him as he passed between the men, but they merely glowered before returning to their posts.

A large fire in its center illuminated the interior of the tent. A haze of smoke filled the top of the dome as it sought escape through the broad hole at its apex. Large furs of unidentifiable animals lined the floor like a carpet, leading toward a wooden dais on which sat a throne made of antlers.

The woman sitting on the throne wore a severe expression, one that made Simon wonder if she ever smiled. Her dark hair was cropped close to her head, and her body was covered with furs similar to the ones he and Luthor wore. Were it not for the fact that Mattie had told them ahead of time that Chieftain Kidnip was a female, he wouldn't have known different.

As they walked around the fire, her dark eyes never left the trio. Mattie stopped at the foot of the dais and nodded to the chieftain. She forewent any bowing or saluting, and Simon wondered if it was even a part of their culture.

"Are these the Inquisitors?" the chieftain asked, her voice as rough as her weatherworn skin.

Mattie nodded as she turned toward the two men. "Inquisitor Whitlock and his associate, Mr. Strong."

Simon felt like he was under a microscope, as Kidnip looked them over with a discerning eye. She paused for a second after examining them before shaking her head and sitting back in her throne.

"You should have left them in the snow to die," she said harshly.

"That's not our way," Mattie retorted. "We don't turn away those in need."

The chieftain leaned forward and bared her teeth. "Then maybe it's time we changed our way."

"If I may," Simon said, stepping forward. "I get the distinct impression that you don't much like me."

Kidnip shifted her ire toward Simon. "Should I? You're an Inquisitor. You exist solely to kill people like us."

"I've also come to ask for your help and to offer you mine."

The chieftain laughed mockingly. "The wolves don't need your help, Inquisitor. March back to Haversham and rejoin your own kind."

Simon placed a foot on the dais and leaned forward, resting his elbow on his knee. "My kind no longer exists in Haversham, thanks in no small part to Gideon Dosett."

The mention of his name drew the reaction for which Simon had hoped. The chieftain's sour expression softened.

Simon continued before granting Kidnip a chance to respond. "We share a common enemy, Chieftain. We should be combining our knowledge and abilities, rather than quibbling amongst ourselves."

Kidnip stared at Simon for a second before leaning back in her throne. "So you're now our benevolent benefactor? Is that what I'm to believe?"

"Believe what you want. We've only come to help."

The chieftain put a finger thoughtfully to her lips. "We've all heard about the way Inquisitors help, Mr. Whitlock. You find things you can't explain, like the werewolves of Haversham, and you slaughter us all. Answer me this, Inquisitor. Let's assume that I accept your help against Gideon Dosett. Let's assume that, as a combined force, we march on Haversham and remove this vile threat. What happens then? Do you personally speak on our behalf to the other Inquisitors? Do you tell them how we are as much victims as we are monsters? Will you guarantee our lives and our continued safety once all this is finished?"

Simon flushed bright red, knowing that he couldn't guarantee any of those things. He had already been battling such questions in his mind since deciding to come to the werewolves for help.

"I thought not," the chieftain said. "You would use us for what we are, and then discard us when you're finished. You're as much a monster as we are."

"There's only one monster here," Luthor replied angrily. "If we don't work together, he'll destroy us all."

The flap was thrown aside, and a pair of fur-clad warriors entered the tent. "The warriors are ready, Chieftain."

Simon noted the large patches of recently healed burns across the man's face and exposed arms. A knot formed in his stomach as the men locked eyes. The warrior's eyes narrowed, and he snarled at Simon.

"It would appear you two know one another," Kidnip remarked.

Simon swallowed hard, remembering the powder horn he shot in the werewolf's hand during the assault on the oil-drilling site. "It would appear that I set him on fire recently."

The snarl became an aggressive growl.

"In my defense, he tried killing me first," Simon said, turning toward the chieftain. "The fact that neither of us succeeded should make us even."

"Silence," the chieftain ordered, her eyes locked on the furious warrior. The man immediately fell silent. "Go tell the others to be prepared to march."

Chieftain Kidnip stood from her throne and retrieved a broad sword from the ground beside her. She strapped it around her waist before stepping from the dais.

"Where are you going?" Simon asked.

"You were correct that Gideon Dosett needs to be eliminated," she said as she took Mattie's arm, leading the redhead toward the front of the tent. "That's exactly what we wolves have been doing. We'll destroy everything that Mr. Dosett dares build on our stolen lands, to include any people who dare to be under his employment. We'll take back everything Gideon has taken from us. More importantly, Inquisitor, we'll do it without you."

Simon hurried after her, chasing both women out of the tent. "Don't be daft, Chieftain. Before we left Haversham, Gideon said he would personally be setting a trap for you. You're going to get slaughtered if you go after him."

"Or worse," Luthor remarked. Mattie turned knowingly toward him with sympathy reflected in her eyes.

"I'm begging you," Simon continued. "Don't do this."

The chieftain stopped before a collection of warriors. Her gaze never left the tribesmen, even as she addressed Simon. "You can revel in your cowardice if you want, but that's not the way of the wolves." She drew her sword and raised it over her head, her voice rising in pitch as she yelled to the warriors. "Wolves aren't cowards. Let Gideon come and we'll tear his throat out with our teeth!"

The warriors howled excitedly. Across the group, men and women stripped away their furs until they stood naked, carrying only the weapons they had in their hands. Luthor averted his eyes even as Simon stared on in fascination. With clawed hands, the warriors reached to their skin and tore away large swaths of flesh, stripping away the skin from their forearms or chests as though it were paper. White fur jutted from the exposed wounds, even as they dripped with bright red blood. Piles of flesh joined the piles of furs at their feet until snow-white werewolves replaced all the once human warriors. Loud barks and howls filled the air as they prepared for battle.

The chieftain turned toward the two men and frowned. "Stay if you want, though your departure would be preferable."

"We should go back to Haversham," Simon said. "Can you get us there?"

Kidnip looked away. "A tribesman will take you by sled. I don't expect I shall see you again."

Simon sighed, thinking about the implications of an entire tribe of werewolves being thralls to the demon. "I most certainly hope not."

The chieftain tore away her skin, growing in stature even as she did so. As she stood upright once more, the werewolf she had become towered over both Simon and Luthor. She raised her sword over her head once more.

"We march on the oil refineries," she yelled, though her voice was far more guttural than it had been before.

The other werewolves howled in response and turned, strapping weapons to bandoliers and belts as they dropped to all fours and sprinted from the village.

Mattie stepped forward to follow, but Luthor grabbed her arm. "You don't have to do this, Mattie. Please stay here. You know what he is, and you know what he's capable of. If he's truly waiting for you, then Kidnip is going to be leading the whole tribe to a slaughter."

Mattie appeared genuinely saddened as she turned toward the apothecary. "The tribe has spoken," she replied morosely. "I have to go. I'm sorry."

She slipped free of Luthor's grasp and bounded down the hill after the retreating werewolves. In mid-stride, she slipped off her fur parka. Luthor turned away from her nakedness and didn't watch as she transformed into the wolf.

Simon placed a hand on the apothecary's shoulder. "Come on, Luthor. We need to devise a new plan."

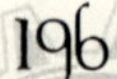

CHAPTER Twenty-six

THE SLED BOUNCED OVER THE SNOW, LEAVING SIMON feeling nauseated once more. He had certainly hoped that their last trip to the refineries would be the last time he would have been strapped into a sled, bouncing merrily amongst the snow dune. He raised a handkerchief to his lips to cover the clammy sweat beading on his upper lip.

"Be honest with me, sir," Luthor said over the howling wind. "How much of our prior plan hinged on the inclusion of the werewolves?"

Simon patted his lip once more before removing the handkerchief. "Damn near all of it, I'm sad to say."

"Then when you said we needed to devise a new plan, you weren't speaking in vague generalities?"

Simon shook his head, though he immediately regretted moving even in the least. "No, I meant quite simply that our previous plan has turned to absolute rubbish."

Luthor turned toward his mentor. "Is it safe to assume that within your massive cranium, you're already formulating a new plan?"

Simon arched an eyebrow but kept his gaze firmly locked on the horizon. "Firstly, my head is not at all abnormally large. Secondly, of course I'm already formulating a new plan."

"Will this be another situation where I'm not privy to your plan until later in the future?"

"Don't be preposterous, Luthor. The plan as it stands is absurdly simple. We're going to send the telegram to the Inquisitors. If the werewolves won't assist us, then we'll rely on those who will."

"Sir, isn't contacting the Inquisitors exactly what Mr. Dosett wants? Isn't bringing more of the Inquisitors here the exact thing we didn't want to do?"

Simon nodded, moving his head as little as possible. "You're absolutely correct, but what choice is left to us? We can't face the demon and his army alone, and we have no one on which to rely left in Haversham. The best we can do is to warn the Inquisitors of the threat so that they might arrive prepared."

Luthor fell silent and returned his gaze to the endless snow ahead. The walls of Haversham were quickly approaching to their right, though their angle of approach was clearly away from the main city gates and toward one of the numerous tunnels that led underground.

The sled slid into the shadow of the tall walls as they slowed. The tribesman pulled on the reins connected to the dogs and yelled something indecipherable. As one, the sled dogs slowed to a trot before coming to a stop. Simon quickly climbed out of his seat and rubbed his lower back. He never thought he would miss the wicker seats of Mr. Parrish's sled until he had to go without on this trek. Everything ached, which only further fueled his queasiness.

They collected their belongings, to include their weapons that had been returned once the tribe had marched toward battle. Simon swung the saber in a graceful arc, feeling glad to have its familiar weight in his hand. He slid the blade into a sheath at his side, where the hilt of the sword pressed against the concealed revolver on his hip. Luthor stuck the tip of his cane in the snow as he adjusted his bowler cap.

Simon bade the sled driver good day as the man turned the dogs and raced back onto the tundra. The man had hardly said a word throughout their trip, which had suited Simon perfectly well.

The two men turned back toward the wall. At the base of the large stones, a dark recess marked the entrance to one of the underground tunnels. Neither man knew if it was the same tunnel from which they'd emerged the few days prior. Leaving hastily and at night had hardly been optimal conditions. Even Simon's sharp mind was cloudy on the exact passages and turns they had taken.

Simon led the way down the steep incline leading into the rocky tunnel. The entrance was dark, though he could see electric lights in the distance as another tunnel bisected the narrow entryway. The entrance was slippery with ice, and they were forced to hold onto the wall as they walked. Simon swore silently to himself, promising that he would purchase shoes with far better soles once they completed their mission in Haversham. Though, he realized, it would be practically a moot point by then. Once he left Haversham, he had no intention of ever returning to the abysmal city.

Beyond the initial entry, the ice disappeared, replaced by the more familiar loose-packed dirt that made the floor of many of the side passages. Though the way directly in front of them was dark, Simon kept his eyes firmly locked on the illumination in the tunnel ahead.

He stopped abruptly as a shadow passed between him and the lights in the distance. The silhouette was large enough to block most of the illumination, though Simon clearly saw the reflection of light off the polished metal blade in the man's hand.

The shadowy guard rushed forward wordlessly, raising his sword high above his head. Simon shoved Luthor aside as he stepped against the wall. The sword passed cleanly between them, and the blade struck hard on the ground in the middle of the tunnel.

Closer, the man's features were more apparent. Though Simon didn't recognize him, his gubernatorial guard uniform was unmistakable.

The guard turned toward Simon and tried to bring his sword to bear, but it struck the wall of the narrow tunnel. Swinging overhead had been simple enough with the tall ceiling but the closeness of the sidewalls made maneuvering difficult.

Simon tried drawing his blade but frowned as the hilt struck the far wall before the sword was fully out of its sheath. He turned in a panic as the guard shifted his position and drew the blade over his head once more.

Before he could swing, Luthor grabbed both the man's arms, pulling them painfully over his head. Simon could see the strain on the man's face as his triceps and shoulders were stretched beyond any reasonable level of comfort. The guard tried to turn and address the new threat, but Simon was far quicker.

He pulled his blade again, knowing that it would still be difficult to fully remove it from its sheath. Instead of drawing the sword as he would have normally, he drove the hilt forward like a club. The pommel struck the guard in the bridge of the nose.

Blood flew from the broken nose, dripping freely down the guard's face. His knees buckled as Luthor kicked him in the back of the leg, dropping the guard to his knees before Simon. Replacing his blade, Simon brought his knee forward, catching the guard under the chin and lifting him from his kneeling position. The man groaned once before falling limply to the ground on his back.

Luthor pulled the man's sword out of his limp hands and tossed it further down the passage. He knelt forward, checking the man's breathing and pulse.

"I presume he'll survive?" Simon asked quietly between hitched breaths.

Luthor nodded. "He'll live, though I don't envy the pain he'll feel in his face when he wakes."

"I think this is what we can expect throughout our infiltration back into the city. Gideon knows we escaped, but he also knows we have nowhere else to go. His minions will be awaiting us at every turn."

Luthor stood and brushed the dirt from his pants. "Then where do we go from here, sir? If Gideon is waiting for us, then we are moving blindly into a hostile city."

Simon nodded in the darkness. "You're right, of course. We'll need to find somewhere to establish a base of operations near the edge of town until we can properly examine the city. He may have most of the town under his thumb, but he can't guard everything all the time, can he?"

Luthor shrugged, unsure if Gideon did have the capability to guard all the major entrances in and out of town.

"We need to find a way to the surface," Simon said, turning toward the lights in the main passage. "Preferably an entrance far away from the estate."

The two men paused at the intersection. Simon peered around the corner and was glad to see the tunnel abandoned in both directions. They both took a deep breath to calm themselves and Simon ran a hand through his hair, pushing it from his face, before replacing his top hat. When they stepped into the passage, they looked once again like the dapper gentlemen they had been upon their arrival in Haversham.

The tunnel wound its way underneath the city wall before they were able to find an ill-used surface stairwell. Dirt and snow accumulated among the spiraling stairs as they climbed, which were to Simon's liking. They emerged in a small, outlying building near the city wall. The tunnel exit showed the same level of disrepair that they had noticed on the stairs themselves.

They stepped onto the street into deep shadows. The sun was setting behind the wall, leaving the nearest roads cast in a premature twilight. A few people walked the streets, though little gave a second glance to the two gentlemen taking a casual evening stroll.

"They don't seem hostile," Luthor remarked while barely moving his lips.

"It would be absurd to think that Mr. Dosett had managed to cast his spell over everyone in the city. Quite unfortunately, it will only take one or two of his thralls to alert him to our presence."

The streets quickly began looking familiar to both men. As they turned a corner, they found themselves in an open marketplace, the same one through which they had passed when paying a visit to misters Orrick and Tambor. Indeed, across the square was the inn at which they had shared a drink.

"Do you think it's safe to enter?" Luthor asked.

"I don't know of another inn within Haversham, so I don't see that we have much of a choice. Regardless, it was where Orrick and Tambor had found sanctuary before becoming thralls, so I would think it the safest option at this point. After all, beggars can't be choosers."

They walked into the tavern, letting the small bell jingle overhead as they entered. A few faces turned toward them, though the expressions were inquisitive at the sight of strangers rather than aggressive. The bartender nodded to the two men before returning to the glasses he was cleaning.

Simon led them both over to the bar. "Excuse me, sir. We're looking for a room for the night."

The bartender set down his glass and threw his stained towel over his shoulder. "We have some available. Just for the night, then?"

Simon nodded and retrieved a gold coin from his pocket. He placed it on the table, to the amazement of the innkeeper.

"Sir, you realize this is far more than the room itself is worth?" the bartender asked.

Simon nodded. "I do, but I'm not merely paying for a room. Discretion is the watchword for today. Do you understand?"

"For this coin, I could understand whatever language you wanted to throw my way."

"Excellent. I appreciate a man with a keen understanding of the finer points of business."

The bartender retrieved a key from underneath the bar and set it on the wooden table in front of him. "Room three, at the top of the stairs. Please let me know if either of you fine gentlemen require anything further."

"Your silence is good enough," Simon replied.

The man made a motion as though placing an imaginary lock over his lips. They turned away and climbed the stairs at the back of the tavern. Mostly oil-burning lamps lit the upstairs and the pungent aroma stung their eyes. The walls above the lanterns were stained black with soot. Simon wrinkled his nose at the sight but continued to the upstairs landing.

Their room was one of only four upstairs, the fifth room being a communal bathroom and water closet. Simon unlocked their door after giving a cursory glance around the upstairs corridor. The room itself was compact and offered few amenities other than a narrow window through which they could see the street below. Simon took his over-the-shoulder bag and set it carefully on the bed. Luthor set his doctor's bag on the room's small writing desk, resting his cane against the chair.

Simon walked to the window and glanced over the city. His view mostly consisted of the street below and the unlit windows of the building across the cobblestone road, though he could catch the faintest of glimpses of the estate between the sloped roofs. The sun was already setting and the long shadows of the wall now stretched over most of the city.

"What are we to do now?" Luthor asked as he tossed his hat onto the bed. "Shall we turn in for the night?"

"No," Simon replied as he leaned against the windowsill. "Our first priority is notifying the Inquisitors. The longer we wait, the more likely they are to send someone to investigate our silence, people who will arrive completely oblivious as to what is really transpiring here."

"Will the telegraph office even be open at this late hour?"

Simon turned around with a broad smile. "Does it truly matter if they are or are not? One way or another, we need to send that telegram."

Luthor picked up his hat from where it had so recently been discarded and placed it back on his head. He grabbed his cane as well, spinning it deftly between his fingers. "Shall we then?"

Simon adjusted the sword at his hip before patting the top of his top hat. "Let's be off."

The bartender looked up as they came back downstairs but true to his word, said nothing at all. They exited the tavern and emerged onto the street as the electric street lamps flickered to life. Their glow pulsed as it intensified, illuminating the street.

Simon led them back through the square, remembering the telegraph office as being only a few blocks away. They walked as though they were hardly out of place taking an evening stroll, though their eyes darted constantly toward every approaching man, woman, and child. Simon loathed the thought of fighting either a woman or child but saw no other alternative, if they were pawns of the demons.

Without incident, they reached the intersection of streets that would lead to the telegraph office. Simon pulled Luthor against the nearest building before peering around the corner. His anxious expression collapsed into a disheartened frown. Six men stood guard at the front of the building. They carried an assortment of makeshift weapons, to include pickaxes and haphazardly constructed clubs.

The other passersby glanced oddly at the unmoving men, clearly put off by the sight of the uncharacteristic guards. Despite the stares, the men said nothing and moved only when shifting their weight.

Luthor stole a glance around the corner as well, furrowing his brow at the sight. "Is that Mr. Tambor?" he remarked, pointing at the heavyset man.

"It is, and Mr. Orrick beside him."

"Then the motley crew is in the service of Mr. Dosett?"

Simon stepped back around the corner, pulling Luthor along. "It would seem so. It appears that Mr. Dosett has anticipated our move. He's a shrewd tactician."

Luthor glanced back around the corner, appraising the guard force. "Could we defeat them in a fight?"

"No doubt," Simon replied, "but we won't. Defeating six men who aren't trained in combat is hardly difficult… if I were allowed to use deadly force. A well-placed blade can easily slip through clumsy defenses. Defeating them while only subduing them, however, is a different argument. I can't guarantee their safety, or our own for that matter, if we only use non-lethal force."

"Then what is our recourse?"

Simon sighed and pointed back the way they had come. "We move on to plan B."

Luthor furrowed his brow. "I thought this was plan B, or potentially even plan C at this point."

Simon frowned at the apothecary. "If you're quite done, I believe we need to have another strategy session back at the inn."

Simon brushed past his friend, not noticing the smirk on Luthor's face.

CHAPTER Twenty-seven

LUTHOR LOOKED OUT THE WINDOW BUT HARDLY acknowledged the soft glow of the streetlamps. His mind was elsewhere.

"I think it's safe to assume that this whole plan has gone tits up," he remarked without turning around. "Gideon will be blocking the zeppelin dock by now, not that there's a scheduled flight for some time. He's blocked the telegraph office, so we can't call for help. I'm sure he's surrounded the estate with a plethora of minions, making himself inaccessible. To top it all off, our own army has turned tail, so to speak, and left us in the cold. Rubbish, this whole speech didn't sound so full of clichés when I was thinking it through."

Simon laughed as he took inventory of the few belongings he removed from his over-the-shoulder bag. Nothing seemed glaringly helpful, mostly articles of clothing and a few notebooks.

"I won't misdirect you, Luthor," Simon said as he neatly folded his clothes and placed them back in the bag, "the situation most certainly appears grim. However, there's always an answer if one looks hard enough."

Luthor turned from the window and walked over to the bed. "What exactly is our answer here, sir?"

Simon looked up from his belongings. "Well, I don't know just yet, do I? I haven't had enough time to look quite hard enough."

Luthor threw up his arms in disgust. He walked over to his doctor's bag and opened it, sifting through the chemicals even though he knew each of them by heart.

"The answer lies with Gideon Dosett," Simon explained. "Destroy him and his spell will be broken."

"And how, pray tell, do we destroy this demon?" Luthor asked sarcastically. "Shall we march up to the gates of the governor's estate and kindly ask him to join us for tea?"

"Sarcasm is very unbecoming of a gentlemen, Luthor. At any rate, you're the expert on mythology and the mystical. What do your books tell you about destroying a demon?"

Luthor frowned, though he knew every possible reference to defeating demons by heart. "They're susceptible to silver, like the werewolves were thought to be. Depending on whether we're dealing with a demon or devil depends on the effectiveness of holy relics like blessed water."

"You believe this to be a demon, though?"

"Firmly, sir," Luthor replied.

Simon shrugged. "Then we'll need access to more silver."

"Silver, I might add, that proved completely ineffective against the werewolves, whose mythology much more strongly supported its use as an effective means of destroying the creatures."

"We won't know until we try," Simon replied with infuriating calm.

"We still don't have a means to reach Gideon, but I know what the answer has to be for what to do next," the apothecary said. "We try our best not to cause grievous injury to those guarding the telegraph office, but one way or another, we send out our request for reinforcements. With the Inquisitors' support, we stand a chance of storming the estate."

Simon shook his head. "I can't justify severely injuring or killing innocent men who are guilty of nothing other than having their mind controlled by a demon."

"You know, sir, I'm starting to think that all these people—Gideon, Mattie, Kidnip—are all correct. You truly are an atrocious Inquisitor. What Inquisitor places the lives of six people over the opportunity to kill a demon?"

Simon turned brusquely toward his friend, his calm quickly replaced by barely contained rage. "Do not mistake my compassion for a lack of dedication to my craft. Unlike you, whom I might add sounds deliriously like a Pellite, spouting your nonsense about the ends justifying the means, I was trained to examine all possible outcomes and pick a course of action that minimizes civilian casualties. Until I am absolutely satisfied that killing or maiming those men is completely necessary, I won't authorize that plan. Do I make myself clear?"

Luthor was stung by Simon's sharp retort but quickly regained his composure. "Abundantly, sir. If it's all the same to you, I think I'll take a walk and let the winter air cool my blood."

"I think that's a brilliant plan."

Luthor angrily pulled on his long coat and retrieved his cane and hat before walking out of the door. His feet echoed loudly on the wooden steps as he strolled downstairs. It wasn't yet obscenely late and the tavern was still half-full of drinking patrons. They barely gave Luthor a glance as he walked out, and the bartender offered only a nod of his head.

As he stepped outside, he realized how frigidly cold the night had become. Though the walls blocked the howling wind, the air was a stagnant cold that settled over him like a wet blanket. He pulled his coat tightly around his torso and turned away from the inn, choosing a direction at random.

The streets were mostly empty, though he knew the catacombs beneath the city would be livelier, out of the chilly night's air. The few people he passed eyed him as warily as he watched them, neither sure of the other's intent. Despite his obvious concerns, everyone passed by him without incident, intent only on returning to their homes.

When he was far enough away from the inn, Luthor glanced over his shoulder to make certain no one was around to hear him. The inn was no longer visible and the streets both in front and behind him were empty.

"I truly wish I could just tell him the truth," he muttered to himself. "It would make life infinitely simpler if I could just tell him that I belong to the Cabal and that he should take my advice on all things demon related. Instead, I'm treated as a second-rate citizen whose advice always seems to be given but never asked for."

His personal monologue made him more frustrated. As he walked,

Luthor wished there was a loose rock or piece of debris he could kick. Though Simon was opposed, it would have made him far happier to release some frustration subduing armed guards at the telegraph office.

After a few more steps, Luthor paused. He didn't know exactly why, but he knew immediately that something was amiss. He turned slowly, examining the nearby buildings and looking up and down the streets, but he saw nothing out of the ordinary. Still, he couldn't shake the feeling that he was being watched.

"Hello?" he said, immediately cursing himself for sounding so juvenile. A killer certainly wouldn't respond to his query.

He took a few more steps but could feel the eyes upon him once more. Luthor stopped and turned around slowly again, but he still saw nothing and no one. He was, for all intents and purposes, alone on the street. Except that he knew that wasn't true at all; he wasn't alone, he just couldn't see his pursuer.

He tightened his grip on his cane, shifting its pommel until his thumb was resting on the button that released the hidden blade. He walked forward slowly, letting his cane clack loudly on the cobblestone street. From within himself, he began channeling his magic, ready to call down an eldritch blast on whoever revealed themselves.

A rattle of a pebble bouncing against the stones of the road sounded behind him. He spun quickly, drawing the sword from his cane in a fluid motion. In the street behind him, a dirt-covered naked woman stood in the middle of the road. Her arms hung limply by her side and curly locks of muddy, red hair concealed her facial features.

Luthor quickly glanced away, while keeping her in view through his periphery. "Madam, you appear to be quite in the buff. Are you in need of help?"

He waited for an answer but heard none. Slowly, he turned his head back toward the naked woman. She stood impassively in the middle of the road, unmoved since her first startling appearance.

"Madam?" he asked again. "Are you hurt? I could contact the constabulary if you are in need of assistance."

The woman slowly raised her head, and her hair parted around her face. Luthor cursed himself for being so stupid, having not recognized Mattie by her locks of red hair alone.

"Mattie? Are you all right?"

He took a step toward her but paused as he heard a low growl rolling down the street.

"Mattie, I don't know what happened, but you seem to be in need. Come back to the inn with me, and we'll get you properly bathed and clothed."

He looked at the blade, the tip of which was still pointed threateningly toward Mattie, and gently lowered the sword. His gesture was met with a more savage growl than the one before.

Though he dreaded admitting the truth, even to himself, Luthor knew what he was facing. Her few movements had seemed stiff and unnatural. She obviously didn't recognize Luthor, though they had spent some involved moments together at her village. Even in the dim glow of the street lamps, he could see her wide, wild eyes staring through him rather than at him.

She was a thrall.

"Mattie, I can help you," he said nervously. He didn't want to hurt her but saw few other options if she attacked. "Come with me and I can break Gideon's spell."

At the mention of his name, Mattie tilted her head back and howled into the still night air. The tips of her fingers spread wide at her side. The fingers elongated and thick bone claws emerged from the tips. Her clawed hands tore her flesh from her chin to her groin. She thrust her bloody claws into the wound and pulled the skin apart, peeling away her dirty flesh in a single animalistic pull.

The werewolf stood in her stead, even as the tattered remains of her former skin drifted lazily to the road. Her lips pulled back as she growled, exposing rows of dangerously pointed teeth.

Luthor raised his sword again but held his other hand aloft, exposing the empty palm. "I don't want to do this. Don't force my hand by coming any closer. If you do, I'm going to have to do something we'll both regret."

Mattie snarled before charging at him, her teeth bared and claws extended, clearly intent on eviscerating the apothecary where he stood.

CHAPTER Twenty-eight

MATTIE CHARGED AT LUTHOR, HER CLAWS EXTENDED and mouth agape, showing long, pointed canines. Luthor raised his sword again, though his hand shook.

"Stop this madness," he yelled in an attempt to be heard over her guttural growling. "I don't want to have to hurt you."

She didn't hesitate in her charge. Froth formed in the corners of her mouth as she closed the distance to her prey.

The tip of Luthor's blade wavered with uncertainty as his mind debated the finer points of harming Mattie in an attempt to preserve his own well-being. Sensing his weakness, she increased her speed, nearly dropping to all fours as she reached Luthor.

A single gunshot rang out, splitting the night air and silencing Mattie's incessant growling. The round tore through her shoulder, spinning her madly from the bullet's momentum. Her feet tangled around one another and she collapsed hard onto the cobblestones, sliding to a halt at Luthor's feet. The werewolf looked up at him confusedly as bright red blood began to stain the fur on her left shoulder. Luthor pointed his blade at her but looked as equally confused.

"For God's sake, Luthor," Simon reprimanded as he hurried down the street toward the pair. "Knock her unconscious before she gets her bearings and actually decides to devour you."

Luthor looked at his mentor, but his thoughts were disconnected from his actions. He was struggling to piece together all that had transpired during his short evening walk.

Simon reached his side and pushed Luthor out of the way just as Mattie placed a fur-covered hand on the ground and attempted to stand. Simon reared back and lashed out with his booted foot. The toe of his shoe connected solidly with the werewolf's temple. Mattie's head rocked to the side and her eyes fluttered backward as she slumped to the ground.

As she slipped into unconsciousness, the concentration necessary to maintain her transformation failed. The fur began to slough off her in droves, spilling into the street around her like gelatin. It lost its consistency shortly thereafter and the stones around her once again naked body became slick with viscous filth.

Luthor's mind finally came to terms with the situation as he looked down on her unconscious body. An angry purple welt was already forming against her temple, and blood still seeped from the bullet wound in the delicate skin of her shoulder.

"What the bloody hell did you do?" he demanded as he knelt down beside her. "This is Mattie. You shot her, not to mention kicking her in the head."

Simon shook his head reproachfully. "My good man, I don't care if she was the Queen of Khovus, she was trying to eat you. I did what was necessary."

Simon's gaze trailed past the apothecary to the naked redhead sprawled across the cold street. He quickly turned his head away and coughed politely. "It does appear that she's quite naked."

Luthor was already removing his long coat, which he draped over her body. Lifting her gently, he wrapped the jacket fully around her to try to stave off the cold.

"Will you quit being so damnably proper and help me lift her?" Luthor demanded. "We have to get her back to the inn."

"We're not taking a savage monster intent on our destruction back to our living quarters."

Luthor cradled her in his arms but glared sternly at his mentor. "Yes, sir, we are. I can create another concoction like the one I used on you to break the demon's hold. I cannot, however, do much of anything worthwhile so long as she is lying limply on the cobblestones."

Simon bent down and grabbed her legs gingerly, though he appeared squeamish at the touch of her soft skin.

"Were you not the one who was staring blatantly as the entire tribe transformed earlier?" Luthor chided.

Simon cleared his throat. "I was, but that was merely an investigation for scientific purposes. It's something quite different when I know the subject personally."

Together, they lifted her and began walking briskly back toward the inn. Luthor's shorter legs had trouble keeping up with Simon's long strides, and he moved in constant fear of dropping Mattie's shoulders. As he shifted his grip, he felt her squirm uncomfortably as he pressed against her wound.

"I don't have a very good grip, sir," Luthor warned.

"Then find a good one because I won't let you drop our patient before we get a chance to treat her properly."

Luthor flushed angrily. "She's only our patient because you shot and kicked her."

They both glanced toward a storefront and noticed an elderly woman watching the two men confusedly. Simon released Mattie's legs with one hand and tipped his hat to her before they hurried past.

"We're here," Simon said as he pushed open the tavern's front door. The bell above the door chimed as they entered, and the few patrons within the tavern looked startled by their appearance.

They paused just inside the door as the entire room held their collective breathes. Simon glanced from face to face as he tried to judge their obviously worrisome expressions. Near the back of the room, a man pushed away from the table, his chair scraping on the wooden floor.

Simon stooped over and gently rested Mattie's legs on the ground. He stood again with both hands splayed before him disarmingly. "Gentlemen, there is nothing for which to be alarmed. I am a trained doctor and this woman is in need of care."

"That's not what it looks like to me," the burly worker said as he stepped around his table. "Looks to me like you've got a young poppet and are planning some immoral things between the both of you."

"I've never, sir!" Simon replied.

He wanted to tell the man that he was a Royal Inquisitor, which would have been enough of an excuse for them to continue, but he was hesitant to reveal their identities. If word were to spread of the whereabouts of the Inquisitor, Gideon would send his hordes after them both this very night.

"This woman is in my charge as a physician," he continued. "She's been shot and assaulted, and I intend to treat her injuries."

The stocky man stopped before Simon and scowled. He was quite a bit taller than the Inquisitor was and had a significant weight advantage, most of which was corded muscle from working in the nearby mines.

"I think you ought to leave her with us, and we'll take her to a proper doctor," the man said matter-of-factly.

Simon gritted his teeth together, knowing they didn't have the time to deal with such a Neanderthal. "I told you, sir, that I am a doctor and this woman is in need of my attention."

The man poked Simon in the chest. "And I'm telling you that this woman isn't going anywhere with you."

Simon's hand moved faster than Luthor could follow, grasping the burly man's finger and twisting it painfully backward. The bone snapped as Simon twisted it awkwardly to the side. The miner screamed in both pain and surprise, cupping his healthy hand to his chest.

Taking full advantage of the opening provided, Simon kicked outward, driving his hardened shin into the man's groin. The yell of surprise was immediately silenced, replaced instead by a wet heaving as the man doubled over. Simon grabbed a handful of the man's hair and drove his knee into the man's face.

The miner was driven upright by the strike and stood unsteadily on his feet a brief moment longer. Simon reached out and pushed him hard in the chest, sending the man tumbling to the ground like a felled tree.

Simon smoothed away the sweat above his moustache and turned his attention back to the room. "As I was saying before being quite rudely interrupted, I am a doctor and now there are two people in need of my attention. Will there be any others?"

The rest of the tavern returned their attention to their respective drinks, refusing to make eye contact with either Simon or Luthor. Satisfied, Simon bent down and collected Mattie's legs before lifting them again. As they walked past the bar, he retrieved a second gold coin and placed it in front of the bartender. The bartender's eyes widened before he once again mimicked placing an imaginary lock over his lips.

Through much struggling, they maneuvered Mattie's limp form up the stairwell and to their room. They placed her gently on the bed, and Luthor replaced his bloodstained coat with the bed's sheet, pulling it up over her exposed breasts while leaving the gunshot wound visible.

"We have to stop the bleeding," he said, turning toward Simon.

"Nonsense," Simon replied. "You need to brew your potion to break Gideon's spell."

Luthor placed his hands on his hips. "She'll bleed to death if I don't treat her injuries."

"Nothing personal, but I'm not overly concerned about her physical well-being at the moment. I'm far more concerned with your physical well-being. Bleeding or not, if she comes around while you're treating her wounds, nothing will stop her from reverting to her previous murderous intent which, in case I need to remind you, was trying to eat your face."

Luthor frowned but knew the Inquisitor was right.

"Now that you've evidently been swayed to my side of the argument," Simon said, "what can I get you in preparation?"

Luthor opened his mouth to tell his mentor that everything he needed was in his doctor's bag but quickly realized that he couldn't possibly create his brew with Simon watching. The mystical components alone would reveal far too much of Luthor's abilities.

"Scotch," Luthor blurted.

"Come again?"

"Scotch, or whiskey, or bourbon," Luthor continued. "Anything with a high alcohol content that can mask the foul taste of the concoction."

Simon arched an eyebrow. "You need me to go down to the bar and retrieve alcohol?"

"If you please. I'll leave the specifics of the type to your discerning palette."

The Inquisitor shrugged. "You are the apothecary and know your craft better than anyone else. Do you require anything else while I'm there? Perhaps some assorted nuts to go with your assortment of booze?"

"A towel would be nice. In fact, anything you can find to help stem the flow of blood would be much appreciated, though I don't have to tell you such frivolities, since you are the doctor."

Simon could sense the gentle ribbing and turned toward the door.

"I'll be back momentarily."

As the door clicked gently closed behind him, Luthor hurried to his bag and began pulling vials from its interior haphazardly. The definitive measurements he had used with Simon's brew were disregarded completely as he rushed through the chemical amalgamation. The colors swirled madly and for the briefest of moments, he feared the glass in his hand would explode from poorly measured elements, but the liquid eventually settled. As quickly as he would allow himself, he added the plant and watched with both surprise and satisfaction when it ignited in a vibrant blue flame, as he had intended.

From the hallway beyond, Luthor could hear Simon's booted feet climbing the stairwell once more. Sweating profusely as much from stress as from exertion, he lifted Mattie's head and gently parted her lips. He poured a small amount of the brew into her mouth, massaging her throat and forcing her to swallow. He repeated the action twice more, ensuring enough of the potion was in her body to counteract the demon's magic.

As he lowered her head back to the pillow, his hand hovered above the gunshot wound. The bullet had passed cleanly through her shoulder, which meant she would require little in the way of surgery. A blinding white light emerged from beneath his palm, glowing so brilliantly that it was no longer possible to see her wound. Mattie stirred uncomfortably from the intensity of his healing magic but remained asleep.

As the door opened and Simon stepped into the room, Luthor hastily removed his hand and the bright light faded. Where the gunshot wound had moments before been weeping blood in small rivulets, the blood had clotted and the injury was on the mend.

"The bartender was very forthcoming with the alcohol selection," Simon remarked as he closed the door behind him. "He delivered a remarkable twenty-five-year single malt scotch, which I think might be slightly overzealous for something as simple as a healing draught."

Luthor stood, his forehead soaked with sweat and his mop of hair matted to his skin. "Then I'm pleased to announce that you and I can share the scotch between us, rather than waste it on something as nonsensical as a patient. I was able to complete the brew while you were downstairs."

Simon frowned. "That's fairly remarkable. I guess I should set this aside then until I'm able to provide the proper attention to her wounds."

"Absolutely," Luthor said as he stepped away from the bed. "Though

I was able to stop the bleeding as well."

Simon furrowed his brow as he stepped past the apothecary and sat on the edge of the bed. He leaned forward, examining the bullet wound on her shoulder.

"This is remarkable," he said. "The wound has already begun to scab. I doubt I'll need to do anything in her treatment except for monitoring the wound for signs of infection."

Simon turned toward Luthor. "You say you were able to stop the bleeding?"

Luthor picked up the towel Simon had brought with him from the tavern downstairs and blotted the sweat from his forehead. "I might have overstated my role in her healing process. I did little other than to wipe away the pooling blood."

Simon turned his attention back to the wound. "This is a remarkable rate of healing. Do you think that this is a direct indication of the werewolf's physiology, that they have a rapid rate of healing? I noticed the burned werewolf in their village had recovered remarkably since I set him ablaze at the drill site. Perhaps it's a side effect of an elevated metabolism necessary to maintain transformations."

"It certainly seems plausible," Luthor remarked.

As Simon began musing about the multitude of theories, Luthor collapsed into the chair at the writing desk and sighed with a mixture of relief and exhaustion.

CHAPTER Twenty-nine

SIMON SAT IN THE CHAIR WITH HIS FEET PROPPED UP on the edge of the bed. His top hat was pulled over his eyes, and he snored faintly with every exhalation. Luthor looked disapprovingly at the Inquisitor but felt the bone weariness as well. He would have much preferred to sleep but refused to rest until he was sure Mattie would recover from her injuries. Much like Luthor and Simon when they had been rescued from the snow, Mattie had slept solidly through the night and well into the next morning.

Luthor lowered his head to his arm and felt the weight of his exhaustion settling over him. He should have slept after expending so much magic but had opted to stay by her bedside. In hindsight, knowing how thoroughly and deeply she slept while recovering, he could have rested.

He was nearly asleep when he heard the bed sheets rustling. He lifted his head as Mattie moaned softly, a sound more akin to awakening rather than pain. She lifted her arms above her head to stretch and her upper torso slid free of the sheets. Luthor blushed at the sight and hastily grabbed the sheets, pulling them up to cover her.

Mattie's eyes opened at the sudden movement, and she screamed as she realized she was exposed and that strange men were sitting by her bedside.

The scream startled Simon, whose feet flew from the bed. His backward momentum toppled the chair, and he collapsed unceremoniously into the corner of the room.

"Mattie, relax," Luthor said as he released the sheets. "It's us, Inquisitor Whitlock and me. You're safe, just calm yourself."

"Yes, do calm yourself," Simon remarked grumpily as he untangled himself from the fallen chair.

She pulled the sheet up to her chin and glanced back and forth between the two men. Though recognition was evident in her expression, she was still clearly wary of the situation.

"Where am I?" she asked nervously.

"In our room," Luthor replied, "though not for any reason that would be ungentlemanly. You were hurt, and we treated your wounds."

Mattie furrowed her brow and lifted the sheet slightly. She could see the puckered scab from the gunshot wound on her shoulder and still felt the throbbing in her head. "What happened to me?"

"You were shot," Simon replied matter-of-factly.

"And kicked," Luthor added, staring at the Inquisitor.

"And kicked," Simon conceded.

"I don't…" She grasped the side of her head and shook it slightly. "I don't quite recall what happened. Everything seems to be a blur."

Luthor retrieved the rest of his potion from her bedside and offered her the drink. "Take a sip of this. It will help with the pain and confusion."

Mattie took the glass hesitantly and sniffed the brew. Her nose wrinkled as the scent of strong alcohol reached her. "I have no doubt this will help with the pain, but I doubt it will do much but further cloud my mind."

Luthor smiled. "It's a compound of my own design. The alcohol merely masks the more pungent of flavors."

She looked at him hesitantly before raising the glass to her lips. Taking a long draw from the glass, she finished half of the remaining liquid. Simon nodded appreciatively, knowing the alcohol Luthor added to the glass once the Inquisitor returned from the bar would have been so potent that few people would do more than sip the drink. He respected her constitution.

She shook her head and blinked away the burning sensation that settled in her chest. “Thank you. This is exactly what I needed.”

“What are you doing back in Haversham?” Simon asked abruptly.

Luthor shook his head. “Give her a moment to wake up, recover, or both before we start berating her with questions.”

“No,” Mattie said, “it’s fine. I’d rather find those very same answers myself.”

Simon righted his chair and moved it beside the bed before sitting once more. “What happened after your pack left the village?”

Mattie narrowed her eyes as she concentrated. Simon knew the feeling all too well, as she slowly pulled aside the veil covering her memories. They would come in time, he knew, but for now, she would instead suffer through bouts of confusion.

“We…” she began, before pausing and pinching the bridge of her nose. As she began again, her words were slow and deliberate as she struggled to recall the memory. “We went to the refinery, intent on destroying the structure this time rather than merely damaging it like we had done before. Only it was a trap.”

Her eyes widened as the memory became clearer. “It was a trap, just like you had warned. It wasn’t just Gideon’s men waiting for us; it was Gideon himself. The sight of him sent us into a frenzy. We knew that we now had the chance to end this war between our people once and for all.”

Her voice trailed off and Simon frowned, already guessing what occurred. “What happened then, Mattie?”

She shook her head as though the memory itself didn’t make sense. “He spoke to us. Nothing more, merely told us to stop and that he wasn’t our enemy.” She flinched at the thought, as though it caused her physical pain. “His words pierced us far worse than had we been stabbed. One moment, I wanted nothing more than to kill the man and the next… the next I stopped, just as he asked.”

“He’s a demon,” Luthor said. “We warned you of his power before you left, warned you that you were rushing headlong into a trap. His words are like venom to the mind, infiltrating your every thought.”

“His words are fingers that massage their way into your mind,” Simon added, having experienced the effects first hand. “No matter how physically or mentally strong you may be, your mind is far more susceptible to attack than you would believe. Trust me.”

"How did you arrive in Haversham?" Luthor asked.

"I don't recall," Mattie replied. "The last thing I remember was Gideon's orders to transform, and then I woke up here. How did I get shot?"

"That's neither here nor there," Simon hastily said. "What matters is that you're cured of Gideon's hold over you."

"Until I see him again," she remarked. "What's to stop him from enslaving me once more?"

"My concoction," Luthor explained proudly. "It not only severs his connection to your mind, it protects you from being enthralled once again. Once you've been treated, you're for all intents and purposes cured of the demonic power."

Mattie started to sit up but quickly paused as she recalled her nakedness beneath the sheet. "Then we need to find the others with all haste and cure them as well. And you need to find me clothes. In fact, let's start with the second of those requests."

Simon and Luthor exchanged glances. "We were able to procure some clothing for you, though I'm not entirely convinced you'll approve."

Simon stood and walked toward the closet, pulling the doors aside. From within, he retrieved an off-the-shoulder blouse, long skirt, and leather bodice. He held the articles in one hand while collecting knee-high leather boots with the other. He turned toward her and held them aloft for her to examine.

Mattie immediately frowned, but motioned for him to bring the clothing closer. The Inquisitor returned to his seat and set them down beside her on the bed. She sat upright and sorted through the articles with one hand while keeping the sheet pressed against her body with the other.

"Neither of you have ever had the pleasure of dressing a woman before, have you?"

Simon flushed, and Luthor frowned. "Simon has watched many a woman undress at the burlesque house, if that counts for anything at all."

Mattie sighed. "These will have to do."

She looked at both men, who sat unmoving in their respective seats.

"Perhaps I made myself unclear a moment ago," she continued more deliberately. "I need a bath and will be dressing now and since I am starting from a state of complete undress, neither of you will be present for this process."

"Of course," Simon said, climbing quickly to his feet.

"That makes perfect sense," Luthor added as he slid off the bed.

Both men walked to the door and nodded politely to the woman. "We'll be just outside if you need us."

They closed the door behind them as she stood to dress. With nothing else to do while they waited, they stepped over to the banister that overlooked the stairwell into the tavern below.

"She's looking well," Simon remarked.

Luthor nodded. "Yes, she looks rather exquisite. You'd hardly known you shot her."

"Come off it, Luthor."

"Or kicked her in the head, for that matter," Luthor chided.

"You're truly not going to let this go, are you?"

"So long as I have breath in my lungs and the ability to privately ridicule you, I will never let things like this go. These moments are the only thing that reminds me that you're capable of fallacies and, therefore, still a human and not merely an Inquisitor automaton."

They stood in relative silence, listening to the sound of chairs being moved aside and plates of lunch being served in the tavern below. They had wiped away much of the dirt from her face and the mud from her hair while she slept, but neither man felt brave enough to clean the rest of her body while she was unconscious. Her own level of cleaning, they realized, could take some time.

The door behind them eventually opened, and they both turned. Mattie stood in the doorway, looking far better in their amalgamation of clothing than either man would have presumed. The off-the-shoulder blouse exposed the healing gunshot wound, but both men agreed it was a good thing to allow it to heal without the irritation of fabric over it. Her curls of red hair, now cleaned and brushed, flowed in ringlets over her shoulders.

"Do I look acceptable?" she asked.

"Fantastic," Luthor remarked before immediately blushing. "What I meant to say is that you look well, all things considered."

"Thank you, Mr. Strong. So tell me, Inquisitor, what do we do next?"

"We have much to discuss," he replied, "but I would feel much safer discussing such things in our room, if it's all the same."

Simon glanced over the railing once more before ushering the group back inside. Once in, he closed and locked the door behind him.

CHAPTER Thirty

"NOW, MS. HAWKE, I NEED YOU TO CONCENTRATE AND try to recall a memory for me," Simon said. "If you are here in Haversham, is it safe to assume the rest of your tribe is here as well?"

Mattie sat down on the edge of the bed and shook her head. "I honestly don't know."

Simon knelt in front of her and took both her hands in his. "I know this is difficult. I've been in very similar circumstances recently. Right now, however, I need you to break through whatever fog remains in your mind and search for those memories."

She nodded. "I'll try."

Mattie closed her eyes. Her eyelids fluttered, and her brow creased with concentration. Simon flinched as she squeezed his hands tightly, as though battling through mental anguish.

"Yes," she said softly. "Yes, I remember. He loaded us like cattle onto the back of a trailer and brought us back to the city. We were patrolling the streets, looking for the two of you." Her eyes flew open. "They're here, in Haversham. That means we can find them and free them as well, correct?"

Luthor crossed his arms over his chest and leaned against the wall. “We can, but it won’t be quite as easy as freeing you.”

She let go of Simon’s hands and looked toward the apothecary. “I don’t understand. Why wouldn’t it be as easy?”

Luthor shrugged. “Because we’re not dealing with a single demon-enthralled individual; we’re dealing with a large, hostile group. I seriously doubt we’ll be able to subdue so large a group and convince them to drink the concoction. I’m sorry, Mattie, but I just don’t know how to free them without addressing them individually and, forgive me, but your pack mentality doesn’t lend itself toward finding too many of them alone.”

“I was alone,” Mattie corrected.

“Indeed,” Simon interrupted, “but I believe that’s a side effect of your personality rather than a fluke. When you’re under Gideon’s servitude, who you are isn’t overwritten by the demon’s power. He manipulates parts of your personality, bending the whole to his will. You were by yourself because, dare I say it, you wanted to catch us alone, rather than as part of the pack?”

Mattie glanced toward Luthor, who arched his eyebrows inquisitively.

“There has to be a solution,” she begged. “We can’t leave them as his slaves.”

“I couldn’t agree more,” Luthor said, “but I just don’t know another solution.”

“There’s always another solution, my good man,” Simon remarked with a knowing smile.

“What are you getting at, sir?”

Simon stood from his kneeling position before Mattie and walked over to his chair before sitting again. “The werewolves are here in Haversham, which means that our original plan B is no longer a lost cause.”

“It was plan C, if it’s all the same,” Luthor replied. “Though need I remind you that this whole discussion is still a moot argument? The werewolves may be here in town, but they’re hardly our friends. Truth be told, they weren’t our friends before falling under Gideon’s sway. Now instead of merely distrusting and disliking us, they’re actively trying to kill us.”

“Semantics,” Simon said dismissively with a wave of his hand. “They will help us if we can free them.”

"Which, bringing the argument full circle, is impossible. We lack the time and abilities necessary to subdue and convert them one at a time."

Mattie politely raised her hand, interrupting the growing back and forth between the two men.

"Yes, Mattie?" Simon asked.

"Gideon Dosett converted us as a group; the whole pack in a single metaphorical wave of his hand. Can't we do the same to release them from his spell? Perhaps we could spray them with the liquid as though from a hose?"

Simon shook his head. "If my understanding of Luthor's brew is correct, and feel free to correct me if I'm not, the concoction has to be absorbed within the body. A spray would soak the skin but hardly enough would get into their mouths or absorbed through the mucus membranes of the eyes and nose. It would be an exercise in futility."

Luthor shrugged apologetically. "He's quite right, unfortunately. It has to be fully absorbed within the body. Ingestion seems to be the most effective technique."

Simon sat upright, his face breaking into a broad smile. "It's the most effective technique we've considered to date, and that's only because we've had no need for a more effective delivery system."

Luthor pushed away from the wall and walked toward the bed. "I know that look all too well, sir. What are you getting at?"

"The chemicals have to be properly absorbed in the body, correct?"

Luthor nodded. "They do."

"Is fluid intake truly the most effective way to introduce a chemical into the blood stream?"

Luthor frowned. "Sir, you know I hate when you ask questions the answers to which you already know. Please do get to the point."

"My point, dear chap, is that there is a far more effective way to introduce foreign chemicals into the body: through a gas. Inhaled through the mouth and nostrils, a gas is absorbed directly into the membranes of both the nose and lungs, transmitting quickly and efficiently directly into the blood stream. In this case, carried rapidly to the brain to… well, to do whatever it is your strange brew does when it destroys Gideon's tenuous hold over his thralls."

"It's brilliant," Luthor said, though the sarcasm was evident in his voice.

Mattie looked back and forth between the two men as though observing an intense tennis match.

"You don't approve?" Simon asked.

"It's not that I don't approve, sir, it's merely that we lack any way to deliver an aerosolized version of my liquid. In order to do so, we would need some sort of contraption that could take a liquid state and turn it into a gas. Unless I've greatly misjudged you, sir, we lack both the tools and the skills necessary to do something of the sort."

"The skills, yes," Simon said excitedly, climbing from his chair. "The tools, however, we might just have. In order to aerosolize a liquid, you would need pressurized canisters with some sort of hose work through which you could transmit the gas, correct?"

"Fine, I'll pull on this string and see where it leads. Yes, sir, you would need pressurized canisters."

"Tell me, Luthor, where have we seen pressurized canisters, mounted to backpacks, with already designed spraying capabilities?"

Luthor opened his mouth with a rude retort before being struck by a recent memory. "The flamethrowers."

"The flamethrowers," Simon confirmed. "The same ones they use to melt the thick layers of ice from the zeppelin docks and the doors leading in and out of the city. We have the tools readily available."

"And the skills to modify the flamethrower?"

Simon smiled broadly. "I believe Mr. Orrick would have the skills necessary to convert the flamethrower."

"And he just happens to be standing guard at the telegraph office," Luthor concluded.

Mattie cleared her throat politely. "Do either of you realize how disturbing it is to see grown men finishing one another's thoughts?"

Both men looked at her as though surprised she was still in the room.

"I understood next to nothing of what you just said," she continued, "except that it appears we have a way ahead, correct?"

"Yes," Luthor replied, "and yet at the same time, a resounding no. We may know where Mr. Orrick is, but that hardly answers our other conundrum from earlier about how to subdue six men without lethal means. Did we not discuss that we couldn't do it alone?"

"Then it's a good thing we're no longer alone," Simon said, turning toward Mattie. "Tell me, how are you feeling? Are you feeling up for a fight?"

Mattie stretched her wounded shoulder and nodded. "If it means freeing my people, then I'm ready to help however necessary."

"Then it's settled. We'll leave tonight, collect Mr. Orrick, send the telegram, steal a flamethrower, create an aerosolized version of your concoction, and free the werewolves." Simon sighed. "We have a busy night ahead of us."

"I know where to find a flamethrower," Mattie offered. "We saw a collection of them when Gideon brought us into the city."

"Excellent," Simon remarked. "That's one less thing on our list."

"We should get some rest between now and then," Luthor offered, stifling a yawn.

"Indeed we should," Simon agreed.

He started to return to his chair when Mattie stood, tapping Simon gently on the shoulder. As the Inquisitor turned, she swung her open hand, slapping him solidly on the face. Simon staggered, catching himself on the headboard of the bed.

"That was for shooting me, you ass!" she said, storming off toward the other side of the room.

Luthor suppressed a laugh as he walked after Mattie. "Yes, sir, I will be adding this moment to your list of private ridicules."

CHAPTER Thirty-one

THEY WALKED DOWN THE DARK STREETS, LUTHOR and Simon shoulder to shoulder as they passed the empty storefronts. Only the clicking of heels and the tip of Luthor's cane on the cobblestones broke the silence of the evening.

Simon ground his teeth in anticipation, as he fidgeted with the hilt of the sword strapped to his hip. He ran scenarios through his mind, attacks and counters, thrusts and parries. A multitude of strategies circulated, both dealing with armed and unarmed opponents. He recalled a myriad of pressure points that would disable a man without doing lasting harm. Of all the things Simon disliked, and there were plenty, he most of all hated the unknown.

They rounded a corner, passing onto one of the city's major thoroughfares. The street lamps glowed brightly overhead, illuminating the road in both directions. Behind the pair, the road was empty, which was not uncommon at the late hour. Before them, however, six men stood in a horseshoe shape protectively in front of the telegraph office.

Simon and Luthor pulled their hats low over their faces, letting the glow from the streetlamps overhead cast dark shadows over their features. They continued walking forward without slowing, their pace marked by the maddening clicks of Luthor's cane.

One of the men looked over, noticing the two men approaching. He looked to his counterparts, who motioned for him to deal with the strangers. The man hefted a crude club, formed by applying coarse engineer's tape to the bottom of a wooden beam. Resting the weapon on his shoulder, he broke from the other guards and approached the two.

"You're out after curfew," the man said hoarsely. His skin was red from standing in the cold night's air. "You need to return to your homes immediately."

Neither man responded. They continued forward, the cane clicking in rhythm with their steps.

The man shifted his club from his shoulder, patting the top in his open hand as a warning.

"I won't tell you both again. Mr. Dosett has set a curfew, and you're in violation. Go home, or I'll send you there in a body bag."

Simon lifted his head and pushed back the brim of his top hat. He smiled calmly to the guard, who stared at him in surprise. "The youth of today clearly have no manners, Luthor."

Luthor lifted his cane, ceasing the incessant clicking. "None at all, it would seem."

"It's them!" the man exclaimed.

He shifted his grip on his club, preparing to swing it in a wide arc when the lights on the street suddenly went out. The entire road was plunged into darkness, leaving bright blue spots dancing in everyone's vision as their eyes struggled to adjust.

Simon recollected the number of paces to the guard, refusing to let his limited eyesight hinder his ability to fight. He closed the distance quickly, drawing his sword as he moved. Rather than turning the blade toward the man, he drove the hilt forward, catching the guard under his chin. The man's head snapped backward and blood flew from his mouth as he fell limply to the ground.

Night vision was restored to everyone left standing nearly simultaneously as their eyes adjusted to the moonlight. The five guards stared at Simon and Luthor, their gaze passing over the unconscious man at their feet. Simon nodded to the guards before the two sides rushed one another.

Simon spun his sword, pointing the blade at the approaching men.

Tambor broke from the pack and charged at Simon, a pickaxe held threateningly over his head. Just before they crashed into one another, Simon slid to the side and let Tambor's swing pass inches from his shoulder. The pickaxe struck the stone street with bone-jarring force, stunning the head of the Miner's Guild.

The Inquisitor flicked his blade behind him, slicing cleanly through the heavyset man's belt. Tambor's pants fell unceremoniously to the ground, and the man released his pickaxe in an attempt to save his decency.

Luthor parried the first strong swing by the nearest guard, though the force of the impact reverberated through his cane. A second guard flanked him, swinging a wrench toward Luthor's head. The apothecary ducked and struck the man's knee with his cane. He howled in pain and clutched his leg, hopping away from the battle. Luthor was able to stand in time to parry the next swing. He wanted to release the blade in his cane but knew the temptation to use it effectively would be too great. Instead, he used the exterior of it effectively to block the heavy, but slow swings of the guard before him.

The night filled with the sound of clashing metal, as Simon parried a knife thrust from another guard. His gaze shifted over the man's shoulder as he turned his long knife aside. Mr. Orrick hurried to join the battle, though he struggled to find an opening amidst the chaos.

Simon struck forward with the flat of the blade, catching the knife-wielding man on the side of the face and drawing a thin line of blood across his cheek. The guard seemed infuriated and drew back his knife for a thrust. The Inquisitor easily sidestepped the jab and struck the man across the other cheek. The guard reeled, granting Simon the opportunity to drive the pommel of the sword into the top of the man's head. His eyes rolled upward as he fell to the ground.

Simon spun quickly and kicked outward, catching Tambor in his rotund belly. The miner groaned loudly before dropping to his knees, his pants slipping forgotten back to his ankles.

Luthor struck his opponent across the neck with his cane. The man grasped his neck immediately as the muscles seized, causing lances of pain to shoot through the right side of his body. He reared back to strike the guard again when he heard a low growl behind him.

The apothecary spun as the guard he had struck on the shin rushed him from behind. No sooner had Luthor spun, however, than a white form crashed into the man, driving him to the ground. Mattie tumbled with the man before pummeling him with oversized paws.

Luthor turned back to his first opponent just as the man drew his weapon over his shoulder for a powerful swing. Luthor jabbed his cane forward, smashing the pommel into the man's nose. The guard's weapon tumbled from his hand as he clutched his ruined face. Luthor dropped to his knee and swung his weapon low, sweeping the man's legs. He crashed hard onto the ground, where he rolled around in pain.

Orrick saw the hasty defeat of his other guards and turned to run. Mattie leapt from her unconscious foe, barreling into Orrick, driving the tall man to the ground. She placed a paw on either shoulder, pinning him to the ground with sheer weight. He tried to struggle momentarily, until she lowered her snout to within inches of his face and growled threateningly. He immediately ceased struggling and lay perfectly still.

The relative silence of the street returned, save the chorus of assorted groans. Simon picked up his top hat from where it had tumbled from his head and replaced it, canted as always.

He strode over to where Mattie snarled above Orrick and knelt down beside the pair.

"Well done, Ms. Hawke," he commended. "Captured but not seriously injured."

The werewolf glanced over toward him, its eyes smoldering darkly. "Sorry it took so long," she said, though her voice was hardly recognizable as the feminine woman's. "It was a longer run from the breaker box to here than I first imagined."

"No worries. Your timeliness with shutting off the lights was impeccable. Now I do believe you can let our good friend Mr. Orrick up. He won't try to run away, will you, sir?"

Orrick turned his head slowly toward Simon before glancing back at the werewolf's maw hovering over his face. "No, sir, I don't suppose I will."

"Excellent," Simon remarked, clapping his hands together. "Then I won't be obligated to say something dreadful like, 'if you try to run, I'll let the werewolf eat the skin from your face while you're still alive.'"

Orrick visibly shook as he stared at the pointed canines. For effect, Mattie opened and closed her mouth, snapping her teeth together.

"I believe you can let him go now, Ms. Hawke."

Mattie climbed off the man slowly, keeping her long snout pointed at him as she did so. To his credit, Orrick refused to move even the faintest bit until Mattie was well away from him. The werewolf skulked toward the darkened alley nearby until her figure was consumed by the dark shadows.

Simon snapped his fingers before Orrick's face, drawing the man's attention. "Do look over here, Mr. Orrick. There are things that you and I must discuss."

The sound of wood connecting with flesh was followed by a dwindling groan of pain. Simon looked over his shoulder as Luthor stood over the now unconscious Tambor.

"My associates and I," Simon said, pointing to both Luthor and the darkened alley down which Mattie had disappeared, "have use of your unique sets of skills."

Orrick's eyes suddenly dilated, and his worrisome expression grew emotionless. "I will never help you. I'll kill you all and bring your heads to Mr. Dosett. I'll—"

Simon drew back and punched Orrick in the chin. The spell faded at once, and the fear returned to the artisan's face.

"Please don't interrupt me again," Simon warned. "In a moment, Mr. Strong is going to come pay you a visit and he's going to offer you a drink. You will drink, Mr. Orrick, or he will beat you unconscious and force the fluid down your throat. Trust me when I tell you that I have observed him do exactly that, and it is not your preferable course of action."

Luthor approached them as Mattie emerged from the alley. She was human again, dressed in the clothing she had concealed in a bag down the street. She carried Luthor's medical bag, which she handed to the apothecary.

"Send the telegram, sir," Luthor said. "Mattie and I can handle Mr. Orrick, should he become rowdy once more."

Simon stood and nodded to the other two. "Be on your guard, both of you. If Mattie was correct, there is a pack of werewolves roaming these streets and no telling what sort of human guards may be with them. If you see anything at all, don't hesitate, just run."

"What about you?" Mattie asked.

"This should take but a minute," Simon explained. "I'll be back out before you have time to grow concerned."

Mattie frowned. "I'm already concerned."

Simon shrugged as he turned toward the telegraph office. "Then I shall have to work quickly."

Glass clattered to the ground as Simon smashed a hole in the store's front window. He reached through and unlocked the door, pushing it open and disappearing into the gloomy interior.

Mattie looked to Luthor, who smiled confidently.

"Watch him," Luthor said, pointing at Orrick. "I'll have this put together in a matter of seconds."

Mattie looked down at the still prone man. "Do I need to turn back into a werewolf so that you behave?"

Orrick shook his head without reply.

She turned her attention back to Luthor, but lowered her voice so as not to be heard inside the store. "Is it safe to assume that this is not an ordinary apothecary concoction?"

Luthor lifted the twig and smiled before dropping it into the glass. It ignited in a brilliant blue flame before falling to ash.

"Clearly not," he replied.

Mattie took the glass and knelt beside Orrick. The man flinched at her very presence, as though he could see the lingering mass of the werewolf concealed within her diminutive frame.

"Drink this and don't try anything foolish," she ordered, "or I will have to follow through with the Inquisitor's previous threat."

Orrick reached out with a shaking hand and took the potion. He brought it to his lips and drank deeply, his eyes never leaving Mattie. As soon as the liquid rushed down his throat, he seemed to visibly relax and blinked heavily, as though intoxicated.

"Is he all right?" Mattie asked.

Luthor took the man's glass before it spilled. "He'll be fine. Being released from Gideon's spell is taxing, to say the least. Everyone responds differently, though it appears to have sapped most of Mr. Orrick's coherent thought."

Orrick laid his head on the road and covered his eyes with his hands. He rolled his head slowly from side to side and slowly opened and closed his mouth.

"He's drunk," Mattie remarked.

"He seems drunk, but it's merely a side effect of the draught."

"You're merely arguing semantics. He looks drunk and is certainly acting drunk. I'm not overly concerned with whether he is or isn't. I'm far more concerned about the fact that we now have to get a drunkard back to the inn."

Luthor sighed. "Yes, I can see how this truly is an argument of semantics. Come, help me get him up."

As they slipped their hands under Orrick's armpits, the bell above the telegraph office's front door jingled and Simon emerged.

"Done already, sir?" Luthor asked as he strained to lift the uncooperative Orrick.

"It was a simple message to send," he said, walking down the two stairs that led to the building's front door. "What seems to be the matter with him?"

"A rather unfortunate side effect of breaking the spell, it would appear," Mattie explained through breaths as she threw Orrick's arm over her shoulder.

"Come now," Simon said, rushing over and taking Mattie's side. "It won't do to have a woman carrying an inebriated man back to the inn, even a woman as physically capable as yourself."

Mattie smiled and patted the Inquisitor on the shoulder. "It would appear that the slap to your face has done wonders for your disposition toward me."

Running to the alley, she hefted the stolen flamethrower onto her back. She hurriedly caught up as the two men began carrying Orrick down the street, his feet alternating between steps and merely being dragged over the stones.

They all sighed with relief when they encountered no one else during their return trip. Stopping at the front door to the tavern, the men allowed Mattie to open the door. They were forced to turn sideways to get everyone through the narrow doorway, which made dragging Orrick even more complex than it had prior been. Mattie followed them through the door and was immediately met with an utter silence in the bar.

The group paused at the doorway as all gazes fell on the motley crew, one of whom was blindly drunk and the woman who carried a flamethrower on her back, its nozzle clutched in her hand.

Simon caught sight of the bartender, as the man shook his head disapprovingly.

"Don't look at us judgingly," the Inquisitor chided, "as though this were the worst thing you've seen us do."

The group walked past the dumbfounded patrons and dragged Orrick up the staircase to their room.

CHAPTER Thirty-two

MR. ORRICK LOWERED THE JEWELER'S LENS, increasing the magnification as he scrutinized one of the valves on the flamethrower. He probed the seal gently with a dental pick, nodding in satisfaction at the resistance.

"Can you please hand me the soldering iron?" he asked without looking up.

Mattie reached toward the row of tools, but her hand paused with indecision. She bit her lip as she looked back apologetically. Orrick glanced up from his work, his one eye grossly magnified under the lens. He quickly gestured toward the nondescript metal rod.

"Do grasp it by the handle," he offered. "The rod itself is abnormally hot at the moment, hot enough to melt metal."

Mattie cringed as she grasped the tool by its rubberized handle. She untangled the long cord that ran from the base of the handle to an electric box. The box hummed with energy. Watching them work, Luthor quickly cranked the handle on the side of the box and the speed of the humming increased.

Orrick took the soldering iron with a polite nod and placed it against the seal while pressing a thin coil of metal to its tip. The metal liquefied from the heat, dripping and pooling around the clamp holding the hose in place. He moved cautiously and deliberately, ensuring the seal was complete between the two pieces of metal.

"Are we nearly done?" Simon asked from his seat on the bed.

"Inquisitor Whitlock," Orrick replied, though his words were muffled from his stooped position, "I am working with canisters of highly pressurized gas. A single wrong move will result in either a puncture, which would send the canister rocketing through this room with severely destructive force or, in a worst-case scenario, actually explode. Need I remind you that these canisters are currently filled with a highly flammable fluid? As an Inquisitor, I'm sure you can extrapolate the potential strength of the blast, should those gases ignite."

"I could," Simon confirmed, "I merely choose not to in an attempt to save my sanity from inevitable boredom."

"It sounds as though your mind has already been consumed with boredom, sir," Luthor remarked.

Simon scowled at his companion. "Shouldn't you be drafting more of your brew?"

Luthor nodded. "I should but like you, I'm saving myself from the tediousness of my work. Besides which, my drafting of the concoction takes mere moments, the most laborious of which won't be required until the final moments before loading the flamethrower."

Simon leapt to his feet excitedly. "Excellent, then you're currently free from any obligations."

Luthor frowned, sensing an impending trap. "That depends wholly on your intent."

"We should leave Mr. Orrick to his work. I believe Mattie can serve well enough as an assistant?"

Orrick didn't bother looking up from his soldering. A faint wisp of smoke rose from around her stooped frame. "She's been a fine assistant thus far, and I most certainly could do without either of you sighing heavily or moaning about your boredom."

"You haven't answered my question," Luthor remarked as Simon pulled him toward the door. "Where exactly are we going?"

"Even aerosolized, your gas will dissipate unless it's confined to an enclosed space. We're going to secure a space."

They walked through the tavern without drawing odd stares from the patrons for once. The midday sun was shining, and Simon frowned at the sight. He had hoped to complete the vast majority of their tasks the previous night, but the modifications on the flamethrower had consumed far more time than he had anticipated.

The two men walked through the streets, making small talk as they went to appear as normal as possible, though they constantly perused the faces of those they passed. The citizens seemed normal, lacking the wrathful glares seen on the faces of Gideon's puppets.

Through twists and turns in the streets, they walked the perimeter of the city, staying as close to the walls as possible. Ahead, the massive, metal doors of the main gate towered overhead. A pair of guards were posted nearby, though they chattered inanely amongst themselves, paying little attention to passersby. Not eager to tempt fate, Simon and Luthor pulled their hats low and acted as though they were examining the storefronts on the far side of the road as they passed the gate, avoiding exposing their faces to the guards.

Once well clear of the gate, they two men angled toward a large, metal barn set against the city wall. The doors were open, and the braying of the sled dogs echoed from within.

Mr. Parrish sat on a stool by one of the barn doors, retooling a broken leather harness. He worked diligently, his focus entirely on the work at hand. As Simon's shadow fell across the street in front of him, he looked up absently. Only upon recognizing the Inquisitor did his expression harden and malice appear in his eyes.

"You," he hissed as he stood, the leatherworking awl grasped in his hand like a knife. "I'll kill you for—"

Simon kicked the man in the chest, sending the sled master sprawling into the barn. They followed him inside, pulling the barn doors closed behind them as they did.

Luthor tugged once more on the straps around Mr. Parrish's feet. The man groaned as the wet leather pulled on his skin, biting slightly into the flesh. The strip of cloth tied firmly around his mouth muffled his complaints, however.

"He's secure," the apothecary remarked. He turned his attention back to Mr. Parrish. "Again, Mr. Parrish, forgive us for treating you so harshly. Once you're freed of the hold Gideon Dosett has over you, you'll surely thank us for what has transpired."

Luthor couldn't decipher the exact words of Parrish's response, and his gentlemanly sensibilities were glad of that fact.

The wolves barked loudly around them, excited by the flurry of activity within the barn. Simon stood beside one of their pens and stared up toward the ceiling. As Luthor joined him, the Inquisitor gestured toward the tin roof.

"There's a skylight," Simon remarked.

"It could work," Luthor agreed.

Simon nodded and climbed onto the narrow wooden divider that separated the canines' pens. Holding his arms out wide, he balanced as he moved gingerly down its length to the barn's wall. Reaching only slightly above his head, he unlatched the narrow window, letting it swing inward. A cool blast of air poured through the open window, but Simon ignored the discomfort. Turning rather acrobatically, Simon walked back down the divider's length before jumped back to the ground.

"I think we're ready," he said, "though I believe we should cover poor Mr. Parrish with one of the parkas. He's going to be lying in a rather cold barn for some time before we return."

Luthor nodded and collected one of the thick parkas, draping it over the angry sled master. The length of the parka covered most of Parrish's exposed skin, his pants and long-sleeved shirt having been stripped away to ensure a better hold of the leather restraints.

Satisfied, Luthor and Simon exited the barn, pushing the doors closed behind them lest someone stumble upon their captive. They walked back to the inn nonchalantly, even nodding politely to the gate guards as they passed.

Once they reached the inn, they hurried through the tavern and up the back stairwell. The door to their room was unlocked, and they entered quickly. Mattie still stood at the end of the table, watching Mr. Orrick like a prison guard. Orrick, for his part, seemed oblivious to Mattie's impatient stares. The flamethrower had been reconstructed with various new nozzles and hoses connecting the canisters. The spray handle had been removed, and the smoke stack was wrapped protectively in fabric. Most notably, there were a series of tall pint glasses on the table before him, all filled to various levels with the gasoline mixture that had previously been housed within the pressurized containers.

As they entered the room, Mattie looked up to greet them. "Is it done?" she asked.

"It is," Luthor replied.

Simon smiled as he sat down on the edge of the bed. "The guards have seen us as well. Coupled with our attack on the telegraph office last night, word should reach Gideon of our general location within the city."

"Now we just have to hope he sends the werewolves after us," Mattie said, ignoring Orrick's obvious shiver at the mention. He stopped his work to glance cautiously at the redhead standing at the end of the table.

"He will," Simon confirmed. "Everyone is expendable in Gideon's eyes, but none more so than the werewolves. Humans are malleable whereas werewolves—other mystical creatures like himself—are a threat. He'll send them. Now we must ensure we're ready when they arrive."

"One of us already is," Orrick remarked. He turned the smokestack toward Simon and turned one of the valves. A cloud of white smoke poured from the stack, enveloping the Inquisitor.

Simon coughed and waved his hand rapidly in front of his face. "Is that steam?"

Orrick nodded. "I replaced the gasoline with water. It will act as a filler for Mr. Strong's mixture, helping increase the overall volume of the gas."

Simon coughed once more as he felt the moisture settle on his skin. "Well done, sir."

Luthor clapped his hands. "Then I suppose it's time for me to get to work."

He walked to the far side of the room, collecting the large pot Simon had acquired from the tavern earlier that morning. His doctor's bag was open on the nightstand, and he withdrew the required vials. He frowned as he observed the quantities of what remained, noting that many of his vials were already less than half full.

"Is everything all right?" Simon asked, noting Luthor's sour expression.

"Everything is fine," the apothecary remarked. "My supplies are quickly dwindling, however. If this doesn't work, I doubt I'll have the supplies necessary to recreate this endeavor."

"All the more reason not to fail."

Luthor poured the entirety of his chosen test tubes into the pan, filling it nearly a quarter way once he added the distilled water. He glanced over his shoulder to where Simon sat, ensuring the man couldn't see the odd color changes occurring within the pot. Though the current mixes were merely mundane reactions, he knew it would be difficult to explain the next stage of the process.

Reaching into his bag, he withdrew one of the remaining leafy twigs. "I should warn you all that this stage of the process involves a rather significant and violent chemical reaction. Like Potassium when it's added to water, this will produce a rather impressive flame. There's no reason to be alarmed, however."

Without awaiting a response, he dropped the flora into the pot. The reaction was immediate. Blue flames leapt toward the top of the pot, illuminating the corner of the room in a vibrant cerulean. The flames quickly died away, leaving the yellowish brew behind.

Simon stroked his chin thoughtfully at the sight. "Out of curiosity, would that be the same brew you had me ingest?"

"And me?" Mattie asked.

"And me as well?" Orrick added.

"Obviously, which only goes to show that it's completely harmless," Luthor added hastily. He glanced to Orrick, eager to change the subject. "Are you prepared with a funnel?"

Orrick glared at Luthor a moment longer before nodding. He held the funnel aloft before placing it at the mouth of one of the canisters.

Luthor lifted his pot and carried it to the artisan, careful not to spill any of the draught. Together, they cautiously poured the brew into the metal cylinder, shaking the pot at the end to ensure every last droplet of the mystical compound was captured.

Orrick removed the funnel and threaded a hose onto the end of the container. With a spin of a valve, pressurized gasses flooded the canister. The artisan raised his head with a smile.

"It's ready for field testing," he remarked.

Simon stood. "Gideon Dosett wants to hunt us with a tribe of werewolves. I believe it's about time we let them find us."

CHAPTER Thirty-three

THE SUN WAS BEGINNING TO SET AS SIMON STRODE alone through the streets of Haversham. He shoved his hands further into his pockets as he lowered his head against the cool breeze pouring through the streets. Gone was his telltale top hat, and his dark hair waved gently in the breeze.

Unlike the night before, the streets seemed fuller and busier than they had been in days, though the nervousness in the air was palpable. Citizens hustled from their work as businesses closed for the night, rushing home only to lock their doors and shutter their windows once inside. The people of Haversham knew something ill was brewing. Even Simon could taste it the air and hear its whispers on the wind.

He turned away from the market square and walked toward the city gates, keeping his head low even as he searched the nearby streets and storefronts for movement. In stark contrast to the square or even the streets down which he had already passed, the road that ran the circumference of the city wall was abandoned. Shuttered windows and a forgotten newspaper blowing down the street gave it the impression of a lost ghost town rather than the lively city carved into the tundra.

Pushing his hand deeper into his pocket, he felt the reassuring coldness of the silver revolver. Though it had already proven only partially effective against the werewolves, it added a level of comfort he wouldn't have had walking through the city unarmed.

The first howl split the night, and Simon tensed. The sound echoed off the wall to his left, concealing the true direction of the call. It mattered little, as moments later the howl was picked up by others. Soon the entirety of the night air was filled with the barking and braying of wolves, stalking through the street.

Simon increased his pace, stopping just short of running. The howling grew closer as the pack hunted; they moved in an attempt to trap the Inquisitor.

From the corner of his eye, he saw the first sight of white fur. The werewolf stopped at the entrance to an alleyway, crouched on all fours and growling at Simon as he hurried past. Once beyond the alleyway, the werewolf tilted back its head and howled loudly into the night sky. Its call was quickly answered as more werewolves approached.

Simon knew that the wolves he was now seeing with some regularity weren't there to capture him, but rather to prevent any chance of escape. They blocked alleyways that led away from the perimeter road, knowing that his left side was already obstructed by the impassable wall.

As more of the werewolves appeared, blocking escape routes, Simon picked up a light jog. His fingers closed over the handle to his revolver, though he was loathed to draw the weapon unless absolutely necessary.

The massive, metal doors of the gate rose before him, dwarfing even his tall stature as he hurried along the edge of the wall. He could hear padded footsteps behind him, keeping pace. Their speed increased or decreased in response to his actions, telling him that they weren't yet ready to attack.

The gate, however, offered him a chance at escaping their tightening net, so it was no surprise at all when a large werewolf emerged before him, standing impassively in front of the gateway. The guards Simon had seen earlier that day were not so curiously absent, leaving him with little recourse but to face his pursuers.

With the werewolf before him, Simon slowed his pace to a walk. The padded footsteps behind him were joined by low growls of anticipation.

Simon came to a stop and turned toward the stalking pack. His frown deepened for a brief moment at the sight before him. A muscular werewolf stood on its hind legs before him, though most of the fur on one side of its body had been stripped away, replaced by a series of rapidly healing burns. Though the sight of a normal werewolf was horrible, the sight of a partially hairless monster was practically terrifying. It helped none at all that Simon knew this particular werewolf, and the indelible hatred it had for him.

"I guess talking about this is out of the question?" he asked.

The burned werewolf growled threateningly before dropping to all fours. Its nose twitched, as it smelled the air, taking in Simon's scent.

"Before you attack, and it seems so invariably likely that you shall, do keep in mind that…"

Simon stopped speaking in mid-sentence as he noticed the werewolf listening intently. Before it could react, Simon spun on his heel and raced toward the city gate. The burned werewolf howled in frustration before charging after the fleeing Inquisitor.

The street behind Simon quickly filled with pursuing werewolves. The one guarding the street before him crouched, preparing to pounce on the seemingly unarmed human racing toward it. In a fluid movement, Simon drew the revolver from his pocket and fired a single shot. The bullet slammed into the werewolf's rear thigh. The limb buckled immediately, even as the creature howled in pain. The werewolf collapsed to the street, clutching its injured leg.

Simon bound over the fallen wolf, yelling a halfhearted apology as he did so. As he landed on the far side, he could already see in his periphery that the creature was getting back to its feet, despite the wound to its leg.

On all fours, the werewolves were significantly faster than Simon was. The element of surprise bought him mere seconds of a lead, most of which vanished once the wolves began their pursuit.

The barn was ahead with doors already opened. Simon rushed inside with a pack of werewolves in close pursuit. The burned one led the pack, its powerful jaws snapping practically at Simon's heels as he ran.

The Inquisitor rushed to the back of the barn just as the werewolf reached for him with long, sharp claws. Simon leapt, landing nimbly on the divider just as claws closed on the air where he had been a moment before. Unable to stop its momentum, the burned werewolf slammed into one of the sled dog pens and the sound of angry barking filled the enclosed structure.

Simon wobbled unsteadily as the divider shook from the impact. He dropped into a crouch, using his hands for support to steady himself. Behind him, the werewolf righted itself and began climbing the divider after him.

Feeling properly motivated, Simon climbed back to his feet and rushed toward the narrow window. Despite its elevation, he jumped easily to its height, turning sideways as he slid through its small gap. His stomach and back scraped along the windowsill and he tumbled out the other side, falling the ten feet to the hard ground below. He landed roughly, knocking the wind from his lungs. Staring upward, he saw the fur-covered arm and claw of the werewolf reaching futility out the window as the creature tried to squeeze through the narrow gap.

The pack followed the burned werewolf into the barn before they realized that the Inquisitor had escaped through the window. As the rearmost wolves turned to leave, Mattie and Orrick slammed the barn doors closed, sliding a heavy, metal rod across their length. The wolves slammed against the closed barn doors. The metal rattled, but held.

Their howling and barking was quickly interrupted by the sound of scraping metal as the skylight was pulled aside. Snow fell through the exposed hole, filtering down over the werewolves as they stared upward with a mixture of frustration and curiosity.

Luthor appeared at the hole, looking down on the trapped monsters. Their inquisitive braying quickly turned to anger at the sight of the apothecary. He looked for a moment longer before lifting the flamethrower, which was now thoroughly wrapped in blankets. Twisting all the valves, he hefted the contraption through the skylight even as the first elements of yellow gas poured from the smoke stack.

The flamethrower landed heavily in the midst of the werewolves, gushing a noxious cloud of gas. The pack parted quickly, forming a vacant hole around the odd machine. As the cloud quickly spread, they rushed toward the walls, clawing ineffectually at the metal barn in an attempt to escape. Mattie and Orrick stepped backward as the thrashing against the barn doors reached a frightening crescendo, though the heavy, metal bar held against their assault. Simon limped over to the pair, listening happily to their furious howling.

Luthor watched as the creatures ran in fear until the cloud consumed them. Their howls and barks turned to coughs of confusion. They tried to cover their long snouts with their arms, but the gas seeped past their meager defenses.

Slowly, the pack succumbed to the aerosolized potion. They dropped to their knees, some vomiting onto the hay-lined barn floor while others convulsed. The floor of the barn grew slick as the transformations began and fur sloughed from the werewolves as they returned to their human forms.

The howls and coughs became moans and retching. As the thick yellow smoke began to clear, Luthor looked down on a large collection of naked and confused indigenous people.

The apothecary stood and walked gingerly to the back of the barn, where a ladder had been propped against the building. He climbed down carefully before walking around and rejoining the other conspirators.

"It's done," he said. "They've all transformed."

Simon and Orrick removed the locking bar from the door, dropping the metal rod unceremoniously to the ground with a clatter. They grasped the handles, pulling the barn doors open.

A cloud of lingering yellow smoke escaped the open doors, filling the air above it as though the building had caught fire. The cool wind rolled through the barn and the naked tribesmen within shivered from the cold.

Simon stepped inside and walked toward the building's center, scanning the faces as he walked. Near the back, he stopped and extended his hand. Chieftain Kidnip reached up gingerly and took it, using his leverage to pull herself to her feet.

"Welcome back to the land of the living, Chieftain," Simon remarked as the woman pulled herself to her full height. "We have a lot of work ahead of us."

CHAPTER Thirty-four

SIMON PULLED THE STRIP OF CLOTH TIGHTLY AROUND the man's leg wound, tying it firmly in place against his upper thigh. He patted the man's knee once complete and smiled.

"That should do it," he said. "This will stop the bleeding and you'll be as good as new in no time at all. If it's any consolation, I intentionally shot you somewhere that would have no lasting detriment to your well-being."

Luthor shook his head as he moved past the groggy and nauseated wolves, covered now as they were in assortments of loose fitting clothing and spare parkas. He walked to the back corner, where the loose hay was piled higher than throughout the rest of the barn floor. The apothecary quickly brushed aside handfuls of the coarse straw, revealing a parka concealed beneath. With a flourish, he pulled it free.

Mr. Parrish squinted as the barn's sole naked fluorescent bulb struck his sensitive eyes. Luthor knelt beside the man and untied the cloth gag wrapped firmly in place over the sled master's mouth. Parrish coughed and spit onto the ground as his mouth was finally freed.

"Tell me, Mr. Parrish," Luthor said. "How do you feel?"

Parrish glared at the apothecary. "If you're asking me if I still have the urge to kill you, then the answer is a resounding yes. However, it's no longer because of Gideon Dosett's prerogative. I want to kill you solely for my own reasons now."

Luthor smiled apologetically as he pulled a knife and began cutting on the thick leather cords binding the man's hands and feet. "I truly wish there had been a better way to expose you to the compound. Trust that everything we did was in your best interest."

Parrish merely snarled as the last of the leather straps were cut and his limbs were freed of the restraints. The sled master brought his hands around quickly and Luthor flinched, preparing for the inevitable punch to his face. Instead, Parrish merely rubbed his wrists to bring back circulation. He stood and pushed past Luthor without another word before storming toward the far end of the barn.

Luthor rejoined Simon as the Inquisitor knelt before the werewolf chieftain.

"Your pack is recovering quickly," Simon remarked. "Perhaps the concentration wasn't as severe in the gas as it was in the liquid the rest of us were forced to ingest."

"We also heal quickly," Kidnip replied. "We'll be back to our old selves in no time." She stared at Simon, though the Inquisitor struggled to determine if she was angry with him or merely angry at the situation in which they found themselves.

"We owe you our lives," she said finally. "For free people like the wolves, there is little worse than being someone else's pawn in a game in which we have no control. Working for the man, no matter how much it seemed to be of our own volition, was a living hell."

"Then seek your revenge against Gideon Dosett," Simon offered.

Kidnip narrowed her eyes as she watched the Inquisitor. "I can't thank you enough for what you've done, but it still doesn't answer the question of 'why'. You're an Inquisitor and, if the evidence before me is to be believed, a rather good one. Why even offer to help the wolves? Why free us at all when you just as easily could have destroyed us with Gideon?"

"The enemy of my… never mind," Simon conceded. "The simple truth is that I cannot defeat Gideon without your help. He has an army protecting him and to be competitive in this war, I needed one of my own."

"Then you're using us," the chieftain replied. "Tell me, Inquisitor, how is being your pawn any different than being a pawn of that creature?"

Simon shrugged and gestured to the men and women around him, who were in various stages of recovery. "Of the two of us, who do you wish to see dead more? You could kill me now if you so desired. Your wolves have recovered enough that your pack could easily overpower Mr. Strong and me. If you do, however, are you not still left with the very real threat of Gideon Dosett? You've spent every waking breath since his arrival trying to destroy him. I'm offering you not only the chance, but my tactical genius to plan that very assault."

"You can trust him," Mattie said as she approached from the front of the barn. "He's risked his life for everyone here, myself included."

Kidnip glanced back and forth between one of her closest advisors and the Inquisitor, as though weighing and measuring her options. "If we charge into the governor's estate, what's to stop Gideon from merely enslaving us once more?"

Luthor raised his hand as he fielded the question. "I can answer that. The gas that you inhaled, the one that severed his connection to you, also acts as a vaccination against his future attempts. Try as he might, he won't be able to reassert his dominance over you."

"You're free," Simon added. "I can't make you stay and help us, but I'm begging for your aid. If you know anything at all about Inquisitors, I want you to grasp the significance of this moment as I beg, on bended knee, the assistance of werewolves to overcome a far greater threat."

Chieftain Kidnip stared at Simon intently, her gaze boring into him. After a long moment, she rose and turned toward her wolves. Her pack saw her and rose as well, facing their alpha female.

"The Inquisitor has freed us from our enslavement," she said. "He has given us our freedom. We can return to the tundra to continue our lives as they have been. I, for one, don't want to return our lives to the way it was before. I don't want to return to our homes, knowing that tomorrow we march on yet another of Gideon Dosett's holdings. I don't want to know that every time we attack, we risk injury or worse to our wolves."

She raised her fist above her head. "The Inquisitor has asked for our help, a chance to stop skirmishing on the outskirts of the city and take the fight to the demon's doorstep. I intend to go with him. Who's with me?"

A rousing chorus of barks and yelps sounded from the group as one by one they raised their fists into the air.

Kidnip lowered her hand and turned toward Simon. "You have our answer. What do we do first, Inquisitor?"

The werewolf padded back to the assembled group, only rising to his full height when he was securely out of sight from the estate's front gates.

"There are at least twenty gubernatorial guards within the estate with at least the same number of armed civilians," the werewolf reported, his rumbling voice a mere low whisper. "They're ready for a fight."

Simon turned toward Kidnip. "This won't be easy. Gideon will do everything in his power to maintain his position. He knows that he fights for his very existence and will stop at nothing."

"The wolves fight for our existence as well," she replied. "An animal, backed into a corner, is dangerous. It will do everything it can to escape harm. An animal protecting its home is twice as dangerous. We're both, Inquisitor. If the demon wants a war, it's a war we shall give him."

Simon shook his head. "These aren't two opposing armies marching to war. Those men in the estate are thralls, much like you and your kin were not an hour ago. Subdue them and stop them, but don't kill them. When Gideon dies, and he will, the spell will be broken. Those men deserve to return to their former lives when all this is done."

Kidnip snarled angrily. "You tie our hands as we march to battle? Do you honestly believe that those thralls will hesitate to kill us? You can't have one army showing restraint while the other has none."

Simon glowered at her. "Promise me. Promise me that your wolves won't kill without absolute reason."

The chieftain turned away and glanced around the corner of the building, which offered a direct view to the gates of the estate.

"Promise me, Kidnip," Simon repeated forcefully.

"I promise," she replied without turning around. "We won't kill without reason."

Simon knew that her words were hollow, but he had no other recourse. He needed the wolves to cause the distraction so that he and Luthor might slip inside unnoticed.

"Sir, we have to go," Luthor said, placing his hand on Simon's arm.

Simon took a step to Kidnip's side, taking a chance to look at the estate himself. "As we discussed, give Mr. Strong and me five minutes, then begin your attack."

Kidnip huffed but refused to meet his stern gaze. Simon sighed, afraid of the repercussions of the bloodbath to come, before turning away and joining Luthor. The two men walked away from the pack, heading toward one of the main entrances to the tunnels beneath the city.

Mattie rushed up behind them, stopping only when she was walking in step with the two men. Simon stopped in mid-stride and turned toward the redhead.

"Where do you think you're going?" he asked.

"With you," she replied matter-of-factly.

Simon shook his head. "Contrary to what you clearly believe, this is something for Luthor and me alone."

"Being contrary is what you do best," she retorted. "You've already proven that you need my help. If you go to face the demon, then I intend to be by your side."

Simon opened his mouth to respond but Luthor placed a hand on his chest, stopping him before he could speak. "Please, sir, allow someone with a little more tact."

Luthor slipped his hand around Mattie's waist and led her away from the irate Inquisitor. "I'm not going to stand here and refute what you say. You've been invaluable during our capture of Mr. Orrick and releasing the rest of your tribe from their captivity. You've proven yourself time and again. Even so, I'm asking… no, I'm begging, you to stay with your tribe."

"Why?" she asked, dumbfounded. "You're a contradiction, Luthor. You say that my help is invaluable, yet you would prefer I didn't join you?"

Luthor shook his head and glanced over his shoulder, ensuring Simon wasn't within distance to hear his conversation. "What the wolves will be facing will be dangerous. People will die, of that I'm sure. Whatever danger they may face, however, pales in comparison to what we'll be facing when combating a demon lord."

"All the more reason for me to join you! Why shouldn't I be by your side?"

Luthor flushed as he tried to find the words. "I don't want you there because I hate even the thought of you getting hurt," he blurted, the words rushing from him before his good sense could pull them back.

Mattie paused, her mouth still hanging open in response. She slowly closed her mouth and blushed herself, her face matching the scarlet of her hair. "Why Mr. Strong, do you fancy me?"

Luthor cleared his throat. "If it's all the same, could we not make this more than it already is? I have a lot to worry about before we will ever get the opportunity to continue this conversation. Just please listen to me, I beg of you, and stay with your tribe. It would be incalculably more calming knowing that you're safe."

Mattie smiled and placed her hand on the side of his face. She leaned forward and kissed his cheek. "Promise me you'll be safe."

Luthor nodded before turning away and hurrying to Simon's side. Simon smiled knowingly as the apothecary returned but, to his credit, he refrained from comment as the two men rushed toward the tunnel's entryway.

They reached the entrance within seconds and hurried inside. The spiral staircase descended into gloom below. They looked at one another before rushing down the stairs.

Mattie watched them both depart, hurrying into the building which housed the spiral staircase. She smiled thoughtfully as she counted the passing seconds in her head. When she had reached a full minute, she rushed off toward the tunnel's entryway and descended the spiral staircase in pursuit.

CHAPTER Thirty-five

THE WEREWOLVES STORMED THE COURTYARD, surprising the thralls who stood guard at the estate's front gates. The chieftain led their charge, rushing across the open field with all haste toward the line of gubernatorial guards who stood watch at the mansion's entrance. The guards raised their rifles in unison and fired, sending a barrage of lead bullets through the air. Wolves faltered and fell around Kidnip. She offered them a sympathetic glance over her shoulder, but their injuries merely fueled her anger.

With long strides, she covered the last of the distance as the guards reloaded their rifles. She crashed her massive bulk into their line, tossing aside the significantly smaller men. The rest of the werewolves reached the guards, and the previously organized combat descended into chaos.

Far below the battle, Simon and Luthor reached the tunnels, which branched into a multitude of directions so close to the estate. Luthor scratched his head inquisitively as he perused the many tunnels, trying to find landmarks that would seem remotely familiar.

Simon, in contrast, wasted no time at all turning toward one of the smaller branches. He entered the tunnel without hesitation, despite its relative gloom compared to the more mainstream thoroughfares.

"It's here," the Inquisitor remarked.

"How can you be sure?" Luthor asked as he hurried to keep pace with his mentor. "They all look the same."

Simon smiled knowingly. "When am I ever not sure? It helps that I have an impeccable sense of direction."

Luthor stopped and stood at the entryway to the darker tunnel. "You once got lost while attending a formal dinner invitation only a few blocks from your house. I had to roam the streets of Callifax just to find you."

Simon ran his hand along the wall as he continued walking. "In my defense, I had been drinking heavily that night." He paused and turned toward his companion, flashing a broad smile. "Regardless, the passage is right here."

Simon stepped around a nearly invisible corner and disappeared from sight. Luthor sighed and rushed after the man, lest he invade the estate alone.

The tunnel was very familiar, narrow and dark as it led to the secret doorway into the estate. After a brisk walk down the passage, it ended in a nearly perfect stone edifice, one that blended seamlessly into the surrounding rock walls.

"The entrance is here somewhere," Simon remarked quietly. "Help me find the release lever."

Luthor stepped beside his friend and felt along the rough wall. "This would be far easier if the access on this side was as obvious as the wall sconce was within the fencing room."

"When are we ever so lucky, Luthor?"

Luthor was forced to shrug in agreement. Simon's hands moved impossibly quick as he searched every protruding stone and pressed every indention along his part of the wall. The dead end appeared as crudely worked stone, which left the face of the wall coarse and rough. There were far too many individual indentations.

"We don't have time for this," Simon swore as he struck the wall with his open hand. "Our diversion on the surface will only last so long. We need to find our way inside!"

Luthor glanced at his infuriated friend and placed a hand on his shoulder. "Sir, step away for a second and take a breath. Sometimes, situations like these require space and perspective, perspective you just can't attain while staring at the same unchanging wall."

Simon sighed but nodded. He walked away, throwing his hands above his head.

Luthor glanced quickly over his shoulder to ensure Simon's back was turned. The apothecary touched the frame of his glasses and a soft green light poured over the lens. Immediately, an innocuous stone by Luthor's right hand glowed with an unearthly light. Reaching down, he pressed the stone and a series of clicks sounded from behind the false wall.

"What did you do?" Simon asked as he rushed back to the secret entrance.

Luthor lowered his hand and the light faded from his glasses. "I told you, sir, it's all about perspective. I found it much easier to peruse the wall without your constant complaining."

Simon patted Luthor on the back. "Remind me to berate you for your obvious lack of respect later."

The Inquisitor placed his hands on the wall and pushed. The stone wall, which had seemed so solid and heavy moments before, swung easily aside on well-worn hinges.

The dark tunnel was flooded with light as the door opened to the wide, square fencing room. The electric lamps burned brightly across the ceiling and within sconces across the walls, illuminating the six men who stood in the center of the broad dueling mat.

Simon paused at the doorway, warily eying the assortment of swords held in the men's hands. "It appears that Gideon Dosett shrewdly anticipated this course of action."

The two men stepped through the doorway and spread apart, granting both the space necessary to draw their weapons. Simon pulled his saber from its sheath, as Luthor released the narrow blade concealed within his cane. Only after they were in position did Simon recognize the man standing at the forefront of their adversaries.

"Mr. Mulvane," the Inquisitor said. "It's been some time since last we met."

The governor's assistant nodded slowly. "Sadly, this will be the last time you and I meet, Inquisitor. Truth be told, I never much cared for you. You're far too arrogant a man."

"I look forward to making you regret those words," Simon replied.

Mulvane chortled and glanced at the five swordsmen standing behind him. "Those are brave words when you are so clearly at the disadvantage."

"I agree that the fight is far from fair, but we hardly have time for you to call for more reinforcements."

Simon could see the anger blaze in Patrick Mulvane's eyes at his blatant mocking. Though Mulvane was correct that Simon portrayed arrogance, it was mostly for show, as a way to unnerve his opponent. An angry opponent was a careless opponent and easily defeated.

"I look forward to presenting your head to our master," Patrick hissed.

He rushed across the room, the other guards in tow. Simon sidestepped Patrick's charge and drove his shoulder into the man as he passed, sending the assistant sprawling to the ground. He turned his attention instead to the two other guards who rushed at him.

From his periphery, Simon could see Luthor similarly detained. The apothecary removed his bowler cap and threw it into the face of one of the guards, distracting him as Luthor parried the first swing from one of the remaining swordsmen.

The two men before Simon were skilled at swordplay but clearly faltered when fighting as a team. As one thrust, the other hesitated for fear of striking his partner. The man's hesitation created openings that Simon exploited; the Inquisitor drove first his knee into the man's exposed hip before following with an elbow to the side of the man's head. The guard crumpled, but Simon had little time to savor his victory before he had to parry another frustrated swing from the other swordsman.

Though disoriented, Mulvane quickly regained his feet as well. Simon backed away from the two men, giving himself more room to maneuver. Patrick placed his hand on the guard's back, practically shoving him forward to engage the Inquisitor. The man staggered, his swing coming without finesse. Simon blocked it, their blades ringing as metal struck metal. Simon slid his sword downward until their hilts struck one another. He grabbed the swordsman's wrist to keep him from pulling away before rearing back and slamming his forehead into the guard's nose. He rocked backward as Simon released the man's sword. The Inquisitor followed with a kick to the man's chest, which sent him sprawling onto the mat.

Patrick Mulvane watched the guard fall before hesitantly stepping backward. Simon angled his blade toward the governor's assistant, pointing the tip of his sword toward the slowly retreating man.

Luthor stepped behind Patrick and struck the man across the neck with the haft of his cane. Mulvane lurched in surprise and stumbled forward. His feet tangled over one another and he tumbled forward far quicker than Simon could anticipate. The assistant struck the tip of Simon's saber and slid painfully down the length of the blade. As he slowly came to a stop and his knees buckled, he looked up pleadingly into Simon's surprised face.

Before Simon could respond, Patrick's eyes fluttered closed and he slumped heavily, his ability to remain upright possible only by the support of the sword piercing his chest.

The Inquisitor turned his blade, and Mulvane's body slid free before collapsing limply to the ground.

"Sir, I didn't—" Luthor began.

"Duck!" Simon yelled as one of the guards regained his feet behind the apothecary.

Luthor immediately dropped to his knees and Simon flung his sword like a projectile, striking the guard in the chest and driving him to the ground. The swordsman lay unmoving, the hilt of Simon's saber protruding skyward from where it had pierced the man.

Luthor slowly stood and looked behind him. "I thought you were hesitant to kill those enthralled by the demon."

Simon knelt beside Patrick's body as he felt for a pulse that was no longer there. "I was and still am. However, you were right before and though I was loathed to admit it, sometimes the ends truly do justify the means. When we kill Gideon Dosett, and trust that we shall, at least some small part of these two men's deaths will be redeemed."

Simon walked past Luthor without looking at his friend. He paused beside the prone body of the guard and pulled his sword free from his chest. Kneeling again, he placed his hand on the man's chest before taking a piece of his tunic to wipe the bright red blood from the saber. Wordlessly, the Inquisitor stood and sheathed his sword once more.

"Come now, Luthor," Simon said flatly, though his lack of emotion merely betrayed the flurry of anger barely concealed beneath his surface. "Let's find Mr. Dosett and repay him a thousand fold for everything he's made us do in his name."

CHAPTER Thirty-six

THERE WAS BLOOD IN THE AUTOPSY ROOM AS THEY walked past, fresh blood that streaked beyond the darkened doorway as though something had been dragged inside. A part of Simon wanted to explore, to find out the most recent of Gideon's victims, but a greater part of him realized it didn't matter. Nothing mattered aside from destroying the demon and severing his abyssal control over Haversham.

The light flickered to life in the autopsy room as Simon walked past, and he spun rapidly. Luthor stood in the doorway, his hand frozen against the inner wall, his fingers still grasping the light switch. The apothecary tensed and made a retching noise before bringing his arm to his mouth and backing out of the room.

Curiosity getting the better of him, Simon returned to the doorway and peered within. He understood Luthor's revulsion. What remained of a man was pinned to the metal table with hooks pierced through his wrists and ankles. The once-obese man had been vivisected, carved upon until he was properly autopsied. The spray of blood that marred the walls and the smear that led from outside the room to the table itself told Simon that the man was most likely alive when the surgery began.

Arching his eyebrow curiously, Simon stepped over the trail of viscera and approached the side of the table. The smell was hideous, a combination of feces and gore. He wasn't sure if the man defecated himself during the torture or if the smell merely exuded from the piercing of the man's bowels, but it lingered in the air like a noxious cloud.

Simon arrived beside the table and turned the deceased man's head toward him for identification. His fears were founded as he finally caught a glimpse of the man's face. Though he had always seemed jovial during their meetings, the horror now permanently cast on the governor's face barely concealed the man's features.

"Is that who I think it is?" Luthor asked, covering his nose to block the atrocious smell.

"Governor Godwin," Simon confirmed. "Mr. Dosett is truly becoming desperate if he's begun eliminating his closest allies. He must realize that his plan for control of both Haversham and the crown is unraveling quickly."

Simon walked out of the room, turning off the lights behind him as he exited. "He's growing desperate, which means he's growing equally dangerous. We have to put a stop to him with all haste, which means we no longer have time for petty distractions." He turned toward Luthor and stared intently at the apothecary. "Next time I avoid a room, do me a favor and leave the light in its original off position."

Before Luthor could reply, Simon stormed toward the staircase at the end of the hall.

They walked up the stairs slowly, weapons drawn as they listened intently for any noise from above. The stairwell ended in a narrow hallway, one direction from which led to the kitchen while the other led to the foyer.

Simon stole a glance around the corner but found the first floor abandoned. He motioned for Luthor to follow as they crested the stairwell. The soles of their shoes clicked on the hardwood floor as they entered the foyer.

"Where is he hiding?" Luthor whispered as they rounded the corner and stood before the stairwell leading to the familiar second floor landing.

"Up, most obviously," Simon replied, equally quietly.

"In his office, you presume?"

Simon shook his head. "Potentially, or perhaps he's in the ballroom.

It's impossible to tell in such a grandiose mansion."

Luthor tightened his grip on his blade. "Then shall we separate and explore as much of the mansion as possible?"

Simon turned toward the apothecary sharply, a look of absolute horror portrayed on his face. "Split up? That is one of the worst possible plans I've ever heard you offer. You never split up, certainly not when hunting a demon. There is strength in numbers." Simon huffed in disgust. "Split up, indeed."

Luthor clenched his jaw, uncertain if this ridicule was merely retribution for his earlier disrespect or if Simon was genuinely disappointed. "What would you have us do then, sir? Shall we slowly and deliberately search every inch of the estate until we uncover where he has concealed himself?"

Simon's features relaxed and he smiled softly. "Of course not, Luthor. You are correct, of course, that would take far too long."

The Inquisitor sheathed his sword and cupped his hands against either side of his mouth.

"Gideon Dosett!" he yelled, startling Luthor badly enough that the apothecary stumbled away. "How dare you wallow in your cowardice, sending minions instead to fight your battles? You're an abysmal demon, and I don't mean that in the slightest bit as a compliment. Show yourself. Come and face me!"

Luthor regained his composure and clenched Simon's arm tightly, pulling his hands away from his mouth. "Have you taken a leave of your senses?"

Simon raised a finger to his lips, encouraging silence on the part of Luthor.

The sound of heavy furniture being tossed aside echoed from high above them. They craned their necks backward as they sought the source of the noise, but they saw nothing on the landings above them.

"You have been a thorn in my side for far too long, Inquisitor," Gideon's voice boomed from the floors above them. His voice sounded deeper and more malicious than it had been during their previous encounters. "I should have killed you when I had you alone in my office, rather than bending you to my will. I see my error now, one that I don't intend to repeat."

Simon and Luthor looked at one another.

"The ballroom," Simon confirmed. "Now wasn't that far easier than searching the entirety of the estate?"

"You're a fool," Luthor scolded, "and you take far too many liberties."

"I do what is necessary, as I have always done," Simon retorted. He placed his hand on the small of Luthor's back, guiding him toward the stairwell. "Now let's make haste before he has a chance to set a trap for us."

Simon and Luthor rushed to the stairwell and bounded up the marble steps, their footfalls echoing through the vaulted central passage. They quickly reached the second-floor landing. Though both men still felt the need to rush, they slowed their pace as they examined the hallway and rooms that extended from the wide landing. They could see the doorways to their previous rooms in the distance, the doors ajar and assorted broken furniture strewn into the hallway.

"I don't see anyone," Luthor remarked.

Simon nodded and pointed toward the next stairwell, the one that concluded on a landing before the ballroom. "Then let's not delay the inevitable. I would so hate to keep him waiting."

Luthor nodded and rushed toward the base of the next stairs. He ascended two stairs at a time, his hand clenching the pommel of his cane tightly and the tickle of magic coursing through his free hand.

As he reached the third-floor landing, the burning in his forearm returned with a vengeance, sending searing pain through his bicep and into his shoulder. Without pulling up his sleeve, he knew the dangerous black tendrils had already reappeared around the edges of the inflamed rune. Simon's estimation had been correct; Gideon Dosett was evidently in the ballroom.

The door was open, offering a clear view across the expansive formal hall. Luthor lowered himself, using the top stair as protection as he examined the room beyond. Gideon Dosett stood in the center, without any attempt to conceal himself.

Luthor turned toward Simon, ready to describe the scene before him, only to find the stairwell behind him empty. Simon was nowhere to be seen.

"Simon," Luthor hissed. "Simon?"

He strained to hear anything coming from the floors below, but the mansion was blanketed with utter silence.

The silence was shattered by a frighteningly commanding voice that rolled from the ballroom. "Mr. Strong, I know you're there. Please do come and join me."

Luthor turned his attention slowly back toward the ballroom, his eyes widening as he saw how much closer Gideon now appeared. The man stood just within the doorway to the hall, a broad smile cast upon his face as he extended his arms in invitation.

No longer seeing the need to hide, Luthor rose from his position on the stairs, cursing both himself and Simon as he walked toward the ballroom's entrance.

CHAPTER Thirty-seven

LUTHOR CLENCHED HIS BLADE TIGHTLY AS HE STEPPED onto the landing before the ballroom. Gideon sensed his hesitation and slowly walked backward, granting ample space for Luthor to enter the large room. The apothecary descended the few stairs into the ballroom proper, keeping his blade pointed at the demon's heart.

The apothecary stole a glance over his shoulder again, almost expecting Simon to materialize, though the stairs and the second-floor landing were all still empty. A litany of profanity rolled through Luthor's mind as he turned his attention back to the demon.

For a moment, it was easy to forget that he was staring into the face of evil, that the man before him wasn't a human of flesh and blood, but a demon lord of bile and effluence. Gideon exuded charisma in abundance and even his smile was disarming. Only the rapier bouncing carefree on his hip held any semblance of danger.

Luthor noticed the tip of his sword dipping and quickly raised it again, keeping it pointed at the demon.

"There's no need for such hostilities," Gideon said, crossing his arms over his chest. "We've merely come to talk, have we not?"

Luthor shook his head. "We most certainly have not. I've come here to put an end to your dark magic."

Gideon's smile faltered for the briefest of moments before the warming smile reasserted itself.

"*Put down your sword*," Gideon said, his tone suddenly inhuman.

His words carried weight, as though they were living constructs that attempted to infiltrate his mind like a parasite.

Pain lanced through Luthor's arm as his ward protected him. He flinched from the discomfort, but was otherwise unaffected by Gideon's charismatic words.

Luthor shook his head. "I think not. Your powers have no effect on me, monster."

Gideon frowned deeply as he stared at the apothecary, any semblance to the friendly human moments before were erased. "So they don't."

"I know what you are, demon," Luthor said, holding his blade aloft.

Gideon sniffed the air, his nose wrinkling with disgust. "Of course you do. You have the stain on you; you stink of magic. I can smell it on you like a perfume. You absolutely reek of it."

Gideon uncrossed his arms and clenched his hands into fists. "Clearly, I underestimated you, apothecary, though clearly we both know that's not what you truly are. Had I realized sooner, I wouldn't have wasted so much of my energies on the Royal Inquisitor, when I should have been focusing solely on destroying you."

"You'll never destroy me, nor will you ever stop the Cabal."

Gideon snarled and drew his rapier. "I should have known the Cabal would come for me in due time. I will enjoy flaying your flesh from your bones. I will savor your screams of anguish."

"You'll never have the chance, demon," Luthor replied, crouching into a fighting stance. "Even now, the werewolves are destroying your meager armies. Soon, you'll have nothing left except your life, which I fully intend to take from you as well."

Gideon stepped forward and halfheartedly swung his blade. Luthor easily parried it aside and both men returned their swords to the defensive position. Luthor jabbed immediately afterward, but Gideon turned the blade aside.

"This is nonsense," Gideon mocked. "We have such greater abilities than to resort to fighting one another with mundane blades. Come, wizard, use your magic."

Luthor clenched his teeth and swung his sword toward Gideon's head. Gideon's rapier appeared quicker than Luthor could follow, blocking the cane sword a mere inch from the side of his head.

The apothecary stepped back, granting some distance between the two duelists. He wanted nothing more than to heed Gideon's advice and use his magic. Though Gideon certainly had protective spells of his own, Luthor stood a far better chance of defeating the demon with magic than he did with the sword. Of his many skills, he never mastered the skill half as well as Simon. Simon, however, was the sole reason he didn't release his magical prowess. Luthor had spent over a year concealing his abilities from the Inquisitor. Though as Simon had found, the ends sometimes did justify the means, he wasn't yet ready to expose himself to the Inquisitor if at all avoidable.

"You can't defeat me with the sword," Gideon mocked as Luthor circled, taking the fight further away from the doorway. "If you insist on maintaining this façade of being a mere apothecary, I most certainly will destroy you."

Gideon swung his blade, and Luthor parried. The parry reverberated through Luthor's arm, leaving the muscles aching from the impact. It was evident that Gideon was using his own magic to amplify his strength. The demon swung again and Luthor parried once more, but the impact left his hand aching. He wasn't sure how much more he could manage without accessing his reserve of magical abilities.

"Fight me," Gideon demanded. "No more of these falsehoods. No more of this mockery of your true abilities. Fight me as you were meant to or I will shatter every bone in your body with strike after strike."

Luthor smiled mockingly. "I would tell you to go to hell, but I fear you wouldn't take it as the insult it was meant—"

He was interrupted as Gideon swung his blade overhead. The rapier, a weapon normally used for finessed strikes, became a brutal club in the demon's hands. Luthor raised his narrow blade to block, and the force nearly drove him to his knees. He heard metal ricochet off the ground, and he looked up to see a sliver missing from his blade.

Gideon breathed heavily, though Luthor doubted it was from exertion. "Fine, you fool! If you want to play the role of the mundane, even unto your death, then so be it."

Gideon grasped his sword's hilt in both hands and drew it over his head. Luthor's arm ached even as he started raising his blade above him in anticipation. He wasn't sure he had the strength to stop another swing, and he flinched even as Gideon began his brutal downward strike.

A howl split the tension in the ballroom and a werewolf slammed into Gideon, knocking him from his feet. The two figures struck the floor and tumbled apart from one another, both scrambling quickly to regain their feet.

Gideon stood and brushed wayward strands of hair that had cascaded over his face. His well-kempt visage was ruined, as was his well-maintained demeanor. He looked enraged as he stared at the wolf.

The werewolf rolled gracefully, coming up on all fours in a low crouch. It emitted a low growl that rolled over the marble and hardwood floor. Though the werewolves were fairly indiscernible from one another when they were transformed, there was little doubt in Luthor's mind as to the identity of his savior.

"Mattie," he said appreciatively. Previous thoughts of telling her to stay behind flew from his mind as he realized she had just saved his life.

Gideon glanced back and forth between the two adversaries as he bent low and retrieved his rapier. Mattie shifted forward as he reached for the blade but Gideon was far quicker, standing once more and pointing its tip at the werewolf.

"You and your motley crew are certainly full of surprises," Gideon said as he regained his composure. "Does your Inquisitor know that you're cavorting with such monstrosities?"

Mattie snarled in response.

"He's willing to turn a blind eye so long as we bring back your head," Luthor threatened.

Gideon pointed threateningly toward the werewolf. "It's good to release your inner monster," he said. "I have one of those, too. Would you like to see it?"

The veins on his neck bulged as he tilted his head backward. Dark splotches formed on his skin like liver spots, though the blackness spread quickly. Smaller spots were consumed by the larger spread until all his exposed flesh was the inky blackness of a moonless night. The color of his hair faded to stark white while his fingers stretched to elongated claws. Spikes ruptured from the skin on the outsides of his arms and legs, leaving open sores that wept viscous, black blood. The skin on his forehead bulged, straining to hold back the horns that threatened to tear through. As the tips lengthened, the skin split apart in a spray of gore. The horns grew from his forehead, curling into a spiral that ended beside his ears.

The demon lord who had once appeared as Gideon Dosett glared at Mattie and Luthor with eyes that smoldered with an internal fire.

“Now, mortals,” the demon lord growled, his voice rumbling like an erupting volcano. “Come and meet your doom.”

Mattie snarled and charged the demon on all fours. As she neared him, she leapt, stretching clawed fingers toward his exposed face. Gideon moved blindingly quick, dodged her outstretched hands, and countered by slamming his forearm into her shoulder as she soared overhead. The spikes protruding from his limb tore into her flesh, and the impact sent her body twisting.

Mattie let out a yelp of pain before crashing heavily to the marbled ballroom floor. Bright red blood oozed from the wounds on her upper arm, soaking and staining the white fur. She whimpered as she tried to stand again, but the shoulder refused to support her weight.

A sizzling filled the air. The fur around the wound smoldered, and wisps of smoke rose from the injury. She looked down at the gash in horror. As the sound intensified, Mattie threw her head backward and howled in pain before her body began to convulse.

White foam formed at the corners of her snout and spilled onto the floor as her tongue lolled from her open mouth.

“Mattie,” Luthor cried in horror. He leapt to his feet but Gideon’s blade appeared before him, blocking his way.

“Not yet, wizard,” the demon threatened. “We’ve not yet finished our duel.”

Luthor clenched his blade even as his eyes drifted again to the werewolf as she was consumed by another seizure. The entirety of her body convulsed awkwardly, and her head slammed into the floor.

“Defeat me and you can save her,” Gideon mocked.

Luthor turned his attention to the demon and raised his blade. “I’ll kill you for this, monster.”

Gideon smiled wickedly. “You’ll try.”

Luthor swung his blade. Gideon didn’t bother blocking, instead merely leaning backward until he was outside the range of the sword.

The blade passed within inches of the demon's black throat but failed to connect.

Gideon laughed maliciously before swinging his rapier. Luthor knew the risk he took in parrying the blow, but it came too quickly for him to duck the swing. He raised his sword into the path of the rapier. The two crashed together. Luthor's blade was driven backward until it slammed into the apothecary's shoulder. The sharpened edge of Gideon's rapier quickly followed, slicing into Luthor's jacket and drawing blood.

Luthor hissed in pain and stumbled away from Gideon's onslaught. The demon pressed his advantage, giving chase. Luthor switched his blade to his off hand and swung feebly at Gideon's assaults. Gideon's strikes were deliberate, pushing each of Luthor's respective blocks wider and wider, exposing more and more of the apothecary's torso.

"Enough!" Luthor yelled as the magic poured through him. The blast struck Gideon in the chest and hurtled him through the air. He crashed through one of the round ballroom tables and slid across the floor.

Luthor breathed deeply as he leaned forward, resting his hands on his knees. A commotion drew his attention to where the demon had come to rest. A black hand emerged from the debris and fallen chairs. It grasped the nearest heavy, wooden chair and threw it aside as though it weighed nothing at all. Soon, the air was filled with flying debris as the demon unburied itself.

Standing, it bellowed with rage and stared at the apothecary. "I'm going to kill you slowly for that."

Gideon charged across the room, kicking aside a table as though it were nothing more than a minor inconvenience. Luthor channeled his magic and swung his arms in an arc. The demon was thrown from his feet once more, rolling to a stop near the wall.

Luthor began another blast as the demon stood, but it charged far faster than Luthor could have believed possible. There was little more than a dark blur as the demon covered the distance, slamming his hands into the apothecary's chest. Luthor flew backward before collapsing onto the ground in a heap.

He scrambled to his knees before the demon reached him once more. As Luthor started to summon another blast of magic, Gideon swung his rapier and Luthor had to hastily block the attack. As he tried again, the cycle repeated itself. Every time Luthor tried to summon magic, Gideon brought his sword to bear, leaving Luthor's arms aching with fatigue.

"I'm glad to see you finally revealing yourself to me, wizard, but you're a fool," Gideon mocked, thrusting his blade toward Luthor's chest. The apothecary was barely able to parry it aside before it pierced his chest. "You can't cast if you can't concentrate. Even the lowliest apprentice knows that. I have no intention of giving you another chance."

The demon reared back and swung his rapier toward Luthor's exposed hip. Luthor shifted his weight and brought his sword to bear with as much strength as he could muster. The two blades connected in an explosion of metal fragments. Luthor's blade shattered from the impact and the demon's momentum brought his forearm around, where it struck Luthor in his shoulder. The apothecary was thrown from his feet, where he collapsed heavily onto the floor.

Though the magic in his body counteracted the toxin coursing through him, every nerve in his body felt as though it were ablaze. His gaze shifted to Mattie, as he understood the anguish she was in. Her concentration broken, she had reverted to her human form. Her naked body was curled into a ball to protect against the pain that ravaged her. He longed to crawl to her side, knowing his own magic could help relieve her misery.

Instead, a dark shadow fell over him and Gideon straddled his prostrate form, lifting his sword high above his head.

Luthor raised his hand weakly, hoping to summon magic to his defense, but his mind refused to focus on anything other than the pain.

"This ends now," Gideon said.

His blade started descending, but a figure suddenly appeared by the demon's side. A saber flashed outward, turning the rapier aside.

Gideon howled and stepped back as he turned to face the Inquisitor.

"Sorry for my tardiness," Simon apologized. "Have I missed anything important?"

CHAPTER Thirty-eight

"I'VE BEEN WAITING FOR YOU, INQUISITOR," THE DEMON hissed as it withdrew its blade.

"I'm sorry to have kept you," Simon replied.

Gideon swung at Simon, which he easily parried. Luthor knew the pain he must have felt from its impact, but Simon showed no signs of discomfort. Instead, he rolled the saber in his hand, driving Gideon's rapier wide before going on the offensive. He slashed, parried, and reposted with incredible precision.

"I've longed to taste your blood," Gideon said.

The demon swung his rapier at Simon's neck, but the Inquisitor quickly blocked the strike.

"You'll be waiting for some time, hell spawn," Simon replied. "I was always the far better swordsman."

Gideon howled angrily and attacked again. After a volley of parried strikes, the two warriors separated. The Inquisitor looked over his shoulder to where Luthor lay, fighting through the poison coursing through his system. From his periphery, he saw Mattie shivering on the floor, her convulsions significantly weaker than they had been minutes before.

"Are you well, Luthor?" he asked.

Luthor nodded as he rolled onto his belly and began dragging himself toward Mattie. "I've certainly felt better, sir. Be careful. Gideon is deceptively faster and stronger than he was during your last encounter."

As Simon turned back toward the demon, Gideon reached out with his free hand and grasped Simon's wrist. With a powerful jerk, he lifted Simon from his feet. The Inquisitor flew through the air, landing awkwardly on the top of a table. Unlike the heavier demon lord, Simon bounced off its surface rather than smash through. He slid off the other side, tangling with a series of chairs as he fell.

"Duly noted," Simon replied as he pushed the chairs aside.

He could feel an angry welt forming across his shoulder from his landing, but he miraculously maintained a grip on his sword without accidentally injuring himself during his landing.

Simon looked around the room, taking note of the layout of the furniture, the open spaces around the dance floor, and his fallen associates. He worried most of all for Luthor and Mattie, who were clearly weak and exposed. Should the demon choose to turn his attention back to the pair, there would be little anyone could do to stop him.

He bit his lip as he glanced across the room toward the large, closed double doors that led onto the ballroom's balcony. It hadn't been so long ago that he had followed Mattie onto that balcony, though it seemed like a lifetime ago. At the time, he would have never expected a camaraderie to exist between himself—an Inquisitor—and a werewolf, much less their entire pack. The idea was preposterous, yet there he was, risking himself to protect a wounded werewolf.

Gideon stalked the Inquisitor. As he reached the table behind which Simon was kneeling, the demon simply grabbed the wooden top and tossed it aside. It crashed into the wall, splintering and shattering into pieces.

Simon knew he was the better swordsman, but skill would matter little in this encounter. He needed to find a way to exploit Gideon's burgeoning confidence.

The Inquisitor tried to stand, but his foot slipped on a splintered piece of wood. Rather than cursing, he smiled and turned, grasping the wooden chair beside him. As Gideon strode toward him, he threw it at the demon. It shattered against Gideon, who growled as he staggered backward. Finding a splintered piece of wood beside him, he hurtled it like a spear at the monster. The fractured table leg struck one of Gideon's curled horns, forcing his head to the side.

With the demon distracted, Simon leapt to his feet and rushed across the room, weaving carefully around the jumble of furniture, leaping nimbly across tables when the way was impassible.

"Coward!" Gideon bellowed. "Get back here."

The demon tried to follow but found himself blocked by protruding chairs and broken tables. As he maneuvered through the maze of furniture, Simon threw pieces of fallen debris, taunting Gideon as he retreated.

Simon looked over the demon's shoulder and saw Luthor crawling ever closer to Mattie. The further he could retreat, the greater the distance between the demon and his fallen friends. Moreover, his true goal was growing steadily closer the further he ran.

A pair of chairs had fallen across his path, and he leapt easily over the pair. While he was in midair, however, a broken shard of a table struck him between the shoulder blades. Simon grunted as he pitched forward, landing in a heap amidst the discarded furniture.

The air had been knocked from his lungs and his chest screamed for air. He opened his mouth, but the muscles refused to relax. Simon rolled onto his elbow and looked behind him, for once feeling the panic of the situation settling over him. Gideon smiled at him as he pushed tables aside, though it seemed far more like a violent sneer when set against the jet-black of his skin.

"Two can play your game, Inquisitor," Gideon mocked. "I hope I haven't broken anything too vitally important. I'm not nearly done with you yet."

Simon forced his muscles to relax, holding at bay the threatening panic attack. As the muscles around his lungs finally eased, blissful oxygen flooded his body. Coughing hoarsely, he cringed at the pain that he felt up his spine. He moved his legs slowly, ensuring no lasting pain or, conversely, numbness. When he was satisfied, he pulled his legs underneath him and climbed to his feet.

He stumbled forward, listening closely as Gideon gave chase. The crashing of chairs and tables marked the demon's progress. Simon's legs didn't seem eager to cooperate as he hurried forward, his eyes never leaving the balcony doors. When he reached the dance floor, the clearing for which led all the way to the balcony, he ran as fast as his body would allow, stopping only when he reached the double doors.

"Where is your brashness now?" Gideon chided as he threw another piece of fractured table. Simon leaned to the side and let the debris fly past, shattering one of the panes of glass in the door. "Are you at a loss for words or is it possible you've finally learned to respect your betters?"

A frigid wind blew through the ruined window, caressing the Inquisitor's exposed skin with its icy breath. Simon forced himself upright, despite the discomfort it caused along his injured back.

He smiled at the demon and raised his sword before his face in a salute. "I'm a Royal Inquisitor, you bastard. I have yet to find anyone better."

Gideon snarled and charged Simon, intent on driving him through the doorway and onto the snow-covered veranda. The demon was a blur, moving nearly quicker than the eye could follow.

As soon as Gideon moved, however, Simon dropped to the ground, rolling forward and out of the demon's path. Gideon rushed past him, his momentum carrying the demon through the doorway, which exploded under the assault. Splinters of wood and shards of glass sprayed across the balcony. Gideon fell into the snow and slid unceremoniously to the metal banister, which stopped him from toppling the three stories to the ground below.

Infuriated, Gideon slammed his fist into the stone floor before climbing to his feet. He turned toward the Inquisitor with murderous rage reflected in his smoldering eyes.

Simon was already on his feet, his sword lying forgotten on the floor. In his hand, he held his silver revolver, which was pointed at Gideon's chest.

The demon stared for a brief moment before tilting his head backward and laughing heartily. "A gun? You threaten me with a gun? Clearly the injuries you've taken have greatly affected your common sense."

Gideon grasped the center of his shirt and pulled it apart, dislodging the buttons from both his shirt and vest as he did so. With the buttons removed, he exposed his inky black chest and abdomen invitingly.

"Do it then, Inquisitor. If you think a pistol will save you where your sword and razor wit could not, then shoot me."

Simon pulled the trigger without a reply. The bullet flew from the barrel, striking Gideon in the stomach. The demon doubled over, his clawed fingers rising to conceal the wound.

For a moment, Simon felt a flood of relief. As quickly as it appeared, however, the feeling dissipated as Gideon rose to his full height once more. The guttural laugh started deep in the demon's chest and reached a crescendo as he tilted his head backward.

"For a last act of a desperate man," Gideon chided, "this moment properly sums up the entirety of your existence—ineffective and pointless. You'll die now with the knowledge that you couldn't save yourself, you couldn't save your friends, and you most certainly couldn't save Haversham."

Gideon took a threatening step forward but immediately paused. The mocking expression on his face melted to bewilderment as he raised a hand to the gunshot wound. His clawed finger touched the edge of the wound, and he raised his hand to his face. His fingertip was stained with silver.

The demon lowered his hand and looked at Simon confusedly. In response, Simon pulled the trigger twice more, striking Gideon in the chest with both shots. The demon staggered backward as liquefied silver dripped from both of the new wounds as well.

"Impossible," Gideon said as the first lance of pain tore through his stomach. He looked down as silver tendrils wormed their way beneath his skin, starting from the oldest wound. By the time the veins of silver had snaked their way to his chest, new tendrils were emerging from the two newest gunshots as well.

"This isn't possible," Gideon said as he clawed at the tendrils. His sharp claws sliced his skin but did little to impede the spreading sickness. "I won't be killed by a mere mortal."

Simon lowered his pistol, placing it in its holster on his hip, and walked toward the broken doorway leading onto the balcony. "There's nothing 'mere mortal' about me."

Gideon howled in rage and staggered toward Simon. The Inquisitor leapt upward and grasped the frame of the balcony door, kicking outward as he did so. His feet connected with Gideon's chest, driving the demon backward. Gideon staggered until his back struck the railing. His weight carried him over, flipping end over end as he plummeted the three stories to the estate's courtyard below.

His screams filled the air briefly before ending abruptly upon impact.

Simon rushed to the railing. Far below, a dark stain against the purity of the white snow, the outline of Gideon Dosett was barely visible, unmoving as falling snow collected on his back.

CHAPTER Thirty-nine

THE MUSCLES ACROSS SIMON'S BACK SEIZED AS HE returned to the ballroom. He paused, leaning heavily on a table for support as he caught his breath. The room itself was in utter disarray. Upturned tables greatly outnumbered those still upright. Broken chairs and shattered table legs mired amidst the wreckage like tangle foot, threatening to trip the Inquisitor as he made his way across the room.

"Luthor?" he called out.

He had left the apothecary on the side of the room nearest the ballroom's grand entrance, crawling toward the equally injured Mattie, though it was impossible to see either from where he stood.

"Luthor, answer me," Simon called out again.

An unsteady hand rose over the wreckage. "Here, sir. We're here."

Simon rushed as quickly as his body would allow, brushing aside chairs and debris as best he could as he hurried to Luthor's side. As he rounded a tilted table, he came upon Luthor and Mattie laying side by side, their hands intertwined even in their prone position.

Mattie's eyes were closed, but her breathing was strong and steady. Her naked flesh was covered by Luthor's long coat.

Simon cleared his throat and wiped the dirt and sawdust from his eyes. "I was worried about the state in which I'd find you both."

"As were we," Luthor said. "It appears that whatever poison with which we were injected was short-lived, dissipating quickly in our blood. My strong constitution and Mattie's werewolf physiology seem to have overcome the pronounced sickness."

Simon wanted to eye them both warily, unsure of such a convenient answer, but he thought better and merely sat down heavily beside them both.

Mattie's eyes fluttered open and she looked up at the Inquisitor. "Is it done, then?"

Simon nodded. "I certainly hope so. He seemed on the verge of death when he tumbled from the balcony. I have every intention of going downstairs and confirming his death myself momentarily, but couldn't in good conscience depart without ensuring both of your safeties."

The Inquisitor glanced toward his companion and noticed Luthor's disapproving glare. He needn't ask Luthor the problem, since he was most certainly aware of the apothecary's complaint long before he arrived in the ballroom to face Gideon.

Simon shifted his position so that he was staring directly at his friend. "Luthor, I can't apologize enough for my delayed arrival. It was clearly a necessary evil, but a position in which I regret having to place you."

"Where did you go?" Luthor asked.

"Gideon searched our rooms, no doubt trying to find anything that could be used against us in our upcoming battle. In our haste to leave, I had packed abnormally lightly, even for someone like myself who travels with so little. I was unable to take my Inquisitor's kit, so I hid it as best as possible, with the hopes that Gideon and his minions would be unable to locate it."

Luthor furrowed his brow. "Your kit? Why your kit? It's proven completely ineffective throughout our investigation."

"It was because of something you said. It was you who told me that mythology showed silver as a demon's weakness."

"Yes, as it did for werewolves, which clearly proved to be a falsehood," Luthor said, exasperated.

"Yet, it was clearly not incorrect against demons. It was the silver that overcame his defenses and led to Gideon Dosett's demise."

Luthor took as deep a breath as possible, though his body still ached from the residual toxins. "Had the silver proven ineffective, then what would you have done?"

Simon shrugged. "I clearly would have moved on to plan D, or are we now on E?"

Luthor laughed, despite himself. "And plan E consisted of what, exactly?"

Simon shrugged. "The kit was filled with dozens of other useful weapons capable of killing magical abominations regardless of their disposition and affinities."

Luthor suddenly stopped laughing and arched an eyebrow inquisitively. "Your secondary plan was to merely overcome him with a massive assortment of weaponry?"

"Sometimes brawn truly is more effective than brains," Simon said as he climbed to his feet. "Will you both be all right as I go recover Gideon's body?"

Luthor craned his neck so that he could look at the weak and pale Mattie. "I believe we're past the worst of it. Go, sir, and make sure this is over once and for all."

Simon nodded to them both before ascending the few stairs to the ballroom's main entrance. He glanced back once more before exiting and beginning the long walk down the staircases.

Once clear of Luthor and Mattie's sight, Simon began walking with a much more pronounced limp. His lower back felt as though acid had been poured into both hips and every step sent pain rolling through his shoulders and neck. He knew he needed medical attention as much, if not more so, than his two companions upstairs, but he refused to succumb to his injuries until he saw Gideon's corpse for himself.

After an eternity of descending stairs, he stepped onto the foyer's hardwood floor and strode toward the front door. It was only as his hand closed on the door handle that he paused, realizing that if he were incorrect, that if Gideon somehow survived the silver bullets and the three-story fall, then the battle could very well be raging still beyond the doorway. Though he was a warrior at heart, he doubted his body could withstand much more fighting today.

With a deep breath, he pulled the door open. The estate beyond the door was blanketed in silence. There were bodies strewn across the snow-covered courtyard, both humans and werewolves. Red blood was smeared across the roadway directly in front of the mansion. Amidst the bodies, however, werewolves padded softly through the snow. The humans still on their feet milled about confusedly, as though unsure of how they had come to be on the estate in the first place, much less embroiled in a battle with fur-covered monstrosities.

Simon smiled and stepped onto the covered porch. One of the larger werewolves broke from its pack and strode over to the base of the stairs. It looked up at him and shivered as it began its transformation. The fur fell away in droves, crashing to the ground in gelatinous chunks that dissolved on the ground. With a final sturdy shake, the last vestiges of the werewolf disappeared, replaced by a short-haired, naked woman.

"Chieftain Kidnip," Simon remarked.

He glanced over his shoulder and noted a winter jacket hanging from a peg just inside the estate's doorway. He retrieved it and offered it to the woman, who quickly covered herself.

"It seems that it's finally over, Inquisitor," she said, glancing over her shoulder to where a small group of werewolves huddled around a fallen form.

"It would appear that you know far better than I," Simon remarked as he walked gingerly down the last couple stairs that led to the road beyond.

Despite the pain, he stood upright as he walked toward the throng of wolves. Sensing his approach, they quickly parted, allowing Simon his first view of the deceased demon. Gideon's dark skin remained as it had been before his fall, though its surface was marred with hundreds of the silvery tendrils, extending as far as his neck and face. One horn had shattered in his fall and pieces of the curved bone were strewn across the roadway. His eyes remained open, though a droplet of liquid silver pooled in the corners like tears.

"Then it's finally done," he remarked.

He turned toward the stupefied humans wandering the ground and pointed at a pair of burly men.

"Come here," he ordered. As they approached, they paused nervously before the demon's body. "Find a wagon and collect this body. I'll give you disposition instructions once that task is complete."

The two men stared at one another before glancing down, once again, at the vile darkness of the demon at their feet. Neither man seemed keen to move, as though frozen in place now that Gideon's spell was broken.

"For God's sake," Simon chided, "act like men instead of schoolyard children. It's dead and not likely to rise from its grave. Treat it as a corpse instead of what it once was and go find me my wagon!"

The two men nodded quickly and hurried off. With their departure, Simon could sense other eyes upon him, boring into his back even as he examined the corpse. He turned slowly and found himself facing the chieftain. A number of her werewolves were behind her, having never transformed back into human appearances.

"What of us now, Inquisitor?" Kidnip asked, a tinge of threat staining her words. "We formed an uneasy truce so that we could bring down a much larger threat."

"Now that the demon is dead, our truce is at an end," Simon surmised. "Is that what concerns you?"

"You called more of your kind to Haversham. The mention of both werewolves and demons will bring them in droves. What of the werewolves now, Inquisitor?" Every mention of his title was said with slightly more vitriol.

"Now nothing," Simon replied cryptically. "Now you return to your villages or even roam the streets of Haversham in your human forms for all I care. I ask only one thing of you—allow me to keep the two autopsied werewolves."

Kidnip bristled at the request. "Those are our kinsmen. Is it not vile enough that you cut them apart for your examination? Now you want to deny them a proper burial amongst their own kind?"

Simon raised his hand to calm her ire. "I understand your hesitation far more than you would believe. Had I known the truth of your kind at the time of my autopsy, I would have never proceeded. However, those droves of Inquisitors that you mentioned will need to be placated. They expect werewolves and demons. I have a corpse of a demon to satisfy their curiosity but if they arrive and there is not a werewolf to be seen, they will march their army across this land, from mountain range to mountain range searching for you and your kind."

He stepped forward and lowered his voice so that only Kidnip could hear him. "I offer you a choice, albeit a difficult one to make. Say your farewells to your two fallen comrades and let me present their bodies as an appeasement to the Inquisitors, or risk bringing the full wrath of not just the Inquisitors, but the Order of Kinder Pel down on Haversham and all your kind."

Chieftain Kidnip blanched at the thought of the Pellites, whose reputation for brutality had spread to all corners of the kingdom, no matter how remote. She swallowed hard before replying.

"Let me consult with the rest of the tribe. You'll have my answer by morning."

Simon nodded. "I would expect nothing less. Thank you, for everything you've done here."

Kidnip stripped away the winter coat and transformed into a werewolf once more. She turned and howled, the other wolves echoing her call as they ran toward the exit to the estate.

Simon watched them depart before turning his attention back to the deceased demon at his feet. He frowned at Gideon's body before rearing back and kicking it painfully in the ribs for good measure.

CHAPTER *Forty*

SIMON AND LUTHOR SAT IN THE RESTORED SITTING room of the governor's estate. The mansion had hastily been restored following Gideon's death, though parts of the estate still showed the wear of combat. Simon stood at the window, staring across the courtyard. His back ached and he preferred to sit, but his mind was a jumbled mess of thoughts. He found it easier to think staring absently outside rather than sitting before the roaring flame.

Luthor looked up at his mentor before shifting in his cushioned seat. The sling on his arm was awkward, not allowing him to properly rest his hands on the broad armrests. Though the injury to his shoulder was nearly completely healed and no lingering effects of the poison could be found, he wore the sling for affect, especially in the presence of the other Inquisitors.

Voices filtered through from the dining room, where the recently arrived Inquisitors discussed all that had transpired and poured over Simon and Luthor's written reports. Their reports had been meticulously similar, discussed at great length long before the first zeppelin arrived in Haversham. Each successive zeppelin, and there had been many, had disgorged new Inquisitors and medical professionals, eager to examine the corpses.

Simon turned as the voices in the dining room reached an excited crescendo. He had already sat before their panel once, answering questions about his report as though he were being interrogated. As unpleasant as it had been, he understood their concern and even mild skepticism. Though hundreds of reports had been filed through the Inquisitors claiming supernatural occurrences, nearly all were unfounded. For the werewolves to have been proven true but, more importantly as Simon's report indicated, they were subservient to a demon, he understood why the Inquisitors were eager to explore all aspects of his investigation.

He glanced toward the apothecary and saw the strained expression on the man's face. He understood his pain all too well. A budding conflict ate at Simon's insides. On one hand, he had come to care for the werewolves far more than he would have believed possible. Yet, equally as strongly, it had been easy to forget about his obligation as an Inquisitor after all that had transpired in Haversham. Only now, with more of his own kind present, was he able to look objectively at his actions over the past few weeks and wonder if he had truly made the right decision.

"How are you feeling, Luthor?" Simon asked. The apothecary had only recently returned from his own scrutiny.

"They don't believe our reports," Luthor replied flatly. "They don't believe it was merely two werewolves serving as personal guards to Mr. Dosett. They think there are more, and they won't stop prying until they discover their whereabouts."

Simon frowned but understood his friend's concerns. The Inquisitors had been equally hard on Simon during his questioning, not because they believed Simon or Luthor was concealing the whereabouts of more werewolves, but because they wanted to ensure two deceased wolves was the extent of the threat.

"If they pry further," he said, "then we'll address that problem as it arises."

Luthor shook his head. "You can't kill them," Luthor said, as though sensing the conflict broiling in Simon's mind. "That's exactly what you would be doing if you reveal the existence of the tribe."

Simon paused and turned slowly back toward the window.

"You can't kill her."

"The laws of the Inquisitors are quite clear. I can't allow a magical creature to survive, circumstances be damned. If they discover our deception, there's little I can do to stop them."

"They're not monsters from the Rift. They aren't threatening the citizens of the kingdom. They *are* citizens of the kingdom. You may have an obligation as an Inquisitor to destroy magic in all its forms, but you have an equally strong obligation as a human being to save and protect those who cannot defend themselves. Mattie and Kidnip need you, not as an Inquisitor but as a friend."

"What would you have me do?" he asked, spinning toward his shorter counterpart. "I care greatly for them both. If I didn't, I certainly wouldn't have lied in my report. However, Mattie and her tribe are proof that the threat of magic is far greater than any of us could have foreseen. If this is truly an airborne contagion now, then no one is safe. Look at this objectively, rather than with the rose-tinted lenses through which we've both been looking. If the werewolves are carrying an airborne contagion and we can stop the infection now before it becomes too viral, then isn't that exactly what we should do both as part of an Inquisitor team and as human beings?"

Luthor shook his head. "I would agree with you if I thought that killing the indigenous population would contain the outbreak. The truth is… if magic is spreading and infecting people in our kingdom, then Mattie and her tribe are merely the tip of a much deeper change occurring throughout our lands. We shouldn't be looking for ways to kill them. We should be using them as a tool to convince the crown that blindly destroying magic is no longer the way. If hundreds, if not thousands, of people within our kingdom are already infected, then the idea of killing everyone who demonstrates magical potential is no longer a viable option."

Simon bit his lip as he considered his friend's position. "The way of the Inquisitors won't be so easily changed, not with the Order of Kinder Pel at the reins. You say that killing everyone isn't a viable option, but the Pellites won't see it that way."

"Then we take Mattie with us," Luthor blurted, his mind reeling as he considered other options. "We make them confront the truth. If they won't listen, then we'll present her to the kingdom and win our case in the court of public opinion."

Simon paused, his mouth agape. He was dumbfounded that Luthor would even offer something so brash as a plan.

"It's daft."

"It'll work," Luthor countered.

"You'll get us all killed, is what you'll do."

"Maybe, but the cost of our lives might save thousands more just like Mattie and her tribe. I think it's a small price to pay."

Simon walked over to the tooled-leather couch and collapsed heavily onto its cushions. He looked up at the apothecary, who beamed with excitement. Simon knew that what he was proposing was practically a coup against the doctrine of the Inquisitors. The plan had little chance of success. Yet, his mind also drifted to the redheaded woman and her fiercely independent nature. He couldn't imagine ordering her death, much less thousands of others throughout the kingdom. He chided Luthor for looking at the world through his newly applied rosy tint, but the truth was, his mentality had changed as well. Mattie and Kidnip were friends and he couldn't imagine ordering their deaths, the doctrine of the Inquisitors be damned.

He also knew that killing thousands still wouldn't solve the problem. The infection was among them already. It was only a matter of time before the crown realized the full implications of its viral spread. Maybe—and he was loathed to admit anything other than a reserved "maybe"—their plan could be the catalyst that drove the change.

"All right," he said.

"You'll do it?" Luthor said, practically dancing with enthusiasm.

"*We'll* do it," Simon corrected. "However, there are some stipulations. First, Mattie stays with us at all times. Until we can force some change in the system, we're practically inviting the Pellites to send assassins after us."

"Agreed, though you'll have a much harder time convincing her to stay practically handcuffed to your side. What other stipulations?"

Simon stood and walked over to his friend, forcing Luthor to look up to see him. "We do this my way. My way is slowly. The last thing we need to do is march Mattie in front of the king and demand change. The both of you will have to be patient until we can bring our plan to fruition. Are we agreed?"

Luthor smiled and stood, grasping Simon's hand. They shook firmly.

"Let's be finished with these horrible lines of questions so we can tell Mattie," Luthor said.

They stepped out onto the wooden platform. The zeppelin hovered in the air overhead, a small gangplank descending to the dock on which they stood. Simon led the way with Luthor and Mattie close in tow behind him. They lowered their heads as the large turbines on the back of the zeppelin sent a torrent of snow into their faces.

Simon handed the conductor all three tickets, which the man perused before handing them back to the Inquisitor and welcoming them all aboard. The three moved as quickly up the gangplank as their various statuses of health would allow. Neither Luthor nor Mattie still wore slings for their wounded shoulders, though they clearly still favored the limbs. Simon's limp was less pronounced but still evident as he moved between the horizontal planks nailed in place for traction.

As they entered the warm interior of the zeppelin, a valet led them to a private cabin. As they took their seats on the benches by the window, the valet closed the door, offering them privacy.

Simon removed his top hat and placed it on the table between them. He looked up at Mattie and Luthor, sitting side by side on the opposite bench, and smiled.

"I must say, Mattie, you look simply divine. Your transformation to right and proper lady is nothing short of miraculous."

Mattie looked down at the dress she wore, with an abundance of laces and frill. She reached up with her hand and felt the small hat, pinned in place by a multitude of clips. "I feel simply preposterous," she replied as her hand drifted over the strip of fabric and crystals tied around her neck. "Is this truly how the women of Callifax dress?"

"It is," Luthor said, "though they don't manage the look half as well as you do."

Mattie flushed but turned her attention back to Simon. "This won't be easy, will it?"

Simon laughed sadly. "Not even in the slightest. People are going to try to kill us for what we've done, make no mistake. If we can convince anyone of the truth, and that is a very fragile 'if', then we will be a growing minority against a very vocal and violent majority."

"It doesn't matter," Mattie replied firmly. "This must be done. Who knows how many others just like us have suffered and been slaughtered because of narrow-minded Inquisitors. The truth must be told."

Simon smiled and reached across the table, patting Mattie's gloved hand. "And so it shall."

The zeppelin jerked slightly as the gangplank was removed and the ropes untied. It rose quickly into the air and the ground seemed to fall away as the passengers gazed out of the window. Haversham turned from a burgeoning city filling the entirety of their view to a rounded mass below, set amidst a sea of icy and snowy tundra.

Mattie's breath caught in her throat at the sight, and she pressed herself as close to the glass as her body would allow as she watched the landscape grow smaller beneath her.

She sat back in her chair with a broad grin on her face. "When we arrive in Callifax, what is the first thing we shall do?"

Simon leaned back in the cushioned bench and retrieved his top hat, placing it on his head and lowering the brim over his eyes to block the light. "First, I'm going to take a hot bath that lasts for a few days at least, and then eat a meal fit for king. Then, once I feel much more like a man, I'm going to call upon Veronica and return to my simple life."

Luthor sighed. "That's not what she meant and you know it. Be serious, Simon. What is the first real thing we intend to do?"

Simon pushed back the brim of his hat and winked at them both. "You're correct. The first thing we're going to do is to enjoy a proper teatime. You wouldn't believe how long it's been since I've had a properly brewed cut of tea."

Epilogue

THE DEMON SAT BACK IN HIS HIGH-BACKED CHAIR and drummed his fingers on the armrests in frustration. He was alone in the vaulted bedroom, the only sound the crackling fire burning in the fireplace.

As he slammed his fist onto the armrest, he roared into the expansive room. His voice echoed, drawing out his howl of anger.

Slowly, he stood, allowing his broad wings to unfurl and stretch. He walked past the broad four-post bed and stopped before an oddly adorned vanity. Four gilded mirrors hung above the marbled surface, the two on the ends turned slightly inward to form a horseshoe that nestled around the room's only occupant.

With a wave of his hand, faces began to materialize in three of the four mirrors. To his right, a dark-skinned demon appeared, the majority of his face concealed by a tattered and filthy cloth. Only his glowing, red eyes were visible beneath his coverings. Beside him, the image was consumed by swirling shadows. A pair of vibrant violet eyes stared back at the standing demon. The third was a brutish figure, appearing to be carved fully from stone. His squared face was barely contained within the confines of the large mirror.

"One of our kind has been slain," the demon lord stated, gesturing toward the empty mirror.

An assortment of hisses and grunts were the other lords' only replies.

"We have clearly underestimated the humans and their prowess. We have also underestimated the Cabal, a mistake I don't intend to repeat. It is time to crush the human resistance once and for all. Leave none alive that aren't your slaves, to be ground beneath your heel."

"What of the ones that have destroyed our brother?" the shadowy figure asked, his voice as wispy as the air around him.

"Leave them to me," the demon lord replied. "I intend to take a special invested interest in the goings on and the eventual fall of the Inquisitors."

END OF BOOK 1

About the Author

Jon Messenger, born 1979 in London, England, serves as a United States Army Major in the Medical Service Corps. Since graduating from the University of Southern California in 2002, writing Science Fiction has remained his passion, a passion that has continued through two deployments to Iraq and a humanitarian relief mission to Haiti. Jon wrote the "Brink of Distinction" trilogy, of which "Burden of Sisyphus" is the first book, while serving a 16-month deployment in Baghdad, Iraq. Visit Jon on his website at www.JonMessengerAuthor.com.